THE
Seraphim
ENIGMA

JAMES C. MARLAS

ARCHWAY
PUBLISHING

Archway Publishing books may be ordered through booksellers or by contacting:

Archway Publishing
1663 Liberty Drive
Bloomington, IN 47403
www.archwaypublishing.com
844-669-3957

ISBN: 978-1-6657-0645-2 (sc)
ISBN: 978-1-6657-0644-5 (hc)
ISBN: 978-1-6657-0643-8 (e)

Library of Congress Control Number: 2021908361

Print information available on the last page.

Archway Publishing rev. date: 11/29/2021

☥

Be the King a Prophet, or the Prophet a King, what was broken remains true since truth cannot be broken ... Until I am found, you must seek something in which to believe ... I alone shall lie with the truth ... somewhere between twelve twice and the One God.

1

October 1938 and earlier

*S*omething moved. Then nothing. He almost fell back asleep. A click changed that. Lights shattered darkness and his strange dream. At this final insult, Michael Caridis pushed himself up on an elbow, rubbed his eyes, and glared through the mosquito netting at the intruder.

Imperturbable, Suleiman crossed his arms. "Effendi, the foreman, he calls. Needs you—at the dig. He says, come right away."

This was curious. Their latest worksite had been through several frustrating months without a hint of success. The taciturn sands of the Nile Valley guarded their secrets well.

"They found something? Tell me. There's a problem?"

The Turk shrugged and raised black eyebrows that could have been brushed in wide strokes of ink above his significant nose.

This was enough. He glanced at the clock—2:15 a.m.— parted the netting, and gave himself a mighty stretch before pulling on the khaki shirt and trousers from a chair where he'd thrown them the night before. A small open carriage already stood at the front steps of the villa. Some years ago, he'd had this charming place built up in the western hills. A fine retreat from the hurly-burly of Alexandria.

He stroked the head of the horse and walked around to the passenger seat. They set off on an eastward course, winding down from the heights, until they came to the great river. The bargeman roused himself from his chair and lazily secured the carriage's wheels with blocks before pushing off with a shove of his pole. Silence enfolded them as they floated across the sleeping Nile, in the background only the electric motor's soft purr.

Caridis stood at the flat bow of the barge, straight, athletic, and trim, silver-white hair, close-cropped curls like an ancient member of his race and glinting in the light of his cigarette and of the moon. He wondered what this night would bring. On landing, Suleiman guided the horse off on foot. The carriage wheels dropped with a jolt onto the broad ramp.

Unnoticed, a pair of shutters opened in the shadowed facade of a low building next to the river landing. A flash of eyeballs burnt into the darkness, furtive and alert. As he closed the shutters, the man turned to another in the darkened room and nodded. "Tomorrow, then?"

A shake of the other's head. "No, now."

Suleiman whipped the horse over the pebbled roadbed. They clattered through fertile, palm-fringed fields that hugged the nurturing river and then drove out into the hardscrabble moonscape of desert.

Impatient, Caridis frowned. "We should've taken the Overland."

"Too noisy this late, Effendi. Attracts attention."

After half an hour, they neared an ancient uninhabited

city studded with ruins like random stalagmites. Suleiman looked over at his boss as he lurched the carriage onto the uneven paving stones of its principal avenue. Ahead loomed the remains of a majestic temple blocking the end of the avenue. Caridis's heartbeat quickened as it always did when he reached this point.

Suleiman jerked the reins and made the horse mount seven broad steps of the temple designed to enable their buggy's wheels to roll up onto the platform. Two parallel rows of giant stone columns had once stood there. Now just their two dozen massive bases squatted in perfect ranks, reminders of the once-great power of the city's founder. Right here, on this spot, that flash of inspiration had finally struck him after almost thirty-five years of guesswork. Decades when he'd struggled to think exactly like the person selecting the place to bury the treasure.

Tonight, Pharaoh himself seemed to haunt the moon-begotten shadows of his temple. Michael could almost see him thirty-three hundred years ago, eyes gleaming with conviction, proclaiming, to the surprise and even horror of his subjects, there was only one true god.

What? Just one true god? Was he out of his mind? The priests, of course, had become apoplectic. They burned incense and threatened damnation by all the ancient gods he was betraying. Didn't he know what he risked? The old gods had already served Egypt well for two thousand years. You don't just cut them off at the knees. Growing ever more angry and more desperate, the priests had at last invoked the ghost of Pharaoh's mighty father, the empire builder who'd expanded the boundaries of Egypt to twice its size. A father's terrible curse would now befall the apostate son, they declared.

Ignoring his detractors and putting an individual stamp on this whole business, the heretic and only ever Pharaoh of the One God had decided he needed a new name. Something special. It was to be *Akhenaten*. It meant *the servant of the sun*. And to round things out, he'd called his new capital, now this brooding husk of a metropolis, *Akhetaten, the horizon of the sun*. It was in this very temple he'd worshipped Earth's star with a fervor that changed the world. As for priests' empty curses, Pharaoh Akhenaten gave not a fig.

Michael looked about, haunted by a sensing. Was he being watched, bewitched in these lightly moonlit ruins? Then he'd ask Akhenaten outright if he'd been roused tonight to good purpose? Would his obsession's mystery finally be unveiled? Captivated by that thought, he perversely tantalized himself by staying put and indulging an almost erotic feeling of ecstatic delay before learning why he'd been awakened.

He stayed Suleiman's whip hand and settled back against the padded wooden seat of the buggy. Ah, that special day thirty-five years ago. His awakening had come on a warm evening in Alexandria. It was his nineteenth birthday. He had just showered after a soccer game with several friends who had come back like him from college in Beirut for a spring break. As he was drying his hair, his father had peeked in the door with a smile and said, "Miko, get dressed. We're going to dinner, just you and me. I've got a little surprise."

As they drove through the city in a landau drawn by a pair of horses, lamplighters raised their torches to the streetlamps, and merchants busied with closing up their stalls. His father pulled reins beside a magnificent building along the sea drive bordering Alexandria's harbor.

Michael's excitement mounted as he entered the bronze doors of the Society of the Seraphim. He'd always wondered what was inside this impressive portal. They were greeted with a nod by the hall porter in a white burnoose. Striding through the arcade surrounding the fountain courtyard open to the sky, his father led him through a series of elegant smoking and card rooms to the extraordinary library at the heart of the building. Michael looked up with awe. The paneled ceiling soared three stories above them with a balcony reaching out to embrace every wall from a grand double staircase at one end. They mounted the steps to a pair of massive ebony doors. On the front of each was carved in relief an impressive vertical rod, three meters tall. On the upper third were two rows of twelve leaves arranged in perfectly equal spacing that flanked each side of the rod.

His father stood before the door and gave him a proud smile. "Surprised? You should know I've thought about this since the day you were born." He reached out and touched the door. "Inside's the private sanctum, called the Sanctuary. Next Friday—if you agree of course—you'll be a postulant there. Now you've turned nineteen, the earliest eligible age, and the committee's accepted my only son as a member of the Seraphim." His expression became a bit serious. "But there's a special responsibility attached to your membership. We all must take vows for life to serve in a brotherhood. It's a remarkable and secret cult called the Aaronites. You're going to be intrigued by the almost incomprehensible level of its power in every corner of the world."

"My god, Papa, this staggers me. Of course I accept. I'd no idea at all about any of this, but count me in. I'm honored, really excited."

He hugged the boy. "Our family members going far back through the ages would all be very proud." He let him go and said, "OK—to dinner."

The maître d' led them to a table near the tall arched windows overlooking the central courtyard. When they were seated, his father pointed at a man sitting alone. His strong face bore a large mustache, small intense eyes, and a military bearing. One notable feature. The man's right arm was held bent up high and tight to his side.

"Now there's a good example of the world you're entering."

"Who is it, Father?"

"The German Kaiser, Miko. He's taking a holiday. His yacht's anchored in the harbor."

Then his father had recounted a fragmented story, with a mystery he had no idea would soon set the course of his son's life. It concerned a tantalizing conundrum passed down since the founding of the Seraphim some three millennia before.

"We've been told it involves two historical personages. First was the Hebrew prophet Aaron. You probably remember him from Sunday school, no? He was a terrible scold of the Pharaoh, making miraculous pestilences befall Egypt to get him to release the Hebrews who'd been captive for over four centuries. Happened to have a pretty famous brother."

"Moses, of course," Michael popped in.

"Yes. But for fascinating reasons, it's Aaron who's the central figure of our cult—the Aaronites. And what you saw carved on the Sanctuary doors imagines the famous and magical rod of Aaron. He used it, according to the Old Testament, to make those miracles. As to the other historical figure of our cult's legend? Not so clear at all. In fact, quite confusing, really." He shook his head and speared a tiny scallop on his plate. "Debate rages whether he was the great—indeed the strange and charismatic—Pharaoh Akhenaten or, in fact, the person the Bible says is Aaron's brother, the prophet Moses. People have argued both possibilities, but the whole thing remains just as much a mystery today as ever."

"Baba, where's this story going? Why do people care who was who?" His logical mind was busy organizing what he was being told.

The older man smiled. "Nice question. There's indeed an

exciting part to whet your appetite. You see, the legend tells us something important is buried out there in Egypt's endless sands. We call it the Seraphim treasure. It's meant to contain all the answers to the mystery. And when revealed, we're told it will have a seismic effect on the world. As of now, the only clue we have to the whole business is an ancient conundrum in hieroglyphs. Translated, it says: *Be the King a Prophet, or the Prophet a King, what was broken remains true since truth cannot be broken ... Until I am found, you must seek something in which to believe ... I alone shall lie with the truth ... somewhere between twelve twice and the One God."*

Upon hearing the riddle, something had clicked. A chord was struck. Michael's curiosity caught fire with a sudden vengeance. He was impatient for his initiation. And when the time came, he kneeled among the sanctum's thousand flickering candles reflecting from the polished golden statue of a bull calf on the altar at its center and overflowed with an immense excitement. He swore to himself every ounce of his being would be poured into finding that treasure. He would solve this riddle, no matter what.

He made a quick start. During his next summer vacation from the American University in Beirut, Michael persuaded his father, a descendant of a Greco-Egyptian banking family, to help sponsor digs in the Valley of the Kings. Experts were hired, and he studied at their feet, eagerly soaking up the ins and outs of ancient ruling dynasties. He learned details of their burial rites, and he inspected objects taken from tombs already discovered or invaded by poachers long ago and sold. He absorbed the histories of as many royal families of the pharaohs as could be sorted out with the scraps of information that had come to light from time to time. These were mainly the products of the Egyptomania firmly gripping Europeans in the past two centuries. He also developed an expertise in ancient Egyptian artifacts that led to a career spent buying and selling and collecting these things for his own pleasure.

He never confessed to anyone, even his father, how driven he was to solve the riddle. But that summer following his initiation into the Seraphim, when he'd started working on that important dig, a mesmerizing young Englishman, Rupert Delacorte, came recommended by his Cambridge tutor to work on the same dig. Michael had been asked to pick up the new fellow at the railway station in Luxor. The lively Brit, wearing a wrinkled beige lightweight suit emerged onto the platform, suitcase in hand, and looked about through the rumpled blond hair that had fallen over his eyes. Spotting Michael and guessing who he was, Rupert smiled. Both men were twenty and hit it off from the start.

They found it easy to confide, and a bonding friendship blossomed quickly. In due course of several years and visits, the two discovered to their delight what was to become a lifetime connection they'd, unknowingly, shared from the beginning. The Seraphim.

2

September 1889

*R*upert Delacorte had lived until the age of eight in what was regarded as the most beautiful Palladian house in England: Ravenstone Park. His father, the Marquess of Ravenstone, happened to be the richest peer of the realm. As if to balance the scales against these superlatives, little Lord Rupert had an only sibling. His brother was older by nine years and, as heir to their father's grand titles upon his death, had in the meantime been given the courtesy title of William, Viscount Cressy. From Rupert's birth, Cressy resented him with a fierce, pathological envy. This bitterness grew stronger as time passed. With a certain irony, the more Rupert was persecuted by his brother, the more he tried to please him, which only added fuel to Cressy's spite.

Fate took an inevitable and cruel hand in this relationship when Rupert was only eight years old. He was playing hide-and-seek with kids from the village one fine autumn afternoon. It had come his turn to hide, and he'd raced to hover in a ditch running along one end of the estate's famous formal garden. Where he hid was meant to keep animals that grazed in the meadows from coming across into the manicured lawns and flower beds. For some reason he never fully understood, people called this sort of ditch a "ha-ha."

Hiding in what he felt sure was a place safe from his pursuers, Rupert would occasionally raise his head to see if anyone was nearby. Excitement gripped him, and his cheeks flushed with his fear of being caught. The last time he peered about to see if his playmates were getting warm, he was startled by the sounds of two shots exploding in quick succession.

A cold shiver of alarm overtook him for reasons he couldn't explain. He crawled out of the ha-ha with both hands grabbing onto vines on the sloping side of the ditch. Oblivious now to the game, he ran in the direction of the shots, the sharp little pops that still reverberated inside his pounding heart. Ahead was Ravenstone Park's famous seventeenth-century maze. It was tall and composed of impeccably sculpted yew hedges. The sounds could have come from the other gardens nearby, but something made him enter the maze with an intuition that fired his limbs with fear.

Although he'd long before mastered its complexities, he now got lost, and the more wrong turns he made, the more terrified he became. The maze loomed above him like the labyrinth of the Minotaur, but he might have preferred confronting the Minotaur to whatever it was that drove him now. He ran this way and that, sometimes up against blank walls of yew, and then into openings he was certain, in error, would lead to the center of the maze, drawn by a premonition to which he would not give a name.

At last, drenched in sweat, with legs trembling and knees weak, he saw ahead the opening into the central room of the maze. He abruptly slowed down, having now to will himself to proceed. Upon stepping into the space, his eyes deliberately elevated to the white marble statue of Aphrodite who he'd been told was the goddess of love. He didn't wish to lower his gaze, but he managed to force himself to see, with a dizzying act of self-control, the bodies of his parents at the base of the statue.

They lay on the grass. His mother looked surprised and even more beautiful than ever when she was animate, as if she had now become a marble version of herself, for all time to be placed next to the ancient Greek goddess looking down upon them. The small inlaid gold handle of one of a pair of exquisite pistols, peeked from the folds of her long white dress. He moved slightly and flinched when he saw the other side of her turned face, a thin scarlet rivulet crept along the grass beneath her head.

His father lay facedown with one arm extended beyond his head. The other pistol glistened on the grass not far from his open hand. He was dressed in a blue velvet smoking jacket. His thinning, light brown hair was stained with a streak of crimson on the right side of his head.

The boy dropped to his knees and held his face in his hands, convulsed with grief. He remained thus for hours. None of the other children ever found him. As the day yielded to twilight, they all left puzzled at the absence of their young host. The shadows deepened to darkness engulfing the two beloved creatures beside Rupert. He was able now to pull himself together and kiss each forehead before he selected the only one of the four exits from the Aphrodite Garden that would take him out of the maze.

He crossed the lawn through the spreading cedars of Lebanon that branched out in lush dark horizontals like the protective arms of Druid goddesses ready to take him to safety. Entering through a pair of French doors into the library, he felt the presence of the man lying in the maze. It was filled with trophies of his father's fascination with ancient Egypt. Marvelous portrait busts of pharaohs and charming sacred animals perched on pedestals. Rupert walked over to his father's desk and sat in the green leather swivel chair. He let his eyes wander over the paneling and columns and books as they became increasingly blurred by his tears. He sobbed with the recollection of stories Papa had told him here. Through his tears, he saw a small envelope tucked into a leather corner of the blotter. Squinting in the shadows, he read his name scrawled across it. He turned on the desk lamp.

> *My dear boy, it is only for you that I regret what we will do today. But you are young, and with time, this selfish act of ours will recede, leaving you perhaps mature beyond your years and, I pray, stronger, because of what we have just now made you endure. Know that our love will not die today or ever after. You must now go to the bookcase, to the left of the fireplace. On the fifth shelf from the bottom, look for the book entitled Moses and Monotheism by an Austrian called Sigmund Freud. As I have long been intrigued by the early history of the Near East, and told you many stories of my adventures there, now I bequeath to you the question that has long puzzled me. Who really was Moses? As you grow up and awaken to thoughts such as mine, perhaps you will find the time and interest to pursue this inquiry.*
>
> *When you are older, say, at university, you might wish to send this letter to the head of the Society of the Seraphim in London. The address is a handsome building at 98 Saint*

James's Square. It is home to an extraordinarily powerful and secret cult. Discreet to the point of paranoia. So, you must never discuss it with anyone unless it is clear, by some chance, they are a member. If you are so inclined, ask that you be considered for its membership as I have been and my father and his and so on going back for centuries. And if you have joined, ask for them to tell you the story of their ancient mystery, the one that has been unsolved since the Society began thirty centuries ago. This will give you something to look forward to in the years ahead, a focus for your very good mind and a treat for your love of puzzles.

Behind the book on the shelf is a little scarab, which I give to bring you luck. It shows an Egyptian queen placing a crown in the form of the sun on the head of a young boy. Find out what this meant at the time of its creation. Your mother and I now place the sun upon your head, dearest Rupert. Our love will never die.

Signed,
Daddy

The next day, the family chauffeur picked up his brother from boarding school and brought the new master to Ravenstone Park. Eton's Head Master had notified him early that morning of the tragic events. It seems the young Lord William, Viscount Cressy, had smiled and retorted, "Well, sir, I guess you'll now address me as milord Marquess of Ravenstone, won't you?"

When William strutted into the great oval entrance hall with the awkward arrogance of an arriviste, his brother was about to experience, in one of its ugliest forms, the fullness of evil. It unfolded like melodramatic scenes from some gothic novel.

William heard rumors among the staff and found the letter left to his brother—but not the scarab. His tantrum set everyone's nerves on edge. Screams from all points in the house made people cover their ears. "Why not me? No letter, nothing!" Repeating this plaint over and over, he hunted down his brother in his quarters. He pummeled the locked door until his fist hurt all the while screaming for the steward with a master key. Pushing the door open with a vicious swing of his arm, he found Rupert kneeling by his bed and saying prayers for their parents.

"Get up this minute, Rupert. Stop that crybaby stuff. Want to speak to you." When his brother remained on his knees, William grabbed him under the shoulders and hauled him to his feet. Spinning him around, he pushed him back on the bed. Standing with hands on hips, curling his lower lip, he addressed the young boy as if he were a judge sentencing a criminal. "All right, so you lost your mummy and daddy. What of it? They didn't really love you. If they did, they wouldn't have left like that. Right?" He bent over and leered into the child's face.

Rupert turned his head from his brother's and continued to weep.

William raised his hand and slapped him across the cheek. "Stop sniveling, for God's sake. It's not the end of the world. Listen to what I've got to say." He straightened and crossed his arms. "Now you're going to live with Grandmam in the dower cottage at the other end of the park. I don't want you anywhere near me. You're on your own, little Rupie. Don't expect a penny from the estate. I'm in control now. The parents should've stayed around if they wanted to protect their little favorite." He gave a high-pitched laugh. When this subsided, he continued, "As for taking advantage of Papa's oh-so-thoughtful last minute 'bequest' to you, forget about trying to join the Seraphim. I won't let it happen. I suspect it's usually the oldest son, anyway."

Rupert could tell his brother had known nothing of the Seraphim before reading the letter. But he held his peace. Pushing his deep golden hair back from his eyes, he asked, "Can I take my favorite things with me to Grandmam's?"

In a shrieky, clipped voice, William said, "Let me see whatever it is. If I disapprove, it'll stay here." He paused and reacted to something he'd just recalled. "Yes, that scarab. I want it. Give it me now."

Rupert shook his head aggressively and whispered, "No. Never. It's all I'll ever have left of Papa."

William reached over and slapped him again. "You will hand it me. Now!"

Rupert's large, bright blue eyes filled with tears, but he gave another determined shake of his head.

William shouted an order to ransack Rupert's quarters. Linens were torn off the bed, contents of drawers were emptied onto the floor, and clothes were pulled out of the closet and searched in every pocket. The servants made him remove what he was wearing to check if the scarab could be secreted anywhere on his body. With some nervousness, they had to report the offending object was nowhere to be found.

William shrieked at them when he received this report. "Tell him I'll never see him again. He must be out of here within the hour." William was sitting at his father's desk in the library, going through every imaginable hiding place, in a state of frantic disappointment. His anger seemed to have drained away his youth and drenched him in ugliness.

When the carriage had finally passed through the outer gates onto the main road, Rupert reached behind one of the back cushions where he'd hidden his little treasures from time to time. He felt in its dark recesses the object of his search and pulled it out with a feeling bordering on reverence. The scarab Papa had left to him was tiny and beautiful, exquisite to the touch.

3

September 1889
and July 1902

His grandmother opened the front door of her dower cottage and took the boy tightly in her arms. They wept together on the stoop for their sudden, inexplicable loss. Taking him by the hand, they went into the little parlor where she lifted a photograph from the mantel. It was in a simple silver frame she kept brightly polished. His parents glowed upon each other on their wedding day, a beautiful, happy pair of young people with everything in the world to live for. They sat together on the sofa, each holding one side of the frame, and she recounted what his father had been like as a child, how he'd met the woman he would marry and brought her to Ravenstone Park to meet his parents. Grandmam's tears splashed on the glass, and, along with his own welling eyes, the image of his mother seemed to dissolve into an abstract form.

The family grave site covered the flat top of a hill overlooking miles of the estate's verdant meadows and woodlands, William had glowered from the other side of the two caskets at his younger brother. Malice radiated toward Rupert as the priest intoned the ritual of interment. This malign energy was entirely wasted on the boy. All he could think of was the statue of Aphrodite, serene witness with him to the tragedy. This scene would haunt evermore.

Grandmam provided for him on her modest dower income, which had now been reduced out of spite by her other grandson. Fortune, if suddenly now stingy, had the kindness to give him a good mind and an enthusiastic character. He won a scholarship to Eton, and then to Cambridge where he earned a double first degree. He was, and would always remain, a survivor. One of his greatest gifts was an uncanny mastery of Egyptian hieroglyphics and other ancient languages of the Near and Middle East, especially Hebrew.

When he left university, Rupert returned to Eton as a teacher. Passionately attracted to ancient Egypt like his father, he decided during their first summer to take some of his students to dig in the Valley of the Kings. By a happy coincidence, his expedition had brought him back in touch with Michael Caridis.

One evening after a tough day in the desert heat, they sat together at a village coffee house near the excavation. Michael looked every inch the young Alexandrian Greek. He wore his curly brown hair in full long waves reminiscent of the poet Byron. His features hinted at a certain voluptuousness, full sensuous lips, somewhat heavy-lidded light brown eyes that watered slightly, and a huge laugh when he felt amused or excited.

By contrast, Rupert bore the inner traits of an ascetic. This turned out to be especially attractive combined with his boundless charm and good humor. It gave him an aura of credibility and authenticity. His self-restraint came from the discipline of a superior intellect that had enabled him to deal with events in his early life that might have shattered weaker spirits and sent them into a spiral of depression. One scar did remain that opened from time to time when he would find himself jerked suddenly up in his bed, awakened by the sound of his own screaming, a kaleidoscope of images tumbling over each other: his parents lying on the grass, Aphrodite turning through the air in cartwheels, his brother laughing hysterically and trying to strangle him.

Rupert found himself this evening in a rare frame of mind, far from his normal surroundings, enjoying the company of a kindred spirit and suddenly wanting to recount the saga of his parents and his brother. It seemed apt given they were digging in the Nile Valley—and the easy and open person across the table.

"So, Father collected stuff that fascinated him from the Egyptian dynasties. They were all over the house. Growing up surrounded like that, how could a kid resist wanting to know more? He could see I was hooked. I even learned from his last letter of a conundrum. It'd intrigued him so much he needed to pass it on to me. Imagine, here it was at the very end of his life, and that's what he needed to tell me. He wanted me to read Freud's speculations on Moses. The part he plays in the evolution of monotheism. It seems Moses might not even be the person documented in the Old Testament."

Michael held his breath. "Where did that come from? Freud?"

Rupert hesitated and shrugged. "You see, Father's letter said I wasn't ever to mention this to anyone." He toyed with the metal cradle of his Turkish coffee glass. "I suppose it's OK just to say it involves a secret cult he thought I should join when I grew up. Anyhow, as I was only eight, I'd have had to wait years. But I never did. Probably because my brother found

Father's letter in my room the next day. He threw a gigantic tantrum and swore to do anything to stand in my way of becoming a member. Father's letter said our family's belonged for generations. It was from this cult, Father wrote, he'd first heard of a treasure somewhere here in the Nile Valley perhaps containing the true identity of Moses."

Michael stared at him without speaking. Finally, he said, "Would that be the Seraphim?"

Rupert smiled, pleased, "Why, yes, so you've heard of this before?"

Carides nodded. "Indeed, I have. Rather uncanny, I've got to say."

Rupert shook his head. "How do you mean?"

Michael leaned forward, intense. "Very simple. Like you, my dad exposed me to the Moses mystery. Couldn't wait to have me initiated into the Seraphim. And I confess, to you— really just you alone—this mystery's set the course for my life." His eyes glowed. "You're going to join someday. In fact, you must. So, let me say what to expect."

Rupert felt a surge of excitement. "Please, go ahead."

"Members of the Seraphim's cult are called Aaronites. Hebrew texts said Aaron and Moses were born in Egypt—to the same Jewish mother. Accepted texts say these two led their people away, the famous Exodus, from four hundred years of slavery in Egypt. The historic Moses gets most of the credit as their leader, and Aaron ends up the bad guy because he committed the inexcusable heresy of allowing their people to worship a tangible idol, the golden calf. They'd begged him for it after waiting so long for Moses to receive the Lord's Word."

Rupert had a thoughtful expression. "You know, I've wondered how Aaron could ever have allowed that. Physical images of God are forbidden by Hebrew canons. Rather nervy of him."

Michael smiled. "A paradox. And you just put your finger on it. Our cult started because its first members felt sympathy with those who'd begged Aaron out there at the bottom of Moses's mountain to create something for them to worship. They were all searching for something to believe in, something they could see and touch. By the way, if you want further reasons to become an Aaronite, the Bible also tells us Moses got so mad when he found what they'd done that he had several thousand of these idol worshippers slaughtered by their friends and brothers. Nice guy, eh? All in the name of Orthodoxy."

Rupert's expression showed his distaste. "Christ! Poor bastards would've been better off staying back in Egypt!"

Michael laughed wryly. "Damn right. Some ideology's at the root of most acts of terrorism."

Rupert was intrigued. "So, Aaron's the cult's champion for dissatisfied people. People who resent authority—but still want something to believe in."

"Exactly! A paradox of humankind." Michael was getting into storyteller mode. "You see, members, even atheists, joined from all walks of life. They've faithfully paid their tithes to the cult's treasury. So, over three thousand years, the cult's wealth has grown, as you Brits might say, beyond the dreams of avarice—"

Rupert said, "Amazing how any group, especially one that values—how to say it—improvising its own spiritual solutions, could have survived for that long. A millennium older than Christianity."

"Exactly. It's got no dogma like a religion, mind you. Evolved into something quite curious. Took full advantage of its paradox. For a long time now, its goal's been to control the levers of political power. This has given it the means to build the wealth of the Aaronites. Its influence would astonish the billions completely unaware of its effect on their lives." Michael spread his hands flat on the table. "The Seraphim's used every empire since its founding to exercise power. These include Rameses II, Alexander the Great, the Ptolemies of Egypt, the Caesars of Rome, the emperors of Byzantium, Charlemagne, and many more. The Seraphim have stood behind Napoleon, Bismarck, and now Hitler and Mussolini—whatever great mythmaker chooses to grab for power. The Seraphim are agnostic. Whatever 'ism' that's moved the masses and looks like a winner, they use it to spread the Seraphim's power."

"So, what happens if the supported empire turns on the Aaronites as an institution?" Rupert's eyebrows went up. "Most of these empires were vehicles for a tight leadership to control everybody, which doesn't necessarily exclude their enablers."

Michael smiled. "If things get too tight for our institutional health, then we move over and support whoever appears to be a likely opposing winner. We also make sure our cult's run only by agnostics, never influenced by the dogmas it may support."

Riveted, Rupert felt a kindred spirit. "Amazing! It's pure, really cynical, paradox."

Michael nodded. "Yes. As for my effort to solve the Seraphim conundrum, it's quite independent; the Aaronites haven't a clue."

"You know, I bet you're going to find it—the answer."

Michael laughed and tilted back in his chair. "You alone have a clue what I'm looking for. And, happily, I can trust you." He reached over and thumped Rupert on the shoulder.

"Of course you can. When you've done it, I'm sure you'll tell me." He delved into his pocket and pulled out a small object.

"What's that?" Michael leaned over the table.

"My good luck charm. Always carry it." He smiled

impishly. "People governed by reason aren't supposed to practice superstitious rites, but you never know, do you? It's like wearing a belt and braces together. So, I'm rubbing this to bring you luck in your search."

Michael took the scarab from Rupert's hand. He studied it for a few moments and then asked, "How did this come into your life?"

"Father. He told me in that letter where to find it in our library, hidden behind Freud's *Moses and Monotheism*."

Michael fixed him with an intense gaze. "You mean the same letter you found after your terrible story?"

Rupert's eyes suddenly filled to his own surprise, and he nodded with a swipe across his cheek.

Michael put his hand on Rupert's arm to comfort him. "You know, I think your father maybe gave you a real clue. See the flat bottom of the scarab—this Egyptian queen crowning her son with the eagle-winged sun—this could in fact be part of the story we're trying to fathom. It's so unusual. It hints at something I've suspected. But, you know, like many Greeks, I'm really more superstitious than your average fellow. So, I'll say no more. Just this, may your kind wish for me in fact come to pass."

Just then, a man with almost albino-like coloring appeared like a ghost in the twilight beside their table. It was one of their fellow young diggers, a German, Lothar von Vranken.

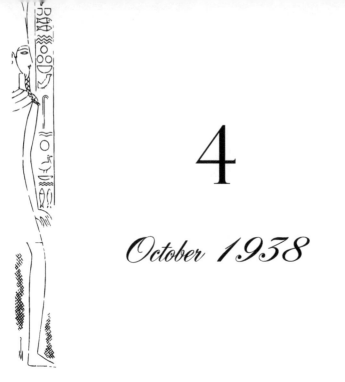

4

October 1938

$\mathscr{S}$uleiman cinched the reins and resumed their drive. He guided the carriage horse through the enfilade made by the two rows of twelve empty stone bases that flanked the length of Akhenaten's Temple of the Sun.

Michael felt once more that same thrilling rush as the momentous day he'd seen a new significance to this axis of columns. The idea had come when he'd stood outside the door to the Sanctum of the Aaronites, as he had so many times before, but for some reason, this time, he'd focused on the two rows of twelve leaves flanking the top of Aaron's rod on the ebony door. In his imagination, the rod's two rows of leaves were now overlaid on the two rows of twelve columns at the Temple of the Sun. That day he'd taken his pencil and ruler, and, with a firm hand on a paper plan of the temple site, he drew a straight line between those flanking column bases. Using the ratio of the space taken by the twelve leaves to the rest of Aaron's rod, he'd carried this same axis line 250 yards out beyond the edge of the ruined temple, directly toward the rising sun. And right there, at the point set by the surveyors' theodolite in the anonymous sands, he'd decided to insert the first shovel.

The surrey rattled out once more onto the desert. Lanterns at the site threw pools of golden light behind the figures milling about. The scene resembled a magical panopticon of moving silhouettes. His lanky British foreman approached, and Caridis leaped down from the carriage to greet him.

"Well, sir, I think we may've done it. Yes. She could be here just like you suspected." His accent had a soft Devon burr.

"Show me, please, Thomas." Michael Caridis spoke with emotional urgency, as if the moment had to be grasped before it fled.

He led Caridis past several cavities where they had probed earlier and come up with nothing but sand and rocks. They walked a good eighty feet beyond, continuing the exact axis Michael had insisted they follow. And now he saw what he'd had faith in all along would be there. In a small crater surrounded by a flimsy, makeshift fence, a flight of eight cut-stone steps dropped down into darkness. They presented an almost whimsical anomaly. Steps to nowhere in the barren wastes.

Caridis said, "Even the orientation of the steps follows the axis." He strode forward. "Let's keep digging tonight and see what this is all about. There'll be more steps, of course."

Thomas pointed at the crew clustered together with their shovels, looking at the two bosses. "They'll work as long as you like, but I suggest you relieve them as usual at dawn and bring in the next crew."

"Of course. I'll stay here till we've got a clearer picture of what lies at the bottom of those steps.

"Is it appropriate to ask the one thing you've never let us

discuss with you?" The British foreman was jumping eager in his curiosity. "Who's the *she* we might find—that mysterious woman you've referred to only by her pronoun?"

Michael paused as if to make up his mind. "Hmm. I've hated to jinx it, Thomas. That's why I've said nothing all this time. I suppose your question's only fair now we've got a shot at success." He smiled. Stories get out, and this red herring was perfect for his purposes. He had deliberately referred to the object of their search as a woman, nothing to do with Aaron or Moses. Satisfied his explanation would pass muster no matter what they found, he said, "The wife of Akhenaten. There hasn't been a trace of her death found anywhere before now. She disappeared from all records after her husband was said to have died around 1335 BC. I've always suspected she'd got to be buried here in Amarna. As you know, Akhenaten too has never been found. Several empty Akhenaten graves have been alleged around here, which could mean perhaps none was his grave."

"Splendid! Then I guessed right all along. Imagine finding the sublime Nefertiti herself? Finding his wife would be just as exciting as the discovery of Akhenaten's son, Tutankhamun. What a sight that was! One can never forget finally opening the sarcophagus and beholding the magnificent golden mask of young King Tut!"

Caridis shrugged and waved his hand over the excavation. "I doubt whatever we find will quite match the opulent trappings of Tut's tomb." He smiled. "Anyhow, you're right, she'd be one hell of a prize—if perhaps a bit more wizened than the bust in Berlin." He laughed. "First things first, of course. Grave robbers could have got here before us."

Thomas was startled to notice over his boss's shoulder, a swarthy fellow, one of the diggers, standing close enough to overhear everything they'd just said.

5

Later that night and dawning day

The diggers were ordered to be particularly careful. They inserted their shovels upright into the dense, gritty sand and pressed as delicately as possible downward and emptied them above onto a growing pile that was systematically examined by Michael and his foreman.

As they took more and more sand away, a wall began to emerge across from the flight of steps. The digging changed, now directed from the wall toward the steps. Everyone was tense. The workers breathed hard as they tried to be swift and careful at the same time, driven by the same curiosity that had gripped the others. Their sweat-covered faces glowed in the light of lanterns hanging above the pit from stakes in the sand.

Desert dogs howled in the distance, and one or two packs, invisible to the diggers, came nearer. Their unseen presence could be felt. Vibrations in the earth radiated from swarms of feral paws thumping on the ground as they ran in search of food, and the nearby hills echoed with their random and ever nearer wailing.

Apparently unconcerned by the presence of these animals, two shadowy figures emerged from the barren sands beyond and quietly moved toward the activity buzzing about the pit. They crept forward in the open and crouched behind one of the vehicles ranged near the site.

Outlines of an entrance slab of stone began to emerge in the light of the various lanterns arranged about.

After another hour or so, a worker shouted the Egyptian word for *platform*. They had hit the bottom of the steps. He tapped his shovel to clang on stone underfoot that was quickly uncovered and shown to lead from the wall to connect with the steps. Michael took a lantern and held it above the platform. He used his other hand to wipe sand away until he saw the edge of an inscription. "Bring me a brush," he commanded a worker. Taking it, Michael cleared away most of the sand from the center of the stone. He put the lantern down and withdrew spectacles from his shirt pocket. Kneeling, he leaned over to peer at the intaglio carving now completely revealed. It was of a woman standing with both her arms lifted, hands cupped under a disc of the sun from which the broad wings of an eagle were spread as if in flight. He looked up at Thomas standing on the rim of the excavation. With an elated smile, he nodded. "I think we maybe found her."

Early signs of morning began to brighten the eastern sky. Vapors wafted upward as the heat of the rising sun struck the night-cooled sands. Desert dogs ceased their howling, and several scrawny creatures approached the busy group, hoping to find scraps of food. The uninvited pair of visitors had by now disappeared. The only trace of their presence lay on the spot from which they had watched and listened. A crumpled cigarette pack.

The morning shift arrived, yet those who had been digging all night were now too curious to leave. One of them, a man who spoke with a weaning smile, went up to Thomas and asked if they could stay and help.

He turned to Michael and said, "Shall we double the force?"

Caridis shook his head. "I don't think so. Look, we've found the door. This is going to be delicate work. They'd only be in the way." He paused to light a cigarette and lowered his voice. "Also, let's be extra careful now. Too many eyes and hands means more risk of pilferage. If this turns out to be what we think, what we hope, we're going to have to get round-the-clock armed guards. They'll inspect everyone whenever they leave the site—and watch for unwanted intruders."

Thomas shrugged and told the weaning smiler to return next sundown.

Put out, the man slouched away. After a few steps, he turned his head with a malignant expression.

Thomas turned back to the business at hand. "Pray not too many've got in there before us."

Michael gave a little laugh. "That entrance, crack and all, looks pretty pristine to me. I'd bet in favor of being first for at least three thousand years."

Suleiman materialized. "Effendi, found something." He held out the crushed cigarette packet.

Caridis took it and smoothed out the paper enough to study it. "Private, luxury brand, German. Here, see the writing on the back? Where was it?"

"Next to the truck for bringing the workers. No dead butts to see. Maybe fell from someone's pocket."

Thomas frowned. "You've had so many dealings with the Germans. What is it, for at least the past thirty years? Could any of them really be spying on us?

Caridis shrugged. "Spy on us? Why for Christ's sake? They know me well enough. They'd hear from me if I've got something of interest to sell. No need to play games."

"Why on earth bother to hide here in the middle of the night?

Caridis's cheek muscles tightened. "You've got a point. Evidently, someone suspects we're getting close to a discovery—something important. Got some locals to spy on us. Maybe gave one of them the cigarettes. Without being exactly paranoid, we could even speculate they got wind of our search for a female's tomb. The body of Nefertiti maybe, to go with her bust in Berlin? A nice prize for those fucking kleptos running Germany."

With a look of disgust, Thomas said, "Certainly throw their weight around in Alexandria, like they're masters of the world."

Michael shook his head. "Exactly what they've got in mind."

Stone by stone, the entrance of the tomb began to be dismantled. It involved slow and careful work and took all that day and evening.

By the next morning, a first small opening was made. Flashlights were aimed through it.

"What do you see?" Michael had just appeared in fresh khaki shorts and shirt at the rim of the excavation. "Couldn't get here any sooner. Had an interesting call from my majordomo, Stephanos, in Alexandria, apropos our conversation yesterday. Anyhow, found something worthwhile?"

"Come down and see for yourself." Thomas smiled.

"Damn right I'm coming down." Practically tripping on the steps, he took the flashlight and shined it through the small opening onto a jumble of sand and scattered items, one of which was an effigy of a crocodile. Standing out amid the chaos was a chair made of wood, gilded in places, with two fully carved women's crowned heads flanking the bottom of the seat. "Thomas, is that chair what I think it is?"

"I'd say very likely so. Too close to be anything else."

"Just like the ones James Quibell found years ago in the tomb of that old couple who're supposed to be the grandparents of Akhenaten?" Caridis squinted into the poor light cast by the electric torch.

"You bet. One and the same. What does that suggest?"

Michael raised his eyebrows. "This isn't Nefertiti's tomb."

"Exactly. That chair makes me think it could be Akhenaten's sister, Princess Sitamun. Those other chairs—identical design, different sizes—found by James Quibell in several of her relatives' tombs—did belong to Sitamun. Sitamun herself, or one of her relatives, could be buried in here along with this version—evidently her largest throne chair so far. A very important lady. Adored by her father—for a while he even made her his queen. Not a bad find if that's the case."

"I suppose you could be right. Come on, let's get this wall down so we can know for certain."

By day's end, the opening had been cleared so they could walk directly into a small room. "Some uninvited folks were here before us—long before us, maybe thirty centuries ago." Michael glanced around the space and the debris from the last ancient break-in. He stared fixedly at two life-sized bas-relief statues of a queen set several yards apart against a wall with piles of dirt, sand, and stone at its base. Each of the statues held upright, at chest level, a disc of the sun. Michael approached the wall between the statues, as if mesmerized, and used his hands to wipe away layers of dust. This soon revealed hints of a carving cut into the wall. When he'd cleared more with an intensity Thomas had never seen in the man, Michael stood back and folded his arms as if to stop himself from trembling with excitement. Centered between the statues, carved into the wall surface, was a tall staff broken halfway down so the bottom piece sat at a forty-five-degree angle to the straight vertical upper part. Sprouting from each side near its upright top were two parallel rows of twelve evenly spaced leaves.

Thomas walked up to him. "What do you think this could mean?"

Michael verged on choking up. "It seems—well, you see, I've always had special hopes for what we might find—and now it actually seems possible the greatest prize just might lie here. Why do I say this?" He pointed. "That, Thomas, on the wall, is the rod of Aaron. Broken, it seems for reasons which I can't yet begin to imagine. I confess complete surprise at its connection with Sitamun—if this indeed's her tomb. I can't see any conceivable connection between those two and the rod." He gestured at the pair of statues looking out from the wall. "You see, as much as I would have loved to, I never really believed we'd find Nefertiti here—those statues of Sitamun pretty much confirm that." He pulled himself together. "OK, enough speculating. Let's check this place out."

Peeking from the rubble were two low long rectangular platforms made of stone running perpendicular to the two statues, set some two yards away in front of each statue. Caridis put his foot on one of them and leaned forward with his forearm resting on his knee. "Thomas, these seem somehow misplaced. They look like platforms for the burial of the dead. Catafalques to hold sarcophagi. If that's the case, you'd expect them to be in another room, less accessible; the usual burial chamber should be much deeper inside this place, not the anteroom, don't you agree."

Thomas pressed his lips tight, preoccupied. He idly pushed some of the thick pile of dirt and pebbles from the flat top of one of the platforms. Then he lowered his head and pushed some more away. Finally, he took both arms and embraced as much rubble as he could drag away to fall to the floor. His arms and clothes were powdered with the dust and sand. Without speaking, he pulled away more and more of the debris until the major part of the platform's top was exposed. By now, an arm had been used to wipe away sweat from his face, which was also streaked with powdery residue.

They both stood and stared at what had been revealed. Faces of the workers were stuffed together peering through the doorway at the two men in the light of flickering lanterns.

A small cartouche had been cut into the stone, the stylized profile of a women wearing a pharaonic headdress with the hieroglyphic caption: "Our Beloved Queen and Daughter."

Thomas and Michael looked up at each other and without a word turned together to face the other platform, which they started to clear at almost frenzied speed. And as the billows of dust from their exertions settled, another cartouche appeared. The two men, covered from head to toe with dust, looked like statues themselves. They rubbed away some from their eyes and blinked at the inscription: "Our Son and King and Glory."

Thomas called out to the men in the doorway to move away and let in the light and air. "Michael, it's pretty clear a pair of coffins must have rested on these. But where are the bodies now? Inside there somewhere?" He pointed at the other walls sheathed in plain plaster devoid of decoration. "A king and queen, evidently married, have their catafalques in the first room you enter, which was practically never done, especially for the rulers. It's as if everything had been constructed with enormous haste. Perhaps there was never anything much to steal, and the disappointed robbers just took the bodies. If so, who were these two creatures, this royal couple?"

The workers were called back in to clear away the debris, sifting for clues or artifacts. By nightfall, a large part of the room had been cleaned and swept, enough to reveal the only things of consequence were the two statues, the pair of platforms, the chair of Sitamun, and the small carving of a crocodile. Michael cradled it in his hands and turned it over and over. "Is this a clue of some sort or just another artifact for use in their afterlife?"

"Maybe we'll find out behind here." Thomas was running his hands over the wall between the statues. Except for the carving of Aaron's rod, it was smooth and blank, like the expressions on the stone faces flanking it. "I think this wall's our best hope. If I'm right, I'd like to think we'll find something pretty revealing."

Michael nodded. "Let's go then. Of course we'll preserve that." He pointed at the carving of the rod.

6

That same night

homas was giving directions to the night shift, which had just arrived. Suleiman came close and gestured to Caridis to follow him to a quiet place behind the truck that had moments before delivered the night workers. "Effendi, one of these Egypto-dogs from tonight's crew spoke to me just now. He wanted us to know something. So, I can say in all fairness he showed himself to be above the rest of that dirty, dishonest bunch." Preening himself with a sense of his own superiority as he pronounced these judgments, the intense Ottoman Turk stared with large, watery eyes into his master's waiting gaze. "It would seem, Effendi, the dog was approached near the river landing by someone with a German accent. He says he knows well the sound of a German who speaks Egyptian Arabic. The man said there was money by reporting every day what was going on here. A pittance—so our dog bargains for a better deal from us instead. I took the liberty of handing him a few piastres. For similar amounts, he'll provide misleading information to the German from which the dog will also profit, thereby proving the Egyptian dogs have an innate talent for both bargaining and cheating."

"Spoken like the Turk you are. You did exactly right, Suleiman. Point out this man to me—discreetly."

Suleiman guided him out into the open area and described the man in question without pointing. Michael realized immediately it was the same man who had gone off the night before in dudgeon because he was required to leave the excavation early with the other workers.

"Suleiman, try to find out any shady types behind this. The identity of the curious German. Does he live in Egypt? In Cairo, Luxor, Alexandria, or somewhere else? We'll naturally pay extra for any accurate information."

Suleiman bowed slightly, touched the tip of his hand to his forehead, and turned away with a small smile.

☥

The delicate work began of chiseling into the surface of the wall, trying to isolate and remove intact the carving of the broken rod of Aaron. The wall had never been touched or tampered with, which led Thomas to sigh and say, "I hope we're not barking up a tree. The plastered wall covering, if that's what it is, seems pretty thick. Or it may just be an outside wall, which means we'll have to try the other two walls to see if we can find an inner doorway to another room."

Two surgical penetrations proceeded within patches of the wall on either side of the carving of Aaron's rod. These were made, one at eye level and the other about three feet to the right of it and about a foot off the floor.

After an hour or so without seeing any change in the material that was coming from the wall, the man working on the lower incision gave out a shout. The others gathered round and aimed two lamps, now powered by a generator, at the scarred wall. The barest outline of what appeared to be the corner of a brick had been revealed. Soon after, the upper incision revealed a similar change of material.

Thomas patted both men on their backs and told them to work together to extract the patch of wall surrounding Aaron's rod. This time, they worked with larger and cruder tools, which soon enabled a larger area of brick wall to be uncovered, and the large plaster section containing the rod was eventually ready to be removed.

Michael touched Thomas's arm and gestured to join him outside. They emerged from the stuffy chamber where a number of the workers had huddled, riveted with curiosity as they watched the two men working on the wall.

"I've got something to tell you before we try to break through that inner wall of bricks." He related his conversation with Suleiman. "It's almost as if somebody out there's expecting us to find something we've never yet fathomed. I think that should give us pause."

Thomas looked around them to see whether others might be listening. Several workers milled about, drinking in the fresh night air after the closed atmosphere inside. The major sounds above the murmur of their voices came from the ranging desert dogs trampling the ground as usual in their packs and trumpeting their nocturnal howls. "I'm getting strange feelings about what's going on. Can't explain exactly when it began. Probably this morning when we were cleaning away debris from the statues. A growing aura's coming from inside there. Like those statues were guardians of a great secret they wanted us to learn right now."

Michael nodded. "All right, then, I think in a way we've been forewarned. My man, Stephanos, in Alexandria, received a call from a German aristo who's now the head Nazi there. While college students, we worked for a summer on some digs. An arrogant pain in the ass, full of himself and his family tree. Now he's dropped some bizarre hints that suggest he might know more than he should. Let's double our guards and give out as much disinformation as we can with the workers. Am I right? They don't read old inscriptions or understand ancient symbols?"

"Absolutely not. Come on, let's start removing those bricks."

☥

All the new electric lights were aimed at the brick wall, which they proceeded to open. The lamps pulsed slightly with the cycling of their gasoline-powered generator. A workman gingerly struck the first brick with a hammer and chisel around its edges. The grout had dried over the millennia and was reduced to powder by the attack. As a result, the brick was fairly easily knocked forward into an unknown space. The sound of its fall to the floor on the dark side of the wall sent a small echo—and a thrill through the men crowded about the tiny opening. A second brick was more easily pried away and pulled out on their side of the wall. As were several more.

Nobody had yet aimed a lamp through the opening, as if reserving that moment to be savored later, but Thomas could wait no longer. He took his new electric torch and switched on its intense beam. The others stopped their movements, suspended in time like a snapshot catching a runner in midair. They were distracted by the swinging streak of light as it swung toward the opening. It caught several of their faces, startled and blinded for an instant. The beam steadied, and those who could peered into the other space.

The room was slightly smaller than the anteroom in which they all stood. Its walls, covered with a whitish plaster, simple and undecorated, showed none of the colorful hieratic formulas that were standard for several thousand years of Egyptian preoccupation with the afterlife. It all gave the impression of a hasty effort to create a secure hiding place. But for what? The room appeared to be empty of any evidence of coffins or other funerary objects. There were no catafalques, no furniture, and no food or drink to nourish passage into the great unknown. Only three objects were gathered in the center of the room on a square stone platform about thirty inches high. The larger item was a simple rectangular wooden chest apparently made of ebony, undecorated with paint or carving or ivory, about thirty inches tall by thirty-five inches long by twenty inches deep. The lid was gently curved and bound by three bronze bands that ran from three hinges on the lid and appeared to circle the chest. They could not make out whether it had locks and seals on its other side. The real shock came from what was set directly in front of the chest. Two busts about twenty inches tall faced each other, their profiles immediately recognizable. This royal husband and wife had been placed just this way to gaze at each other for all eternity.

Thomas gasped. "My God, it really is Akhenaten and Nefertiti after all!"

Michael whispered in Thomas's ear, "Careful now."

Thomas turned off his electric torch, and they both stood up to their full height, having leaned over to inspect the inner space. He pointed at the two workmen who had been removing the bricks. "You two stay now and finish opening the wall down to the floor. You others can go home. You'll be paid for the entire shift, and your wives will be glad to see you home early." He paused for a moment. "What you've seen today must stay with you—and you alone. If anyone questions you about the excavation, you'll say nothing. Leave everything to us. After a year has passed, and if none of you has violated my order tonight, everyone will receive fifty pounds each. That's more than you'll ever earn in that year. If any one of you should betray all the others and do something foolish, the others will know whom to punish. I'll see you tomorrow night. We're going to try the other walls to see if there's anything beyond them. Remember no loose tongues."

The two men continued working on the brick wall, while the rest, curious to see what else would be revealed, reluctantly moved outside. They straggled into the truck that was to take them back to their village. Thomas noticed Suleiman catching the attention of one man and signaling him to follow. They disappeared behind Michael's horse feeding from a bucket beside its carriage.

Michael lit his cigarette and Thomas's. "Well, seems this mystery deepens. First, we find Sitamun's statues. Next, we uncover a carving of Aaron's rod. Then, hidden behind a wall, are Akhenaten and Nefertiti's busts. How on earth do we make all these connect? All known evidence suggests Sitamun was Akhenaten's older sister. Then why on earth would a sister's statues guard the tomb of her brother and his wife—if indeed that's what this was?" He paused and frowned deeply. "Good God, what if it's empty? What if that chest has nothing to tell us? We could never know any answers."

Thomas laughed. "What a paradox. Not only are you one hell of a driving optimist, but you're a typical Greek pessimist. Probably superstitious too … It won't be empty, worry not." He inhaled his cigarette. "It's too pristine, too perfectly arranged with the royal busts set just so to guard its secrets. Keep the faith, old man."

They strolled over to the top of the excavation and sat on its rim. Light splashed out from the doorway below their feet onto the steps descending into the sepulchre. They could hear the tapping of the hammer and chisel and the stacking of the bricks being pulled out.

Michael looked up at the constellations studding the inky night sky. Checking the ground behind him, he leaned back till he lay with his hands laced behind his head. "Ah, now this is more like it. From here, it all falls into place. All those bright specks peering down at us. And what do they see? Mere mortals, just specks, are we not? And certainly not as visible as the stars. Yet the busts of two people down there have been guarding a box, probably for more than three thousand years, and their names will be remembered long after ours are forgotten. A kind of immortality, no?"

Thomas hooked an elbow into the sand. "Well, maybe. But there's something else. Knowledge is another kind of immortality. We're seekers. We want to learn more and more, unravel mysteries. Knowledge never dies. It deepens us and elevates us, and even when it may go with us to the grave, there's a part that lingers on, somehow floating out there like a celestial mote in the universe. That's what I care about most. Leave fame to the others. It usually brings its own problems."

The two workmen emerged from the sepulchre and looked up at them. "The wall's open down to the floor, Effendis. May we go home now?"

Michael and Thomas scrambled to their feet and descended the steps. They peered past the men and saw they had also raised the height of the opening and inserted a wooden lintel across the top. Beyond sat the chest and two busts lighted by a lamp they had moved from the anteroom.

"Yes, by all means. Be on your way. Good work tonight. We'll see what we find tomorrow. The driver's returned and can take you now." Thomas patted them both on the back and watched them mount the steps and disappear toward the truck. When they heard its engine roar to life, they entered the sepulchre.

Michael turned to him. "So, where're the bodies now—if there ever were bodies in this place? It's all very strange. Everything's where it shouldn't be. God willing, we'll discover some answers when we open that chest!"

They circled around to its other side and found clasps holding the three bronze bands together. A bronze rod ran through the clasps to keep them from opening.

Thomas touched the three metal clasps and their heavy layers of wax seals that remained unbroken. He raised the casket slightly with a cautious lift of both handles. "Heavy, mainly the weight of the ebony and metal construction, I should think. I don't expect we're going to find any gold statues or jewels in there."

The only decoration on the chest was a disc of the sun carried by the wings of an eagle. This had been carved twice, between the three bronze bands on the lid.

"Interesting," remarked Caridis. "The same motif is carved into the upper back, above the seat, of the chair in the anteroom, Sitamun's chair. Her statues carry the same symbol." His mind teased his memory for something more. There was another example of the symbol, a special, unusual example that he was surprised didn't come back immediately to recollection.

They touched the sides and lid of the metal-bound wood to test its soundness. "Feels like a strongbox, well-constructed and in immaculate condition." Michael lifted the bust of Nefertiti from her place. He noticed the stone, underneath where she had rested. It was spotless, untouched by time. He held her before him at arm's length and stared into her painted eyes. "At least both eyes are intact unlike the gorgeous version in Berlin, which is missing the left one. She's quite beautiful here, but sublimely so in Berlin. I guess the artist hit his best stride just that once."

He put her down as she had been, facing her husband. Crossing his arms and bowing his head before the casket, he retreated into quiet reflection for several minutes.

When he looked up, excitement lit his face. "You described some feelings earlier today. I believe you said those statues appeared to be guarding a great secret. Well, it's been coming over me in a wave, and now we're alone with this. I suppose we're soon going to know. There's more. A power, a force is coming from it. Do you sense what's happening? As if the casket's waking up."

"Indeed, I do. We've got to remove it tonight and take it somewhere safe. Much too risky to leave here."

"The villa's got a steel vault. Put it in when I built the house. You never know what might need to be protected from thieves—even the authorities." Michael stopped and held a finger to his lips. Walking quietly through both openings, he emerged into the night and looked around to check whether the two guards were anywhere within sight or hearing. No one was visible.

Thomas joined him and said in a low voice, "Good thought to check. Tell Suleiman to distract them. Got something to cover it?"

"An old tarp should be inside the rear storage trunk. The casket's too big to fit, but we can put it behind the front seat and cover it like you say. I'll sit with Suleiman, and you can keep it by your feet in the back seat. Stay at my place tonight, of course."

Suleiman, alerted to a task he enjoyed, did his job and took the pair of guards off for a smoke and some ouzo-spiked cold tea from his flask.

Michael and Thomas returned to the sepulchre.

Thomas picked up the bust of Akhenaten. The face was an elongated and thinnish oval with voluptuous, feminine lips and widely spread nostrils. The shape of his head was its most notable feature. The back bulged out as if the king had been hydrocephalic. His eyes were slanted upward. "You, sir, were one exotic-looking fella. I wonder how you ever got the most stunning woman in the world to be your mate." Thomas's eyes twinkled. "Ah, by Jove, I think I've got it. The most powerful king in the world could be a rather fine aphrodisiac, no?"

Michael laughed. "Come on, let's move on before Suleiman runs out of gossip with the guards. We'll leave the two busts placed just the way they were and claim the chest was stolen. We'll show plenty of anger but insist we know the likely culprit and are sure we can get it back, maybe even hint at someone German."

"A nice red herring." Thomas raised his eyebrows and nodded.

They each took a handle of the casket and carried it outside to the steps. Thomas returned to close all the lights and slide a heavy wooden panel over the entrance to the sepulchre. The moon gave enough light to mount the steps and see their way to tuck it into the carriage.

Caridis called with a loud burst, "Suleiman!"

Within moments, he came running and flashed a conspiratorial grin as he leaped up onto the driver's seat. No one spoke during the river crossing and the rest of their journey through the palm trees and up into the hills. When they arrived at the villa, Thomas helped Suleiman carry the casket inside and down a flight of steps into a cave-like space with a long, curved ceiling. At the far end, wooden wine racks covered most of the stone wall under the barrel vault. They placed the chest on a long marble-topped table, and Suleiman discreetly withdrew, closing the double doors behind him.

Wrought iron electric sconces filled the space with a warm light. Wooden armchairs with woven-cane seats bracketed each end of the table.

Several moments later, Suleiman knocked and handed Michael a tray of tools somewhat surgical in appearance.

Thomas touched the wax that sealed each of the casket's three clasps. He picked at it with a fingernail and tasted the little chip. "Beeswax and animal tallow I should think." He searched through the tools and removed what looked like a scalpel, which he wielded expertly in lifting off the wax without scratching the metal clasps or the wooden sides.

The hinged clasps were held in place by a single bar running through three rings that pierced the three clasps. With the removal of the wax, Michael carefully pushed on one end of the bar and, wiggling it slightly, began to slide it through the rings. When it had finally been withdrawn, he lifted each clasp off its ring. The lid was now ready to be raised.

Michael said, "It seems pretty clear nobody's seen what we're about to witness ever since this box was first sealed shut." He held the sides of the hinged lid with the flat of each hand and gently pushed up until it came to rest against the wall behind. A burlap-like cloth lay atop its contents.

Thomas took the cloth with both hands and lifted it to reveal three large papyrus scrolls. These appeared to be the only objects within the sandalwood lining of the casket. His hands began to tremble slightly. He looked confused and dropped the cloth back into the casket. "What's happening to me? Am I frightened? Perhaps not exactly frightened but awed by something I can't begin to explain."

Caridis hesitated. "I wonder. Are we violating something sacred? I really feel we're being tested. As if our intentions must be declared before we go any further."

Thomas interlaced his fingers and brought them to his chin

in an attitude of contemplation. "So, be it. Nothing to lose by committing to respect and do our best to protect whatever we find. So, I do pledge."

"As do I." Michael removed the burlap cloth and gently touched the scroll lying nearest the front of the casket. It responded with a resiliency as if the papyrus were freshly made. Lifting it with great care, he placed the scroll on the cold marble where it lay, loosely curled. "A tiny test. Why don't I hold the open end flat while you see how much resistance there is to unfurling it only a very little?"

Thomas pulled the scroll away from Michael with both hands just a couple of inches and exposed the face of the light beige papyrus sheet. There was no brittleness. The hieroglyphs glimpsed inside appeared vivid and clear. "It's miraculous. No signs of age, at all!"

In the tool tray, lined up like a rank of steel rulers, were two-foot lengths of polished stainless metal weights. Thomas took one and indicated for Michael to open the scroll enough to lay it upon that end. They unrolled it further and placed another weight, and they repeated this action until the entire scroll lay flat on the table. It was at one end of the table where it could be studied from either of two sides.

Michael put on his reading glasses and examined the document without speaking. He remained focused for a number of minutes.

Thomas burned with curiosity.

Finally, Caridis looked up. His manner was somewhat guarded. "We seem to have selected a scroll that begins like a covering letter. It's addressed to Sitamun. So far, most evidence we have shows she was the sister of Pharaoh Akhenaten. Yet here, she's called the Mother of God before saying, 'We weep with the tears of all the heavens to return to you your beloved Son and his Queen after their great flight.'" He followed the hieroglyphs with his forefinger. "Their story is told here for you and for all the ages to come, and to assure they journey through the afterlife recognized forever as Children of the Sun."

Thomas was puzzled. "What you've translated sounds absolutely like the bodies of Sitamun's son, not her brother, and his wife were returned. But do we know if she was supposed ever to have a son—and was that son a pharaoh?"

Michael shook his head. "I've got no idea whether she had a son. But those biers in the anteroom of the sepulchre were created for the coffins of her brother Akhenaten and his wife, Nefertiti. History to date has shown us no pharaoh whose parentage is unaccounted for during her lifetime or after her death. So, if she wasn't the mother of Akhenaten, there can be no other candidates for a son who was a pharaoh."

Thomas wrinkled his forehead with thought. "We do know Sitamun was older than her purported brother. Maybe she actually was his mother at only fourteen or so. And we know he was succeeded as pharaoh by his own son, Tutankhamen. So, the only conceivable inference is Akhenaten is in plain fact, not her brother, but her son, and from what we see here, regarded as some sort of divine incarnation."

Michael nodded. "You're saying, then, she might have been assumed to be a virgin when giving birth to Akhenaten?" He dropped into one of the armchairs and lit a cigarette.

"Yes. Interesting thought that, no? Then on to more mysteries. Their 'great flight' ... what does that mean? Fleeing from what or whom? And to where? And how did they die? From the sounds of this letter, they must have died together."

Thomas examined the scroll. "I don't read these things as well as you, old man, but it seems to speak of passing twice across the river between life and death, pursued by their enemies. It prays: 'May Sitamun be now their great protector,' or some such thing, I think."

Michael flicked some ash onto the stone floor. "I know. We're both dying of curiosity to understand so many things— not the least being the surprising connection between the rod of Aaron and this royal couple—but let's not try to read everything right away." He was forceful. "I think this translation must be got just right. Our most gifted expert to do that is my longtime English friend, a legend in his field of Middle Eastern languages, Rupert Delacorte. I'd never feel comfortable coming to any conclusions on our own without him."

"Of course. Fantastic reputation. His history's rather interesting, I believe?"

"Oh, yes. I heard a lot about it when we were very young, sweltering together on digs. We cut our archaeological teeth in the Valley of the Kings. This was during Eton's summer vacations. He was one of that school's favorite teachers. Utterly charming. Always wore his learning lightly." Michael leaned back in a relaxed posture, hands behind his head, legs stretched out, ready to recount his story.

"When their parents died together, Rupert was very young—and his jealous older brother took revenge by cutting off all funds from the estate to Rupert. From then, he grew up quite poor, and he went on to support himself by teaching and writing. Immigrated to America in his twenties, married a Chicago meatpacking baron's gorgeous daughter, and has two kids now grown up. He expected to live in America for the rest of his years, but fate decided otherwise. It appears his brother was terribly unstable, not the marrying kind, and a complete eccentric. He tried all sorts of maneuvers—except to sire an heir—to make certain Rupert could never inherit should something happen to him. But the estate had by law to remain intact for the next in line. Perhaps caught psychologically between that hate for Rupert and his horror of matrimony, the brother ended his own life with a shotgun. Rupert inherited everything and moved back to England to take up as the new immensely wealthy and popular Marquess of Ravenstone, with his wife and children, a boy and girl. Of course, none of this has ever gone to his head."

Thomas nodded. "Impressive. Think he'll come? You've got to be as anxious as I am to know what this is all about."

Michael tilted his head and smiled. "Let's hope so. If it's at all possible, I can't imagine he won't. A cable will go first thing in the morning. Meanwhile, let's lock up." Michael stood before the wine racks, removed a bottle, and reached to the rear. A motor started humming, and two central portions of the racking, filled with bottles like the rest, swung out on hidden wheels. The massive steel door of a bank vault was revealed. He fiddled over the locks and made it open inward on a curved steel track.

Thomas replaced the scroll and cloth in the casket and closed its three clasps. Together they carried it into the vault and slid it onto a shelf among many shelves crowded with antiquities. Thomas's eyes opened large. "Some collection, my friend."

With a sly smile and a shrug, Michael pointed the way out. He locked the vault and returned the central racks to their normal place. "Let's get some rest. Tomorrow, we'll have some explaining to do at the site, and of course, we must test the other walls to see if something else might lie behind." He paused to switch off the light. "Which is not to say we haven't already discovered Golconda."

☥

After staring at the ceiling for a good hour, Thomas got up and began to pace in his bedroom. Contradictory thoughts raced through his mind. From time to time, he stopped and shook his head with a dissatisfied expression, and then he continued to range like a caged animal.

Michael was also restless. His excitement over the day's discovery made sleep a lost cause. He sat and recorded the day's events. He included his undercurrent of concern that something menaced the entire project. Whatever was going on would require him to be ever on his guard. A wan smile flitted across his face. *Even in Eden, there'd been a serpent.*

With this, he put down his pen and climbed into bed. He fell into an uneasy sleep.

☥

When they appeared late the next morning, the excavation site was abuzz. The workman who had been asked by a German to spy on the excavation made a special point of seeking out Suleiman. Michael noticed the two of them pair off together, and he followed them casually over to the rear of one of the work trucks. Suleiman appeared almost conspiratorial—as if he did not even want Michael to be aware of what he was doing.

The two mortified guards from the previous night shift had remained and grabbed Thomas as he arrived at the site. With excited gestures of hands and eyebrows, they stumbled over their words, asking if he knew what had happened to the box. Defensive, they insisted it had been there all night. As they always were alert on duty, they were certain no one had invaded the site during their watch. What kind of magic had made it disappear? It wasn't their fault.

"Please, Effendi, don't fire us. Bad spirits must be about this place. That's the only explanation."

Thomas affected to frown and be puzzled. He nodded at the suggestion of bad spirits. He crossed his arms and told two of the workmen to look around the site for any clues or signs of the chest. He then entered the tomb as if to check for himself the void where the chest had once been behind the busts of Akhenaten and Nefertiti.

A small shock jolted him, and the base of his skull began to tingle. The royal couple indeed still faced each other—but no longer in the inner room on the platform where the chest of scrolls had been discovered. They sat now in the anteroom of the sepulchre where each bust rested on the catafalque where its mummified body had presumably been placed before the tomb was sealed. Everyone outside denied ever touching the busts.

Thomas assured the workmen he'd take care of finding the chest. They should get back to their jobs. The unpenetrated walls of the outer and the inner chambers were tested to see if other spaces might be concealed behind them. Nothing. The tomb had given up all its secrets. It seemed to have been constructed in haste, without frills and decorations, most likely when the scrolls and bodies had been delivered to Sitamun, fascinatingly addressed in the first scroll's preamble, as the Mother of God.

They speculated how grave robbers had probably stolen the bodies soon after their placement on the catafalques—and how they might have assumed that was all there was of interest. Why would there be other rooms since sarcophagi usually ended up protected in the innermost chamber?

Michael remarked, with a certain wryness, "This probably saved the wooden chest from the thieves."

Thomas shrugged. "Strange for them both, Akhenaten and Nefertiti, to have been here together and then not even the hint of a tomb where Nefertiti might have been moved. We already know of several where he was supposed to have been laid, but no body for Akhenaten has ever been documented."

"You're right. She had to be one of history's most beautiful, mysterious, and elusive of all creatures—even in death."

☥

That evening, Thomas announced all further excavation would be stopped. The object of their search had been found. Sadly, the bodies of the royal couple and the ebony chest had been plundered. There was nothing else to be sought.

Some of the workers grumbled at the loss of work. The one whom Suleiman had spoken to in the morning now engaged him in what appeared to be a heated argument. Suleiman shook his head forcefully and turned away, unaware as the other man took up one of the shovels and swung it at him. He ducked when the others gave a shout of alarm. Suleiman stared at his assailant for a long moment and gave him a saturnine smile and an obscene gesture.

Driving the Mercedes-Benz four-by-four back to the villa, Michael turned his head toward the back seat. "So? What was that all about, Suleiman?"

"That unspeakable Egyptian swine, Effendi, says he knew how the box was taken last night because he hides, instead of going home in the truck, and watches us. And he swears now he's going to tell this to the German who would pay him much more than we were paying him to confuse the German. I told this double-crossing traitor it didn't matter what bullshit he told the German because any information he gave would be a lie. All his stories were wrong. The man swears he knows the truth and wants big money to stay quiet. I say no, and the rest you see with your own eyes."

"You did right, Suleiman. It doesn't matter what he tells his paymaster. It will only be speculation. They cannot know where the casket is kept—and not even we really know its contents yet. Just stay on your guard in case anyone comes calling, uninvited."

"I'm always on the alert, Effendi, do not fear. But you don't know already what's inside the box?" With that question, Suleiman's eyes perhaps belied his seeming sincerity.

Was it the sly look of a man playing a double game? Michael seemed not to have taken this in. After so many years of service from the Turk, he'd no reason to question his full trust in the man. He responded with candor, "No, not quite yet, Suleiman. We're waiting for someone to help us, my old friend, Rupert Delacorte."

7

October 1938

*I*t had taken some thirty-two years of speculation and false starts and hours of discussion with his old friend for the announcement finally to come. This morning, Rupert awoke to a timid knock on their bedroom door. Turning to see his wife had not been disturbed from her sleep, he pulled on his dressing gown. Opening the door, he found the cheery face of their housekeeper looking contrite.

"Sorry, your lordship, but telegrams is usually important." She handed him the yellow packet, looked over at the bed, and whispered, "Will you be needin' your tea just yet?"

He stepped out into the hall, curious about the delivery in his hand. "No, no. I'll be down in a bit. Thanks, Hattie." Closing the door softly behind him, he crossed over into his dressing room and opened the telegram.

> My dear Rupert, at last uncovered mystery long discussed. Stop. Dark forces already threaten.

Stop. Please come immediately Amarna. Stop.
I know sudden and terribly impractical but am
desperate for your help. Stop. Your eternally
grateful Michael

Rupert looked out the window. He could feel his excitement
rising. The day was misty, and the air filled with Wiltshire's
autumnal smells of damp leaves and soggy earth. A little of
Egypt's sunshine and dry breezes might just hit the spot. He
turned at the sound of someone behind him.

She seemed most beautiful in the morning, without any of
the refinements and adornments ladies have used forever to
enhance themselves. Only two years younger than his fifty-
four, she had the freshness and verve of the girl of twenty-one
when they had met in Chicago. It happened at a dance at
the fancy club the barons of railroads and meatpacking and
agribusinesses had built to celebrate their elevation to new
levels of respectability—having passed the major hurdle of
amassing enormous wealth. He had been invited to attend the
ball when a sketchily informed rumor had got out that the
younger brother of the richest peer in England was working
at the University of Chicago in their department of Ancient
Near Eastern Studies. In fact, he had real advantages as
well. A compact, athletic young man with a lithe grace to his
movements, a face that some women had characterized as
beautiful, which would have embarrassed his deep masculinity
and even puzzled him as he never thought about the way he
looked. His clear blue eyes were set wide apart and slanted
slightly upward under a shock of wavy and heavy golden hair.
An air of seriousness underlay his abundant charm, but good
humor was never far from his eyes.

A young lady, heiress to a great meatpacking fortune,
happened to see him appear at the top of the ballroom's

entrance staircase. With a questioning aura, he was studying an engraved invitation as if to be sure he'd come to the right place. What she saw was some sort of young god. Suddenly attacked by a bout of shyness, she turned to her aunt who stood entranced by the same vision. "Betty, do you see?" She finished by simply pointing.

"I sure do, kiddo. Who? I'll tell you what, I'm going to take this one by the bit and find out, baby."

Several minutes later, Rupert was surrounded by others with the same intentions. Aunt Betty, however, was practiced at getting her way and managed to disengage him from the little swarm and lead him in her niece's direction. Chatting all the way, the two had become animated until they reached the young woman who was to become the mainstay of his life. He had been looking down while they were walking, and when Betty announced "Lizzie, baby, this is Rupert Delacorte, and I think you two should meet," he snapped out of the conversation with his older escort and looked up into the dancing brown eyes of Elizabeth Bierstadt, granddaughter of German immigrants on her father's side, and fell in love. With an unquestioning certainty, he knew deep in his gut this would become his best friend and the mother of his kids, the Fates be willing.

"What's that, darling? A telegram?"

Rupert came out of his reverie and smiled. "Yes, it's Michael. Sent from Egypt. Says he's desperate for me to come. Seems he's finally found what he's been telling us for years he was searching for. I suppose he needs to have translations and the like. Not a very convenient time for me, of course."

"You mean those debates raging in Lords over PM's follies at Munich?" She frowned. "Sleep with dogs like Hitler and Mussolini, and you get fleas. PM harbors delusions that you can change tyrants. So, Nazi gangsters are handed Czechoslovakia like it was ours to give. Just because Hitler promises he'll be a good boy once he gets it. Pathetic—just wait. You'll see. They'll be grabbing even a bigger prize before you know it." She crossed her arms and looked delightfully determined.

Rupert adored her grasp of serious things, things that mattered. When his brother had killed himself, middle-aged and childless, he'd inherited the whole shebang—entailed and, therefore, couldn't leave the family line. So, he'd gone from enabling their family to live just comfortably while he earned the modest salary of a professor in Chicago to return to England where Lizzie jumped in like a duck to water. Without missing a beat, she became his partner and hostess in the management of a great fortune and a political life that flourished from the very start when he made his much-admired maiden speech in the House of Lords. As the new Marchioness of Ravenstone, she was appreciated by many for her convictions and intellect—and reviled by those with their heads in the sand.

She came over to him in her gauzy nightgown edged with lace and put her arms around his neck.

He felt her still-firm breasts against his chest.

"Darling, let's face it, staying here isn't going to change anything to do with this government. You should go and make a real trip of it. You haven't seen Michael in several years, and who knows what he's found? Why, you never know," she assumed a drawl to her voice, "it might even change the course of history—a bit more than anything you can do staying here." She giggled and kissed him first on his eyelids and then his mouth. It had been like this from the day they'd met and married in Chicago. He found himself exhilarated by her very existence.

When she had taken him by the hand back into their bedroom, it had all the magic and prompted all the desire he had felt as a twenty-three-year-old on their wedding night.

Perhaps even better. Lying back on his pillow afterward, he pulled a cigarette from the little silver container on his nightstand and lit it. After inhaling deeply, he looked up at the ceiling and said, "I've had some not-so-marvelous news about our son, I'm afraid."

Her expression went from contentedness to a little frown. "Yes?"

"Jacobson from Scotland Yard called on me at the office late last night—after the debate in Lords. You were asleep when I got home, which is why I didn't tell you then. It seems Orlando's taken his flirtation with fascism a bit far of late. All that silly marching around the streets with Oswald Moseley and his absurd British Union of Fascists in black fencing jackets—imitating that poppycock Mussolini—is bad enough. But things are getting more serious. The Yard's pinpointed a Nazi cell here. They know who the leader is and a certain number of people it's tried to recruit to Germany's cause. Our son's apparently one such recruit."

"Darling, it's that damn Ravenstone curse. Your mom and dad—your brother—now it's sunk its clutches into our son. Thank God our Tessie and you've been spared. OK, tell me," she paused, "what's he been up to with the Germans?" Elizabeth steeled herself for his response.

Rupert sat up, braced himself against the pillows, and shook his head. "He seems to have been spying on me, of all things. Giving them information—my activities, speeches I've prepared before I actually deliver them, conversations among ourselves with the kids. But worse than that, Orlando's very substantial income from the trusts after William killed himself means his life's got no financial boundaries. I'm told he contributes to the Nazi Party, and I'm told for some time, he's been funding some pretty toxic personal habits that you may not want to know about."

"Not to worry. Go ahead." She huddled a bit more under the covers.

"Well, he makes regular trips to Venice where he's taken up with a young woman who's an infamous practitioner of sadomasochistic eroticism. She's said to be in her early twenties, very beautiful, and probably borderline insane. And happens to be from a distinguished Italian family that's got several popes in its tree."

"Our boy's got unusual tastes it seems."

Rupert's jaw clenched. "Sadly, they may've got him into some real trouble this time. No proof so far, but there's a hushed-up situation here involving several of our local fascist types—Orlando and this young woman were said to be present—during which a Jewish boy died in a rather terrible way, which I won't get into. She was thought to take flight back to Venice where she'll be beyond our jurisdiction. She's so well connected with Mussolini's government that she's got virtual legal immunity there." He leaned over and took her hand. "Now, it's altogether possible our son wasn't implicated. They've not yet questioned him. All we can do is pray he's not responsible for the sad fate of that boy."

Elizabeth pulled her hand away, sat up, and pushed the covers aside with a forceful cry. "It's true—he's got the Ravenstone curse!"

8

Late October 1938

Rupert Delacorte stood at the railing of his ship to watch it land in the grand harbor of Alexandria. It was a gorgeous day, comfortably cool. He felt excited as they passed the little island where Pharos, the famous lighthouse, had once stood, built at the command of Alexander the Great soon after his conquest of Egypt. The island was attached by a causeway to the mainland. Built over two millennia ago, that immense freestanding beacon tower was man's tallest thing ever built before the late nineteenth century. At forty or fifty stories high, it had been a wonder of the world. Gone now, felled centuries ago by an earthquake.

His thoughts ranged as the ship rounded its course for the landing. *Here is where it all started. All of Western civilization could find its taproots in this land.* The Nile, whose delta spread before him fertilized not just Egypt but the science, architecture, religions, engineering, and political models that had influenced every Western culture of the past five thousand years.

Winches ground and lowered the gangway to the dock. He joined the festive crowd of passengers thronging off the ship. Alexandria was a bazaar. Commerce thrived everywhere he looked. Caftaned men hawked postcards, jewelry, guide services, everything imaginable of interest to the arriving visitors. Red fezzes, some with black tassels, dotted the teeming crowds like cherries on a cake. Dark mustaches, grizzled beards, black burqas, smells of spices, grilling meats, prominent noses, watery, sun-damaged eyes, strong cigarettes, pungent Turkish coffee, burlap bags of grain piled on the docks, poor children's pleading expressions, tugging hands pulling at sleeves and jackets—a chaos and a symphony of Middle Eastern life greeted him. He kept turning his head at the importunings, laughing, and fending off the urchins. He inhaled the exotic smells, wiped the sweat from his forehead under a panama hat, and had his passport stamped by an official in a uniform straight from a Gilbert and Sullivan operetta. A suave man in his forties carried a sign with Delacorte printed on it. A minion collected his bags, and he was whisked off in an open Bentley to Michael Caridis's palace at the center of the bustling city.

Along the way, Rupert noticed a number of German officers dressed in Nazi uniforms. They sat at sidewalk cafes and strolled in the streets, looking rather snappy, he mused, in a rather sleek Teutonic way. These were well outnumbered by British officers, somewhat more relaxed, whose presence gave reassuring evidence of Egypt's status as a British protectorate. Rupert wondered whether the political rumblings roiling Europe—only temporarily calmed by the British prime minister's signed nonaggression agreement with Chancellor Hitler at Munich—had affected relations between Brits and Germans here in Alexandria.

He was thinking about Michael's many German friends and clients who lived here. Rupert was reminded of a German aristocrat from those early digs, Lothar von Vranken. In the shimmering summer heat of those days, when they were sifting through the detritus of times gone, they'd discovered their mutual cousinage with both the now-ailing deposed kaiser and the British Crown.

Lothar had been a strange bird. Michael could never tolerate him when he'd drop himself down, uninvited, at a table where the two of them had been talking, and launch into criticizing this or that person in the dig, or the Khedive or the Caliph or anything that had aroused his easily awakened penchant for irritability. But the arrogant Westphalian aristocrat had surprised them one day when he'd leaped from their table and raced into the teeming street to save a small girl who had wandered into the traffic and was about to be run down by a mounted man in robes and a turban who was pressing his horse through the maze of camels and carts and could not see the girl as he emerged into her path.

Rupert recognized the familiar facade of Michael's house and the wizened attendant at its impressive iron gates.

The man saluted him with an open hand held to his forehead. He cast down his watery brown eyes in respect and gave a little, tilted nod. "Welcome back, Effendi."

Rupert was escorted by a servant wearing a very short, embroidered jacket and baggy pants tied at the ankles, through the high vaulted passageway to the inner courtyard. This parklike space was crowded with massive black basalt and granite statues of ancient notables and kings, sarcophagi, obelisks, and sacred animals. They entered the house through tall double doors of heavy bronze and glass at the top of broad steps on the far side of the courtyard. After the bright Egyptian sun, his eyes were temporarily blinded by the relative darkness. His vision cleared and was again dazzled as they passed through room after room filled like a museum with antiquities. Mummies, wall fragments, canopic jars, faience vases, jewelry of precious metals and stones, blown glass, coins, bronze weapons, helmets, horses' halters, small models of boats and carts, and other homely furnishings placed in tombs to serve their occupants in the hereafter. Rupert reflected how so many of these objects had survived far more intact than the vain hopes of their owners. Several of these creatures lay in glass cases, withered remnants of skin pulled like thin layers of leather over bony skulls and limbs.

They entered the central hall of the palace to find a handsome, clean-shaven younger man with curly dark hair who had just finished descending the grand staircase.

He strode over and embraced him. "Welcome, Rupert. What a pleasure to see you. I know Michael's so grateful for the way you dropped everything to answer his call."

This was Stephanos, a Greek of ambiguous antecedents, who administered Michael's business and household affairs.

Rupert smiled. "Well, his telegram was pretty compelling. Can you fill me in with a few more details? I must say, he does know how to bait a person's curiosity."

The other man drew him into a small sitting room where they made themselves comfortable and were served refreshments. "Even with me, Michael's being quite mysterious. Apparently, they've now closed the site and placed a guard or two. When he started this project, he hired a Brit, Thomas Lavery, to be foreman. Main qualification's having been a junior member of Carter's team sixteen years ago when they found King Tut. Carter and Carnarvon are no longer with us, so we couldn't do much to verify things. Took him mostly on faith."

With a little laugh, Rupert responded, "Well, it could be Lavery was indeed a good choice. Given the urgency of Michael's telegram, it seems they've discovered something of, let's say, importance?"

"I would assume so. Strangely, all I've heard came from one of Michael's old friends from his student days on digs. The German's now a senior Nazi officer posted here since August. Several days ago, this man called and tried to wheedle information from me about the dig. He said he heard they'd made a find. A chest, bound in bronze. When I told Michael, his rage made my phone rattle. Blamed it on one of the workmen who said a German had followed the truck taking workmen from the site to their village. When the workman got off the truck, the German spoke to him and said he'd pay him well to report everything going on at the site. Michael's so upset that he lets go at me of all things. About not knowing whom to trust."

Rupert nodded. "Yes, probably not a bad idea if he's found something important. Tell me, is this Nazi fellow called von Vranken?"

Stephanos seemed to smile to himself. "How did you know?"

"A good guess. Was with us years ago when we met as students on summer digs."

Stephanos said, "I see. Well, let me take you to your room. Have a rest and a soak if you'd like, and we can continue this at dinner. Your train leaves in the morning at ten."

Rupert, with his finely tuned powers of observation, had noticed the rather artful sincerity of his host, and his enigmatic smile. It all prompted a cascade of reflections about whom indeed his old friend ought to trust.

☥

Late the next day, the steam engine blew its shrill whistle and braked in a welter of sparks alongside the railway station nearest to Amarna. Through his window, Rupert spied

Michael Caridis waiting on the platform. Still well-knit and straight-backed, the man seemed to him preoccupied, also to have aged. The moment he spotted Rupert, he ran for the door of his compartment and wrenched it open. As Rupert got out, he gave him a big bear hug. "My dear, dear friend. You're a saint, an angel. We've got so much to do. And now you're here at last. I feel such a burden's been lifted. Come, come, let me carry your bag."

The two men walked across the tracks to a dark green Mercedes Overland G5. "I've come without Suleiman so we could talk freely. So much to tell." Michael opened the passenger door. "Here, do get in. It's a bit of a bumpy ride, which won't surprise you after those summers ages ago. The roads really aren't much better now."

Rupert settled into the passenger seat and studied the other man as he maneuvered the vehicle over the pitted roads. The elegant head and profile. Skin tanned by a life much in the sun. Hair in more recent years close-cropped and silver-white, covering his head in tight curls. The Byronic waves almost to the shoulders had disappeared long ago. The skin around his eyes had darkened with worry and perhaps not enough sleep.

"How was your trip? And how is Elizabeth taking my selfish kidnapping of her prince?"

Rupert's eyebrows rose. "She encouraged it. Fed up with all the nonsense surrounding Chamberlain's naivete at Munich. Thought it'd be good for me to leave the backbiting at Westminster and forget Hitler and the Nazis for a while." He held back their concerns for Orlando's connections, which he had let recede a little from his top of mind.

"And was it your idea or hers to do the last leg, from Athens to Alexandria, by boat?"

Rupert laughed. "Oh, that was entirely mine. Had a sudden hankering to land the way I did when you and I first met in

'04. Don't know exactly why. Could be your cable. It implied the quest you described to me then, and often after, may have come at last to a brilliant conclusion."

"You will be a most vital key to any such conclusion, dear Rupert."

"Miko, last night, Stephanos mentioned something about a chest and said you were very upset. Awfully sorry. Hope I'm not too late to help."

Caridis gripped the steering wheel and cast a haunted look at him. "It's a long story, my friend."

Rupert leaned toward him and patted him on the arm. "By all means, do tell it—and please don't spare the details."

"Thanks. The search for the Seraphim treasure has indeed ended. I believe we've almost certainly found the answer to our Society's ancient enigma. My quest finally hit its stride when some stroke of luck made me divine something that's so simple. A mathematical connection between Aaron's rod on the doors of all the world's Seraphim sanctuaries and the pillars of the temple of the sun in the ruins of Akhetaten."

"Damned exciting, Miko! As you know, your encouragement long ago to take my father's advice and become one of your fellow Aaronites has made a big difference to my political life. As an Aaronite, I feel as if I've got a stake in your discovery."

Caridis looked over at him. "I must confess I'm pleased to hear that. I think I'm going to need you as an ally. The translation of three large scrolls in that chest will be the beginning. But there's much more afoot here. It's clear that spies have been tracking our actions for some time. And, yes, it looks like they're Nazis. I've no idea how far up their political ladder this goes, or how deeply the Berlin Sanctuary is involved. Berlin is today's power base for the world society, as you probably know."

Rupert turned to him and nodded. "Stephanos mentioned

that von Vranken appeared suddenly this summer in Alexandria. Posted as a Nazi officer, in fact, probably the leading gestapo guy there. And that he called about the chest like he knew just what you'd found."

"He might well be our nemesis. He appears here after all these years and calls me out of the blue. About three months ago, and it seems he's already at the epicenter of the German community."

Rupert frowned. "I see. So, he could be behind the threat to your discovery?"

"I'm certain that's the case. He's the one who phoned Stephanos." Michael gripped the wheel even more tightly. "You've always had a gift for getting to the nub of things. That's just what's happening, as we speak. As of course you're aware, the Seraphim are a major sponsor of the Nazi party."

Rupert nodded. "Several of us in the London Seraphim are very uneasy about this connection. One of our members is a minister of the present government, Churchill. He could even become prime minister at some point if things heat up even more with Germany. He's been warning anyone who'll listen about the looming threat from Berlin."

"Absolutely. Von Vranken and his Alexandrian friends in the Seraphim drink sickening toasts to their so-called Fuhrer. It's disgusting to hear them speak sometimes." Michael shook his head as if to clear his thoughts.

Rupert flicked the ash from his cigarette and was transfixed with interest. "So, now you must put me out of my agony of suspense, Michael. Is the famous secret of the Seraphim revealed? Have you begun at all to translate the scrolls?"

Caridis gave a full description of the events of the excavation, the opening of the chest, and its placement in the villa's vault. Rupert was silent during the narrative until Michael finished with a questioning look at him.

Rupert cleared his voice and said, "So, it seems you've found what was probably the first tomb of Akhenaten and Nefertiti. Even if the bodies are no longer there, they may eventually turn up somewhere else. It wouldn't be the first time something like that happened. I know there's another tomb where he was said to have been buried, but his body has yet to be found. What seems just as intriguing is why would the royal couple have died at the same time? Rather too much of a coincidence. This raises some speculations—were they killed by someone or some event?"

Michael nodded approval. "Your mind's as agile as ever, my dear fellow. How I miss our conversations when you were spending summers here and those times we've been together since in places like Paris and Madrid."

Rupert ran his hand over his blond naval-cut beard. His chiseled profile and the trimness of everything about him gave an aura of youthful vigor and discipline. "You must have been sorely tempted to read ahead. I might not have been so restrained. Frankly, I'm incredibly excited!"

Michael left the main road and turned the Mercedes all-wheel-drive up the gentle hill through olive trees and palms until he pulled into the courtyard in front of the villa. Puzzlement registered on his face. "Why the skid marks by the front door? Why the hell's it open? Where's Suleiman?" He leaped from the car followed by Rupert. They dashed into the house and down the broad steps to the lower level. Along the way, they noticed footprints smeared into the stone pavings. They were fresh smears of what looked like red wine or even something else.

Michael ran the length of the corridor to the opened double doors at the end. The mayhem inside was visible from afar. Wine bottles in profusion lay shattered on the floor, shards of glass everywhere amid puddles of wine and blood. The pair of racks that were hinged had been wrenched open to reveal the steel vault's massive door, which was apparently still locked shut. A chair had its back to them in the middle of the barrel-vaulted space. Tied to it with his hands and feet strapped, Suleiman's head hung slumped away from them. When the two men ran around the chair to see Suleiman, they stopped abruptly. He had been viciously slashed about the head, throat, arms, abdomen, and even groin. It had been a terrible torture by someone impatient for an answer. The devastation was crude, the work of an amateur, and somehow even more horrible because of the angry cuts and the man's completely random ruination. There was no sign of life. Too much of the deep puddle about Suleiman's feet was his own blood. Its depletion had been so complete he was left an ashen gray, the color of old stone.

Michael rubbed his eyes as if to erase the scene. And wipe away a tear. He went to the vault's door where someone had started to arrange wires as if to connect some sort of explosive device. This too was amateurish and apparently thwarted before they had made much progress.

"They must have had a lookout and scuttled from here once our car was spotted," Rupert remarked.

"Oh my God, Rupert. What have I got us into? Poor Suleiman. They must have made him show where we placed the casket. He'd no idea how to open the vault's door, so they probably tortured him, certain he did know. What a catastrophe!"

Delacorte, cool and practical, said, "Horrible. Now, Michael, let's assume this was done by the same parties you suspect have been after this from the start of your excavation.

"Of course, Von Vranken and his ilk. They toast their Fuhrer and say things like 'death to the Israelites.' The legend surrounding the casket smolders with stuff to throw on that fire."

Delacorte folded his arms. "There's something we haven't put our finger on. A peculiar contradiction I can't quite yet grasp. One can only hope the scrolls give us the answers."

Michael nodded. He walked past the ruined creature and placed his hands on the heavy vault door. "This is almost hot. I felt the heat back there. What can be happening?"

"I've no idea, but we must assume Suleiman's attackers are still desperate to get inside your vault. Can we trust the local police to be on your side if they come to inspect the mayhem?" He looked about. "Have you got have any guns? We could be under attack before the police appear."

"You're so right. We've got to leave now. Give me a moment." Michael left and returned with a broom. "Inside the vault are some shotguns for bird shooting. Also a rifle. We can take them. Here, use this broom to clear the area in front of the vault while I call the police. They're a good distance from here so it'll take at least forty to fifty minutes before they arrive. We'll pack up the car and leave before then."

When he returned from making the call, Caridis walked across the damp floor to the vault and entered the several combinations to open it. As the huge door swung inside on its track, a wave of heat attacked them. The casket had fallen from its shelf to the floor where it lay on its side. Only slightly cracked, it had been saved by the three bronze bands encircling the casket.

Both men stood riveted by the scene.

Michael was the first to speak. "Thomas and I placed it firmly on that shelf. Nothing but an earthquake could have moved it."

Rupert crouched to touch the warm casket. "There's an energy coming from this. As if reacting to what happened here. Let's move it to the car. The guns?"

Michael collected weapons and some ammunition from

another shelf, and they brought everything to the table. Michael closed the vault door, and they could hear it locking automatically. They pushed the hinged racks back into place. In spite of the damage, they still hid the vault. Michael took a last look at Suleiman and noticed a crushed pack of cigarettes between his feet. It was the same private German brand found at the site of the dig.

With the casket and the guns stored in the car, Michael climbed into the driver's seat, and Rupert took the rifle and some ammunition and moved in next to him. The engine revved, and they slowly pulled out onto the road that wound its way back down to the main highway running alongside the Nile all the way to Alexandria, many hours to the north.

They came to a stop at the landing normally used by Caridis to cross the river on his way to the dig. This time, they continued on the highway without taking the barge across. As it was dark, and there was practically no other traffic, the sound of their engine stood out and carried across the water. Shutters opened in the shadows surrounding a low building on the other side of the river, from the same window that Michael's surrey had been observed only a couple of weeks before. This time, night binoculars appeared at the window and focused on the driver with his distinctive silvery-white cap of close-cropped hair.

Rupert turned around to check their rear. The casket was under a dark green tarp, and a glow emanated from round the edges. He said nothing, but he felt a thrill of anxiety and excitement. All his faculties had hit high alert.

"The road's empty behind us. I think we managed to elude anyone waiting to go back to the villa after we scared them off."

"Hope you're right." Caridis's facial muscles tensed. "There's another vault in the catacombs beneath the house in Alexandria. Should we hire special guards to keep watch round the clock? Or maybe not, so not to call attention to anything unusual."

"I'd go ahead and get some guards after seeing what these people are capable of doing, Miko."

The primitive highway forced slower progress than they'd have liked. Dark silhouettes of palm trees passed by, barely lit by a sliver of waning moon. Sometimes their black fronds, stark against the sky, seemed to have blown about into the forms of giant claws clutching at the air. Constellations splashed across the heavens, sparkling into infinity. They both remained silent.

The minute hand of the dashboard clock had moved a quarter way round the dial before Michael said, "I've been thinking about poor, unlucky Suleiman. With me such a long time. Loyal. Always trusted him. I don't even want to wonder if someone might have dangled some sort of temptation to make him talk." He paused. "Except, what was he going to say that was new? That workman at the site already told his German paymaster he'd seen us take away the casket. And Suleiman had no idea of how to open the vault. The most he could have done would be to confirm we brought the casket to the villa and where the vault was. No, dear God, he was just their victim, nothing more."

Rupert lit a cigarette. "Let's open up all logical doors to possible motives and actors behind Suleiman's death. We start with this suspicion—the Seraphim Nazis believe something important *to them in particular* lies buried near the ruins of Akhetaten." He exhaled and hesitated. "We know the legend's murky, but the treasure's pretty much understood to concern Moses and Aaron in all likelihood." He thought for a moment. "Both Jews. Could that mean they might have some reason, perhaps based on information we've never heard of so far, to imagine the Jews could be ill served by whatever's revealed in those scrolls?"

Michael nodded. "Yes, it's certainly possible. The legend has hinted huge disruptions could occur because of its contents. But these people have been willing to kill to get whatever they think is there. It's hard to imagine what could make them that determined."

Rupert tilted his head back and said, "The Aaron of the plagues sent against Pharaoh is one of the traditional biblical heroes. We Aaronites, on the other hand, celebrate only the pagan Aaron of the golden calf, the Aaron at the moment he lapsed, not at all the Aaron of Hebrew orthodoxy. Maybe the scrolls will tell us that the Bible story got things wrong. Let's imagine we could discover a completely different slant on Aaron and Pharaoh and Moses that somehow undermines the very fundamentals of the traditional Hebrew faith itself. That certainly could whet the appetite of the Nazi contingent of the Aaronites."

Michael nodded. "And explain why they want to get their hands on the treasure. That's why I needed you so desperately to come and do the translation and give me your advice."

"Which, old friend, I could not be more pleased to do." Rupert put out his cigarette in the dashboard ashtray. "I've got to say, everything here naturally begs the other fascinating question: Where the hell is *Moses* in all this?"

They were coming to a point where the river widened, and the highway swept in an arc around its expanded girth. Rupert remarked, "I thought I saw some headlights just turn off, about half a mile ahead. Across that great bend the road's going to make. First sign of life in a while. Not likely to be a threat now that we've advanced so far without incident. Probably somebody parking for the night."

Two hundred yards ahead, a small truck was blocking the road. A man was waving his arms for them to stop.

Rupert barked, "Looks fishy to me. Let's not take any chances. See if there's a way we can zip by around it."

There was no clear and easy path to avoid the truck.

Michael slowed down almost to a stop some distance from the man waving his arms.

The fellow started to advance toward them.

Rupert held the pistol out of sight, wary and alert.

Suddenly, several other men emerged from bushes on either side of the road.

"Quick, turn around—and let's get out of here," Rupert shouted.

Michael reversed with a screech of tires on the ragged pavement and spun the Mercedes around. Its four wheels gripped the road as he changed into forward gear and pressed hard on the accelerator. The grinding sounds of shifting into second gear were punctuated with thuds of bullets striking the rear door panel. Several more shots zinged past them. Their lead widened.

Rupert turned to look out the back window, which had a nick from a spent bullet. "They're getting into the truck and starting to chase us. We've got to pull off and hide. Let's get out of their viewing range."

The Mercedes bounced into and over the ruts, lifting and dropping the vehicle and its contents like dice being shaken in a leather cup.

Michael's teeth clattered against each other as he said, "Can you still see them?"

"No. Let's put some more distance between us. They certainly can't maneuver like us over rugged terrain without four-wheel drive."

Michael kept searching for a likely place to exit the

highway. Dark cliffs that flanked the great river loomed in the distance. At a grove of eucalyptus trees, he pulled sharply off the highway and onto a narrow dirt road. "We should try to place ourselves out of the way, but where we can see them pass us by."

They drove past several low houses made of mud bricks. All lights were out. Driving a bit farther, they pulled behind a wooden storage barn. They stopped next to a tractor, turned off the lights and ignition, and jumped out of the vehicle. Together, they ran back to the highway and hid behind the trees. In the distance, the headlights of the truck appeared. Holding their breath, they prayed for it to pass them by, exhaling when it did.

Rupert whispered, "We've got to wait a bit … in case they have second thoughts and turn around."

After several minutes, they headed back to the barns. A man with a shotgun was standing next to the Mercedes. He was about sixty, stooped, with gray hair. He pointed the gun at them and said, "What brings you to my house? You wake my family, frighten my wife, and make the grandchildren cry."

Rupert took over. "*Ish shahib*, please forgive us. Some bad people are following us in a truck, and we had to find a place to hide from them. We are so grateful for the protection of your barn. May we show our gratitude?" He withdrew some banknotes from his pocket and took several, which he offered to their questioner with a reassuring smile.

The man stepped forward. "You are *Eengleesh*. Only the *Eengleesh* in uniforms come this way. Are you in army?"

"No, no, *ish shahib*, I am just a simple scholar of your wonderful culture. You should be proud to be Egyptian."

The older man let his gun fall and held it upright from the barrel. He accepted the banknotes and touched that handful of notes to his forehead as a gesture of goodwill. Then all their heads turned abruptly.

The sound of a truck's engine and its gears shifting shattered the calm. Its headlights beamed and bounced down the little road next to them until the vehicle appeared. It drew to a shuddering halt when the driver spied the three men standing in the barnyard.

Michael ran back to get the rifle from the Mercedes, the older man jumped behind the tractor, still holding his shotgun, and Rupert stood his ground.

The driver and two other men came toward him. They were armed.

One of the thugs, thin almost to the point of emaciation, said, "All right, where is it?"

"What is *it*?" Rupert's voice struck a most supercilious level of contempt. His pistol lay gripped and hidden under his folded arms.

"Don't be funny, milord." The man gave his rifle a little jerk upward.

"Frankly, sir, you mystify me. What can you possibly want with two chaps out for a spin in the wee hours of the morning? And doing no one any harm."

"I'll do you harm, you snotty Brit. Want to end up like that Turk who wouldn't talk?"

"So, that's it. You are the sadist himself. Who taught you such crude tricks? Torture should be practiced with more finesse, you know. Perhaps you should speak to your employers. They are becoming rather well known for, shall we say, skewering information from the unwilling."

During this exchange, Michael had taken the rifle and edged over to the gray-haired man hiding behind the tractor. He whispered something in Egyptian, moved between the tractor and the wall of the barn, and crouched down behind its tall tire. He gauged the distance between the head man and the one slightly behind on his right. Turning to nod at the older man who had placed himself to the left of the tractor's cab with his shotgun, Michael took aim at the leader's legs and pulled the trigger. In the next second, he struck his other target in the legs. At the same time, his companion had felled the third man, avoiding any stray shot into Rupert, who had dropped quickly to the ground.

Rupert lay in the dust, slightly on his side, with his pistol arm extended and pointed at the leader who had screamed as he was struck near the groin, collapsing on one leg, and firing in the air. When he had finally fallen completely, the man pulled himself together enough to roll over and look for a target. He spied the old man moving away from behind the tractor and fired. At the same time, Rupert took aim at the man's death's-head of a face and blasted its brains all over the rocky ground. One of the other two men was immobile after receiving the shotgun blast, and the third man writhed in pain from Michael's bullet, which had ripped through his pelvis.

The gray-haired proprietor had not been struck by the leader's second bullet, and he joined Michael and Rupert to examine their assailants. The shotgun blast had killed its target, and the only survivor had dropped his weapon and was unconscious in a mass of blood collecting around his midsection.

"First, we examine these guns for hire and get as much information as possible, then our friend here contacts the local police, and we leave before he does so, and the police arrive." Having said this to Michael, Rupert explained it to the old man who nodded. He promised to say he thought they had headed south instead of north if the police wanted to catch up with them.

Searches of the bodies and the vehicle yielded a modicum

of evidence, the most telling of which was an almost fresh pack of the same private German cigarette brand found both at the excavation site and in the courtyard in front of the villa. The leader carried a German passport, and the other two possessed Egyptian identity cards. There were a couple of telephone numbers that they would check out as well.

Rupert handed their erstwhile partner banknotes for fifty Egyptian pounds. "We're so sorry for all the trouble. Please let this show our gratitude."

The man grabbed his hand and kissed it. "Effendi, you will always be welcome in our house. Always."

They drove back toward the highway, and Michael turned to look at the house. "Ah, I think I understand. This is the only building with its lights on. His family probably switched them on after we arrived in the barnyard and found the old man waiting for us. When the truck returned searching for us, they figured we came here ourselves."

Rupert murmured, "Could be a good thing for us they did. But this isn't the end of our problems. I'm sure people in Alexandria are on watch for us. We should find a phone and have a couple of extra guards waiting when we unload the casket."

They were silent for a while as the scenery changed to more villages. The sky began to lighten, and stirrings of life were evident as people emerged onto the road. "I've been thinking, Miko. How did that sadistic bastard get ahead of us after he did in poor Suleiman?"

"Probably left the house with his goons and waited near the river. Could have seen us coming down the hill to the highway and figured we'd be heading north. So, they took their chances and drove on ahead of us."

Rupert said, "Hmm. There's a missing link. Timing's too neat. How did they know you'd be gone from the house to pick me up from the train? Somebody's playing a key role. Probably close to you. Someone you've trusted. I've been nagged by something you said earlier. It had to do with who in fact could have known you actually found those scrolls? Not someone just speculating?"

With a puzzled frown, Michael thought for a moment. "Suleiman certainly hadn't a clue. The only other person who's ever laid eyes on the scrolls was Thomas, my foreman. He read a small bit of the first scroll. Perhaps he read a little beyond where I left off. It gets pretty interesting at that point in the scroll. But he hadn't time to get much further."

"Any references on him?"

Michael shook his head. "Actually, no, but surely he's straight. A bright, sensitive fella, dedicated to his profession. Can't see him double-crossing me. In fact, quite unthinkable."

"All right, then, did you discuss any of this with someone else—or could Thomas have done so?"

Again, he searched his memory before responding. "Well, perhaps I did mention something to Stephanos when he phoned me about von Vranken's call."

Rupert said, "Any discussion about the contents of the casket?"

A moment of hesitation. Then a sigh. "I suppose there was. But, again, unthinkable that he should betray me. He and I discuss everything, you know. Look, if he was double-dealing, he wouldn't have told me that von Vranken asked about the chest. I was pretty upset, so I guess I spilled out why I'd asked you to come."

Rupert turned and noticed how tightly his hands clenched the wheel and how the color had drained from his face. "My dear Miko, let me be candid. You know as well as I that sometimes we misjudge people. How did Stephanos come into your life … if you don't mind my asking?"

"There's a place where I've spent many pleasant hours. A coffee house in Alexandria. That's where I met Stephanos, a Greek, like myself, originally Macedonian. He was at loose ends, and I needed someone to organize the many aspects of my life—the collections, the accounting, keeping track of correspondence, that sort of thing. I suspect you'll think I was a bit cavalier because I didn't even ask him for references. Now it's been some years that he's done all this, and I'd say he gets high marks overall. As for any private life he might have, I've really never wanted to open that window. You must think I'm a bit of a trusting dotard after hearing this."

"Well, you know people even get married sometimes without knowing any more than your instincts about Stephanos. I'm far from judging any of this. Just keep your eyes open from now on."

"I certainly will." Keen to change the uncomfortable subject, he smiled. "Good image—choosing a spouse—afraid unlikely at my stage in life. As we know, I've chosen my so-called freedom. I must say the steady stream of women over the years sometimes has left me feeling a little empty. You, lucky beast, making the most brilliant marriage, wouldn't have a clue about that. I confess, it sometimes gives me a pang of envy to think how agreeable for you, having two handsome children and a partner who does you such honor."

"Yes, Lizzie's a dream, the center of my life. And there's Tessie, takes after her mother, thank God."

"What about Orlando? Pretty gifted kid, if memory serves."

Rupert ran a hand over his tidy beard. His eyes had lost a little of their good-natured brightness. "Ah, there's a tale. Thirtyish. You may recall, as my heir apparent, he bears a courtesy title, Cressy. Named for an exceptionally brave ancestor who fought under Edward the Third. The British annihilated the French army at Crécy in Normandy. Alas, that heroic streak seems to have warped into something else with my boy."

"How do you mean?" Michael turned from the road ahead to have a look at him.

Rupert lit a cigarette and threw his head back to exhale, as if this would bring some solace to what he was about to say. "First, my brother. We've discussed him often. At eight, he made me poor as a pauper. Refused to share a single farthing of our patrimony. Not that I was remotely unhappy. Fairly easy to make my way. A teacher at Eton, lecturer at Cambridge, writing articles on archaeological subjects. But to be cut off so abruptly after the shock of suddenly losing parents at that age, that wasn't easy, especially on a sentimental level. But I managed to stay a pretty happy fellow—a gift of temperament, I suppose. But not, alas, given to my brother. As you'll recall from my earlier accounts, he ended his life with a shotgun. Blasted his head off in the woods at Ravenstone Park. And I became the marquess."

Michael nodded and passed a slow wagon that had pulled onto the road ahead of them. It was drawn by a single plodding dray. "That was around the time we were together in Grenoble at that archaeological conference? Your kid was in England staying with your grandmother? Twenty years at least?

"Yes, well my son's cut from similar cloth to his uncle. A streak of meanness runs through him. Yes, he's rather dashing, quite handsome and, since reaching twenty-one, very rich in his own right. I hesitate to speculate, but there may also be a streak of madness. The worst of it is he's become infatuated with the Nazi movement. He speaks constantly about the new world Herr Hitler, so-called German Fuhrer, will bring about. A new world that should frighten us all. Populated only with arrogant Aryans. The spawn of selective breeding. Raised like Spartan kids left on a hillside. Only the strong will survive and procreate. Of course, they'll rule that world. It's a megalomaniacal vision of the future. The lad's a preening Narcissus. Not a flicker of compassion. And oh so quick to take offense. Sensitive to the smallest slight he fancies against him. Lives on a tightrope. Makes me wonder how he'll even get through the rest of his allotted years. Something bad, terrible in fact, I fear will be the end of him. Elizabeth loses too much sleep over this as well."

Michael looked over at him from the driver's seat. "My friend, I'm *really* sorry. Had no idea all these years you carried this."

Rupert dragged once more on his cigarette and threw it out the car window. "Thanks. I've not wanted to burden you before." He took a deep breath of the air rushing in the window. "It's just that lately, he may have got himself in over his head." He summoned a faint smile.

At about eleven-thirty, the Mercedes pulled into the teeming square flanked on its east side by the Caridis palace. Rupert studied the situation across the square at the house's entrance, "The guards are just as Stephanos promised when we called. I think they're armed. Yes, I can see rifles at their sides."

"Good." Michael drove slowly around the square through the confusion of carriages, taxis, hawkers, tourists, and camels. Only a few feet away from the palace gates, a swarthy man with a huge dark mustache stared at the car as it pulled up next to him. Adorning his head was a stack of tasseled red fezzes, and more were arranged on a tiny pushcart. He appeared to be selling these to passersby, but his eyes were focused on Caridis. When he saw the porters salute their employer from inside the elaborate forged-iron grillwork and begin to pull open the two sides of the gate, the vendor took one of his fezzes and waved it continuously in a large arc over his head.

Another man stood up from a small table at a nearby café

and trotted through the crowds toward the car. He arrived just as it began to pass through the gates. He stared into the rear door of the vehicle and spied, among some suitcases, a large object covered with a cloth. One of the guards hurried over to check him out. The nosy fellow adjusted his sunglasses, put his hands in his pockets, and ambled past him.

The gates were pushed closed while the guards continued to survey the surroundings with intense concentration. Michael pulled deep into the central courtyard, which was out of view of the street. He climbed from the driver's seat as Stephanos came down the broad entrance steps.

They embraced, and Stephanos turned to shake Rupert's hand. "Glad to have you back. You must be shaken after that encounter last night."

Rupert studied his face. "Yes, we'll tell more inside."

Michael had started up the steps when he stopped and turned about. "By the way, has the Sitamun chair arrived from the excavation?"

Stephanos nodded. "Oh, yes. The Antiquities Ministry have agreed to let us study it as long as we need before turning it over to them. They're sending a team down to the site to study the statues of Sitamun and the stone catafalques. Quite intrigued by the clues concerning Akhenaten and Nefertiti."

"Any further mention of the casket?"

"Naturally. I explained once again how it'd been stolen from the tomb site the same night as your discovery. We suspected the work of some people working for the Germans because we found some suggestive evidence at the site."

Rupert said, "What was their reaction?"

Stephanos gave a wry laugh. "What you'd think. The Brits run the department. This fits their expectations. They like to call the Germans arrogant bastards who've got no place here.

Of course, Mussolini's minions drifting over from Libya next door are now getting much the same reaction."

Rupert shook his head and mounted the steps to stand next to Michael. "Not at all surprised. Those Italian *fascisti*! They've now really gone too far to get Hitler's respect. They've given in altogether, mimicking German policies. You do know about the new Italian racial laws enacted last week?"

"No? What's that all about? I've been a little out of circulation up in the hills," Michael said.

Stephanos interrupted. "That's all they're talking about in Alexandria these days. The new laws forbid Italians from marrying Jews, and they make it a crime to hire a Jew in the government or to teach in the schools or even to do banking. And they're taking away property that belongs to Italian Jews, mimicking just what the Germans have been doing with theirs."

Rupert frowned. "By the way, these laws also apply to African races. Do think a bit about what that could mean here in Egypt. Many of the ancient pharaohs were bred from African blood stock. So, are these fascist brutes going to suggest we start destroying temples and statues built by the mighty Rameses II or Amenhotep III?"

Michael responded, "I suppose once you're warped enough to malign a race for being 'inferior,' whatever that might mean, any barbarity is permissible." He opened the door to the towering entrance hall. "Come on inside. Let's change the subject. This conversation's becoming downright depressing."

The others agreed and laughed. "Stephie, has the vault area been readied?"

"Right you are, Michael. The table and lamps are set up in the conservation room. All you've got to do is open the vault itself."

"All right, then. You and Rupert please fetch our freight

down to the catacombs." Michael moved toward one corner of the hall. "I'll wait for you there."

Stephanos opened the front door for Rupert and followed him outside. "We've given the staff a holiday until dinnertime. Didn't want any curious eyes. By the way, Michael looks exhausted. Did you have a tough time?"

"It's much worse than that." Rupert led the way down the steps. "He's not had time to tell you about the villa last night and our little adventure on the way to Alexandria."

"I hate to think, from your tone of voice."

"All I'll say right now is some pretty terrible people are on the prowl. They're willing to kill gruesomely to have the chest. The Germans seem to be at the crux. Would you by chance have any idea why von Vranken should be so keen to know about Michael's find?" Rupert looked him squarely in the eyes. The other man shook his head and scurried to open the rear door of the four-by-four.

They removed several valises and brought them to the entrance hall. With the rear compartment otherwise cleared, they shifted the casket so as to grab its handles through the covering cloth. Their footsteps echoed through the entrance hall and down the marble steps beyond an arch off a far corner of the hall. After two turns of steps, they came to a steel door, which had been left open for them. Now the steps were made of rough stone. Electric sconces had been placed at intervals on flat portions of the walls. The rest of the wide underground passages were honeycombed with niches filled with rotting cloth, dusty bones, and grinning skulls. Some bodies were more or less intact mummies within their winding sheets, and many others had been shifted into little piles of bones, taking up less space. The pervasive mustiness was underscored by an acrid odor with a hint of dampness. Stephanos guided them to a T-junction where he nodded to the left. After another sixty feet or so, he stopped and gestured to put down the casket. He removed the tarp to reveal the curved ebony lid and the three straps of green patinated bronze surrounding the chest.

Stephanos looked down with hands on hips. "So, that's it. Quite simple, one form of decoration—the winged suns. Well put together. Ebony from the looks of it, probably imported from what we call Gabon today. That's where all the most beautiful, blackest ebony used by the ancient Egyptians comes from." Stephanos bent and stroked the chest with an appreciative hand. "Now to see what's caused all the excitement, no?"

Michael came out of the well-lit conservation room cut into the living rock. An impressive open steel door that would typically be used for a bank vault dominated the room's far wall.

"Like the villa, but much bigger," Rupert said. "Shall we bring this inside?" He leaned down to pick up one end, and Michael took the other handle. They carried it through the doorway and placed it on a long steel worktable in front of the white plastered walls. Several gooseneck lamps sat on the table, adjustable for better viewing of details. He could feel air coming from a ventilator grill above the table. Tilting his head upward, with a twinkle in his eyes, he remarked, "Nice to think I've got something else to breathe than emanations from our grisly friends out there."

He pushed the bronze rod through the loops protruding from the three clasps and laid it gently on the table. His hands almost trembling, Rupert carefully lifted each clasp on its hinge and then held the sides of the lid with the flat of his hands. Looking at the others with a quizzical expression, he lifted it.

As the interior of the casket was revealed, a sighing sound, above and beyond the squeaking of the lid's hinges, wafted out like a spirit released from captivity.

The three men backed away slightly.

"Certainly something going on in there," Rupert said.

"I feel an energy, seems almost alive." Stephanos stared uneasily into the chest. "Dare we touch what's inside?"

Michael wryly said, "Well, we survived the first time, why not now?" He removed the burlap cloth covering its contents and lifted out the scroll that he'd opened before. After laying it on the table, he went to a cabinet and withdrew a magnifying glass and several long, narrow metal weights, which he laid next to the scroll. "All right now, we'll begin to unroll this and pray it won't have become too brittle since the first time." He and Rupert placed the stainless steel weights at intervals to hold the papyrus down on the table. After it was fully unrolled, he stepped back. "My dear Rupert, here it is, all yours. Do you want to have a look now or go upstairs, take a bath and maybe a nap after our all-night escape?"

"Not at all. No, no. I'm on a second wind right now. Couldn't sleep a wink even if you knocked me out. I must have at it." Rupert had taken from a pocket his round glasses and adjusted their curved steel sides behind his ears. "Why don't you leave me alone for a bit. Can I contact you with that phone over there?"

"Absolutely. It's on an intercom line. Press that first button to ring my apartment upstairs. Let me know if you need anything. When you're ready to lock it up in the vault, I'll be down to give a hand." From the same cabinet he removed a stack of clean sheets of paper, several pencils, and a sharpener. "Here, just in case you feel like writing a translation now or after you've had a chance to digest things."

"Thanks, Miko. Will give a call later." Rupert's attention was already on the scroll, and an air of preoccupation had engulfed him.

The other two walked out of the room. "You can lock

this from the inside any time you'd like," Michael called out, rapping the open door with his knuckles.

They mounted the last little flight of marble stairs and crossed the main hall to the principal archway leading to the interior of the house. Stephanos led the way to a large drawing room where on a low platform in the center was placed the chair of Princess Sitamun. The dust of centuries in the sepulchre that had held the sarcophagi of Nefertiti and Akhenaten had been carefully cleaned away. The gold-embossed figures shone in the lamplight, especially the golden sun carried by a pair of eagle's wings spread across the top of the inside back of the solid wooden throne.

"Impressive. In even better condition than the Cairo Museum's—the one James Quibell found in 1905. Wood appears cleaner, fresher, as does the gilding. Really quite a beautiful thing."

Stephanos put his hands on either side of the chair. "I think it's actually bigger than the three chairs found by Quibell. His graduate in size as if for Sitamun's stages growing up. This fourth one's the largest so maybe even her throne chair as Daddy, Amenhotep's, brief queen and wife."

A telephone rang in one corner of the salon, and Stephanos hurried over to pick up the receiver. "Yes, Caridis residence." He paused and stood frozen for several minutes gripping the receiver. Finally, he said, "I see." He pressed the disconnect bar with his other hand and hung up.

"Well?" Caridis stood, hands on hips. "What was that all about?"

"An anonymous caller. They know you've got the casket and the scrolls. They want you to take them to the Society of the Seraphim and place them in the Sanctuary. You should do so on Friday before six o'clock. If done, you'll have no further disturbances from them. Otherwise, there's no predicting what may happen."

Michael thudded down into an armchair. "Damn it! Did it sound like von Vranken again?"

"He didn't give his name, but he spoke with an English accent. It wasn't von Vranken." Stephanos arched his eyebrows. "This doesn't jibe with what we know so far. How do the British fit into this picture?"

Caridis stared at him, as if seeing someone anew. "You do realize, Stephie, only two people have ever known for sure the chest contained scrolls—Thomas, who directed the excavation, and yourself."

A cloud passed over Stephanos's face. Tension mounted. He cleared his throat. "I see, the finger of suspicion may point at me. You know, of course, I knew *only* because you told me on the phone. Why not look at Thomas? He actually read at least part of a scroll, wasn't that the case?"

"You're right. But he's got no motive. To the contrary, he was worried about a looming threat to the project." Michael fixed Stephanos with a stare. "We were already suspicious about the Germans because of an incident with one of the workmen being approached to spy on us, but nobody other than he and you—not even Rupert—was actually told there were scrolls."

Stephanos looked at the floor, and the muscles in his cheeks tensed. "And *I've* got a motive? More than Thomas?" He took a deep breath. "Come on, we've got to expand the circle of suspects a little. First, Rupert suddenly comes on the scene. Raises the question. Why Rupert? Couldn't someone who's learned you've discovered a large chest conclude he's here to translate something? What would be inside a chest that needs translation? Scrolls with hieroglyphics, his greatest expertise. This would be a simple deduction for someone like von

Vranken who was probably made aware of Rupert's arrival and his reputation. After all, he's top dog of the gestapo cell here in Alexandria. It's no secret."

He drew a deep tense breath. "OK, here's another explanation—all those workmen who knew there was a chest in the tomb. You've said one admitted he'd been paid to spy by a German. Maybe Suleiman was in cahoots with him—maybe with those Germans as well. Could he have spied on you when you opened the casket? Did you and Thomas mention anything about its contents in front of Suleiman that night or the next morning?" Stephanos paused, and his look of desperation matched the urgency of his voice.

Michael rose and walked to a tall window where he looked out at the city square, his hands pressed together behind his back. After a few moments, he turned. "Of course, you haven't yet been told about poor Suleiman." He proceeded to describe the scene of horror at the villa. "And what you say could have been the case. Suleiman could have overheard or even spied on us and learned about the scrolls. I'm sorry. It really can't possibly have been your doing. I'm just so bothered by what seems a betrayal among my most trusted people." He stopped and turned again toward the window. "There's a scuffle near the gate. Ah, yes, our guards have pinned someone to the ground."

They left the grand salon and rushed through the courtyard to the front gate. Police were handcuffing a small, muscular man, snarling in Arabic.

"Is he armed?" Michael asked his guards as they stood aside to let the police take the man prisoner.

"Yes, Effendi. A pistol. Tried to climb the fence while another distracted us by lighting a fire in that steel can." They pointed to a small can of gasoline-soaked rags that was still sending little billows of black smoke. "Now he's gone, disappeared." They gestured at the thronging crowds, some of whom had gathered to watch.

One of the arresting officers was in the British military police. "Mr. Caridis, any idea who this character might be and why he's so keen to get inside your place?"

"No idea. Not very clever if he'd got burglary in mind. Just to begin with, the place is wired to the gills with alarms."

"Well, I see you've got some extra guards. Is there something special that might attract people you'd rather not have in the house?"

Michael laughed. "As everyone knows, there's a lot inside to interest the wrong sorts. Lately some rumors and phone calls have made us a bit more alert. I suppose this ruffian could be connected to those."

"I see. Well, give us a call if you feel you need even more protection. Glad to be of service." He touched his hand to his cap in a brief salute.

Michael smiled and shook his hand. "Very civil of you, Lieutenant. Many thanks." He nodded to his guards and took Stephanos by the arm. When they reentered the gates, Michael leaned over to his companion. "I think it's time we call the police near Amarna. Could be they've got some leads on who's behind yesterday's tragedy."

That telephone conversation carried its own surprises. When Michael hung up, he turned to Stephanos with an amazed expression. "So, our adversaries are, if nothing else, fastidious."

"How so?"

"Police arrived quite a time after our call yesterday—several hours later, they admitted. Found the villa locked after we said we'd leave the front door unlocked. They looked everywhere for any evidence of disruption. There was no body in the wine cellar space. No broken bottles, no wine on the floor, no blood anywhere, including the pavement in the front courtyard. In short, all was perfectly normal and peaceful. Of course, there was no Suleiman either to let them in. Just hate to think what someone's done with his poor body."

9

Late October 1938

Rupert sat back in his upright chair at the long metal table and smiled with satisfaction. He had been there almost ten hours. An uneaten sandwich sat on a tray at the end nearest the door. Next to him, a jug of water and a crystal drinking glass were both almost empty. Before him lay a neat stack of paper covered with his writing. On the floor nearby were sheets that had been crumpled and thrown away. He suddenly felt both elated and weary. His right hand ran down the side of his face and around the chin and throat. His naval-cut beard, golden with flecks of gray, was similar in color to his hair, which was worn in full gentle waves and parted in the middle. It was a likeable, kind, and shrewd face with widely spaced blue eyes and a broad forehead. He was, in middle age, a dashing aristocrat with a charming common touch.

He rose to his feet and stretched his arms with a yawn. He began to roll up the third and last scroll he'd just translated, by removing, one after the other, the polished steel bars that held it to the table. Its suppleness, like the other two, still amazed him. As with the others, he numbered it faintly in pencil on the outside and returned it to the casket. After closing the lid and replacing clasps on their protruding bronze half rings, he ran the bronze rod through them. Picking up the telephone, he pressed the intercom button several times, which signaled all the other phones in the house.

Stephanos answered. "Yes, Rupert. Everything all right?"

"A bit weary, but ready to have someone help me put the casket into the vault."

"Does this mean you've finished the translation?" The voice sounded both hopeful and guarded.

Rupert responded, "For all important purposes, we can say I've done it. Certainly, when I've got my full library available, there may be some fine-tuning, as they say, to a few minor points."

"Fine. We'll be right down."

Moments later, the two men entered the room in a state of excitement.

Michael grabbed Rupert by the shoulders. "Well, well. What do you think? What do we have?"

Rupert grinned. "Oh, nothing in particular, Miko. Really just a small change to an old story."

Crestfallen, Caridis let go of his shoulders. "Really, you can't mean it. So much sound and fury for nothing?"

Rupert laughed. "All right, I'll stop my teasing. Dear friend, you happen to have discovered one of the most important, and perhaps revolutionary, documents in human history. Value's incalculable. In today's environment, it could also be incendiary. You must find a secure, secret place and let it be known soon that this is no longer in your possession. Otherwise, you really do run the risk of ending up like poor Suleiman."

Michael was jubilant. "I understand. Of course we're going to follow your advice. But now, now we must hear the translation. Are you too worn out to do that?"

"Indeed not. Too excited, I suppose. Read it to you upstairs after we put this in your vault."

Michael nodded, hurried over, and turned the main wheel of the vault door to open it. "Left it unlocked so as to act quickly if we were being pressed by something unforeseen." He and Stephanos took the handles of the casket and carried it inside. When they emerged and pushed closed the heavy steel door, Michael turned the wheel to the lock position and spun two large combination locks. They could hear the tumblers fall into place.

Rupert observed the somewhat stressed expression on Stephanos's face. "Does anyone other than you know the way to open that, Michael?"

"No one but me." He laughed. "They'll have to dynamite it open if something happens to me." When they had closed and locked the conservation room door, Michael took Rupert's arm to slow him down, letting Stephanos stride further on ahead through the catacombs. In a low voice he said, "The combination doesn't die with me. I've left a series of clues in a riddle form just in case something were to happen. These were posted only to you the same day you received my telegram. Should be at Ravenstone Park by now."

They hurried to follow Stephanos back through the catacombs, up the stone steps to emerge from the steel door, which they locked, and then they mounted the circular staircase with marble steps up to the entrance hall. Stephanos carried the sandwich, carafe, and glass through a door to a back hall leading to the kitchen.

Michael led Rupert to the library. "Staff returned at six and laid out a small meal in here." Entering the room, they passed between two Assyrian bulls fixed to the walls flanking its double doors. A table had been set for dinner in one corner, and a console buffet next to it bore several platters and chafing dishes with food. Candles had been lit on the table and the console. Lamps and sconces also lit the paneled room and highlighted endless colorful book spines.

"I think it'd be helpful to have something to eat before we go over the translation," murmured Rupert, placing the stack of sheets on a small marble lamp table.

Stephanos entered and closed the double doors. He carried a carafe of red wine. "A decent claret for our sins."

They dined. Rupert was ravenous and ate as a starving man given food at last. He was brought up to speed on the afternoon's would-be raider. "Well, you've seen already what can happen because of the casket. I repeat. Best to find a permanent and secret hiding place and then announce it's out of your control. I must say, a power really grips one down there. Strangely exhilarating, you know."

"The great mystery is how some people seem to know or have a hint, at least, of what we'd find inside the casket." Michael put down his knife and fork. "These Germans have been acting like they already know what you're about to tell us, Rupert. While you were working, we got a call from someone with a British accent who threatened harm if we didn't bring the casket to the Sanctuary of the Seraphim by late Friday afternoon."

Rupert scrunched his face in a frown. "I must agree with that suspicion, especially based on what you're about to learn the scrolls contain. These Aaronite Nazis are rightly keen to have it at all costs."

Stephanos appeared restless, if not a little uneasy. He asked, "But then why would those clues, if that's what we're talking about, not have been known to everyone in the Society of the

Seraphim, at least here in Alexandria so close to where it was found?"

Michael said, "You'll have gathered—because Stephanos answered the phone with the threatening call—I've had to make him privy to some facts about the Seraphim. And I want to emphasize we're definitely not going to deliver the casket to the Sanctuary regardless of their threats."

Rupert nodded, "Understood, Miko. Well, to answer his question, I think we can construct a logical theory. If there are such clues in existence, they're probably known only in Berlin. I say this because Michael's never heard a word about any such clues, and the only people so far implicated in this scheme to steal the casket are German and well-connected." He rose from his chair. "I'd say it's time for me to share my translation. It's going to help us all to understand just how much is at stake here."

Rupert picked up his manuscript and found a comfortable chair in a small grouping, and the other two sat down with their claret glasses and the carafe at hand.

He placed his small round spectacles on the bridge of his nose. Leaning forward, intense and excited by what he was about to reveal, Rupert began in his best storyteller's voice. "I will give you my translation in today's vernacular. The original is written in two languages. This first part, which Michael briefly saw, is in Egyptian hieroglyphics. It takes the form of a report personally addressed to Sitamun, princess and then queen to her father, Amenhotep III. As we know from Michael's brilliant excavation, Sitamun's statues adorn the wall of the sepulchre. And her throne chair sits now in this house awaiting further analysis. As you'll realize from what you are about to hear, some major assumptions of history are going to be thrown out the window."

All blessings to you, oh Mother of God. This humble report accompanies the saddest freight imaginable to your Greatness. We weep with the tears of all the heavens, having to return in this way your beloved son and his queen after their great flight. Their final story is told here for you and for all the ages to come, and to ensure their undisturbed journey through the afterlife, recognized forever as children of the sun.

I, Ishmael, followed my Lord king on his last journey to a far land with the same devotion that I gave when I was his eyes and ears in his holy city of Akhetaten. It behooves me now to relate the final story of your son, a tale, tragic and beautiful, which will explain much that would otherwise have remained unknown to you, his holy mother.

How can I ever cease to think of that auspicious morning along the mighty river's edge where the blessed Akhenaten and his guards were strolling, and he saw my desperate plight? With his own hands and the spear of his attendant, your godly son saved me from the maw of the crocodile. At that moment, my fate became bound to his. I was indeed born with the name of Ishmael. But my Lord soon honored me with another name. It was the private name you bestowed upon him at his birth, calling him Moses in remembrance of your brother Thut-Moses who had just passed to the other side on that very day when my Lord was born. For as I became my Lord's most devoted shadow and follower, and I weep now as I write this in his remembrance, he told me something that made me fall to my knees and kiss his hand. "Ishmael, I now feel as close to you as my beloved mother felt to me, so my private name for you shall henceforth be 'My Other Moses.'"

Rupert removed and held his glasses. "Most historical research confirms it was Akhenaten's older brother who was named Thut-Moses. In fact, this scroll tells us he was really Akhenaten's uncle, Sitamun's younger brother. The unfortunate young man seems, according to our narrator, Ishmael, to have died mysteriously on the very day his sister's son, Akhenaten, was born." He replaced his spectacles.

Your son's final days in Akhetaten saw much intrigue. It was inflamed by the outrageous goings-on in Luxor, our ancient and unlamented capital. There, the treacherous General Horemheb stirred up conspiracies so vigorously his eyes began to bulge with the effort. He could not contain his ambition. His solemn oath of loyalty to Pharaoh was shown only to be a hollow pretense, a cover for an all-consuming desire to usurp the throne. And as you will by now already know, poor Nefertiti and your young grandson, Tutankhamun, were to be his pawns.

The ever-crafty Horemheb had made a cabal with the high priests to overthrow Pharaoh. But he wasn't motivated by their theological indignation over the apostate Akhenaten's heresies. Horemheb cared not a fig for all the hocus-pocus of the priests. He simply found it convenient to make common cause with other aggrieved parties. Each of them had a special axe to grind—and grind they did.

One night, when sleep had overcome most souls in the royal palace at Akhetaten, the smell of treason infected the air like the fumes from unbathed bodies covered with sweat. I made my normal nocturnal rounds, an ephemeral ghost unseen and all-knowing.

A wall of marble filigree divided the queen's bedroom from her private garden. The soft splashings of several fountains were meant to lull the ravishing Nefertiti to the realm of happy dreams. Blending with their soothing sounds came the murmur of two quiet voices. What I overheard through that stone filigree was calculated, in this moment, to bring nightmares to my Lord.

I was greatly relieved when Queen Nefertiti recounted everything to Akhenaten the next day. The night before, General Horemheb had proposed a nefarious bargain. She would become his queen, and Akhenaten's son, Tutankhamun, would be acknowledged as the crown prince. Pharaoh would be permitted to organize his safe escape without interference from the great forces now turned coat and loyal to his marshal of all the armies, Horemheb, who would crown himself king.

She had promised to lay this proposition before her husband. As part of the bargain, Pharaoh would be allowed time to prepare his departure. It would be a bloodless restoration of the old regime. As Horemheb declared to her that fateful evening, Akhenaten's sun-blinded monotheistic revolution would be brought to its dramatic end.

I met with my Lord alone after Nefertiti had left his presence. At his bidding, I had taken my place behind a screen and listened to the queen's case. She had begged him to save his own life even if it meant sacrificing hers to the monstrous Horemheb.

When my Lord asked my advice, I presented a plan devised earlier in the day as I was reflecting on that treasonous conversation overheard in the shadows of the night before.

My plan was just as opportunistic as Horemheb's. I am a Hebrew by birth, and my people had been prisoners in Egypt for more than four centuries. It was well past time to leave the yoke of Egypt. Time to fulfill our singular godhead's command to reach the lands of Judea and take by force our own place in the sun. To find at last our Zion.

With all this in mind, I proposed to my Lord that we ask for enough time to rally my people who had lived in their squalid camps in a state of ignominious servitude for far too long. I pleaded for his recognition of their belief, like his own, in the supreme place of the One God. And I knelt before him and beseeched blessed Akhenaten to lead us to Judea and become our just and compassionate ruler.

Our side of the bargain with Horemheb would be cleverer yet. We would gather the Hebrews along with their moveable possessions into a massive exodus of some several hundred thousand souls, and Pharaoh would direct his loyal palace guard to join us with enough armed men at least to discourage a surprise attack by Horemheb midway along our route.

Nefertiti and Tutankhamun were the keys to this arrangement. Their new destiny was as Horemheb's hostages to his imperial ambitions. They would be sent under Horemheb's own armed guards from holy Akhetaten to perfidious Luxor to be received by him as the seal to his claim to the great double crown of Upper and Lower Egypt. He would then be the most powerful ruler of empire in the world. Until, of course, his own usurper should repeat his travesties in the usual manner of ambitious mankind and make a similar move to unseat him.

My Lord was mightily pleased when I added a final stratagem not, of course, to be discussed with Horemheb. It was the capstone to the architecture of a perfect escape and a poke in Horemheb's eye.

Horemheb predictably accepted my Lord's terms. He was careful to confine knowledge of its terms to his coterie of intimates, the future oligarchs of his reign. He would afterwards spring on the old Council of Nobles the news of the successful transfer of power. By that point, any who objected would be overruled by numbers of new members loyal to him.

The day arrived when the grand plan was launched. Yes, there were predictable objections among certain of the Israelites. The one person most vocal of the few Hebrews who showed any signs of displeasure was Aaron, my older brother. He had been used by my Lord in the past to frighten the Egyptians with the pestilences he delivered by means of his great staff, the rod of Aaron. Pharaoh used Aaron's powers to punish Egypt for its priests' and nobles' failure to recognize the singular nature of God.

As for my brother Aaron, he has always wanted the tribal power for himself, the right to lead our people. He has also been immensely jealous of my remarkable relationship with my Lord Akhenaten. And most bothersome to my brother, my Lord Akhenaten was not even a Hebrew. He was from another race—and the leader of our longtime oppressors.

On that fateful day, my Lord waited in a state of supreme calm outside his palace at Akhetaten. A veiled woman was helped up into his chariot while he stood by. The two horses harnessed to his chariot were to be changed for rested animals already sent to stations along the way.

Prince Tutankhamun mounted a horse after embracing his father, and his eyes had a somewhat blank stare. They were tense with fear, which he manfully attempted to master. My Lord assisted another veiled woman to step from the palace terrace into a canopied chariot of her own. He whispered something to her when he briefly lifted her veil in the sight of Horemheb's soldiers to show it was Nefertiti. Tutankhamun pulled his horse abreast of the canopied chariot and signaled his entourage to proceed.

Pharaoh then leaped into his chariot, pulled the reins of his horses, and turned north. With an ache that all could feel, he turned to watch his son and the other veiled woman head south for the many days' journey to Luxor and to an anxious Horemheb who must have been beside himself with expectation of his imminent glories.

I rode in one of the many wagons that followed my Lord. Our loyal Egyptian guards and those Egyptians who were followers of Akhenaten moved with us from Akhetaten and across the endless sands to our point of convergence with the Israelites who had quitted Luxor some many days before. Indeed, as had been planned so carefully during the past weeks, we came to a small range of hills and rode up to their crest. Such a sight it was, that once seen, it must remain seared forever upon the book of memory. Spread before us were my people, the Hebrews, in their ragged tens of thousands. When they saw us appear above them against the burning sky, a mighty shout went out that carried across the sands and brought salty tears to my own eyes and those of my Lord. He raised his arm in greeting, and the shouts resounded in waves upon waves.

My Lord rode down the hill to take his place among his loyal imperial troops at the head of the mass of Israelites. A host of other seasoned warriors gathered as a rear guard a league away. They urged the people to move now that Pharaoh had arrived to take the lead. Wagons, oxen, household belongings, and countless accumulations of simple lives testified to the massive uprooting that was taking place. My Lord had taken his loyal attendants, physicians, musicians, priests of the One God, embalmers, cooks, and others vital to the operation of the royal household. But my Lord wore none of the regalia of his former office. He appeared in the simplest tunic, belted with a rope, almost relieved to have left all that behind for others to sport in pride and arrogance. A royal pride that is darkened by the uneasiness that must attend, and diminish, some, if not all, the pleasure that might come to the fiercely ambitious from the possession of great temporal power. Indeed, one gives up completely any peace of mind to be a king.

My Lord had traversed before my eyes the path between earthly splendor and mythic simplicity. He now commanded a different kind of power in his face and gaze and bearing. It was indeed a passage to godliness. Like the others, I was struck by the change. Its rapidity was both startling and intimidating. My Lord had become another man, a vessel for a divine spirit. If I may say, for the divine Spirit.

The people—my people and many Egyptians as well—followed him with joy. All were touched by what I had perceived in him. Their eyes were lighted from within and also by reflection of his gentle power. And we marched from day to day, strengthened and secure in my Lord's purpose.

Rupert lifted his head. "Now the text changes. It is written in Hebrew rather than hieroglyphics. You will see why."

My lady, the time has come for me to revert to the tongue of my fathers. My clay is theirs, even though my form is of the divine Akhenaten's making. It is to my clay I am now given after all we were to go through on this journey toward Judea. It is a journey that I fear I shall never complete after sending you my report. Should that be the case, should the Hebrews succeed in reaching Judea, and you receive what I am sending to you, my mission will have been done. For I shall have served well my Lord who saved and gave me my new life.

Our march of the multitudes through the blazing sun took its toll. Several older pilgrims gave up their lives for a dream that they would never realize. Of even greater concern was the bitter realization that was with us from the start. Until a certain moment, the threat remained unrevealed. But its revelation was always inevitable. The question was never in doubt. All that was unknown was the timing.

As it turned out, the timing could not have been worse. We were amazed it had not happened sooner. Our path at this point lay along the edges of the sea that divides us from the way to the outer dominions of Pharaoh that reach to far-off Babylon. We had not quite yet come to the place where the sea ends, and we could cross over by land to the Eastern reaches that would take us to Judea.

That day, the sun had started to fire the rays of dawn in golden and rose-hued streaks across the rolling dunes. I had awakened early and was roaming the camp to make inspections as was my custom. With no warning, sounds of thunder began to make the ground reverberate under a crystal clear sky. It took only a moment for me to realize I was hearing at last the hoofbeats of Horemheb's army. Now they were the drumbeats of our doom, trapped as we were against the sea.

Soldiers on horses surged up like a rolling tide to appear along the rim of the steep plateau, its vertical heights towering above our camp. We were at a complete disadvantage, caught between the looming army and the drowning sea. My Lord emerged from his tent with his veiled lady. They looked up at Horemheb's army, over the heads of my fellow Israelites who were now on their feet and showing alarm as they turned back and forth in silent questioning from my Lord to Horemheb's triumphant smile.

The veiled lady stepped forward and with both hands lifted the heavy gauze that had hidden her from view for the many days that we had already traveled. The most beautiful face in the world was revealed to the amazement of multitudes who began murmuring among themselves. It did not take long for the truth to make itself apparent. The lady riding with Prince Tutankhamen was a look-alike for the queen. She had probably only been discovered when Horemheb lifted her veil in what must have been a short-lived moment of triumph. Heaven knows what fate awaited her after that, and I tremble with sadness at the thought of her possible sacrifice for my Lord and his lady.

But the ruse had ended. There we were now, trapped, denied the slightest chance of escape. Without hesitation, Nefertiti stepped forward, prepared to go with Horemheb, tacitly understanding that this would save the lives of the rest. My Lord put a hand on her shoulder to restrain her from leaving him. She turned and gazed with that lovely, all-knowing intelligence, which was the greatest ally of her beauty, and shook her head. She lifted his hand from her shoulder and continued to walk toward the plateau where Horemheb smiled at his soldiers. He wore an expression of such smugness that only a man of his egotistical pretension could summon.

The people parted to let her pass. Not a sound could be heard other than the breathing of the tense multitude who followed her every step as if it were each of them being led to be sacrificed. She did, with her famous compassion, turn to smile this way and that and touch the heads of small children in her path.

And then like a visitation by all the angels of heaven, the impossible happened. It defies my powers of description. With sublime timing and no warning whatsoever, the great powers of the One God were manifested in all their magnificence.

It was a phenomenon undreamt of and beyond all language to describe. Far off in the western sky, it seemed another sun had suddenly been born to rival that which was now arcing up in the east. It was for a moment a silent spectacle, utterly strange, transfixing. A pair of suns? But the interloper was speeding closer and closer. And then the thunder came. Not as the intermittent howlings and clappings of the child's terrors, but as a surging, ever loudening, onrushing, roaring force that grew and grew in size and sound and burning light. I could see the startled face of Horemheb spin around to look behind him, and how he cringed and sank with his horse to its knees, bowing before the anger of God. The vast ball of fire blasted its deafening way overhead and toward the sea behind us. And as it reached the shore above the marveling eyes of the Israelites and our Lord, its great power attracted the waters of the sea. It pulled them up in a gigantic swell as if drawn by some powerful magnetic suction to this celestial phenomenon and spread them out in two vast waves that surged away from the awestruck multitudes.

I ran toward the base of the plateau and took Nefertiti by the hand. She looked startled as from a trance. I urged her to hurry. By merest chance, she now faced the possibility of a fate far different from the one she had just been prepared to accept with Horemheb. She looked up at the broad plateau where his forces were spreading apart and charging in all directions to find ways down to the plain below. We ran to my Lord's chariot where he helped us up with a smile and reined in the terrified horses to point them toward the exposed floor of the miraculously exposed seabed.

The multitudes followed us into the breach. The towering walls of water made a virtual canyon sliced into the sea. We stumbled and pushed our desperate way through the mud and rocks, conscious of our pursuers who must soon be entering the divided waters. I kept on looking over my shoulder at our people struggling to carry their goods, their small children and elderly parents, and my heart still aches for all near the rear about to receive attacks by the soldiers who had finally appeared at the opening of the waters.

Sad to say, some of ours were lost. Too weak, too slow, and too unfortunate to avoid what happened next. Most of our multitudes managed to reach the other side, damp, hearts pounding, and gratefully alive. The laggards alas went the way of our pursuers. Some were *slaughtered in anger by the soldiers who delayed their own egress from the watery canyon to carry out these atrocities. They paid dearly for their cruelty. The great walls of water began to tremble and shudder, about to topple, now released from their hold by the passing ball of fire. Just as the greatest number of our vicious pursuers had managed to enter this miraculous passage, it began to collapse upon them with relentless efficiency. Without mercy, the waters poured down like the wrath of God to cover Horemheb's army in a cataclysm of flailing horses snorting for air in the engulfing waves. All were captured in a desperate jumble floating up through the turgid waters, mouths agape, eyeballs exploding, limbs akimbo in a grotesque ballet of death.*

I believe Horemheb himself had the good sense like most generals to leave pursuit to the others. I will probably never live to know what became of him after the loss of his prize, Nefertiti. I have often wondered whether he permitted Prince Tutankhamen to live, appointing himself the young man's all-powerful regent. Or did he grab the whole prize for himself, the heavy double crown of Upper and Lower Egypt and all its dominions abroad?

My Lord patiently led the multitudes onward through the months and years to follow. It was not easy to move and feed and bury and bring to new life so many nomadic souls searching for their final home. My Lord became thinner and more ascetic, eating little and praying much.

Nefertiti never left his side. She would hold his hand and kiss it from time to time.

Aaron fumed around the edges of my Lord's daily existence, anxious for the Word, the telling connection that would confirm the meaning and destiny of our expedition. The day came at last when my Lord summoned Aaron and me to his presence. We had encamped now for some time at the base of a mountain where there was a spring and enough game and other food to take care of our needs. Great Akhenaten announced the time had come for him to receive the word. He turned to me, not to Aaron, and said, "My Other Moses, you will accompany me and be my scribe." And to my brother, Aaron, he admonished, "If the peoples become impatient for the word, tell them to wait upon the will of the Divine, for it will come when it comes and He is ready."

And so the two of us ascended the mountain that the peoples chose that day to call Si'nai which for us meant "the place where it is now time." Once up there, we waited together for many more days, in patience, for my Lord to receive the Word. Our diet soon became limited to the berries gleaned from bushes and whatever waters might come from the occasional evening rainfall. My Lord and I grew thinner and our thoughts more ethereal. We would walk about the mountain's summit searching for food and for the place of divine contact. Our sleep was in a shelter under an overhanging rock with fine sandy ground. Our robes began turning to rags, and our bodies became covered with blisters from the sun and lack of bathing.

One morning, while it was very early and the merest hint of the sun had lightened the darkness, I was awakened. My Lord touched my shoulder. "It is time. Come."

I rose and gathered up my trays of moist clay, a pot of water, and styluses to follow my Lord to the chosen place. It stood above the rest with a withered tree at its crest. I sat on a rock and used another as a table to lay the first tray, which I made even and smooth, so its clay could be incised legibly.

He stood above me. The morning winds surged off the plains below as the warm sun touched the night-cooled land. My Lord faced the east, and his face was suffused with the rose light that shimmered across the sky. His robes were caught by the winds, and he held on to the scrawny tree with one hand. I looked up at him and waited. Another light began to glow, coming from within my Lord. It grew in intensity until his eyes seemed to be shooting out streaks of sparkling crystal, and his body shuddered as if in ecstasy. The tree he was touching suddenly began to sprout from every naked limb, an abundance of tiny, newborn leaves, translucent greens that ripened before me into a full-blown tree of life, lushly verdant and beautiful in its symmetry. I was almost afraid in the midst of my fascination with the miraculous. But a soothing power came from my Lord, and I had visions at that moment of armies at war, and fields fat with plenty to be harvested, and new babies uttering their first cries to a new world, and lovers embracing and cities growing up hillsides and over plains, and the ultimate victory in the form of our peaceable kingdom, strong against all who would menace it, with my Lord at its head.

"Let this by my Covenant with you," my Lord spoke with another's voice. And I inscribed his words. "You shall have no other God besides me." His voice had a music, haunting and deep, almost a chant sounding from within a great domed space in which it carried and carried.

He put up his hands to cover his face and eyes, and he was silent for many minutes, waiting for more to come. When he dropped them to his sides, a warm smile seemed to bring me closer to him so that I felt as if we were one entity. Softly, he spoke, pointing at my stylus. "My dear boy, you must know that you are now the finger of God."

And, holy mother, I did inscribe the rest of the Commandments given by the One God, all of which I have copied for you here in both Hebrew and your own language. We were visited by the One God a number of times over forty days when he would command my Lord to tell me what must be written. When my inscriptions on the clay tablets were complete, and my Lord had recovered from his encounters with the Divine, night had begun to darken the world. Plumes of smoke were rising from the plains at the foot of the mountain. We looked down and were puzzled. Then my Lord shook his head. I did not ask him why. His expression was so anguished, and I knew what was happening down below had greatly displeased him.

The next morning, early, my Lord and I awoke and gathered our few pitiful things along with the tablets now dried and firm as stone. He clutched these to his chest and wound his way down the mountain, moving at speed as if he must come to someone's rescue. We were sighted, and the multitudes began to awaken and assemble in anticipation.

When we reached the bottom, my Lord turned to his right where a fire still burned before a makeshift creature made of wood and clay, with a calf's head and four legs and a golden shawl spread upon its back. He strode over to the altar upon which the creature stood and began to weep cold tears. When Aaron approached him, my Lord dropped the three tablets at Aaron's feet. He practically threw them down, and they shattered. There came from my Lord's eyes the same crystalline beams as those upon the mountain, except now they pulsed with his anger. He towered over Aaron and seemed the incarnation of divine power about to deliver retribution.

"How could you do this? There, lying at your faithless feet, is your Covenant with the One. Could you not be patient? There can be no excuse for this heresy, this travesty against our beliefs."

And in his anger, my Lord drew up his arm and slapped Aaron across the cheek, causing Aaron to stagger in order to keep his balance.

Fury blazed from Aaron's eyes. "Majesty, I had no choice. The people were restless, ready to revolt, tired of waiting. They needed something to worship, something in which to believe that was beyond themselves. You were long, very long, in your absence. Faith needs an object; it cannot exist in emptiness. They pleaded for Baal, the golden calf, which they had known before. They were given to dance about the fires of worship and to chant the forbidden rituals of our forefathers. Do not punish them, only me, if you must." He bent down and gathered up the pieces of the broken tablets. These he hugged to his breast as if they were a child. "Perhaps we can put these back together?"

My Lord bowed his shoulders in dejection. "No, there is no need. I shall return to my place up there." He pointed at the mountaintop. "Who can say what will now be the Word that we may be given to receive? I fear it may be less gentle and forgiving."

Aaron then turned to me in tears and handed me the broken tablets, saying, "I am not worthy of these sacred things that I have caused thus to be ruined." These, holy mother, I also now deliver to you for they must go forever with my Lord on his endless journey.

Rupert looked up.

Michael appeared stunned and muttered, "This is … my God, what have we found?"

Rupert nodded. "Yes, perhaps in this lies the major reason for the fuss over your treasure. Where do you think the fragments may have been placed when the two bodies were put into the sepulchre? Can you imagine in your wildest dreams finding the tablets of the First Covenant, the one that was broken into pieces at the feet of Aaron and replaced by the Second Covenant, which is the standard set we call the Ten Commandments? We must speak later about the excavation site, the tomb, and the catafalques to see if there are perhaps some clues. For now, I'll continue.

> *And so the next day after bathing and changing our clothes, my Lord and I returned to our tree of life whose leaves had now begun to change their colors as if preparing for the time when they must fall.*
>
> *This time, there were but ten commandments given by the One, and they were more harsh, more stern than those before. Holy mother, you have the broken pieces of the original Word. The one message from my Lord's original commandments I most regret not being included in the final inscription is this one: "Whoever does not love does not know God, because God is love."*
>
> *We descended the mountain once again, this time with two, not three, tablets, and presented them to the multitudes who gave a great cheer. When they were read aloud by my Lord, the people were more sober, but they fell to their knees and repeated, "Glory be to the One God."*

Aaron was livid with jealous rage, and he stormed about the camp, muttering to himself words that no one could understand. Humiliated and upstaged, my brother found it difficult to contain his resentment. I thought this would abate after a time as now our people had their Covenant with the One God, and they could build upon this mighty foundation, but abate it would not. Terrible arguments between Akhenaten and Aaron would erupt over matters that seemed not to warrant such reactions. I must say they were, alas, almost always instigated by my brother.

One day, it all went too far. Nefertiti was present at the table with Aaron and my Lord. My brother stood up from his seat and began to preach against the presence of a woman at the table. My Lord then stood up and walked over to Aaron to beg him to excuse himself for the insult against the queen. Aaron refused and leaned over to pick up his rod.

My Lord smiled and said, "So, do you wish now to use your powers to make us disappear with that famous staff that we used to such good effect against the benighted priests of our old regime?"

Aaron could not tolerate this taunt. His cheek muscles tightened, and his eyes burned like hot coals with rage. He lifted his rod and swung it in a mighty arc against Pharaoh, screaming, "You are the heretic, the Egyptian who pretends to be our savior, and by what right? By what right?"

Nefertiti had by now risen and stepped over to stand beside my Lord, perhaps as a peacemaker, we will never know, for the blow that struck Pharaoh struck the queen as well. They fell together and within each other's arms, embracing in death as they had so fondly done in life.

A great cry of horror went up in the camp. Aaron stared at his broken rod, and the multitudes rose up from their fires where they had been dining on the meager evening meal. I have never been so sad, and I hope that I shall stop feeling this way so intensely whenever I recall that moment. Broken, on the ground, were two of nature's most remarkable creatures. One conceived in utter beauty—and the other in a divine state by you, Holy Mother. Their likes may never be seen again.

The embalmers did what they could, but it was almost unnecessary. They had never before seen a man and woman who appeared to be virtually incorruptible by the forces that govern creation and decay. These beloved ones come to you albeit wrapped as is our custom in their perfumed shrouds and completely protected in a layer of wax. I commend them to your care. I did not want to leave them in the lonely desert between their original home and the home that we Israelites hope to build someday—probably after even I have departed life as we know it. May they be blessed in the afterlife as they have so blessed ours in this one.

Thus ends my report of the great Moses of the Israelites, called by his own decree Akhenaten, and called Moses by those who loved him and who number in the hundreds of thousands of his followers. These will now build a nation that serves his deepest convictions. There, as he always wished, all men and women shall respect and love each other, as they must also do when they serve the One Almighty God.

Rupert lay down the last sheet of his translation.

The others remained silent, overwhelmed by what they'd just heard. It was as if a sacred event had been taking place before them.

Michael blinked back the moisture that was welling into his eyes. He kept shaking his head slowly from side to side, giving the impression he was trying to digest it all. At last, he tapped the precariously long bridge of ash off his cigarette into the crystal ashtray at his side. He started to speak and had to clear his throat to find his voice. "No wonder the world is after this. Great heaven! We've got a real revolution on our hands. The prophet and greatest lawgiver of the Jews is Pharaoh Akhenaten. Pharaoh! A mystic, a monotheist, a revolutionary—and not even a Jew! How will people deal with this?

"And just as incredible, somewhere there may be the actual broken clay pieces of the Jews' Covenant with God! Their very first Covenant, the one that seems to come from a gentler and less angry God. You do fathom what we're talking about here? This isn't just some fanciful adventure story where the hero's made to discover a sacred object that we know does not exist today. We just might actually be able to find these pieces of the First Covenant.

"So, this is what the Seraphim riddle was telling us. Such a complicated chain of consequences will be let loose by that knowledge. I never imagined when I began so long ago that this could remotely be the result."

Rupert rubbed his weary eyes. "You're so right. Scholars might well split into two factions. One will regard the broken pieces of the first set of Commandments as the holiest of Holy Writ in existence. The other faction may want to destroy the scrolls in the name of orthodoxy before their message about Moses's real identity sees the light of day." Rupert frowned. "Of course, that'd fly against every cherished notion of truth in our Western philosophy. At least since Socrates."

Stephanos shifted in his seat, showing some discomfort. "What will you do with your manuscript, Rupert?"

Michael said, "I think it's best kept in the casket with the scrolls. Perhaps you feel like making another copy, Rupert?"

"Good idea all around. I'll pen the copy tomorrow. Tonight, I'm whacked." Rupert rubbed his eyes again with both hands.

"Of course," Caridis said. "You've been amazing. Two days without sleep. Time to rest now."

Rupert picked up the pages of his translation and stood. "Let's check out the casket tomorrow. Maybe we'll find something that leads us to the broken pieces." He laughed. "Oh, by the way, that phone call from someone who sounded English, you said, not German for a change? So, he says we've got three days before the witching hour." Rupert gave them an impish look. "We can do some interesting work in the meantime to tackle this—perhaps at its very source."

10

The next day

$\mathcal{R}$upert awoke late, recovered fully from his fatigue. After breakfast, he went into the grand salon where Sitamun's throne rested on its small platform. He spent several hours studying its gilded carvings, including the two heads of the queens flanking the seat of the chair. When Stephanos found him, he was on his knees, holding a magnifier against the details on the inside back of the chair, which had been arranged to catch the direct rays of sunlight just then slanting through one of the tall windows facing the square.

"Any inspired thoughts this morning, Rupert? Can you tear yourself away for a late lunch—or shall we have a tray brought in?" A certain archness colored Stephanos's questions.

"Ah, hello. Timing's quite perfect. I've completed my examination with some fascinating results. Will you get Michael and let me explain now before we go to the table?" Rupert gathered together some sheets with his notes and glanced up as Stephanos left the room.

Moments later, Michael appeared, all eagerness. "Yes, yes. You must tell your latest thoughts."

"I've made detailed notes you can read anytime. Here." He wagged the bunch of sheets he had scribbled on. "So, I'm going to give you the short version. This chair has one symbol after another that suggests Sitamun gave birth in a most unusual way. The symbols all point to a maternity that transcends the normal."

Rupert directed their attention to the upper inside back of the chair. "For example, the wings of the sun here are not those of a falcon, which would be the custom. Instead, they are of an eagle. We think of this as the most powerful and noble of all airborne creatures."

He stopped to light a cigarette, which he used now to emphasize his points. Aiming it at the outside of one flank of the chair, he said, "And here's the symbol of maternity, a god called Tawaret usually depicted as a hippopotamus. She is instead shown here as a lion. Guess what? The most noble of beasts. Check out the inside of this side of the chair. The three creatures are carrying gifts. Are they presents for Sitamun or for her child? One appears to be gold. Could others be frankincense and myrrh? Gold for a king, frankincense for his Godliness, myrrh as a symbol of the ointment used at his death. We cannot see if these last two are incense and oil, although the objects carried could be meant to contain them.

"Finally, see these two fully carved heads of a queen jutting out from the front flanking the seat? This throne's about a singular motherhood—and only that. There's no male depiction anywhere on the chair. The eagle wings bearing the sun are also shown on the casket's top. They're also carved into the stone outside the tomb. They symbolize an exceptional woman in any event, but here especially as the mother of a god."

Rupert fumbled in a pocket and withdrew a small object. "And to give further credence to what might be one the more extraordinary overlays of one ancient religious story upon another, I have something here given me by my father, the day he died. Michael, you laid eyes on this years ago. I touched it when you first told me of your ambition, to wish for your success in solving the Seraphim enigma."

"My god!" Michael stood up and took the scarab from Rupert. "I remember what I said then, purely from some instinct, no other reason—that it might well relate to the treasure we were trying to find." His voice almost trembled with emotion as he held out the bottom of the scarab toward the other two.

"It shows a queen crowning her son with the sun itself borne on the wings of an eagle!"

☥

At lunch, the three men continued playing with the idea about Akhenaten's birth suggested by his mother's throne.

Michael was riveted by this possibility as he attacked an omelet. Suddenly, he put down his knife and fork and blurted out, "Aha, I think I've just got it, the important piece to your hypothesis." He gulped some wine and turned to Stephanos, with a wink toward Rupert. "Let me tell you the strangest story you've ever heard about the god Horus. It connects in a way what Rupert's just suggested about a virgin birth directly to the myths of old Egypt.

"Horus was said to be the only child of Egypt's two most important ancient gods, Isis and Osiris. However, before Horus was ever conceived, his father, Osiris, was attacked by a murderous enemy and then dismembered into fourteen parts, which were scattered about the world. Poor Isis, desperate to become a mother, was heartbroken, but a determined lady nonetheless. She searched the world high and low for all the pieces of Osiris. Indeed, thirteen parts of her husband's body were found at last and reassembled. She was only missing the final—and, as it turned out, rather important—one, his phallus. That organ, so necessary to her master plan, had, it seems, disappeared into the stomach of a fish from which it could never be retrieved. So, although her husband was thus restored to most of his old self, he obviously had quite a significant defect."

Rupert laughed. "You've twigged completely." Nodding toward Stephanos, he smiled, and picked up the ball tossed by Michael. "So, then what do you think she did to correct this daunting defect? What else was there for her to do but magically to create a golden phallus? This phenomenal organ most helpfully emitted a sacred fire that made her pregnant with the child Horus. Thus, we've got Horus, whose symbol is the sun borne on wings, emblazoning the back of Sitamun's throne. Horus, *born of a woman impregnated by divine fire*."

After lunch, Rupert gathered up his notes and the magnifying glass and became serious. "OK, now we've got some real work to do. Where are those broken pieces of the original Covenant? That might well be the main prize for which people are being killed. And what about this phone call from an English person warning us to bring the scrolls to the Sanctuary by Friday afternoon? Do we know of any Englishmen who might be involved with the Germans in this? Any thoughts about friends here in Alexandria?"

Michael shook his head. "Not really. You know, maybe it's time to give a call to your one-time digging companion and self-described distant relative, von Vranken. Say you'd like to have a meal together. Study his reactions. We've got zero doubts he's directly involved in a plot to get the scrolls."

"Just what I planned to do. Can you show me a phone?" Rupert followed Michael into a little square hallway nearby.

"There's the phone. Just ask the operator to connect you."

He made the call and spoke for a good quarter hour. When he replaced the receiver, Rupert extracted a cigarette from its case. Tapping the cigarette on it, his thoughts were focused on what had just transpired in his conversation with Lothar von Vranken. The man had not seemed the least bit surprised at his call. Seemed to take it for granted he was in Alexandria.

Slipping the cigarette case back in his inner breast pocket, he saw Stephanos entering the small hallway where the phone sat on a console under a mirror. Rupert's first sight of him was the man's reflection. It revealed an expression unguardedly curious, as if he were coming to check up on him. He turned around with a cool smile and expressionless blue eyes. He was plagued as before by an ambiguity that he could not yet pin down.

Michael, nursing his coffee in the library, waited eagerly to learn how the call had turned out.

Rupert sat. "Quite friendly. Didn't seem to think it odd I was here. Can't imagine why, but perhaps he prefers to hide his reactions. Anyhow, wants us to join him tonight at Sala Sikandra, which he claims is the current hot spot where all the top German brass like to tickle the tits of the belly dancers. Says they're not at all bad-looking, as if I needed persuading." He laughed lightly and put out his cigarette in a crystal ashtray by his place.

"Why not?" Michael glanced at Stephanos who nodded. "Yes, what time did he say?"

"Ten-ish. I did bring my dinner jacket, so not to worry about me. It looks like we'll be able to test the waters with this chap. To be clear, he sounded a bit too smooth. Like he was reading from a script."

Stephanos leaned forward with an eager urgency. "And what do you think we'd best be doing to search for the broken pieces of the Covenant?" His intensity betrayed his effort to make the question seem offhand, even casual.

Rupert's expression became coy. "Isn't that the question of the moment? One's got to imagine there are just three realistic possibilities. Been thinking in my sleep, sometimes not such a bad way to unravel a tangle of things that don't seem to make any sense."

Michael put down his coffee. "Could we have your three theories?"

"Indeed, Miko. You of all people deserve to hear them. So, first, let's imagine Queen Sitamun is handed the fragments of the First Covenant by whoever actually delivers the bodies and the casket with the scrolls. She'd simply see some dried clay bits and pieces, probably inscribed with words in Hebrew, which I'm certain she could not read. So, suppose she's overwrought by seeing the wrapped bodies of her son and his wife, and she simply ignores the fragments or even hands them to a servant to be thrown away.

"The second possibility is the broken tablets were somehow laid inside the winding sheets that shrouded Akhenaten-Moses. If so, we'd have to look for his body, which until now seems to have disappeared from any tomb, which might have been his resting place. So, this, like the first, is a rather depressing hypothesis.

"We come finally to the one that might give us a chance to find the tablets. It could be right under our noses, so to speak. And it would explain why the casket has been dogged by people willing even to murder in cold blood just to obtain it. We must examine the casket itself to see if there might be secret compartments that contain the original Commandments."

Stephanos said, "Oh, I'm sure that's unlikely. Where could

you hide the clay pieces? They'd take up too much room." He waved his hand as if to discourage even bothering with this possibility.

"Really?" asked Rupert, studying the fellow for clues to his inner feelings. "Isn't it worth at least a look?"

Stephanos squirmed. "Well, I just think it could be a waste of time. Really, I wouldn't bother."

Michael and Rupert exchanged glances.

Michael said, "Oh, come now, what can be lost in just giving it a look?"

The fellow slumped a little in his chair and shrugged. "Do whatever you think best, of course."

Michael and Rupert rose at the same time, ignoring their companion, and headed for the stairs to the catacombs. They passed the leering skulls and jutting bones and closed the door of the conservation room.

Crossing in firm strides over to the vault, Michael spun the dials with a dexterity that showed his frequent use. He grasped the long handle with both hands and turned it clockwise until the sound of the bolts being extracted had stopped. They pulled the door open on its curved track and switched on the light inside the vault. The casket rested where it had been placed the night before. They picked it up by the handles at each end and carried it to the stainless steel table in the conservation room.

Rupert remarked, "It's maybe a bit heavier than one might have imagined for its size, even allowing that it's made of ebony, which is dense and heavy. This could be a tip-off to something hidden inside." He drew out the bronze rod from the three locks and then lifted the clasps so they stood straight upright against the top of the casket. As he lifted the lid, they both felt a powerful emanation from the chest.

Michael took a handkerchief from his pocket and dabbed his forehead. "I'm feeling its energy even more than before.

Now that we've read about the broken pieces of the First Covenant, I reckon it's a little heavier than you would expect." With an air of hesitation, he lifted the three scrolls from the chest and laid them aside on the table with a certain reverence now that he understood the possibility of the casket's other contents.

Rupert removed his jacket and rolled up his sleeves. "It's getting warmer. Is the ventilation system working?

"Oh, yes. But it's evidently being outdone by whatever's in there." Michael pointed at the chest. He turned to the cabinet nearby and grabbed the flashlight. His hand trembled a bit as the beam searched both the lid and the sides of the casket. He moved it down to the floor of the chest, which appeared to be perfectly tied into the four sides. "Nothing unusual that I can see." He put down the flashlight and closed the lid of the casket. Lifting it with both hands, he asked, "Do give me a hand to turn this on its side."

Rupert grabbed the middle of the chest on its top and bottom and guided it backward onto its hinged side. They both stopped breathing when the bottom came into view. Incised into the darkened wood was a representation of the rod of Aaron, with its twenty-four parallel leaves flanking the upper third. "Jesus wept! How could we not have had a look here before?"

Like a man mesmerized, Michael placed his fingertips into several of the hollowed-out leaves, which he pressed. He did this singly and then in combinations on both sides of the rod. He tried a number of permutations without result, and when a scraping sound came from inside, they turned the chest back upright and lifted the curved lid. The floor of the chest had been released enough for them to see there was indeed a compartment beneath. They carefully took hold of the floor and pulled it up and away from the walls of the casket. A great sigh of warm wind touched their faces and whistled in their ears. Both men found their hands trembled as they stared into the shallow compartment at the bottom of the casket.

It was filled with flattish objects wrapped in separate folded envelopes of burlap. Of varying sizes, each was tied with a thin string of hemp. Rupert looked at Michael, who nodded, and then reached into the exposed cavity and withdrew one of the packages. With a delicate touch, the hemp pulled apart easily, crumbling into puffs of dust.

He unfolded the burlap covering and spread it on the table. The two men were motionless as they studied the thin, flat piece of hardened clay. It was jagged, obviously broken from a larger matrix. Small, neat lettering was inscribed in three parallel lines cut off at its irregular edges. "Hebrew, ancient script, influenced by Egyptian pictography." Rupert picked up the shard with an unsteady hand. "Can this really be? Am I touching the very Words of God?"

Michael reached over and took it from him. He turned it upside down and looked at the pattern of the woven reeds of the tray in which it had been laid when the clay was wet. "What does it say?"

"Because it's interrupted on each line, the full meaning is not expressed, but the hints are there, Michael. Anyway, after reading the third scroll, we know indeed how to arrange the pieces and how these commandments will differ from those we've been brought up with."

Michael shook his head. "It really doesn't seem possible, does it? The broken pieces of the earlier Covenant between Moses and God! Before the later one said to have been kept by the Jews in their Ark of the Covenant, which has never been found in modern times." He handed it back to Rupert. "No wonder there's such a determined effort out there to possess this. What I want to know is how the hell did the Nazi mafia here in Alexandria find out what I never even suspected?"

Rupert frowned as he placed the shard in its burlap and folded the ends over it. "Can you give me a bit of string? This old hemp's finished."

Caridis went to the cabinet and rummaged until he found what was wanted. "So, have you come up with any theories?"

With an air of preoccupation, Rupert tied and replaced the small package next to its fellows and laid the false bottom back down on the treasure. When it clicked into position, he replaced the scrolls and put a copy of his translation on top before closing the lid and sliding the short bronze pole through the three hoops protruding through the clasps. With this, he turned to Michael. "Yes, I've got some theories, but let's put the chest in your vault first."

The two men lifted the casket and replaced it on a shelf within the strong room.

While Michael pushed down the door handles and twirled the combination locks, Rupert stood to one side. He finally said, "Are you sure no one else knows how to open the vault?"

"Absolutely yes, no one else has the foggiest. As I told you, just as a precaution should something happen to me, I posted the combination to Ravenstone Park when I sent you the telegram. It's probably waiting for you there." He paused for a few moments and then asked with a hint of stress, "May I assume no one else opens or reads your mail?"

Rupert laughed. "Not anybody who's likely to figure out the clues to your combinations, which you said were described in the form of a riddle." He fished for a small notepad in his pocket and a pencil. "Here, perhaps you can recall what it says, your letter, I mean, about the combinations?"

"That's testing me a bit. Let's see. As there are two combination locks, and each needs four correct numbers, and the left-hand lock begins by turning right, and the right-hand lock begins by turning left, there's a play on 'sinister' and 'dexterous.' This is done by the phrase: 'What seems right may be wrong, and the reverse can be true as well.' Then the fact of four numbers for each lock is indicated by 'a couple of handfuls less twenty parts of a hundred for each will help to make a good start.'

"Now moving to the actual four numbers for each lock, the clue reads: 'When Great Caesar ignored what he heard the bell tolled before its time, which he would have wished turned back upon itself for a second chance—'"

"Let me see if I can get that one." Rupert lifted his pencil from the pad. "I assume there's no punctuation to limit your meaning. So, one interpretation can be as follows. What Caesar heard—that leads to his last hours—was on the Ides of March, the fifteenth day of the third month. Thus, we have the numbers fifteen and three. The bell tolled for him at the age of fifty-five, which, for a man murdered, was certainly before its time, and it tolled in the year 44 before the time of Christ. If you turn these numbers back upon themselves, they'd read in reverse: forty-four, fifty-five, three, and fifteen. Now, these numbers could be sequenced a little differently, which would be easy to try, and it should not be long before the right combination was found. Finally, if you took the month and placed a zero before the three, you would have two sets of four single numbers that could be tried, for example, as 1503 and 4455, but that is somewhat inconsistent with his hypothetical wish "to turn back upon itself for a second chance.'"

"My dear fellow, you never cease to awe me with the speed you're able to zero in. Yes, you've certainly got the idea, and the first sequence is quite the correct one. I assume you were planning to apply the first sequence to the left knob."

"Of course. Now, I'm going to tear my page into tiny shreds

so no one could ever decipher those numbers I've jotted." He ripped it from his small bound notebook and noisily carried out his threat over a stone ashtray. When done, he took his lighter and ignited the lot. "There, that's done. Now you and I are the only living souls who know." He glanced at his wristwatch, "I say, we probably ought to be thinking about having tea and getting ready for our evening with the distant Teutonic cousin."

Michael kept his place. "Not yet. We've got time. You've evaded answering how the Germans here could have understood what was so important about the find we made at Amarna. They seem to have known in advance an earthshaking discovery lay in that casket. My God! Moses turns out to be the pharaoh himself, not even a Jew, and the first set of Commandments that he received from God are physically here, here in this house." He shook his head in disbelief at this outcome.

Rupert lit a cigarette without responding. After taking a second drag, he said, "And you've not mentioned how this has cast Aaron. He's the very reason why the first set of commandments was destroyed by Moses/Akhetaten. And then Aaron goes on to slay the great man. What could be more deliriously attractive to the Jew-haters in Berlin. Aaron's got to be their hero. The man who killed Moses."

Michael turned to him with impatience. "OK, that's fair. We can understand all that, but the huge question is *how* did Berlin or Alexandria know so much more about what was inside the chest? You keep evading that, don't you?"

Laughing, he said, "Fair enough. All right, here's what I think. If history can give us any clues, then we do know, for example, that Schliemann, the German discoverer of Agamemnon's mask, and Borchardt, the German discoverer of the magnificent Nefertiti bust, pursued their callings in a culture infatuated with antiquities. People like that might also have discovered something, some sort of reference or clue, relating to the Seraphim treasure."

"And somehow that clue might have found its way to the Seraphim in Berlin. Sounds possible, Rupert, but not very likely. Just a magical explanation, frankly."

The other man pulled the conservation room door shut, and Michael locked it. "So, you say, but just consider all other imaginable sources besides the wild chance someone simply guessed the First Covenant was the major treasure." Rupert smiled. "Not bloody probable."

The two men strolled through the catacombs and upstairs to the library where a service of late-afternoon tea had been set up.

Stephanos appeared at the doorway.

Rupert looked up from his cup and had the sudden impression he might have just overheard their entire conversation through the door of the conservation room. There was something in the way the man looked and the studied casualness of his entrance. "Ah, there you are, Stephanos. I was just saying to Michael we probably ought to be having a bit of rest and dressing for dinner after tea, no?"

Caridis rose from his chair, turned around, and stared at Stephanos. "Have you come to tell us something?"

Stephanos seemed uncomfortable. "In fact, Michael, I've been taken with a bit of a bad stomach, so you two should count me out of tonight, please. I'll just go upstairs with some tea and biscuits. Sorry to drop out like this."

Rupert said, "Not to mind. Sorry you're under the weather. Hope by morning, all has settled itself." He walked over and took Michael by the arm. "Just had a thought. Let me take you to see something in one of your galleries that I've meant to ask you about." He turned back to Stephanos. "Do excuse us and take care to get better." He led Michael out the other end of the room and around a corner and into the next room, which was a square hall leading to three galleries.

"What do you want?"

Rupert held up a finger to his lips and whispered, "Stay here." He abruptly retraced his steps back to the library and was almost struck by Stephanos striding around the corner. "I do say, I thought your bedroom was the other way, no?"

Stephanos, flustered, said, "Oh, I was just going to check with Michael if there's something he'd like me to do while you're at dinner."

"I see, well, I'm sure Michael wants you to spend your energy recuperating. I wouldn't bother him now." Rupert deliberately turned around to go back to where Michael was standing—without explaining why he'd even come back to the salon in the first place.

The other man fled without another word.

Michael said, "Where've you just been?"

"I'm afraid the cat may be out of the bag. Our little game of ciphers may not have gone unnoticed by someone else in the house."

"Stephanos? Think he was eavesdropping on us? The door's pretty thick."

"Very possibly. We could test what can be heard from outside the closed door. I'd also suggest we reset the vault's combinations on both locks tomorrow. Actually, I'd do it right now, if we didn't have to dress for this evening."

♀

The doorman was done up like an Ottoman grand marshal. Resembling an extra in a Rossini opera, he was tall and bowed to them deeply, showing the top of his colorful turban with a billowing egret feather fastened by a fake-jeweled pin to its side. With even more exaggeration, he announced, "Welcome, Effendis, to Sala Sikandra. The beauteous ones await your pleasures with breathless impatience."

Rupert smiled and nudged Michael as they passed through the elaborate doorway. When he didn't react, Rupert could see he remained badly unsettled by the new light thrown on Stephanos.

11

That evening

*E*ntering the cavernous space, they felt an instant assault on their senses. The air was filled with the music of bouzoukis and finger cymbals and pan flutes, the smells of Turkish tobaccos and French perfumes, the chatter of many languages, and the crystalline bell tones of glasses touching other glasses, and the laughter of besotted lechers and hopeful courtesans. Necklines plunged, jewels glittered, uniforms made some men seem fitter and handsomer, and smoke from cigars, cigarettes, and guttering candle flames undulated in swirls up to the peak of the square-tented room. Great swaths of cloth like Jacob's robe of many colors, swooped down from the apex of a giant central Venetian chandelier draped like an oriental tent over to the four walls where they were gathered and fell in irregular folds down to the floor. These were interspersed with metallic palm trees and gilded mirrors in front of which slouched the scented and Macassar-ed inventory provided for the instant satisfaction of a kaleidoscope of lusts.

A man of medium height in a snappy old-regime German military officer's dress uniform of a light blue-gray wool with an upright collar band trimmed in silver threads came up to Rupert and Michael and greeted them in a cool, cultured accent. His eyes blazed above wide cheekbones, and his light-colored hair, albino-like, was parted in the middle and swept back in wings from his pale forehead with its almost invisible white eyebrows.

"So," he drawled the "s" as if it had been a "z," his voice teetering vertiginously on the precipice of sarcasm, "it seems my two favorite *auslanders* are at last together with me after all these years. How nice, I say to myself. Really—a privilege to see my cousin, especially now one of England's greatest lords. What transformation from schoolteacher-archaeologist, yes?" He laughed mirthlessly at this thought.

"And here we are joined together by the catalyst of our youth, our famous Greek, today's Agathon of Alexandria, a man of exquisite sensibility and vast knowledge, perhaps hoping to return us to sifting sand and looking under rocks for signs of ancient life?" He nodded to Michael and extended his hand to Rupert. "Gentlemen, do come and join my table."

Von Vranken led them past tables of German officers carousing with overly made-up camp followers. Hairdos were already beginning to come apart, and cheeks were overly flushed. On one, a bottle of champagne leaned against a flower arrangement, slowly spilling both their contents, and the smell of a burning napkin rose above the other aromas assaulting one's nostrils.

They reached their destination at the edge of the dance floor. Three other high-ranking German officers lounged about the table along with two women, only one of whom seemed to be paid attention to by one of the officers. Two of the men clearly were absorbed only in each other and were making little giggling sounds.

"Please meet old friends from my salad days, everybody. Here we have the eminent aesthete of Alexandria, Michael Caridis, and my cousin of several degrees distance, the distinguished Marquess of Ravenstone, Rupert Delacorte."

Waiters rushed to bring chairs and place settings. Orders were given for drinks. Rupert found himself riveted by the theatrics of their host. The man clearly was on a high of some sort. Cocaine came to mind. Eyes glowed as if they were liquid pools. Laughter came in staccato bursts. Words rushed out like bullets from a machine gun. He was once again amazed by the arrogant self-assurance of Lothar von Vranken. Compared with the much caricatured sangfroid and stiff upper lip of the classic British military officer, their host tonight took the prize for put-downs of every conceivable creature that crossed his mind. His smugness and his heartless dismissal of others, either to their faces or behind their backs after they had stopped by his table, made Rupert imagine a man on a high tightrope, tempting the fates to knock him off.

Michael was placed beside one of the women, somewhat plump arms and shoulders above a strapless dress of smooth pale pink satin to the floor, with curly light-brown hair and cheeks that had too much rouge. She made an unrewarded effort to get him to focus on her. He was studying the feminine inventory on the dance floor and the nearest wall of patient hopefuls.

"What's bothering you, honey?" she finally asked in a faint Cockney accent.

He turned his attention to her and replied, "Would you excuse me? I think I see someone I know." He scraped his chair back and strolled over to a group of Alexandrians standing with drinks.

Von Vranken maintained his bantering tone. He seemed incapable of arresting the onslaught of his chatter. After several minutes, Rupert interjected with the greatest guile. "Lothar, I've a question you might just be able to answer."

The German seemed hesitant to stop his verbal tidal wave, but curiosity appeared to win out, and he responded, "Yes? What can I do for you?"

"Thank you. You see, of late, I've become rather fascinated with a project Michael asked to help him with. And now it's occurred to me, as we are fellow Aaronites, to ask you to help us with something that's come up connected to that project. This involves the Seraphim here in Alexandria."

The German gave him a cold stare and a forced laugh. "Yes? What sort of help could you possibly need? I know you and Churchill are important members of the London chapter —and both rather nasty about your friends in Berlin."

Rupert ignored this thrust and smiled with blatantly affected innocence. "Frankly, it would amuse me greatly to see their building here, which I'm told is quite beautiful, but I fear I'd feel a bit out of place, under present circumstances."

"You know better than that, Rupert. An Aaronite's welcome in every Sanctuary around the world."

Rupert tilted his head and raised an eyebrow. "Well, you know, that may be so, but Michael, poor chap, received a quite threatening call from an Englishman, nameless of course, who wants something very valuable of Michael's delivered to the Seraphim ... or else heaven knows what will follow. Not a little like a Mafia threat?" Rupert stared directly into his eyes. "Can you think who might have it in for Michael?"

Von Vranken remained impassive and icy.

"Can you imagine? Our old friend Michael's been ordered to comply by the day after tomorrow. Of course, he hasn't the slightest intention of reacting to their absurd demand." Rupert gave him another guileless smile.

At that, the German's head gave a nervous jerk, and his ebullient state abruptly began to dissipate into a downer, as if whatever boosted him before had by now worn off. He avoided eye contact with Rupert. Looking into the distance, he remarked, "Ah, yes, I see. The show's about to begin. Best belly dancers in town." Without excusing himself, he scraped his chair back and headed across the room. He threaded his way between the tables and passed through an opening in the draperies.

Rupert rose and followed him. Beyond the curtains were several sitting rooms and small enclosed telephone cabins with windowed doors. He saw von Vranken sitting in the last cabin with his back angled to the door, his hand cupped over the receiver.

Feeling curiously uneasy along with a mischievous touch of satisfaction at having precipitated this reaction, Rupert strolled back into the main room. The youth of twenty in the days of their digs had become a powerful Nazi, apparently walking something of an emotional tightrope. He was going to be a formidable antagonist.

A new musical set was just starting. It began in a burst of bouzouki and woodwind and never let up, increasing in speed and rising through the scales until it finished with a crescendo, announcing the entrance of a twirling woman clad only in a minute jeweled bra and a diaphanous skirt slung deep below her navel. The music changed abruptly to a pan flute and a pair of tambourines that struck the rhythm for the wide swings of her hips and the sensuous movements of her hands and arms. Her breasts were full and firm, and her mound of Venus was taut and flexed with the undulations of her hips and the arching of her body in backward dips almost to the floor.

Rupert could not take his eyes from her face. Mesmerized, he devoured its every contour, from the unusually widely spaced eyes with their emerald green pools framed by long, dark curving lashes to the high cheekbones, small, refined nose and heart-shaped mouth, almost pouting in the clearest, silkiest pale skin he had ever seen. The mane of shining black hair swept this way and that as the music pulled her in a heady, antic orbit around the dance floor. When she got to his table, she stopped before him and began to move her hands palms facing each other, up and down in circles through an elongated trajectory that carried them from high over her head, arching back away from him until her breasts hid her face from view, and then downward, bringing her hands to make their circles over her groin. The music had now reached a level of pulsating urgency that called for an imminent climax.

"Enjoying the scenery, Rupert?" Lothar sat down next to him with a self-satisfied smile and the restoration of the moist glow to his eyes that seemed to be part of his periodic bouts of electric energy.

Rupert gave a quick smile to the dancer and turned to respond with a breezy, "I do believe I'm ready for a martini."

Lothar summoned a waiter with a commanding wave of his hand. He gave him the order as well as a bit of paper from the telephone booth's notepad. The waiter nodded and withdrew. Turning to Rupert, he preened with self-satisfaction. "I suspect you may be pleased with receiving your cocktail along with, shall we call it, an appetizer? In the meantime—" He took champagne from a bucket and filled Rupert's glass with an ingratiating lift of his eyebrows.

Some minutes after reaching the twirling finale of her dance, the object of Rupert's fascination magically appeared at their table to a flurry of scraping chairs and stiff bows from the German officers. Her breasts nippled barely into the folds of a Lucien Lelong gown, draped from her shoulders in a large V open to the navel with a similar plunge at her back to the waist. It was gathered at the bottom of the V just at her navel with a large, shimmering aquamarine brooch that matched the blue-water nuances of the silk. It slinked around her perfect hips and down to the floor in a spreading center double fold.

"My dear Solange, may I present my distant cousin, Rupert Delacorte." With a sly smile, he added, "Rupert, perhaps you recognize our performer whom you so admired a few minutes ago? Do meet Solange Falkensberg, our refugee from Vienna."

Offering a narrow, graceful hand to Rupert, her profound green eyes were given a faint blue cast by the teardrop aquamarines dangling from her earrings.

He held it for a moment before bending to brush her hand with his lips. The musky notes of her perfumes billowed into his nostrils. He looked into her eyes. "You do belong here, I suspect, more than staid old Vienna." He helped her be seated, admiring the flawless skin of her back, which appeared to have no pores whatsoever across its velvet-smooth expanse. After pulling up his own chair close to hers, he said, "So, you must tell me, why a 'refugee' as our friend has described?"

"Well, I'm Jewish. After recent events especially, Vienna's rather uncomfortable. So, I'm here. Ballet lessons as a child, perhaps even my ancient heritage, think Salome, made it natural to do this." She hesitated slightly. "And it gives me the means to be independent." Her voice was quiet and firm, with more than a tinge of an English accent coloring the Viennese German of her upbringing.

Rupert's blues twinkled. "There surely've been attractive opportunities along the way—shall we say—to become quite comfortably dependent. No?"

She laughed a little and softly hugged her arms. "It seems my standards are perhaps a trifle too particular." She paused.

"And that, not to be too indiscreet, describes my present state as well."

He gave an understanding nod, looking at Lothar. "You sound as if you've spent time in my country."

"Oh that. Father loved your country, so my nanny was British. From Wiltshire, in fact."

Rupert leaned back. "Exactly where I live. Ravenstone Park. Nice country, but it rains a lot, so it's good to be here right now." He gave her a somewhat puzzled look. "Strange. You strike me as someone who's really been part of things that happened ancient ages ago—in these parts. Uncanny, you know." He ran his hand along the side of his short naval-cut beard. "I've a mental image of Nefertiti, the Berlin bust, and you keep merging into it as I sit and stare like a gawking teen."

She did not respond, and her smile remained mysterious and guarded. Finally, she said, "You're an old soul, aren't you? Wise in ways not well understood in these times. And something's recently come into your life. Something so remarkable it puts you into some danger, doesn't it?"

This charged him with curiosity. He looked at the dance floor, which was almost full. "Do I dare ask you to join me there?" He tilted his head toward the fox-trotters.

"Of course. Delighted." She gave him her hand as she rose from her chair. A thrill of sexual desire pierced him like a sudden arrow. The anticipation grew as they stepped onto the dance floor and faced each other. He took her into his arms and was overtaken by a cloud of her scent and the beating of his heart.

They moved as one. She wasn't there, so light did she seem.

After several minutes, he looked into her eyes and asked, "Your last question about present danger, what did you mean?" At this, he noticed a film form over the green pools. "Has anyone mentioned to you about my life's work?"

She nodded. "Yes. It's true. They have. I think, after this briefest meeting, you're a good man and must not be hurt. Forces are trying to take something from you, something of staggering importance. They will go to any lengths. Be on your guard. Your distant cousin is not your friend. Nor, deep in his nature where it counts, is he mine."

Rupert held her closer. "Then you've heard him give his disgusting Nazi salutations to the other Jew-haters in his circle?"

She nodded again. "They want to touch, to caress, to make and profess love to us, and a moment later, they'll shatter our windows, steal our treasures, brutalize our bodies, and try to extinguish the inextinguishable candle that burns in our souls."

Rupert studied her. "Well, what these gangsters want from us, Solange, will both shock and surprise your people. It is the most profoundly sacred object for them in existence. Perhaps for all people. The question is, how did the Nazis ever learn of it, even before we learned the full extent of what we had?"

She glanced over his shoulder at Lothar staring at them and looked up with a huge smile. "We're being noticed. Be lighthearted—as if you're having fun."

He laughed. "But I really am, and I'll try to make it look even more that way." Grinning, he twirled her about and leaned to be close to her ear. "Now in this tender embrace, as the poets say, we can continue whispering what might be assumed to be sweet nothings. So, any thoughts as to how the Germans may have come by their information predicting what would be in the treasure unearthed by Michael over there?"

"Yes. Naturally, when they talk among themselves, they don't imagine anyone else could have the slightest idea what it concerns." She gave a mysterious smile. "I may be unusual in how much I do understand." She put her hand on the back of his neck with a tender look. "See what a good actress I am? Now, back to our point. There's a man here in Alexandria named Fritzi Vogel who's been a member of the party since the early twenties—when they were just starting to strut about the streets of Munich and knock down Jews and insult them whenever they felt like it.

"I feel something about him, the way he addresses me when I'm around Lothar. He seems almost sympathetic to my position. Anyway, I suddenly need to spill out to you, a nice, kind stranger. Makes me feel less the Nazi whore." Her eyes teared over a bit. "Lately, Lothar and Fritzi have been locked together in meetings. I've been able to pick up that a recently opened document this August revealed many details of something buried in Amarna that must be the very treasure you mentioned. And they know your friend Caridis has found it."

Rupert saw Lothar approaching them on the dance floor. He twirled her again and said, "Save the rest for our next dance."

"All right, you two, enough of this smooching about. Dinner's on the table." Turning to her, he said, "See what I meant? An interesting chap, my cousin, eh?" Putting his hand on Rupert's shoulder, he guided them back to their seats.

Across the table, Michael was locked in conversation with one of the more voluptuous and exotic denizens of the waiting wall whom he had selected with the eye of a connoisseur. He looked over at Rupert who raised eyebrows approvingly and elaborately lifted his left arm to examine the time on his watch.

Solange Falkensberg was clearly popular among the Nazi officers. She told amusing stories and kept up her lively and intelligent dialogues throughout the rest of the meal. When she and Rupert said good night, the clock had reached two o'clock in the morning, and they had not had another opportunity to dance together. He slipped her his calling card with Michael's house phone number jotted on the back.

At their parting, Lothar von Vranken was visibly on edge— and not just from the lapse of time since his last hit.

12

Later that evening

*D*riving back from the Sala Sikandra, Michael entered the large square and pulled his small open roadster up to the gates of the house. He looked about, alarmed. "I say, what's going on? No one's here to open up? Lights are out?" They jumped from the car and rushed to the tall iron grillwork. Not a soul in sight. No night shift of armed guards. Michael rang the bell several times, and its clear chime seemed to resonate throughout the entire deserted square. At last, he returned to the car and pulled a rather large iron key from a compartment under the seat.

After he unlocked the gates, and they pushed its two leaves open, Michael drove into the motor court and parked next to his small fleet.

Rupert pushed the gates together until they noisily clicked back into their locked position.

By now, both were on high alert. They moved cautiously into the arched passageway between the landscaped front and central court of the mansion. The glass and steel door to the porter's office and lodgings was set into the left wall of the stone passage. Lights had been turned off in both the passage and the office, which were normally left burning all night. They opened this door and pushed the switch down. In the wash of light that suddenly sprang from the pitch darkness, their eyes were blinded for a moment. They soon saw a porter's feet sticking out from the end of the tall counter. When Michael and Rupert looked behind the counter, the two men were wrapped in ropes and asleep.

Rupert sniffed. "Gassed, I'd say. Probably wrestled to the ground, tied up, and then given a heavy dose. Chloroform. This should be aired out now with the door open." He walked around the counter, dropped to his haunches, and untied their bodies. The men were still limp and unconscious. "Just leave them here to sleep it off. I suspect they'll survive and be all right."

"Good God! What on earth's going on here? Where the hell are the armed guards?" Michael picked up the intercom telephone and pushed all the buttons on the little switchboard panel so that he could address every corner of the house. "Stephanos! Can you hear me? Are you there? Please pick up. We're calling from the porter's phone." They waited, both of them tense and alert.

Rupert finally left the porter's office before the men began to stir, and he crossed the central courtyard. In the dim ambient light of the sky and the sleeping city, he noted the ancient monoliths and sarcophagi looming like strange, fantastical creatures in a frightening dream. Michael joined him with a flashlight, and the pair walked up the broad steps and entered the soaring entrance hall now draped in darkest mystery.

Michael groped to one side and found the switches underneath a heavy brocade curtain. He pushed several of them down without effect. He aimed his flashlight at the large, suspended bronze lantern, sending its beams through the tall panels of carved and beveled glass. The light quivered into the shadowy corners of the space. The rest of the house also seemed to be unlit. As if sharing a single mind, the two men bolted across the marble floor to the staircase leading to the catacombs.

The light switch just inside the bronze door to the final flight of steps did not work. Since this had happened before, a shelf had been installed on the right-hand side with several flashlights. Rupert grabbed one.

Michael shouted, "Stephanos! Are you here? Stephanos!"

Just silence. A stillness of eternal oblivion. Their moving shafts of light darted from side to side, picking out the leering sightless eyes and ashen bones of the endless stacks of the dead. They held their breath as they approached the door to the conservation room. It was closed as usual.

Rupert pushed down on the lever handle and pulled it open. They were startled as their flashlight beams revealed straight ahead the wide open, fearful eyes of Stephanos who had been strapped by his feet and legs to a heavy chair with his arms and hands tied over its back. A gag covered his mouth. He moaned and jerked his head in the direction of the vault.

The aimed their beams behind him at the massive steel door of the vault. It stood wide open and showed no signs of forced entry. Their lights swept in and out of the cavity inside.

Michael said, "Oh, Christ!"

They untied Stephanos, removed his gag, and stood in silence before him, waiting.

He rose, moved his arms up and down like wings, massaged his shoulders, and staggered over to the wall where he pushed the light switches. He spoke as if to the entrance door, "Of course, the central power control must have been turned off."

Rupert, in a quiet voice, asked, "Is that switch nearby?"

A furtive shadow passed over Stephanos's face. After hesitating a moment longer than expected, he answered over his shoulder, "It's in the porter's lodge." Stephanos turned to face them. "I've been in pitch blackness for hours. Horrible, horrible. They wore masks. One was blond. British voice, young, quite tall. The other was clearly German, light reddish hair, medium height. Seemed to be in charge. The tall one directed the opening of the combination locks. He had a piece of paper and read off several different sets of numbers, which they tried until they came up with the ones that worked. It was clear they knew exactly what they were after.

"They asked me if everything was in the casket. Of course, I pretended I'd no idea what was in it. When they opened it and took out the scrolls and felt about the inside of the chest, one of them swore, the blond one, I think. He said to the other, 'You told me the pieces would be here, but I don't see them.' The other one turned the casket over and pushed in several places until there was a noise inside the casket. They turned it back up and lifted the cover. They reached inside, I couldn't see, but they must have pulled up the floor of the chest. When they did this, there was a long, whistling wail. A blast of heat seemed to rise with it into the room. The blond one jumped away and said his hands were burned, but the other one had no problem with touching whatever was there. The sound was so strange. The German said it was like a hundred angels weeping. He fell to his knees and covered his face for a moment. The Englishman spoke to him scornfully. 'Come on,' he said. 'Get up now and let's take this where it belongs.' The German responded, 'Don't worry. I've got it all arranged. We'll be off tonight.'"

Rupert stared at him. "So, how did these two make it into the house?"

Stephanos turned abruptly to face him. "Well, didn't you see?"

"See what?"

At this, the other caught himself and became guarded again. "I suppose, that is, it only seems logical, doesn't it? They must have taken steps to overcome the porters at the gate, no?"

"True. They were overcome. Seems some sort of sleeping gas. By now, they should be coming out of it, I'd guess." Rupert continued to study the man who had now cast his eyes down. "Somehow, they got rid of the armed guards—another mystery, no? Can you be more precise in your description of each man? Did you feel you'd ever seen either of them before?"

Stephanos shook his head. "Never, I'm sure. Both wore black eye masks and looked to be quite fit. The blond Englishman had a rather entitled way about him, used to authority, I'd say, impatient, arrogant. Upper-class accent. The German was more humble and practical. Businesslike, not much like the officer types we see here in Alexandria. But he did have a dueling scar—even if he might not be from the elite families who are licking Hitler's boots."

Rupert's expression darkened. Conflicting currents were running through him. "Clearly they knew what they were looking for. Did they make any references to their sources?"

Stephanos looked carefully at him. He seemed to be making calculations in advance of giving his response. "No, I don't think they referred to any such sources of information. But I recall now, when von Vranken called while Michael was in Amarna, he asked me something strange, which I'm afraid I neglected to report to you, Michael."

"And what was that?" Rupert asked.

Stephanos glanced at Michael. "He asked if I thought the Jews would be happy with the discovery. Of course, there was nothing I could say to that. I guess there was a sneering tone in his voice, which probably meant he'd got a fair idea of what was meant to be in the casket."

Michael said, "It's still a mystery to me. I keep on asking myself, how could von Vranken know anything more than I? My father and my ancestors were members of the Society of the Seraphim. As Aaronites from the upper echelons of the Society, we all should have known whatever the most informed would have known. And Father would have told me anything and everything." He shook his head as if the alternative was unimaginable.

"May I speak to you alone, Michael?" Rupert studied his hands and looked up at Stephanos. "Would you mind if we had a private word with each other?"

Stephanos stood and scowled for a moment. He turned, grabbed a flashlight, stumbled slightly, and walked out the far end of the conservation room. "I'll throw the main power switch," he said as he closed the door behind him with a small slam.

Rupert gestured to say nothing for a few moments. He then opened the conservation room door and looked up and down the aisle of skeletons. A flashlight beam flickered in the distance. Satisfied, he turned and spoke in a low voice. "Tonight, I came straight out and told von Vranken about that call demanding the chest's delivery to the Society, by Friday afternoon, or else terrible things would befall you. The fellow reacted as if he hadn't heard a word. Pushed his chair back and strode off. I followed and found him making a call in one of the little telephone rooms. I'd bet anything it was straight to those characters who tied up Stephanos, seemingly against his will."

"It's obvious that reptilian Nazi invited us to Sala Sikandra just to get us away from the house. And you say 'seemingly.' You don't really think Stephanos could have been in cahoots?"

"Seems possible."

The room's lights went on, and the telephone bell sounded on the marble worktable.

Michael picked up. "Yes. I see. Hold on. Here's Rupert." He held his hand over the mouthpiece. "The lady you danced with tonight. Most anxious to speak."

"Solange?" Rupert smiled into the phone.

"Yes. It's important, Rupert. I'm sure you must know by now what's happened at the house where you're staying." Her voice was muted to the point of being almost inaudible.

"Are you in danger making this call?"

"There are risks. This is important." She stopped speaking. The sound of a male voice, someone entering a room and surprised to find her. The high-pitched voice was angry and shouted, "Do you know what the hell's going on? Where's Fritzi? I've wondered how cozy you two were—"

The phone was apparently grabbed and thrown to the floor, and sounds of scuffling could be heard with pained cries and then screams from Solange.

It was picked up, and a male voice demanded, "Who's this? Speak up. Speak up, damn you!"

Rupert remained silent, and even Michael at some distance could hear the cruel voice crackling out from the receiver. With a delicate touch, Rupert depressed the cut-off cradle and hung up.

"That poor, poor woman. Sounded like von Vranken. What brutes. Nothing we can do, I'm terribly sorry." He frowned. "The fellow who attacked her shouted about a 'Fritzi.' Interesting—while we were dancing, she spoke of a Fritzi who'd meet for hours with von Vranken, and they'd plot together, presumably to pull off the heist tonight. That's all she had time to tell me because von Vranken interrupted and pulled us back to the table. After that, we were never alone again.

I passed her your phone number. My guess is honor among thieves hasn't necessarily improved with the Nazis. This Fritzi probably decided to take the spoils for himself. Wonder what happened to the Brit, evidently Fritzi's partner? And how on earth did they ever get their hands on the combinations for unlocking the vault? Someone must have overheard you or spied on your mail before you sent it to me."

Michael shook his head. "I can't begin guessing how they learned the codes. Thank God, we thought to keep a copy of your translation. But the originals? What if they're destroyed?" He was finally showing the full impact of the loss. His voice trembled. "The proof's been taken. Moses's extraordinary true identity, and worst of all, the very tablets themselves, the record of that first encounter with his God." His voice broke. "The most precious, the greatest imaginable treasure gone, just like that ..."

Rupert placed a comforting hand on his shoulder. "They weren't stolen to be destroyed. I think we can depend on their survival. History will forever show you alone were their discoverer. These remarkable things are out in the world." He paused and looked him in the eyes. "And don't doubt for a moment, we'll move mountains if we have to, to retrieve it all."

Michael's jaw tensed with anger. "Let's be realistic about what's been taken from us. Major wars have been fought over much, much flimsier causes. We've just lost to these bloody criminals nothing more nor less than the earlier, the very first, of the two Covenants of God with the Israelites."

13

Later that same evening

The athletic man is dressed like a cat burglar. His muscles bulge under a dark turtleneck and tight trousers, and a knitted cap covers his red hair. He scales the architectural rustications on the Nazi aristocrat's urban villa, sure of his footing and his objective. When he reaches the ledge desired and stands up with his back to the outside wall, he cranes his neck around the edge of the window. The room is dark. He moves along the ledge to where a shaft of light passes through a crack in the curtains. What he sees fills him with anger and pity. He moves on to the next room, dark, with curtains completely opened. Faint light under the door from the hallway reveals no one inside. He tests the jamb and finds the French window has not been completely shut. With a tool from his belt, he pries it open and climbs through.

His ear pressed to the hall door senses nothing. Pushing the lever handle down with care, he pulls it open to inspect the immediate hallway. He peeks out in both directions. No one. With a deep breath, he tiptoes to the next door and tries the handle. Locked. With another glance in both directions, he returns to the dark room and pulls the door closed. Climbing back onto the ledge, he edges over to the lighted window and taps it with a fingernail. Moments pass, and a long, pale hand pushes aside one of the curtains.

Solange peers out at him, her face bruised and her dress torn to ruin. She gradually smiles at seeing him perched as if in midair. After fiddling with their handles, she opens the French windows, staggers back to a chair, and collapses.

He holds a finger to his lips, moves over to the door, takes out a tool, and addresses the lock. After a moment, he pulls the door slightly open to listen for any activity in the corridor. Hearing nothing unusual, he inspects the still-empty hallway. Turning back to her, he says, "I suppose *he* did that to you? Can you make it down and several streets away where I've got a truck? It may be a little rough before we get there."

Solange nods, answering in a breathless whisper. "Anything to be away from that monster. Anything." She pushes herself up with both hands, walks to a closet, and removes some clothes.

He remains in the bathroom while she changes. After several minutes, he returns with a wet facecloth and sponges up the blood and blotched eyeshadow and makeup from her face. She ties a turban around her hair and inserts her feet into low pumps.

He opens the door once more, turns off the room lights, and summons her to join him.

They pass quietly through the hall to a back stairway and descend a flight.

When someone starts up the stairs from the ground floor, he glances into the nearby hallway and gestures for her to leave the staircase. She hides in a service closet he points to before turning to stand just around the corner from the staircase landing. As luck would have it, it's only an Egyptian steward carrying a tray to the floor above.

As he passes, Fritzi, realizing it is probably intended for Solange, steps behind the man, clamps a hand over his mouth, and grabs the tray with the other. There is little resistance. The man's dark eyes roll upward to see who has done this. Fritzi whispers in the man's ear. After he recognizes who it is, he nods and takes back the tray. Fritzi crosses the hallway and gestures for Solange to follow them down the stairs.

The three make it to the kitchen where the Egyptian steward opens the back door to let them out. With a whisper of good wishes, he locks it behind them and stares at his wristwatch. It is three-thirty in the morning. His private act of compassion for the beaten woman has suddenly become something much bigger. But he's got his explanation ready if ever asked.

Out in the alleyway behind von Vranken's villa, the darkness is relieved only by the ambient lights of the city, which have dimmed down mainly to its streetlamps. Fritzi holds her as she stumbles over the uneven paving stones. He feels her shivering more from fear than from the temperature which is barely night cool. They round a couple of corners to a small, deserted square surrounding a tiny park. They approach a black and brown truck. He helps her up into the passenger seat and climbs behind the wheel. He glances over his shoulder behind the front seats at the quilted moving blanket spread over an object. With his left hand, he feels the reassuring surface of the ancient casket underneath.

Shifting the transmission into gear, he draws slowly away from the curb and circles the square to the street leading down to the harbor. Figuring by now the corniche would have been placed under observation by von Vranken—as would have been the train terminus and the airport—Fritzi smiles to himself and turns right on a boulevard before the harbor road.

They drive straight toward the east through the sprawling environs of Alexandria into the outlands and delta beyond.

By the time the November dawn begins to tint the sky, they have arrived at a quiet fishing village on the coast. In a cove protected from curious eyes, Fritzi draws the truck up to the beach. A small rowboat is tethered to a spike in the sand.

A man in his late teens helps Fritzi bring the casket down to the water's edge, and they tie up the ancient chest inside a tarpaulin and lay it in the stern of the rowboat. They return to the truck, carry Solange across the sand and pebbles to the rowboat, and help her onto a seat. Fritzi puts his foot on a thwart and, with hands on the gunwales, swings down beside her and envelops her in both arms. She is still trembling.

The young man throws off the line and rows them out into the center of the cove's waters. Moments later, a periscope thrusts up through the dark waters, and a small submarine begins to emerge. When complete, its hatch opens to let two sailors in turtlenecks and jeans clamber out onto the little deck and grasp the railing surrounding the hatch.

The oarsman ties his boat to the railing where it pitches and rolls a little in the restless waters. Working to maintain their balance, he and Fritzi pass the tarpaulin-encased casket through the railing to the sailors. When the casket has been handed down the hatch, Fritzi and the oarsman hoist Solange up to them. The sailors hold her firmly on the slippery deck while Fritzi gives the young oarsman an envelope and joins them to bring Solange into the depths of the small sub.

The men carry her with gentle hands to a bunk and cover her with a blanket.

Fritzi leans down and says, "You must rest now. Try to relax. We'll be several days. No one has the slightest idea where we are. You're safe now."

She reaches up to touch his cheek and smiles.

14

Autumn 1922 and
August 1938

O ne morning, some sixteen years before, a boy just verging upon manhood made a decision that changed his life. His mentor, a gentle Catholic priest, was stupefied by what he'd just heard. Especially because of the stories the boy had told him about his upbringing.

Father Stanislaus had taken to this athletic young stone mason from the outset when he appeared at his door to help with restorations of the parish church. The boy had been only sixteen, but he showed a wry sense of humor that belonged to someone who has already seen much.

His name at birth was Friedrich Vogelhardt. On the eighth day after his birth and following the custom of his people, the baby was prepared for his ritual circumcision. All the preliminaries had taken place when the rabbi came to the high point of the occasion. He leaned over the tiny creature with his scalpel in hand to amputate the tot's foreskin. Out of the blue, the sly arrow of fate intervened.

The rabbi, knife raised, clutched his chest with his other hand and let out a horrible cry. He fell forward upon the child and grazed the baby's left cheekbone with the scalpel. The blood began to ooze from the cut, and the rabbi fell to the floor. His fatal heart attack in the midst of this ancient ritual was interpreted as an omen for the child. The cut on the cheek had accomplished the requirement that blood be drawn from the child. And the fact, almost unique in all Hebrew lore, of the rabbi dying while he cut the child was interpreted to mean that any attempt to repeat the ceremony of circumcision would deny the omen from God received that day. It was seen by sages to be just like Abraham who was stopped by the Lord at the moment before he plunged his raised knife into his son. This obedience to the Lord's command to sacrifice his beloved son, so dramatically confirmed by his actions, had satisfied the Lord. Isaac, designated as the sacrificial lamb, would be permitted to live. By the same token, tiny Friedrich was never circumcised because the rabbi had fulfilled the will of the Lord. And it would be bad luck and an affront to the Almighty to take any further action of this kind.

When little Fritzi was only five, his father died and was buried in Danzig's Jewish cemetery. Sensing the hatred growing in the prevailing undercurrent of anti-Semitism, his mother decided to change their name to Vogel. She declared from that moment on the family were Lutheran. It rather pleased her, the symmetry between Martin Luther's rebellion against his church, and her apostasy from the faith of her fathers.

Fritzi grew up to be a robust teenager, full of fun and always good with his hands. Like his father, he became a stonemason. The rabbi's cut on his left cheekbone had healed into an elegant scar. As he approached the age of eighteen, it was assumed by many observers he had been marked during a duel. Dueling was the province of elite young men who engaged in the sport at universities where they were members of exclusive clubs. Whenever asked about his scar, he would simply respond it was a matter of ritual honor, and he had come out ahead.

His conversations with Father Stanislaus went on for two years while Fritzi cut pieces of stone to replace decayed portions of the ancient entranceway of the church. The priest learned much about the boy's life, which was told without apparent hesitation. The young man seemed to be craving a way to find new meaning, a new purpose, a calling perhaps, which had yet to be heard. In response, the priest recounted to him the story of another youthful Jew who famously had experienced his conversion to the Roman faith while he was visiting a brothel in Venice, the city of his birth. That Italian Jew was only nineteen at the time. He was called to Rome to be ordained and serve at the Vatican. His inside track led to rapid promotions within the church's hierarchy to the point now where he had become a monsignor. One expected he would soon be given his own diocese and be made a bishop. Giovanni Camberini was his name.

The boy seemed impressed, and Father Stanislaus was waiting with hope for the moment when Fritzi would ask to be baptized. But luck would have it quite another way. Several men had recently met Fritzi at a beer hall and filled his ears with stories about a new political party that was just getting started in Munich. These men were soldiers from the defeated German army who had not found jobs to their liking and were persuaded that a totally new order for Germany was needed. The voices of these men touched a part of Fritzi that he had never before confronted. The seductive appeal of power. Not just the power to remake one's own life, but to change the world. And this is what was being offered.

The boy could not resist. He said farewell to Father Stanislaus with a hug and an embarrassed smile, packed his meager belongings, and hopped the train to Munich where he sought the address he'd been given. There, at five o'clock one afternoon, he entered the back room of a pub and joined about thirty other young men. They were sitting and standing about the room at the center of which was speaking the most mesmerizing person he'd ever seen. He listened, enthralled, to a prescription for the birth of a new Germany, one that was mighty in its military and pure in its racial makeup.

It did not take long for the leader to discover the talents of this new recruit. Fritzi was popular with everyone. He hid his intelligence with a screen of good humor, often choosing to play the buffoon for laughs. He was appointed to a cadre of select men who were given the job of performing subtle and complex tasks. The Special Operations unit brought Fritzi into close touch with men destined to become future leaders of the German nation. Those who would go on later to be regarded as the famously cynical and cruel founding fathers of what they had just now decided to call the "Nazi" Party, short for National Socialists.

Yes, there were times, perhaps too few, in the ensuing years when he would arrange events to go differently from that directed by the party. Conscience long deliberately muted would then raise its voice above a whisper and call him to save the lives of people being persecuted by the Nazis for such transgressions as being Jewish or foreign or homosexual. He could never overcome the sense of leading a double life.

In August 1938, he was called into the office of Josef Goebbels, whom he knew well from those early days, and Goebbels delivered a series of surprises. First, the Reich minister of propaganda described an ancient document that had just come to light, unveiled several days before at a society called the Seraphim. It contained a remarkable message, which he proceeded to recount. Because of the sudden urgency for action inspired by that message, he'd had Fritzi elected to be a member of the Seraphim and to its secret cult called the Aaronites. Fritzi would be introduced that very evening by Goebbels to his fellow members at a ceremony in the Sanctuary. Time was of the essence, and he expected Fritzi to cancel any plans he might already have for the next several weeks. Everything would soon be explained.

His precipitous immersion into the crowd at the Seraphim that evening had seemed rather surreal. Nonetheless, his discomfort was hardly evident to the many bigwigs present from Berlin society. He held his own speaking with party leaders, top military brass, industrialists, orchestra conductors, opera stars, and men and women of note in the arts and the sciences. These creatures of privilege were allowed to flourish only so long as it was clear they were devoted to the Nazi Party's purposes.

Fritzi was taken from group to group by Goebbels, and the lot of them were led into a dressing area where each person donned a scarlet robe that was held together by a gold chain at the black-braided high collar. From there, Fritzi was taken at the head of the crowd into a large space the size of a ballroom. Its walls, ceiling, and floor were lined with mirrorlike black granite. In the center rose an altar at the top of a flight of steps, also made of polished black granite. On the altar stood the statue of a calf fashioned of solid gold. The flames of countless candles danced in reflections from all the surfaces.

The Aaronites arranged themselves around the altar and began to chant over and over, "Give us something to worship! Our souls are parched. The God we sought has deserted us!"

A sinuous orientalist melody, played on a pan flute, filled the air. When it stopped, there was a roll of kettle drums followed by a blast of trumpets. A procession emerged from the blackness through an arch leading to the room. It was headed by a tall golden-robed man wearing a black and gold miter rather like a bishop's but with a red snake curled around it in a graceful spiral. He carried a staff almost as tall as him, at the top of which was a small leering animal skull. Every other person in the procession carried a lighted torch. They halted at the bottom of the seven altar steps, which the mitered priest ascended. Approaching the golden statue, he raised his staff high in the air and shouted, "Heil Hitler!"

The rest of the group in unison proclaimed, "Heil Hitler!"

The priest turned to face the assembly. "The candidate will step forward."

Goebbels pushed Fritzi toward the altar steps. The eighteen torchbearers divided to line the path on either side. "Thank you, Brother Goebbels."

With a nod, the priest dismissed him and said, "Candidate Vogel, you will now kneel on the first step."

Fritzi obeyed and looked up, waiting for what might come next.

Another roll of drums and blast of trumpets.

"Repeat after me." The priest raised his staff into the air. "Give me something to worship. My soul is parched. My God has deserted me."

Fritzi did so.

The priest bellowed, "Now mount the steps and kiss the right foot of Baal."

Again, he did as he was told and turned to face the priest.

The priest lifted his staff and rested it on Fritzi's left shoulder. "By all the powers of the known and the unknown, by the forces that we can harness and those for which only fate will decree the outcome, I ask you, Friedrich Vogel, do you pledge to join the Brothers of Aaron and be part of his rebellion against Moses?"

Fritzi appeared startled by this pledge and waited several seconds before responding in a quiet voice, "I do."

The priest raised the staff and moved it to Fritzi's other shoulder. "And do you pledge unfailing loyalty and obedience to the Society of the Seraphim?"

"I do."

The priest lifted his staff and turned to face the idol. "Then, oh, Baal, we give to your service our new Brother Friedrich and commend all your acolytes to accept him into their ranks." He turned again and faced the assembly. "Do you accept your new brother, Friedrich, who has pledged fealty to our ancient brotherhood?"

They shouted, "We do!"

"Then, I welcome you, Brother Friedrich, to our ways and rituals and the service of Baal." The priest raised his staff and called out once again, "Heil Hitler!"

After mingling with the other members at the reception following the ceremony—and having touched glasses and drunk toasts with a large number of them—Fritzi was taken by Goebbels into a small room where a small and very old clay jar stood on a table. Next to it lay, between two framed sheets of glass, an ancient papyrus inscribed with hieroglyphic symbols.

Goebbels lifted a piece of paper lying beside the papyrus. "Here's the translation done in 1912 by Ludwig Borchardt. He found this jar along with our sublime Nefertiti's bust. He knew it was the answer to a riddle that had passed down the Seraphim generations for several thousand years. We assume he decided not to reveal its message during his lifetime because he feared the reactions of other Jews. So, he gave it to the Berlin Seraphim in this jar, which he resealed—not to be opened until his death."

"And what's its message, Josef?" asked Fritzi who was fighting a slowly rising sense of alarm.

"Of course, that's why you're here. It's written by the very same man, an architect, who sculpted our bust of Nefertiti. He tells us he was the architect of her sepulchre in the new capital city of Akhetaten. He was commissioned by Akhenaten's mother to build this tomb for her son and his queen Nefertiti. It seems both their bodies had been returned to Egypt from an unnamed faraway place." Goebbels lit up. "Just think. What a triumph for Germany—to have the actual remains of Nefertiti. Not to minimize, of course, Akhenaten's if we found them as well.

"But the story gets better. So, along with their bodies was a casket of ebony and bronze. We're told it contains a description of their journey, which we believe must be the same as what the Jews called their Exodus. Now, for the miracle, the papyrus says it holds the broken pieces of the Covenant the Israelites were said to have made with their God. It seems Pharaoh Akhenaten, of all persons, was their real Moses." Goebbels let out a long, high-pitched laugh that sent shivers through Fritzi. "And, imagine, it describes how Aaron actually killed the man later called Moses in Israelite scripture!" His laughing was almost hysterical. Catching his breath, he pounded his fist on the table. "We must have this casket, Fritzi! Just try to picture it, the dismay, the confusion, the rabbis and the Hebrew rabble will feel when they learn what's in it—and that we have it!"

Fritzi felt almost dizzy. Wild conflicts were at war within him. "You said time was short. May I ask why?"

"Of course. We've received what could be extremely important information. When we learned of the Jew Borchardt's translation, I wrote to inform our highest-ranking man in Alexandria—you've heard of the margrave, Lothar von Vranken—that such a treasure was said to be buried in or near Akhetaten, which is called Amarna today.

"Lothar reported back a remarkable coincidence. Another

Aaronite, a Greek who lives in Alexandria, has launched exploration of an area just east of Akhetaten without giving any clue to his purposes. We know his foreman was heard to say the excavation was based on an ancient riddle. We believe that riddle may well be the very same one Borchardt's translation seems to answer." Goebbels's jaw muscles clenched. "Just think. What if the Greek should find this huge prize for us now? You're to work with von Vranken and keep track of everything going on at that excavation."

Fritzi's voice was strained. "I think all's quite clear, Josef."

"Good, Fritzi. The Fuhrer's made this a top priority. Now pack up and leave immediately. Oh, and don't be surprised by Lothar's sybaritic lifestyle. Spoiled offspring of a degenerate line. Filthy rich aristocrats."

15

Early November 1938

*R*upert and Michael stayed up together in the host's soaring library for the remaining hours before dawn. Rupert paced about the space, among its huge terrestrial and celestial globes cradled in gilded baroque stands, pondering their next moves. It was clear from von Vranken's rage overheard during his brief telephone connection with Solange that the casket had not been delivered as planned. And from his screaming out Fritzi's name on bursting into Solange's room, it probably was taken by this same fellow. Solange had told Rupert he was deep in cahoots with von Vranken. *What would have brought about his betrayal? And what would he do with the casket and its contents? Keep it for himself? Sell it to the highest bidder? Destroy it?*

The telephone rang. Michael hurried to the hallway phone table. Before he reached it, the ringing had stopped. When he returned to the library, Rupert said, "Know who called?"

Michael shrugged. "Either hung up or answered by the staff, maybe Stephanos."

Rupert strode to the same phone outside the library and held up a finger to indicate quiet to Michael. With great care not to alert anyone else on the line, Rupert put the receiver to his ear just in time to hear a click cutting off the connection. He replaced it with a shrug. "Who'd call at this time of the night? Not a wrong number. The connection was kept for too long. Someone heard me and stopped whatever they were saying."

Michael shook his head. "If Stephanos has gone rogue, something must have come along to change him."

"Or someone," added Rupert with a wry tone. "Notice changes with him since we got back from Amarna?"

"Maybe. A little more inside himself, I suppose. Nothing very obvious. Not quite the same easy way between us."

"I see."

"By now, the Nazis must have launched a manhunt for Fritzi. It's a question of who'll get to him first. We want that to be us."

Caridis yawned suddenly, feeling drained but determined. "Of course. How do we go about it?"

Rupert folded his arms. "Find as much about him as we can. I assume his name's Friedrich Vogel. We go to our British military police when they open for business this morning and see what they might have on file. I'll also contact an excellent private investigator, a fellow now retired from Scotland Yard. Finding this sort of obscure information is just his dish of tea. Of course, we've got to assume the Germans are going to be doing the same."

Michael said, "And of course we let none of this be known by Stephanos, do we?"

"Afraid so, old man. I'm afraid he may have switched sides."

"I just don't see how—or why?" Michael tensed his

shoulders. "If so, I'm goddamn disappointed. I gave him such an opportunity. Can't imagine what he's hoping to gain."

☥

By late morning, the British military police had pegged Friedrich Vogel's main residence to Berlin and his city of origin to Hamburg. Given that information, Rupert sent his investigator a long cable with his marching orders.

He also learned the famed Borchardt had fled Berlin and moved to Switzerland five years before, in 1933, hounded by Hermann Goering who wanted to get his hands on the thousands of ancient artifacts Borchardt had collected. Goering had despised him for being the son of Jews, which entitled the insatiable Nazi to grab whatever he liked. Rupert sent his widow a cable asking for a meeting at her home in Basel. With these two feelers launched, Rupert arranged to charter a plane that would leave late the next morning. He then sat and wrote a response to Elizabeth's latest letter which had arrived after an unusually long delay, well after several she had written earlier.

Her news added yet another level of stress to the building tension over their plans to recover the stolen casket. She reported Orlando was now being sought by investigators in the hushed-up death of that Jewish boy. Orlando had apparently left London for Paris the week before and was believed to have gone on to Vienna or Berlin. All contact had been lost.

Rupert paused mid-sentence in his reply, thinking how badly he wanted to find Orlando and make him behave like a Delacorte—and not a renegade. He rolled the pen between his fingers, suddenly dreaming of being with Elizabeth to comfort her. Since their marriage, they had become each other's rock, giving strength and support through thick and thin. He hated to imagine the pain their son was causing her now.

16

Early November 1938

That same evening, they contacted Rupert's London staff to make arrangements for their departure to Switzerland the next morning. Nothing was said to Stephanos. They would pack their own bags and leave without alerting him to any travel details.

The two men then set out in full dress to attend a long-standing invitation that, at Michael's request, had been extended to include Rupert. The young and spoiled Egyptian king, Farouk, just eighteen, had decided to host a party in his kingdom's second city. Excited by the prospect of fatherhood and producing an heir, he couldn't wait to celebrate the imminent birth of his first child with his new wife, Queen Farida, herself only seventeen.

The limousines were lined up in lengthy ranks along the street outside the royal palace gardens. Guards in colorful uniforms, a combination of East and West with pantaloons and short gold-braided jackets and elaborately decorated headgear, stood arranged outside and inside the palace. A band was playing loudly with an incessant oompah robustness. Guests from the diplomatic corps and the local aristocracy and foreign dignitaries had been summoned to share the monarch's jubilant determination to beget a male heir. It was a virtual rite of supplication to the gods and perhaps tempted the fates to frustrate such an outcome without a hitch.

When Rupert was presented to the teenaged playboy, the young man had been prepped. "Aha, the greatest fortune in England, and one of its oldest titles. A cousin to your king on both sides of your family. I am pleased and honored to know the Marquess of Ravenstone. You are seated tonight next to my mistress. As you know, my wife cannot appear in public in her advanced state of pregnancy." His chest puffed out a little at these declarations.

Farouk then waved Michael forward to speak and mentioned his own membership in the Aaronites, aware of the Greek's distinguished father's position in their leadership. "We are Seraphic cousins, are we not?"

Michael gave a graceful bow to this gesture of familiarity and rejoined Rupert out of hearing distance of their host. They shared a discreet laugh at the young monarch's exaggerated self-importance. Michael spied von Vranken and nudged Rupert to watch him cupping a champagne glass in one hand while the other adjusted a monocle, which appeared to have as its primary purpose their own closer inspection. Michael delivered a sarcastic smile, and Rupert made the first move, striding directly over to him. With hands in his pockets, he shrugged and gave a wry smile. "The best-laid plans of mice and men ... don't you know ..." He reached into his breast pocket and pulled out the platinum cigarette case that bore the family's Plantagenet coat of arms. He snapped it open and held it under Lothar von Vranken's nose. "Perhaps this will help ease your disappointment." The other man was frozen to the spot, unable to speak as Rupert snapped shut the case, flicked his lighter's flint wheel, and set fire to his own cigarette.

Finally regaining his poise, von Vranken tilted his head back and sneered at Rupert. "You do know this king's our man, don't you? Resents you British with your arrogant ways, your rule by divine right of the world. He's one of the Fuhrer's admirers because he knows we can liberate Egypt from your onerous self-proclaimed protectorate. The British are so goddam high-handed."

"Protecting whom from what?"

Rupert's eyelids half-closed as if he were inhaling opium not simply tobacco. "If you really want to know, 'cousin,' there's more reason today than ever before to protect innocent people. People helpless against tyrants who go around thieving whatever you please from your citizens, beating them to a bloody pulp because of their religion or sexual preferences, killing whomever you choose with impunity. Perhaps you can get away for a while with that in your own countries. But not anywhere that we can stop such depredations. Oh, by the way, here's a memorial to the ashes of poor, unsuspecting Suleiman." He flicked the long glowing ash from his cigarette into von Vranken's champagne glass and turned his back on the stunned Nazi.

17

Early November 1938

*S*olange continued to recuperate in the small submarine as it plied its steady way under the waters of the Mediterranean. Fritzi sat beside her with a bowl of water and a facecloth, which he used to cool her forehead, touching the wet cloth frequently to her temples, eyelids, and mouth as well. The crew was Italian, and they passed by to admire the great beauty they had brought on board. Her large green eyes would sometimes follow the young mariners and return their smiles with a wan movement of her long lashes.

On the third day, the vessel cut its engines and rose through the surface of the sea in sight of land. A small fishing boat came out from a deserted beach and attached itself to the submarine's railing. First to be handed down to the two men in the boat was the chest, which was tied up inside a green tarp. Next, Fritzi and a sailor lifted Solange down to the boat where two men helped her to a cushion of folded fish netting. She was propped against the gunwale next to the chest. Fritzi shook hands with the submarine crew and climbed over into the fishing boat.

A small Lancia sedan with a woman at the wheel, her hair covered by a scarf wound around like a turban, was waiting on the beach. The two fishermen placed the tarp-covered chest in the boot of the car, and Solange was propped up in the back seat with Fritzi at her side. The driver turned to look at the couple and started the car. She guided it over the bumpy surface of the rock-strewn beach until they reached the main road. They followed the signs north through a series of small villages until the landscape changed from farmland and light industry to the beginning of an urban sprawl. They continued deeper into this for some time, passing through neighborhoods of humble and run-down buildings until they came to Il Duce's new motorway. They joined its traffic and soon came to a bend and rise in the road. Rounding it, there suddenly lay before them the great and ancient metropolis at the center of which rose the dome of Saint Peter's Basilica.

The driver smiled at their reactions and continued into the winding streets of Rome until they reached a pensione near the bottom of the Spanish Steps. The driver helped Fritzi carry the chest inside and then assisted with bringing Solange as she walked slowly through the double doors into the small reception room. Fritzi handed the driver an envelope and thanked her elaborately in quite respectable Italian.

Once Solange had been installed in her room, Fritzi ran downstairs to make a telephone call from a private booth in the reception area. The answering voice replied it was the office of the cardinal secretary of state. Fritzi gave a preordained code name and was immediately transferred to a phone answered by a big, resonant voice, "Camberini here. Who speaks?"

Fritzi gave his code name, and the other voice laughed with

pleasure. "So, you've actually made it, safely I trust. I must congratulate you."

Fritzi gripped the phone. "Oh, Your Grace, everything's due to you, every step of the way. I don't even know how to thank you."

"Well, well. It was all in a very good cause. Can you come to me now? You've got the object with you, of course?"

"Oh, yes. Intact by the grace of God and ready for your inspection."

Forty-five minutes later, Fritzi appeared at the Vatican desk and gave his code name: Viktor Bartos. Camberini's steward was summoned to help him carry the casket up two long flights of marble stairs to the grand entrance of the secretary of state's private suite. Towering double doors were pulled open, and the casket was carried into the magnificent drawing room and placed, still wrapped in the tarpaulin, on a pink marble-topped table. The steward went to another pair of double doors where he knocked and announced completion of their task. He nodded to Fritzi as he left him standing, nervous and expectant.

The other doors opened to reveal a big, rotund man with a large head, prominent nose, and high forehead, on top of which perched the red skull cap of a cardinal. He advanced toward Fritzi with open arms and said, "Welcome, welcome, my friend. By now, I feel we've come to know each other. Just through our correspondence to your special postal address in Alexandria. What a pleasure now to greet you. There were so many ways something could have gone wrong." He took Fritzi in his embrace and kissed him on both cheeks. "Now, let's have a look, shall we?"

They untied the rope and removed the tarpaulin, which was dropped on the floor. Fully revealed, the simple three-thousand-year-old chest sat alone and mysterious upon the elegant table. Camberini touched it in several places. He felt the ebony, the curve of the lid, and the bands of bronze, and he finally withdrew, almost with hesitation, the rod from the three hoops that held the clasps closed. One by one, he carefully raised each of the three clasps. He stepped back with an expression of almost fearful reverence before lifting the lid.

"Here we are, my new friend. I, born a Jew in Palestine, and now a cardinal of the world's mightiest church. And you, a Nazi since you were eighteen, but secretly a Jew who became party to our enemy and finally saw the light. You've made a wonderful choice now."

Fritzi's eyes glowed. "Your conversion inspired me when I was a young stonemason. I helped restore a small church in Danzig for a priest who I came to respect and love. It's this man who told me about you."

Camberini gave him a questioning look. "Do you mean, at that time, that long ago, you experienced a conversion to the church?"

"Not fully. Maybe it would've happened if the guys from the new political party hadn't come along. Long ago, I'd given up thinking of myself as a Jew—even before joining the Nazi party. In fact, you know how it is when you're very young. So, it was easy for the fellows who got me to join. They made it sound pretty exciting. We were going to change the world. It's hard to know when I stopped believing in its promises. Pretty early. When they began to humiliate and beat up innocent people, I felt terrible. I sometimes hated myself for this. That is, till now."

"Why especially now?"

"When the party gave me the job of stealing this marvelous thing, it sparked a flame. I knew right then I was being given the means to atone for everything that had gone before. Funny how I've kept alive your story. It's never been far from my mind. So, you were the one person to help me save it. Thanks to you, I could bring this holiest of holy objects to Your Grace. And now, when I walked into this room, it all came clear to me. I want you to make me one of your flock. I want to serve you and the church from this moment onward."

Camberini stepped away from the table and reached his arms out once again. "My son, what a moment this is. You've truly been called. Come to the arms of Mother Church. You shall become one of us."

Fritzi accepted once again the cardinal's embrace, this time breaking into tears, which made his body heave while the cardinal kept holding him. In a broken voice, Fritzi said, "I've allowed myself to do stuff that's really wrong and terrible. At times, we did things that I'm so ashamed of, so ashamed. Yes, I sort of believed a time would come when I could do something helpful for my people. And that would give me a chance to cancel all the evil. Of course, it's no excuse to say the need to hide I was a Jew justified taking part in those horrors. Your Grace, I can't forgive myself. Please, please, Your Grace, take this shame from me. Give me absolution. Let me start again."

Camberini stepped back and made the sign of the cross. "You've made your confession, my son. In the name of our Lord and the Holy Church, I grant you absolution from all your sins and receive with joy your pledge to start a new life in the bosom of Mother Church."

Both men were surprised by the suddenness of this avalanche of grace.

Fritzi found himself carried almost out of his body, transformed and radiant at these words. "I don't know what to say or how to thank you. I feel I'm being given back my life."

Camberini smiled and nodded. "That's a blessing, my son, for me as well to be a part of it. Indeed. Let's now have a look at what you've gone through so much to bring us today." He turned back to the casket, placed his hands on each end of the curved top, and lifted it onto the table. He withdrew the translation of the three scrolls that lay wrapped in a velvet cloth placed there by Michael Caridis in Alexandria. He glanced at the translation and asked Fritzi, "Who's done this English translation? Do you happen to know?"

"Oh yes, Your Grace, I certainly do know. A famous Englishman, Rupert Delacorte. He's a great scholar of Egyptian hieroglyphics and Hebrew, among other things. The Nazi headquarters for propaganda in Berlin were particularly pleased to know he, of all people, had done it. They felt it would give credibility to the message they've been planning to launch against our Jewish people."

Camberini took the scrolls from the casket and laid them on the marble tabletop next to the translation. "I don't see the most important contents said to be inside this chest?"

Fritzi smiled and closed the lid of the casket. He turned it on its back and pressed the cartouche in its bottom. There was a click inside and a small clatter. He placed it back on its bottom and lifted the lid once again. "Prepare yourself, Your Grace." He lifted the now-loosened interior floor of the casket and stood back. A great sighing sound swept from its depths, and the two men had the impression of ephemera emerging in all directions. A haze of light in surging movement filled the room. They fell to their knees and heard for several moments what seemed a celestial choir.

Fritzi's faintly freckled face lit up with joy. He stood again and ran his hand through the curly reddish-blond hair worn short above his square-cut features. When he realized the large man was struggling to rise from his knees, he grabbed Camberini's forearms and lifted him up with little apparent effort.

"My boy. Who might ever have imagined such a thing

as this could still exist? After all this time. Truly a miracle, a miracle. No other word will do. The broken pieces are gathered into a number of neatly tied bundles of burlap cloth. It almost seems a sacrilege to unwrap them. Does not the faith of our fathers find itself served by the simple knowledge that this is the very first Covenant made by the Lord with our great lawgiver, Moses?"

"A wonderful confidence in the evidence of things unseen, Your Grace. Still, don't you think we should first study Delacorte's translation? It may give us reasons for wishing to study the broken pieces for ourselves."

Camberini sighed. "Yes, so many questions, aren't there? Enough of all this speculation. It's time to see whether the answers lie there." He pointed at the scrolls and translation on the rococo table.

He picked up the translation and gestured for Fritzi to join him on a settee. It shook as the large man sat with a heavy thud and arranged himself. He handed Fritzi the sheaf of pages and reached inside his robes for a pair of spectacles. Having placed them on his imposing nose, he retrieved the pages and squinted at the opening paragraphs. "My, my. What do we have here? Apparently, this is written by a man called Ishmael to a queen whom he addresses as the Mother of God, no less." He pursed his lips and continued to read a bit further, with Fritzi reading over his shoulder.

Camberini suddenly turned. "Do you grasp what this is telling us? How can it be? How can this be true?"

Fritzi nodded. "When I saw Ludwig Borchardt's translation of his own discovered papyrus opened this August when he died, it certainly just alludes to the very different story we see here of our great Hebrew prophet and lawgiver. Even then, I had serious doubts about the truth of Borchardt's dramatic clues hinting at Moses's different identity. But this translation confirms it without doubt. Pharaoh Akhenaten was indeed our historic Moses!"

Camberini appeared shaken. "Yes, and the scribe Ishmael, author of these scrolls, is called by Pharaoh 'my other Moses.'" He paused. "He who, in fact, inscribed in clay the words of God as Akhenaten heard them."

"How strange is that?" Fritzi said.

"Indeed." He mumbled under his breath, "What happens to thousands of years of our history and belief?"

The two men read on to the end. They looked at each other, returned to the beginning, and reread the translation, sometimes selecting something to be said aloud. The daylight outside the windows faded to twilight, and the room darkened until they could no longer make out the words on Rupert's pages. Camberini leaned over and placed them on the table in front of their settee. They remained silent for some time. Outside, the streetlamps were turned on and gave a glow to the night seen through the windows.

Fritzi stood up and found his way through the shadowy furniture to one of them. He pushed aside the heavy draperies and gazed at the remarkable scene before him. Down below was the vast piazza in front of Saint Peter's, embraced by Bernini's curved colonnade. Hundreds of people streamed in and out of the basilica on his right. Its facade was lit to great effect, highlighting its majestic proportions. He looked up at the monumental dome designed by Michelangelo with its enormous cupola and felt a rush of such emotion that he found himself once again in tears. This was now going to be his church.

Camberini appeared at his side. "Yes, Fritzi. It's something this place. You feel the power of the church in a very material way here—at its very center. I'm pleased you'll be a part of it, my son. But we've got a mission before us."

Fritzi turned and gave him a questioning look.

The cardinal clasped his hands together and bowed his head. "Mussolini and Hitler can pervert this revelation. Imagine how these barbarians might improvise."

Fritzi nodded. "I can see. The greatest leader of the Israelites isn't even a Jew. The savior of our race—an Egyptian." He paused. "What a heyday for Goebbels's propaganda blitz. Akhenaten's statue at the Berlin museum. He's got thick lips, wide nostrils—so Moses is found out to be a black. Aryans of Germany, you must unite against the blight of Negro and Jew!"

The cardinal turned on a table lamp, walked over to the casket, and pointed again. "And that isn't all. Here lie the most sacred relics of our fathers' faith. Not easy to accept even though here's the physical proof. Many Jews take literally the tradition that God himself etched his Commandments upon stone. Not simply a scribe writing in wet clay. Such is the way many minds will work. A rock will be removed from the whole edifice of their belief ..."

A loud knocking on the door startled Fritzi. He turned around to see a uniformed steward.

"Good evening, Your Grace. Shall I do the lights?" The man glanced over at the rococo table and the casket and the scrolls. This was not lost on the two men standing in the room.

"Not to worry tonight. Thank you, Giuseppe." Camberini noticed the steward's examination of Fritzi before he closed the door behind him.

The cardinal walked slowly about the large room, hands behind his back. Eventually he asked, "What chance is there that anybody could have even the glimmer of an idea you're here, Fritzi?"

The muscles in his jaw twinged. "The submarine severed my trail. No one can suspect it existed, nor imagine where it landed, even if they did. But I wasn't alone. One other person came with me. It certainly wasn't planned until the night I left Egypt. She's one of us, a Jew, from Berlin, lately living in Alexandria. Mistress to Lothar von Vranken. The Nazi capo in Egypt. She's a remarkably beautiful woman who found me sympathetic. Once or twice, he saw us chatting at his headquarters, so Lothar now thinks we were in cahoots, which was never the case. When the casket wasn't delivered as expected, he beat her badly." He reflected for a moment. "It was vicious and pointless. Vranken's probably our most direct threat—with Goebbels not far behind."

Camberini smiled. "Well, my son, you've not yet taken your vows of chastity. There's always time to change your mind. Believe me, whatever way you choose will be fine with me. But where is she now? I must also tell you there's a coincidence—and not a very happy one, I'm afraid. This Lothar von Vranken is famously friendly with my greatest rival in the Curia, Cardinal Antonio Fiorelli. He shares His Holiness's sympathies with the fascist regime here. If Fiorelli should ever get wind of your true identity, it might well get back to Vranken. So, if you stay here as my protégé, it will be under your assumed name. Papers will be created to substantiate your new identity."

Fritzi strode over to the cardinal and knelt before him. "No, Your Grace. I shall take my vows, and I shall stay with you. I must take both risks, bodily temptation and being discovered. This means more to me than both. It means my very existence. My decision is firm."

The cardinal reached out to touch his head.

Fritzi grabbed his hand and kissed his ring. "Your Grace, we must find a way for Solange to be nursed back to health and kept safe."

"She'll be safe. I'll have her taken to Orvieto, not far from Rome. A school for those who want to find whether their calling is to be a nun. No spiritual obligation. No need to do more than attend classes and prayers and take time for her recovery. Their nurses are quite competent. Do you think she'll be all right with that?"

"Yes, indeed, Your Grace. But can we also find a way for her to start a new life?"

"I should think so, my son. But let's not worry about that right now. It's more important you be given novitiate lessons and made part of my immediate staff in the secretariat."

"What about the casket? Some won't balk at murder to get their hands on it."

"Quite so, Fritzi. For the moment, we'll adopt the principle of concealment in plain sight. Do you see that long box under the beautiful Raphael Madonna? Its front is a predella dating back to the fourteenth century, much younger indeed than this 'Ark of the Original Covenant' as I shall forever call your casket. There are some folded tapestries inside." His eyes twinkled. "But having seen old maxims turned on their heads during my long life, let's make things a bit more difficult for those with malice in their hearts." He went to one of the bookcases that filled two walls of the room and moved a ladder along its brass supporting rail over to one of the sections behind a pair of tall-backed Renaissance armchairs and an elaborate table with a lamp. He reached under its large lampshade and turned on the lights.

Camberini displayed unpredictable agility in mounting the steps to reach the topmost shelf. There, he removed several books at a time and handed them down to Fritzi. He gestured to the scrolls beside the casket.

Fritzi understood and passed them up to be placed at the rear of the shelf.

"Can you bring over the burlap packages now, Fritzi?"

"Not to worry, Your Grace." He collected the tied burlap

bundles from the bottom of the casket with a reverence touched by awe. As he picked up each one, it felt warm, indeed almost alive. He handed them up to Camberini, who kissed each one and laid it along the rear of the shelf. All the books were replaced to appear as if they'd never been touched. The ladder was rolled along the bronze rail back to its original placement.

The two men removed the folded tapestries from inside the large chest and placed the empty casket inside. They arranged the tapestries around it so, without much closer inspection, they appeared to be the only contents. "I've always left this unlocked, and so it shall be for the moment. We'll need a better solution very soon, of course."

Having finished, both stood silent, as if mulling their next steps. They were startled by the sound of loud knocking on the door.

18

November 1938

 R upert led the way across the tarmac to the little two-engine de Havilland DH.90 Dragonfly. The British pilot from Imperial Airways was waiting at the steps to the biplane. He saluted them and said, "Welcome, milord. Would you be sitting in the copilot's seat?"

Rupert turned to Michael and laughed. "Would you feel safe if I sat by the controls?"

He rolled his eyes with feigned skepticism. "How many years have you been flying solo?"

"At least twelve to fourteen, I suppose. Does that comfort you a bit?"

"Just," retorted Michael. "How many stops for refueling?"

"Two," the pilot responded. "Athens and Rome. Shortest way to Basel. If you're ready, we can board now."

The three men mounted the small staircase that had been flipped down and bent their heads to enter the five-seater. Michael took his place just behind Rupert who strapped himself into the copilot's seat. When he had finished lifting the steps and securing the door, the pilot took off his hat, threw it on the empty seat behind him, and arranged himself at the controls.

"All right now, milord. We'll go through the checklist together. You've chartered this gal for a week, so we might as well get familiar with her now."

Michael stared out of the wide window at the gleaming red wings. The little plane was immaculate.

After they had completed the routine drill, Captain Davis announced, "All's good. We're ready. Seat straps secured?" His voice carried on to the control tower, and their responses crackled and croaked as they taxied down to one end of the runway. Davis checked both passengers, turned, and revved the engines. They gathered speed until the small plane lifted off and pulled away from Alexandria's airport. Late-afternoon light slanted across the harbor, touching the tops of endless ranks of rippling waves. They formed jagged diagonal lines across their windows as the plane dipped its starboard wing to arc its way toward Europe.

"Reminds one of Monet. His paintings of the sea at Sainte-Adresse, no?" Michael shouted over the engines.

Rupert turned and smiled. "You're right, all those lines of waves were the same. Makes me long for a beret, palette, and brushes." He grinned. "And finally some talent—like Winston's perhaps." He reached into his jacket and withdrew a pack of Naval Cut cigarettes he hadn't yet bothered to line up in his cigarette case.

The plane leveled off and headed due north.

☥

Back at the airfield, a German noncommissioned officer walked up the stairs of the conning tower. He approached one of the men sitting before a radar screen. "Good afternoon, my friend. May I ask you something?"

The other removed his earphones. "Yes?"

The German pointed out the tower at the field. "Anybody leave this afternoon? A couple of fellows, a Greek and a Britisher?"

The man leaned over to question a colleague. "Do the manifests show a Greek and a Brit leaving today on a private plane?"

After rustling through some papers, the response came back. "Two names, Caridis and Delacorte, could fit the bill. Booked to Athens, thereafter, as directed by the client. No other destinations specified."

The German asked, "Who might know if they'd preselected any other destinations?"

"You could always ask Imperial. They own the plane."

The German nodded with an air of mild frustration. This was not a practical solution. He knew that was going to lead nowhere; Imperial Aviation guarded their clients with true British discretion. "Thank you." He touched the bill of his hat and turned to descend the stairs.

♀

As shadows lengthened and streetlamps lit up in Alexandria, a man approached the gates of the Caridis mansion. Tall, fair-haired, slight of build.

The guard inside saluted and opened the gates, but the guard did have a flashback. Something about the man's build and hair triggered a most uncomfortable memory. But, then, it was only an inkling of a feeling.

The other guard at the porter's office in the passageway leading to the central courtyard had the same brief moment of déjà vu. He, too, allowed it to pass and called on the general intercom to announce the visitor.

Stephanos answered with the order to send him in.

The porter pointed toward the end of the passageway and the courtyard beyond.

The visitor nodded that he knew his way. He walked through the brooding forest of basalt and granite antiquities, mounted the steps, and entered the towering reception hall.

Stephanos stood, waiting, and smiled when he came through the double doors. His arm shot out. "Heil Hitler!"

"Heil Hitler!" the visitor responded in an upper-class English accent. He approached and kissed Stephanos on the lips.

19

Later that afternoon

The de Havilland descended through low clouds to the runway of Athens's airport some five uneventful hours after leaving Alexandria. Rupert marched briskly to the small terminal to make a telephone call, and Michael stretched his legs and idly watched the mechanics insert a petrol hose into their fuel tank's receptacle.

Rupert radiated satisfaction as he strode back across the tarmac to the plane.

Michael asked, "So, what was that all about? Anything interesting about this renegade Fritzi?"

"Indeed so. Rather fascinating as it turns out. When we're finished in Basel, we're going to Danzig. Some pieces are falling into place."

Rupert's private eye was a retired officer from Scotland Yard's Intelligence Division. He'd been lucky. In fact, the tracks led so easily to his goal both he and Rupert wondered why the Nazi authorities hadn't cottoned on earlier to Fritzi's true identity.

"His father was Jewish, and as a young man, he left central Poland for the port city of Danzig. Although Fritzi's identity papers say he was born in Hamburg to Pieter Vogel, in actual fact, his father was one Isaac Vogelhardt and is buried in the Jewish cemetery in Danzig."

"Amazing he got away with it." Michael shook his head. "I'd imagine he'd got to have been circumcised. Surely that would have raised suspicions somewhere along the line."

Rupert shrugged. "If he'd been circumcised, it's obvious it never got in the way. He was there at the very beginning of the Nazi Party, right in the inner circle of what became the Nazi's sadly effective propaganda machine. He spent his youth, before enlisting in the party, as a stonemason." His voice caught a little. His own son, Orlando, had also not been immune to their seductive message. "Our investigator contacted a German associate who searched the Nazi archives.

"He was able to find record of a church where Fritzi was working at the time they recruited him. His job had been to restore its stonework. He worked there for two years and became quite close with its priest, a Father Stanislaus, who was the source of what we know now about his Jewish background. The investigator thinks this might be a useful interview for us. This priest still happens to be in the same church. It's named for Saint Catherine of Siena. He's the closest individual from the man's past our investigator could find. Apparently, he told Fritzi about a Jewish scholar of Renaissance art who became a priest after undergoing a conversion. The man's now a cardinal of all things. Name's Camberini. It seems this left a strong impression on Fritzi. In fact, so much so the young man appeared to have been on the verge of conversion himself. Except, as fate would have it, along came some chaps who dangled stories of a group being formed to change the world. They must have touched the same inner need to be part of something bigger and with a tangible mission that excited him. They managed to persuade Fritzi to join the nascent Nazi movement instead."

Little had he known, Rupert himself had just his own twist of fate. His call through the airport telephone operator had been eavesdropped. The listener had been stationed to await their arrival in Athens. She had followed Rupert into the terminal building, and when he made a request to be connected long distance, she approached the operator and laid before him a pile of banknotes large enough to obtain the use of a small, round receiver plugged into the same line as Rupert's. How easy it had been to fulfill her mandate to learn the destination—and so much more—of the de Havilland being refueled on the tarmac. She smiled to herself as she watched Rupert leave the building and had the same telephone operator go through the elaborate procedure of connecting her with Alexandria.

20

That same afternoon

tephanos handed the young Englishman a tot of whiskey. "Here's a small cure for what he did to you. So, what exactly happened?"

The Englishman settled onto a settee, crossed his long legs, and sipped from the glass. "I've already told Lothar all the gory details of exactly what happened after we left here with the chest. He found it quite hard to believe good-natured Fritz Vogel, a loyal long-standing member of the party, could have planned this right under his rather snotty nose.

"Once we'd got into our truck with the chest, I started to drive. We'd been instructed to take it directly to the Seraphim building on the coast road. He was in the back with the chest hidden under a blanket. When I stopped at the service door in a deserted alley behind the building, it was two in the morning. Before I could turn around, he stuck a needle in the side of my neck. I was knocked out instantly. Didn't know what had happened until I woke up hours later when some fellow making a delivery to their kitchen found me lying where Vogel had obviously pulled me from the van. He shook me to see if I was alive. Happily, I managed to prove any such fears were unfounded." He gave his cigarette a long drag, tilted his head back, and held it in for some time, before letting go a slow stream of smoke directed straight up to the ceiling. His pupils had contracted to little pinpoints.

Stephanos sat down on the small settee alongside him and snapped his fingers, "So, just like that, this Fritzi betrayed everybody. Lothar must have been furious."

"More than furious. He's out for Fritzi's blood. Lothar doesn't like to lose—especially since the traitor took his concubine with him. Pretty cheeky of Fritzi when you come to think of it, no?" A giggle and another long puff and exhalation.

"Well, at this end, I overheard a call from the concubine to Ravenstone. While they were speaking, Lothar apparently came into the room and beat her, accusing her of betrayal with Fritzi. Lothar ordered his men to comb the city's trains, airports, buses, and rental car companies, and the only thing reported was that the small rental truck you two used has completely disappeared. So far, no one's been able to track it down."

The Englishman turned to him. "So, where have Caridis and Ravenstone gone? Any clues at all?"

Wearing a perplexed frown, Stephanos shook his head. "None at all. Ravenstone was on the phone and telegraph all morning. He got some messages, which I could never read or hear properly, but it seemed like he was tracking down a couple of people."

The Englishman shrugged. "And now I'm told they've chartered a plane for Europe, and we've got no idea why. Lothar's cooked up some paranoid theory they were in cahoots with Fritzi. His sense of betrayal after all their planning has unhinged the man. Absurd theory when you consider Fritzi and I actually stole the chest from them. And they'd no idea you were our enabler all along the way."

Stephanos was uncomfortable at this. "I suppose you could say that. It was, of course, for the party. Lothar persuaded me to join in August and to say nothing to Michael who was digging away in Amarna. I could be much more useful, of course, if I didn't."

"And you certainly were. What a coincidence you should overhear that business about the codes to the vault. That made it all possible. Of course, you realize that. When I think what a good actor you must have been to pull the wool over their eyes, it makes me want to laugh. What a shock, no, to find you tied up like a rag doll on the chair in the catacombs?"

Stephanos squirmed. "That Ravenstone's got a sixth sense. I don't know what signals I sent to him, but he was skeptical from the moment we met. I can promise you, my physical discomfort wasn't the slightest bit pretended. You fellows play a rough game. My ankles and wrists still hurt."

The young Englishman's eyes had seemed to glaze as if he had momentarily thought of something else. He left his reverie with a small start to focus on the handsome, dark-haired Greek whose hand had just planted itself on his thigh.

21

Later that afternoon

Lothar von Vranken could not stop fretting. How could his brilliant plan have been stymied like this? What an egregious insult to his trust. There it had been, in his grasp, or at least in the grasp of a most seasoned aide. The man he'd relied upon was one of the earliest members who had first assembled around the charismatic and moody Hitler in Munich back in 1921. How could the man have made such a face-about after those seventeen years of loyal service? And with so much at stake. So very much. What an absolute coup to present this casket himself to the Fuhrer. Far more important than any of the Titians and van Dycks purloined and hoarded by Goering. Gone in a sickening flash, and with it his imagined rewards. Oh, yes, in more fanciful moments, he'd allowed his ambition to soar, perhaps even elevation to field marshal. Now dissipated, blown away, like ephemera that had haunted a dream.

He sensed his moment had passed forever, and yet a tiny

hope glimmered. He sat down to write a letter. It was to his best friend, a man with whom he had gone skiing for years, champions since they were carefree youths, and spent winter holidays together in the Alps. Antonio Fiorelli had been born to a noble Italian family that went back to the earliest years of Christianity. Their scion, Lothar's oldest and closest friend, was now Cardinal Fiorelli, and, like Lothar, an admirer of Germany's all-powerful leader.

The letter pulsed with anger and frustration. He described the casket and its contents, referring to it as the true Ark of the Covenant. "Imagine, Tonio, what it would be like for Berlin to possess this most sacred object in the world to the Jews. Can you believe, Tonio, this Hamburg orphan was one of us for so long that it was unthinkable he could ever become a traitor. And yet he's taken this treasure and completely disappeared. Search your mind. Where do you think he would take it? What could be his motivation? Is it money? Will he simply hide it somewhere for himself? I never thought he was much inclined to any faith. None of this makes sense to me. To you? Any thoughts? The traitor's name is Friedrich Vogel, but he's mostly called Fritzi." And so the letter ranted on to its close.

Von Vranken put down his pen and sucked a spot of ink off his forefinger, not remotely imagining what he had just launched.

22

Three days later

The late-afternoon sun filtered in long beams through the blinds of his Vatican apartment. A knock on the door, and a liveried steward carrying a small vermeil charger stacked with the morning post entered and approached his desk.

"Today's mail, Your Grace." Several envelopes were laid on the desk, and with a small bow, the man withdrew.

Cardinal Fiorelli flicked through the little pile, stopped at some familiar handwriting, and pulled out von Vranken's letter. As he read through it, each sentence seemed to carry its own surprise. The deluge of information struck him like a summer shower. He was amazed from the start to learn what had been taken away by the renegade Nazi named Fritzi Vogel. Antonio Fiorelli gripped the letter's pages, electrified by the story of a man he could never have imagined was the true Moses of scripture. His mind raced through its implications. The ark and the shards of the original Covenant. He felt almost dizzy with their layers of consequence not only for the Jews but for his own mighty church—and, therefore, for himself.

An opening beyond anything in his wildest imaginings. He was suddenly captive to desire; it seemed to catch him in the throat. An obsession leaving no other choice. He must, above all else, possess this treasure for himself. This would be his key to the kingdom. He saw exactly how it could be exploited in his single-minded pursuit of the throne of Saint Peter. This could be the makeweight in his scheme to ascend the papal throne. Who else was better suited than he to purify the doctrine of the church and rid the world of its greatest enemy—the Jews. With this ark, he was God.

Of course, he had to think of the competition. His own greatest enemy was very much in evidence these days. The apostate Jew who had reached the position that made best use of those devious methods of his kind. How could such a man have been made secretary of state of the Vatican government? The church's top diplomat was exerting much energy trying to counteract the present Holy Father's indifference to the purges underway by Hitler and Mussolini. He was trying to put a more tolerant and compassionate face on Mother Church. But of course, wasn't that to be expected, given Cardinal Camberini's Hebraic origins?

But he, Antonio Fiorelli, wasn't such a patsy. He knew the future belonged to the rulers of Germany and Italy. And with the church as their staunch ally, its power over the souls of mankind would be unstoppable. Ah, yes, and whoever was the Holy Father would exert as much moral authority as possible to make those rulers themselves need his endorsement for their schemes. No latter-day Napoleon would ever grab a crown from his hands once he occupied the papal throne. Those crowned and uncrowned heads of the future would bend their knees to him.

He stood and paraded around the room, his dressing gown billowing behind him, transfixed by his daydreaming. He stopped at a mirror and studied its image. The tall, chiseled aquiline features of an impeccable lineage stared at him. His back straightened, and he placed a folded hand on his hip while the other shot forward for the mighty of this world to bow and kiss.

23

Early November

*G*iovanni Camberini picked up the small bowl from the little altar in his quarters and dipped his hand into it. With the holy water resting in its hollow, he poured the contents of his hand atop the head of his new recruit. He dipped his hand once more and dropped holy water on each shoulder. Another dip, and he wetted eyes and lips. With this, the formulas of baptism were pronounced, and when they had been completed, he held both his hands and raised Fritzi to be embraced.

"Welcome to the bosom of Mother Church, my young friend. You are a new Christian and bear a new name. Before taking your first vows as a novice member of the monkhood, you shall have your First Communion." Camberini took up a small silver salver with a piece of bread on it. He instructed him to take and hold the bread. Then the cardinal raised a chalice before Fritzi and indicated the bread must be dipped in its wine and then eaten. The new Christian's first taste of the body and blood of Christ brought tears to both men.

At the conclusion, the vows of a novice were made, and Camberini opened his arms once again. "You are now Brother Andreas, and a whole new life has begun for you. May you thrive in spirit and body and find your truest calling after the teachings which you shall receive."

From that moment on, Brother Andreas became Camberini's personal assistant and was seen to follow him wherever he might go, to meetings within the Vatican, to embassies, to dinners, anywhere the secretary of state was called upon to perform his duties. This did not go unnoticed by Camberini's observant rival and enemy. Fiorelli's spies on the cardinal's staff, moreover, were producing regular reports of this so-called Brother Andreas, which seemed to hint at new mysteries as yet unexplained.

✟

Rome was bathed in the rose gold of a setting sun. The little red plane passed like a gliding hawk over the Colosseum's honeycombed walls and the ruins of the Forum just before dipping its wing to the beating heart of the church, Saint Peter's. The basilica and the Vatican made a serene oasis of parkland, pine trees, and the enormous piazza embraced by the curving arms of Bernini's colonnade, a great enclosed plain in the midst of the cobweb of narrow streets that laced through the city.

At Ciampino Airport, after a smooth landing, they arranged to meet their pilot the next morning for the final leg of the journey to Basel. A car was waiting to take them to the Hassler at the crest of the Spanish Steps.

Their driver was in a jolly mood and jabbered away in

Italian, which they both understood. He took them through his shortcuts to avoid the clogged boulevards. At one point, they emerged at the edge of the Borghese Gardens.

Michael leaned forward and asked him to stop the car. Turning to Rupert, he asked, "You know we've got to spend the night in Rome because of our flight plan. Let's give ourselves an extra reason and see some really gorgeous things" Michael directed the driver to bring them through the iron gates and up to the building, which, he told Rupert, had once been a cardinal's country house right in the center of Rome. It had helped he added, in amassing one of the great fortunes and art collections of his time, to have been a nephew of the pope.

"Nepotism alive and well," quipped Rupert wryly.

"To be sure!" He rubbed his hands together and smiled like a kid about to step into a candy store. "Now let me show you some of the most beautiful sculptures ever made by man."

The taxi stopped at the foot of the double staircase that rose to an arcaded central facade of the grand white villa. Michael bounded out and extended his arms as if to embrace the whole building.

Another vehicle, nondescript and unnoticed, had parked just outside the gates while the others had driven through. A couple of men got out and strolled into the park toward the waiting taxi. They observed Rupert and Michael mount the staircase and started chatting with the driver who let it drop his passengers were heading to the Hotel Hassler.

"It's astounding! They're all by one artist. For my taste, the finest work ever done in marble." Michael raced up one side of the two flanking staircases to the piano nobile. Once inside, he pulled Rupert along to the first room on the left. They found themselves before a miracle of stone filigree depicting the roots and tendrils of an achingly seductive Daphne at the moment she is morphing from her feet up into a laurel tree. To the great disappointment of her pursuer, this stratagem succeeds. She is changing within the ardent embrace of a lusty young Apollo, unbearably frustrated as he is losing her to branches and leaves.

"Now come to see my very favorite." Michael led him into another room. There stood an athletic David, lips pulled tight and inward clenched between his teeth, with fierce resolve to sling his stone against the brow of an implied Goliath. "Not the serene adolescent boy after the battle à la Michelangelo, eh?" Michael looked for his reaction.

"Breathtaking. All energy and poise for action. I want to see the others as well."

They went from room to room admiring Bernini's delicate facility with the medium and his acute psychological insights. In the large central room on the other side of the building from the entrance, they encountered a towering, muscular Pluto in the act of abducting Proserpina.

Michael commented drily, "This time, the fellow gets his prize. She can't, alas, even turn into a tree."

Rupert admired everything about the monumental piece. He let his eyes take in the almost tangible flesh of the desperate victim's thigh as her abductor's strong fingers press hard to hold her while she pushes his head away with her arm. But she can only writhe, helpless, suspended high above the ground in his massive grip.

"Not a very pretty situation, is it?" Rupert and Michael turned together to see who was speaking.

"Sublime skill, no doubt, but what a terrible story. The gods were ruthless, no? Made their own rules. Could do things ordinary mortals mostly only thought about. But the gods got away with it." He wore a black well-tailored clerical gown to the floor, buttoned at the top into a starched white collar circling his neck. A broad-brimmed black hat with a shallow rounded crown made him look like some sort of ersatz chess piece on the checkered marble floor.

Rupert smiled. "Yes. A rather unholy sight in the near reaches of the Holy See."

The other laughed. "Not at all bad, sir. Of course, these are not alone. Countless other immodest depictions of human flesh litter the Roman landscape. But Rome's quite civilized. A tacit pact here between Christian dogma and pagan history lets everything live happily together."

"I suspect even tolerance can be selective." Rupert studied the cleric. Probably fifty-five. Clean-shaven, medium build, long thin nose, knowing dark eyes, graceful, elongated hands. "You'd probably agree so-called heresy can still be punished?"

The other nodded. "Gruesomely, sometimes." He looked at them both. "Too forward to ask whom I have the pleasure of interrupting so callously?"

Rupert and Michael gave names and bowed slightly.

The cleric returned his own bow. "I was once Brother Antonio, a member of the Society of Jesus, as you may have already gathered. My specialty is Italian Renaissance sculpture and painting. May I take it you have some interest in the subject?"

Just then, a woman with a tight gray chignon interrupted them. She fell to her knees and kissed his ring. "Your Grace, my husband and I know you will save the church from those who are confused. We pray for you every day."

The priest took both her hands and lifted her to stand. "And I, dear lady, will do the same for you. May your judgment remain unclouded by doubt."

She pulled a handkerchief from her handbag, dabbed at her eyes, curtsied, and departed.

He turned to the two of them. "As you will have gathered,

my incognito vestments are not always successful. Cardinal Fiorelli, at your service, gentlemen."

Rupert seized the moment. "Ah, yes. To have met a prince of the church in such surroundings. Another happy conjunction of the sacred and profane."

"How else can one govern the souls of men without understanding the voices of their flesh?" Fiorelli gave a rather scary smile.

Rupert responded, "Am I correct? Did I hear *voices*?"

Fiorelli hesitated for a moment and then laughed. "Touché, Signor Delacorte. Very nice. Vices do have their place as well."

Rupert smiled. "Interesting. You're the second Roman cardinal made known to us today. This morning, someone happened to mention one of your brethren with quite a history. It seems he, too, was in youth well versed in Renaissance art. Apparently comes from a rather unusual background, no?" He turned to give Michael a smile as if eliciting his agreement.

"Oh yes," Michael blurted out. "Camberini's his name."

Fiorelli frowned slightly. "Shall we say Camberini's one of our church's more exotic princes? Born into the Hebrew faith and later underwent a conversion. Age of seventeen in a brothel with a woman whose feet he washed and kissed as he begged her forgiveness."

Rupert found this worthy of a riposte. "Before or after completing his ostensible reason for being there?"

The cardinal raised his eyebrows. "Actually, she's the only one who knows. Indeed, there's long been a certain amount of speculation on that very question."

Rupert eyes were mischievous. "Sounds a rather good sort, don't you know."

"Possibly. Frankly, I don't trust him. Something a little theatrical, clearly opportunistic. Prodigal son, errant believer coming to the bosom of the church and all that." Fiorelli glowered a bit. "May I ask what brings you here to Rome?"

Michael shrugged. "Just passing through for the night. Plane leaves early in the morning."

"And might you be free to be my guests for dinner tonight at the Vatican palace?"

Surprised at this sudden reaction to their meeting, Michael turned to Rupert who responded, "How very charming, Your Grace. We accept."

24

That evening

he butler's rather splendiferous outfit, straight from the Renaissance, was quite at home in the cardinal's apartments with its carvings and gildings and murals and marbles of many hues. He asked the two guests to wait. Within several minutes, Fiorelli swept in wearing an elaborate crimson velvet robe unbuttoned over a dinner jacket and black tie. He said, "You are Greek Orthodox, Mr. Caridis? By your appearance, if I may hazard a guess, perhaps originally from the land of Alexander the Great?"

At this little extravagance, Michael nodded. "But certainly of somewhat less consequence."

Turning to Rupert, he said, "Of course, the penny dropped after we parted. The marquess himself. One of England's great scholars and most powerful families. Like me, you will travel somewhat incognito, Rupert Delacorte."

"Simplicity, sir. Less is better at times."

"Come, gentlemen, let me take you for a viewing of

something wonderful. You've heard of the loggia here, painted by Raphael?"

Michael nodded. "Yes, but mostly a mystery to me. Rarely seen by the public."

"True. Another reason why I wish your evening spent with me to be memorable." He laughed. "We must traverse a courtyard and several corridors to get there. Are you up to that small journey?"

"Of course. Please lead on." Rupert was emphatic.

They passed down the grand staircase and out into the quiet reaches of a courtyard surrounded by multistoried buildings with windows, many already lit for the evening. Crossing to the opposite building, they mounted a staircase up to the second story, turned right, and traversed several archways before turning right again. The thirteen vaults before them faced as many windows.

"This was a porch once open to the elements, can you imagine?" Fiorelli pointed at the windows. "These were added centuries later. Now enjoy yourselves." He pointed down the gallery whose walls and arches were encrusted with frescoes. Neoclassical images and biblical tales were depicted in a staggering display of virtuoso painting.

The cardinal kept up a patter, describing Raphael's personal contribution to the loggia's design. "This rivals Michelangelo's Sistine masterpiece. More intimate, crammed with learned references, and so harmonious."

When they reached the last mural, their host turned. "I've stuffed you with too much information, haven't I? Must be hungry after a long day. Come. Time for our dinner."

As they started down the stairs to the ground floor, two men emerged from the double doors of an apartment in the adjacent corridor and headed toward the staircase. Rupert noted the older man was impressively tall and well padded. His large head sported a cardinal's cap. The younger fellow had a tonsure shaved into his thick reddish hair. Fiorelli ignored them and led the way down to the courtyard.

The flames of candelabras and sconces welcomed them into the intimate oval dining room. Two stewards helped them to their chairs where the first course was already arranged on the glittering table.

Fiorelli asked what they thought of Mussolini and received bland, tactful replies. He probed their travel plans and was similarly diverted with nondescript responses. At last, having drawn from Michael his interest in archaeology and residence in Alexandria, the question, long submerged just beneath the surface of their conversation, was asked. "Gentlemen, I have heard rumors. Yes, such rumors even can reach to the Vatican. It has been said there was a remarkable discovery made recently in Egypt. An archaeological triumph, one might call it. Of course these things do get exaggerated in their passage from one to another."

Rupert pulled his cigarette case from his pocket. "Your Grace, would it be all right?"

Fiorelli, sidetracked, turned to him and pointed. "Of course, of course. An ashtray is just there."

"Thank you. May I offer one to you?"

He hesitated, and then he nodded and accepted. Rupert took a small votive candle from his place and held it to light the cardinal's cigarette followed by his own.

Rupert leaned back and smiled at Fiorelli. "You mentioned some sort of discovery. I'm sure we would have heard of it if it's that important."

"All right then. Let me ask whether you might have come across the theory that Moses was really not at all a Jewish boy rescued from the Nile, but rather the Pharaoh Akhenaten himself?" Fiorelli's eyebrows gave a questioning lift.

Rupert glanced at Michael and tapped his cigarette into the ashtray. "Certainly a revolutionary thesis. You do know Sigmund Freud has been exploring the possibility that Moses was not a Jew but an Egyptian who left Egypt with the Israelites. The very name, Moses, was at that time not even a Hebrew, but rather an Egyptian, name. You may also know Akhenaten's older brother who died young was, in fact, called Thut-Moses. So, why not imagine passing his name somehow to the younger brother when he became heir to the throne?"

The cardinal inspected him with an unflinching stare. "Yes, and what chain of events would unfold if there were proof, real proof, Moses was not a Jew at all? Would not the tribes of Israel rise in revolt against such a thing? Would the Austrian Jew Freud be happy at such an outcome?"

Rupert stared back at him. "In the wrong hands, yes, such proof might become a dangerous propaganda tool." The muscles in his cheeks twitched as he continued to look directly at Fiorelli. "Tragic, isn't it, some actually believe it's perfectly all right for Christians to murder as many Jews as possible. So, I should think anything that further arouses passions between people of those two persuasions might best be kept under wraps."

Fiorelli laughed. "I see. You've almost answered my question, haven't you?"

"Really? Well, rumors do get around. If yours comes from Egypt, then there's someone in Alexandria who might be more helpful than us in answering your question. Do you by some chance know a German with the gestapo, one Lothar von Vranken?"

"Perhaps, my Lord Ravenstone." He sported an insinuating smile. "From our conversation, it also seems plausible you yourself might have some inkling of where such proof may lie?"

"Frankly, Cardinal Fiorelli, at this point, I really do not have the slightest idea." Rupert stood. "The hour's late, and we've taken undue advantage of your kind hospitality by staying so long. Let us bid you a good evening."

25

The next morning

nondescript black car followed them the next morning from the Hassler to the Rome airport from which one of its riders called to confirm he just learned a certain small red airplane, now taxiing on the runway, was destined for Basel, Switzerland.

The de Havilland rose from Ciampino and banked to set its bearings to the north. An hour later, it approached the foothills of the Alps. Clouds concealed the great peaks.

The pilot turned to Rupert. "Let's hope we can get some visibility; otherwise, we've got to fly around them into France and come back the long way."

They managed to find enough sight lines through the shifting cloud layers to maneuver their way through the peaks. Both men in the cockpit understood the risk they had taken and were tense as they progressed from valley to valley. The pilot knew the route from past years as a mail carrier and relied on memory to fill in when his views were obscured. Their way was complicated by wind drafts between crags that acted like chimneys with sudden uprushes of air tossing the little craft about as if it were a toy. Breathing became more relaxed as the landscape of the Jura finally softened into rolling hills of green studded with pine forests in patches of darker green like a medieval tapestry. The late-afternoon sun had emerged from the clouds, and the world looked and smelled fresh when they landed on the puddled runway.

From their hotel, Rupert made a call and then rang Michael's room. "We're all set to meet her at seven thirty. I've got the address, same as what we were told."

A man clothed in black trousers and peacoat was hiding in the darkness off to one side of the 1930s modern house on a handsome street of such buildings. He had a good view through its ground-floor windows into any part of the house that might be occupied by the expected visitors. Within ten minutes of stationing himself, the taxi's headlights swept a swath of light across the front before it stopped and deposited two men.

A maid led them into the drawing room, and Ludwig Bordhardt's widow greeted them with a charming smile. After they were comfortable in their well-padded easy chairs, and the maid had delivered a cocktail to each, Rupert raised his glass to her and gave a short eloquent speech of thanks for her hospitality.

She was not tall, grayish hair gathered in a bun, dressed with a taste for Parisian fashion. The room was stuffed with antiquities. Among the most prominent were several busts and painted fragments depicting Nefertiti.

Michael raised his own glass, which he swept around the room, ending with her, and said, "May I be permitted to praise your husband's taste in distinguished women."

She smiled demurely and responded, "Certainly Amarna

let him set the bar very high. Ludie was a true romantic. Nefertiti was, more than anything, a dream that came true."

Rupert glanced at her husband's pipe rack. "Would you please stop me if my smoking a cigarette could even be a tiny bother?"

"Not at all, your lordship. You see, I've done my homework and know rather more now about you. Honored to have you in my house." She nodded to him.

"Very kind of you." Rupert stood and offered her a cigarette from his case, which she accepted, and he lit it for her. After lighting his own, he leaned back and let his eyelids close almost completely. Snapping them open as he finished his first exhalation, he launched into his brief. "In 1912, it seems Herr Borchardt brought back from Amarna not only the magnificent lady, but also a small, sealed jar, which contained a papyrus scroll. He translated this document and apparently resealed it inside the same jar, which he gave to the Berlin Society of the Seraphim of which he was then a member. The only condition was that it not be opened until his death. Alas, as we know, and very sadly, this occurred in Paris while he was on a trip to England just this August."

Mimi Borchardt put on a brave smile. "Yes. Very sudden. It hasn't been easy. But please continue."

"Indeed. It seems the two of you left Berlin and Germany for good in 1933 when Hitler became chancellor. Moved to Basel at that time."

"Yes, milord. It was a terribly difficult thing to do. We were both Jews, you see. The future looked very bleak for our people in Germany, so we left. Ludie tried several times later to get the jar back from the Seraphim, but the new leadership of the Society were Nazi industrialists who agreed with the kleptocratic policies of their party. Nothing of historical or artistic or financial value would ever be given back to a Jew."

"Yes, so you departed Germany without the jar, and five years later, just a couple of months ago, Herr Borchardt's death was made known and the jar was opened. This set in motion a whole train of events, which is why we're here tonight." Rupert pointed to Michael and recounted the history of his discovery and the deaths and thefts that ensued. "So, let me come to my point. Can you remember what Herr Borchardt's translation of the papyrus said?"

She put out her cigarette and walked over to a breakfront between two Greek herms. Pulling a little drawer all the way out, she reached into its cavity and triggered the opening of a panel on the surface of the desk. Lifting the panel, she removed from the space beneath, a sheet of paper.

"Here's the translation. Ludie never let me know what it said while he was alive. I found it with other things when he died. As you'll see, at the end, Ludie explains why he sealed it up again."

Rupert put on his half-glasses and read the page. He pulled off the glasses and took a deep breath. "Ah, yes. In 1913, when he gave the jar to the Seraphim, he thought they should have it because of their connection to Aaron the prophet who is described here as the slayer of Moses/Akhenaten, and, of all things, the husband of Nefertiti herself. Then when you left Germany in 1933, he added another inscription, which he dates in that year. 'Now I regret not destroying the papyrus as we enter an age of the whirlwind that could well sweep away civilization as we know it. As a non-practicing Jew, I failed to see where this all could lead in the wrong hands. How could I not have imagined the discord and doubt it could breed among my people? Worst of all, the original Covenant, albeit broken into pieces, would surely be the most sacred relic in the world to all Jews. And if ever discovered at Amarna, this treasure would most likely be found first by our bitterest enemies. What have I done?'

"And there we have it. All's clear. The Nazis saw this, and the rest we know." Rupert sighed and shook his head. "But Ludwig's spirit should be less disturbed by his actions. The fact is Michael here found the treasure without knowing anything about Ludwig's papyrus. We are ironically still left with the question: where can the casket be now? We've another stop to make, Frau Borchardt, in our efforts to find it. As you would understand all too well, we must keep this treasure out of the wrong hands."

"In August, when Ludie died, my sister and her son disappeared in Berlin. Not a single word from them or to know what happened to them. I pray there's no connection to all this. God help you, milord."

"God help us all, Frau Borchardt. Thank you for receiving us."

After the visitors had departed and the owner and staff had turned off the lights and closed the doors to the drawing room, the man who had observed all that had transpired through a narrow opening in the closed curtains managed to get in through the French windows from the garden and enter the room where he repeated the process for exposing the hiding place of Borchardt's translation. Just as he was crossing the room with it to the French windows, Mimi Borchardt opened the drawing room doors, and at the sight of him, she fell to the floor in a dead faint.

26

*The next day,
November 9th*

A Swiss-German spy stationed himself at the Basel airport and waited for a certain plane. He was a member of a Berlin-controlled network to which Cardinal Fiorelli had access, and he was acting at the request of his counterpart at the Rome airport. He had followed Rupert and Michael to their hotel and later to the Borchardt house. Their prey had not noticed his car pull out to follow their taxi back to the hotel afterward. His colleague, who had been planted outside the house before his arrival, had also remained to steal Borchardt's translation and notes.

Fiorelli pounded his fist when he learned the Swiss authorities had refused to divulge the de Havilland's destination when it departed the next morning. As events turned out, sadly, it did not matter.

Rupert's pilot crossed above the fertile plains of central Germany and passed into Poland, heading for its Baltic coast. They circled out over the sea before landing in the so-called

Free City of Danzig, called Gdansk under Polish administration since 1920. Recently this designation became a euphemism when Berlin had flexed its muscles and claimed ownership of that important port just as their goose-stepping army had recently taken over all of Austria and the Sudetenland with only a slap on the wrist from the rest of Europe's major powers.

It was a chilly November day as they emerged from the de Havilland. Michael shivered and said, "Typical northern European weather, I suppose, for this time of year. So glad to live in Egypt." In the distance, a fog was rolling in, spanning the sea like a giant tidal wave, and the air was damp and salty.

Rupert smiled. "Lucky you don't live in Britain either."

Their taxi navigated the late-afternoon traffic of the central city on its way to the southern outskirts. When they had entered the street where the church they sought was located, the two men looked at each other.

"I hope that's not what I fear it is." Rupert's jaw muscles twinged. Toward the far end of the next block, a stream of smoke spouted in fitful spasms. They arrived at the small church with its graveyard and rectory next door. The church's little steeple was smoldering above the collapsed slate roof, and the understructure had been mostly consumed by fire. It had destroyed the interior, shattering all its windows and devouring the entrance doors, which were now singed sticks of wood hanging from ancient iron hinges. It was set back from the street in a dilapidated neighborhood that had seen more prosperous times.

A young man opened the door after they pulled the rusted doorbell chain of the rectory building next door, scarred but still intact. In his shirtsleeves, which were short, and his bedraggled clerical collar, which was unfastened so that one end flapped free, he presented a sad, haunted image. Gaunt, tallish, with a thin, slightly hooked nose, there was something of the Nordic seafarer about him. One could imagine him crossing through the mists of the North Atlantic in a ghost Viking ship with a huge carved prow, braving uncharted seas to make some new landfall never seen before. "What do you want?"

Michael responded in flawless German, "We'd very much like to meet with Father Stanislaus. We'd no idea this tragic fire had happened. Is he all right?"

"No, he is not all right. In fact, he's dead. Murdered last night by the gestapo police. You're not German, either of you?"

Rupert replied, "No, not at all. Please tell us what's this terrible business all about?"

"Come in," the man said in English. He closed the door and motioned to some wooden chairs in a small room off the entrance hall. He sat behind a desk. "Are you here about a box from an Egyptian tomb?"

"Yes, we are," Michael said, rather startled. "Do you know anything about this box?"

The younger man sighed and wiped a tear from an eye. "I know it's the reason why Father Stanislaus is dead. He refused to give any information about the man who's said to have stolen it. The police tortured him, asking if the thief was a Jew and if he'd been in contact with him. The rector answered in the negative to all questions. The police said he was lying. They did unspeakable things to him. The worst images of hell could not be worse."

Rupert frowned. "Had Father Stanislaus ever mentioned this man to you in the past? You see, we've never met him. So, as far as we know, his name is Friedrich Vogel. Seems to be called Fritzi by his friends. We came here to learn as much about him as we can. Like the terrible gestapo, we want to find him because he's got something of great importance. Unlike the gestapo, that thing belongs to us—and it was taken by this Vogel."

The young deacon shook his head. "I really can't help with any of this. Stanislaus never told me anything about Vogel. All I can say is last night the police kept shouting the name of Camberini at Stanislaus, screaming the question whether Vogel had ever been told by him about this cardinal in Rome. Stanislaus kept on insisting he knew nothing of what the gestapo were talking about."

Rupert turned to Michael with a sudden look of shock. "Eavesdropped in Athens—how else could the gestapo know to ask these questions?" He shook his head and directed himself to the younger man. "We appreciate your openness with us. Can't express how terribly sorry we are for this tragedy. Better for you, I fear, that we go now—"

At this, a loud sound of smashing glass echoed through the darkening street as twilight was turning into night. They all ran outside where they halted on the stoop and remained transfixed for a very long time.

People were scattering in all directions. Down the street, Nazi soldiers marched in loose formation with clubs in their fists. Several hooligans waved burning torches in sweeping arcs. Every now and again, they would stop and smash the windows of a house. "Death to the Jews! No more Jews! Danzig must be pure! Danzig is German! All Poland is German! Heil Hitler!"

Occasionally the Nazi soldiers would inspect someone cowering in an automobile, rip open the door, and demand their identity card. If a Jewish man, they would beat him. If a Jewish woman, they might slap her and demand to see her children. Several cars were set aflame as was a synagogue whose incineration was visible from the churchyard. Its leaping flames of orange and red and blue and white pulsated in the sky beyond the immediate rooftops of houses.

Rupert finally spoke to the young priest. "Do you want to come with us? Will you be safe here tonight?"

"No one will be safe in Europe, my friend. Mark my words. The future of humanity is at stake now. A new beast must be fed, a new king of the jungle. Until it falls or is subdued, peace will be but a faint memory. Go pursue your quarry. I swear to say nothing of your questions or your conclusions to anyone. May the Lord be with you."

"And with you, Father. Goodbye."

Their driver was tense and made a turn away from the mayhem ahead of them. They looked through the rear window and saw flames had spread from the synagogue to nearby houses and were moving greedily in the direction of the church they had just left.

Their route, as with all others toward the center of Danzig, was impeded by islands of chaos. With mad relish, gangs of uniformed thugs and random hooligans smashed windows in shops and homes and set fire to motorcars and particular buildings, their faces contorted by gleeful vindictiveness. People were being dragged through the streets and vilified by others shaking their fists and shouting at them. The scenes resembled visions of hell. Nazi soldiers were everywhere. No evidence at all of Danzig's police. It was the Nazi's first Kristallnacht, and all the monsters of hell had been let loose upon this ancient Hanseatic seaport.

Rupert turned in the back seat to Michael. "My God, Miko. I feel as if I've caused that poor man to die. Who'd imagine the Nazis had planted a spy at the Athens airport? They heard everything. Good God, I must hope Mrs. Borchardt isn't put through a wringer because of our visit."

When they reached their hotel at last, badly shaken as was their driver, the two men alighted and quickly pushed through its doors into the lobby. There were pockets of hysteria among guests clustered at the reception desk, and several people were being ushered, pleading and weeping, from the lobby, where they had sought refuge.

The hotel doormen shouted as they pushed them back into the street, "No Jews hiding in here!"

Michael tried to intervene. "You can't let them go back out there. Inhuman!" He was shoved aside by a large doorman in his immaculate regalia. It seemed the thirst for blood had metastasized and needed more unspeakable violence before it could be slaked.

27

Later that evening

"Did you send your telegrams?" Michael put down his knife and fork and picked up a glass of well-chilled Riesling.

"Haven't heard back yet from London about Camberini's direct phone line. They're trying to get it without revealing my identity." Rupert leaned back in his dining armchair. "I've been thinking since we got to Danzig and witnessed these horrors. This is the future of Europe if we aren't ready to defend our cherished values. Chamberlain must stop his fantasy that Herr Hitler has set any limits on the spreading Reich. His jaws will bite into every new power base his claws can grab. Appetite's insatiable and military machine's on its way to becoming unbeatable."

Michael brooded a moment. "Our minds seem to be in the same place." He waved his hand in an arc. "How are we going to save this continent without the help of your country and probably our spores blown across the sea? The Americans?

I must confess to being quite fed up with the threat of a larger world war than the one supposedly ended just twenty years ago."

"Given our human inclination to believe in false prophets, nothing surprises me. The struggle isn't between the wanna-haves and the haves. It's between shamans and gullibles. These tin-pot dictators are simply prestidigitators with uncanny powers of persuading masses clamoring to believe."

"And all the more dangerous because of the terrible toys in their playrooms." Pointing at his wineglass, Michael encouraged the waiter to top up the Riesling.

A bellhop with white gloves materialized beside their table. "I've got a telegram for Herr Delacorte."

"Thank you. I'll take it." Rupert plucked the yellow paper from the little silver tray. He turned to Michael. "No phone number, but his telegraph address was given. I'll send one right away."

"Well, what's happening here?" Michael gestured with his head and eyes toward the hotel dining room's entrance. Two men in military uniforms were speaking to the maître d'hotel who was pointing toward their table. The room fell silent as they strode toward them.

Michael raised his eyebrows and spoke in German. "Good evening, gentlemen."

They focused on Rupert. "You are Herr Delacorte?"

"Yes. What can I do for you?"

"Please come with us, Mein Herr."

"I think you might explain first. What's going on?" Rupert appearing relaxed, leaned back in his chair and lit a cigarette.

"You're needed for questioning. Everything will be explained. We must ask you to join us immediately."

"May my friend come along as well? He can help with translation if needed."

The SS officers looked at Caridis and shrugged. "I suppose so. Is he Jewish?"

"No," responded Michael in a quiet voice.

They walked from the dining room under the silent watchfulness of the other guests.

At the police station, they passed through a crowded corridor past closed doors. Raised voices could be heard—one followed by a scream of pain—and they were escorted to a large office. Soon a man entered. His rank was evident by the deference paid to him. He smiled and, in English, invited Michael and Rupert to be seated before a large desk. He took the chair behind it.

"Now, Herr Delacorte, may I see your passport" After receiving the document, the officer commented. "So, you travel under several names, it seems. Delacorte and Ravenstone. A habit of the British aristocracy, I would imagine?"

"Quite right, sir. It simplifies things. May I ask, why do you even care about my presence in Danzig?"

"Well, I do care. Why is an English peer here in this city, and why does he bother to visit an obscure Catholic church where the rector has just been found early this morning most brutally beaten to death and burned almost beyond recognition?"

Rupert shook his head and kept his eyes fixed on those of his interrogator. "I imagine you'd have a much better idea of what happened." A touch of sarcasm sounded in his voice.

"You've not answered my question." Through the office windows could be heard the sounds of destruction. Lights were flashing in strobe-like streaks on the walls of a building and a tree opposite.

Rupert vaguely thought of images flickering in an ancient silent cinema as he responded. "I believe my reasons are my business, not yours. Danzig's a free city, and I'm from a free democratic country where we're not required to explain perfectly innocent actions." Rupert leaned back and stared at his interrogator.

The door opened, and a subaltern brought some papers to the officer.

After studying them, he looked up and asked with a restrained triumphant air, "Why are you trying to contact a certain Cardinal Camberini in the Vatican?"

"It's evident you're referring to my recent telegram to my London office." Rupert had an ingratiating smile.

The officer glanced at the papers before him. "Yes. I've got a copy here of the reply as well. So, what's your business with this cardinal?"

Rupert reflected for a moment. "I'm a scholar of antiquities, and Camberini's a scholar of Renaissance art. I've got a question about a fascinating connection that might exist between an ancient personage and a Renaissance work of art. To be precise, the statue of Moses done by Michelangelo intended for the tomb of Julius II, one of that church's greater popes."

The SS officer stared. "Do you also have any interest in a formerly high-ranking member of the Nazi Party named Friedrich Vogel?"

At this, it was clear the fine hand of Lothar von Vranken had reached to the gestapo who were in the process of taking over the police stations of Danzig. Rupert wanted to kick himself for that Athens phone call. Clearly someone had reported the whole conversation to von Vranken. Still, he would behave as if it had never occurred. So, he brightened. "Yes, I do. That's why I wanted to have an interview with the unfortunate Father Stanislaus. You see, this Vogel character has taken something from me of considerable value. It seems the priest knew him many years ago. I was hoping as a long shot he might help me to find him. He's stolen an important translation I've made of an ancient manuscript, and I'd like very much to have it back. My only copy, and it was quite a lot of work."

"Then, Herr Delacorte, what could be the connection today between this Camberini and your thief, Vogel?"

Rupert folded his arms and tilted his head to one side. "Until this moment, sir, the two men were completely unrelated in my mind ... and Vogel's not my thief. He was von Vranken's before he apparently went rogue on his own. I can't imagine what he and Camberini might have in common today—or ever. I shouldn't think they've ever met each other."

The officer raised his eyebrows. "Really? Are you sure? I believe someone has recently mentioned to you that Camberini was a Jew who converted. And that Father Stanislaus had told this to Vogel years ago when, as you know, he learned Vogel was a Jew himself." With a certain air of smugness, he, too, crossed his arms and tilted his head. "So, what should we make of this bit of symmetry—or coincidence as you might call it?"

"*Oberstleutnant*, you've asked me, and I shall tell you. Why should we make anything at all of the coincidence that I wish to meet Cardinal Camberini, and that the priest mentioned his name to the thief almost two decades ago because both men had started life as Jews? Why would your Nazi colleague have any reason to connect with this churchman, as Jews or not? Until you can establish a logical link between those two men today, I think speculation's useless that there may be any connection at all."

The officer appeared disappointed. "You leave me at an impasse, sir. I suppose we must try now to establish that link for ourselves." He shuffled through some papers and pulled one out. Looking at it, he said, "I've been directed by Berlin's top authorities to hold you in Danzig for questioning. You will be under house arrest for the next twenty-four hours. Do not leave your hotel at all during that time. A guard will be posted outside your room—and will go with you whenever you emerge. At any time, I may send a police car to bring you back for further discussion. Have I made myself clear?"

Rupert rejoined, "Perfectly."

He pressed a button on his desk. The subaltern entered and was ordered to show the two men out. A police car drove them back through the inferno.

Michael had wanted to speak in the car, but Rupert gave him the sign to hold his peace. When they pulled up to the hotel entrance, the dramas of the night before were being reenacted with two uniformed doormen pushing people away who were, as Jews, desperate to remove themselves from harm's way. Michael said, "Let's not go to our rooms yet. A drink and maybe some backgammon?"

"Sounds like a good distraction to me. Don't much feel like trying to sleep with this agitation all about us." Rupert's hand swept to include everything.

The bar was crowded, but two people vacated a game table just as they arrived. When settled, Michael looked up from arranging his plaques on the game board. "Today's made me better understand at close hand what lies in store for Europe."

"Not very pretty. Just about impossible for people classified as Jews. It's goddamn madness to treat some of your most enlightened and productive citizens this way, aside from the dreadful inhumanity involved."

At this, a well-dressed man leaned toward them from his small group at the next table. "You British will never understand, will you? If you did, you would be begging to be part of our national project. Your weakness will be your undoing."

Rupert smiled and thought this could well be a plant by their recent hosts trying to provoke a reaction to warrant bringing them back to gestapo headquarters. He reached into his jacket and withdrew his cigarette case. "I don't believe we've met before, sir. To calm the atmosphere, may I offer a smoke. Like the peace pipe of America's Indians, perhaps?" He snapped open the case and held it out to the somewhat startled fellow.

The German waved it away. "There you go. Typical British sarcasm." His color mounted, making his face florid. He grabbed a glass of schnapps and swallowed its contents with a jerk of his elbow. Rupert stood up from the still unarranged backgammon board, with Michael following, and left without another word.

Before turning off his light, he recapped the day's disturbing events in his nightly letter to Elizabeth. "These Germans are playing with fire—and they've got the firepower to back it up. We must step on it with our defenses and get Neville to understand the stakes, or all could be lost."

The next morning, Rupert telephoned their pilot to prepare for departure in twenty-four hours. Their destination would be Bern, Switzerland. Assuming his phone would be monitored, he had no intention of leaving a trail of their actual intended ports of call until he got to neutral territory.

The rest of the day passed without event. That evening, the pogroms of a second Kristallnacht resumed their terrors. Fires threw jagged streaks of light visible from the lobby windows. Sirens, shouting, scattering figures, and confusion reigned on the other side of the panes of glass, like a vitrine displaying for the hotel guests unspeakable visions of hate playing itself out.

Blue-gray morning mists mingled with dirty plumes of smoke from Danzig's forty-eight hours of mayhem. The de Havilland flew low over the devastation as it banked on its way toward the southwest. Rupert looked down from his copilot's seat and felt a chill. He could not shake a premonition that soon all of Europe was to be devoured in flames.

28

November 11, 1938

With Rome's autumn day dimming into darkness, Fiorelli pushed the light switch with a triumphant thump and returned to his desk. Elation surged through him once again. Could this really be? He reread the very long telegram from Lothar von Vranken. Yes. The chase now was on. It named the imposter. The trail was hot. Delacorte had shown them the way. He had even bothered to visit the Jewess Borchardt across the Alps. She probably added nothing Berlin did not already know. After all, Lothar had already explained to Antonio how her husband's find had precipitated this whole business. Then Danzig!

How very clever of Lothar to have his spy eavesdrop the English lord in Athens. That produced their brilliant clue to the priest who had befriended the Jewish imposter in Danzig when the party had recruited him. Stupid man had died refusing even to discuss any mention he might have made of Camberini to the Nazi traitor. The priest's stubborn silence had only confirmed their suspicions.

He settled into the high back of his chair. Who'd ever have imagined his archrival in the Curia might just be playing a vital part in this drama? It would have been far-fetched to invent a scenario so close to home that could produce such a fascinating key to open the gates of power for him. Ambition sets its own rules for those who succumb blindly to its grip. He trembled from passions welling over him once again. Such visions of power and pomp. Imagine possessing the Ark of the First Covenant, presumably now in its broken pieces from being thrown in anger to the ground. The yellow paper with its block capitals slipped from his fingers and drifted like a dried leaf to the floor.

♀

That same day, Vatican telegrams seemed to be in spate. Camberini received his that morning. Its implications brought him both pleasurable anticipation and a stab of disquiet. Could others have reached the same conclusion—or was he just overreacting? Could this simply be a coincidence? In any event, he would take the next step. He was amused by the clever coding of its message.

The telegram was from a man who called himself Charles Wakely. He claimed to be a biblical scholar and to have translated an ancient Egyptian document that might throw a fascinating light on Michelangelo's Moses. Would the cardinal be willing to meet him at the site of the statue? A response could be left to his attention at the Hotel Hassler. For reasons Rupert could only have regarded as having the remotest odds, he was in luck. Camberini picked up his phone and asked for the hotel's concierge.

♀

Rupert turned to Michael in the back seat of their Roman taxi. "I hope Camberini can put two and two together—and doesn't think this is some sort of stunt to get his attention. Who knows how much the Curia spy on each other?"

Michael nodded. "Yes, good plan to meet outside the Vatican grounds. Interesting toss-up whether he'll be tempted to find out what's behind your message. He's not exactly lacking distractions as their chief diplomat."

They both laughed. Rupert pulled a bill from his wallet. "Here's a fiver to say he takes the bait." He paid the driver, and they entered the Hassler.

A telephoned message from Camberini confirmed he would meet them the next day at noon in front of the Moses. Michael shrugged and handed Rupert ten pounds.

☥

Halfway between the Roman Forum and the pope's personal basilica of Santa Maria Maggiore, lies the ancient site of Saint Peter in Chains, San Pietro in Vincoli. Those chains were brought from Jerusalem to the earliest incarnation of this church in the fifth century by a devout Roman empress. They were said to have been used to secure Saint Peter himself from escaping his imprisonment and his horrible fate—nailed to a cross, out of modesty, upside down.

The bells of Rome rang out the noonday hour in a rippling melodic wave. Rupert and Michael entered the arcaded facade of the church. In the time it took to adjust their eyes to the relative darkness, two different doors opened, admitting a young monk and a prelate into the greater calm of the basilica. It was difficult to determine whether they were together. They took up separate positions before the immense statue of Moses. The bearded patriarch looked quite prepared to speak his mind to all four men.

One could envisage the marble figure in life, standing on Mount Sinai, powerful and demanding of himself and others. As he receives the orders of his God, anger is not far from his expression. He appears stern, meditative, disturbed by the worship of idols that attract his spiritually famished people who mill, restless, about the base of the mount for forty days awaiting the Word.

The prelate showed a trace of curiosity as he looked about the area before the statue. The other man remained staring up at the Hebrew patriarch.

Waiting together next to a pillar, Michael whispered, "That's the fellow we saw as we left the Loggia with Fiorelli."

"You're quite right. It might thicken the plot, no?" Rupert stepped forward. "Forgive me, sir, do I have the honor of addressing Cardinal Giovanni Camberini?"

The churchman studied him for several moments, and then he smiled and looked over his shoulder at the monk who nodded. He turned back and spoke. His voice resonated. A big, well-padded prelate with a broad face, small round spectacles, and the square red cap of his office perched on the back of his head. "May I venture my own conjecture, sir? Is it possible I'm speaking with Rupert Delacorte, the Marquess of Ravenstone?"

Feeling an inner surge of jubilation, Rupert responded, "Indeed so, Your Grace. And this is Michael Caridis, who discovered the document mentioned in my telegram." He paused. "Your uncanny recognition can lead to only one, I think most happy, conclusion—perhaps so obvious it needn't be spoken, yet so improbable that I hesitate almost to utter it."

The monk edged closer, looking hard at Rupert as if he were making a decision before speaking. Now standing beside the cardinal, he projected a muscular physical presence not to be underestimated. In a subdued voice, he said. "Please forgive me, gentlemen. It was a terrible insult to you and your discovery. There just was no other way. We had to keep the ark from getting into the worst hands imaginable." He fixed on Rupert. "How on earth did you make a connection between me and this man of God? I'm indeed Friedrich Vogel."

Michael's voice shook as he said, "Speaking for my friend, he had a private investigator uncover as much about you as could be found in a very short time. The fellow took a deep dive into the past and found the priest at the Catholic church where you worked as a mason just at the point the party recruited you."

Camberini smiled. "The full story can be discussed later at my apartments. But I must say, quite clever of you to guess— from such a scrap of evidence—that it just might be with me and then to cover your tracks this way. You must be aware the Vatican is riddled with spies. So, you'll be introduced henceforth as Charles Wakely and his friend. Now please tell me. Other than an ingenious way to tip me off as to who you might be, have you some insights to offer about this work of genius?" He pointed up at the brooding statue.

Rupert replied. "Quite right. In fact, ever since translating the scrolls, I've been evolving some theories. By now, I imagine you've read the translation I made." He advanced closer to the hulking statue. It seemed almost alive. He pointed up at its head. "We see those two rather bizarre stumps protruding from his skull. What do you believe they represent?"

The cardinal moved to stand beside Rupert. "It's an artist's conceit. He probably misread the Hebrew text that said Moses came down from Sinai with his tablets, 'horned.' Later scholarship, as you and I certainly well know, redefined the word to say 'radiant.'"

Rupert opened his arms wide. "All right, sir, so now let's allow our imaginations completely free, unfettered rein.

What if, however come by, Michelangelo himself had some sort of unlikely inkling the Moses of the Exodus was really a monotheist pharaoh? A religious iconoclast who ran from those anxious to usurp his throne? What if the two horns on the head of Michelangelo's Moses are a code for the double crown of Upper and Lower Egypt? What if they also represent the—as you say *radiant*—rays of the sun, the very key object worshipped by the earliest true monotheist monarch in recorded history?"

Camberini said, "I suppose in light of the monumental discovery that's now been made about the true identity of Moses, it's reasonable to ask if others may have had this knowledge before us. Or at least had the evidence perhaps without even understanding it." In a quiet voice, he added, "I've got a personal story. When I was a young priest, fresh from my conversion, I came to this very church simply to meditate and pray. As you can see, there's a special feeling here. There were tourists about. I overheard one mention they'd seen something peeking up slightly from behind the tablets held in Moses's right hand. I waited until they'd gone and the church was empty. Being much more agile in those days." He laughed. "I climbed up onto the plinth that holds the statue and, indeed, found a piece of gray paper, the color of the stone."

Michael asked, "Was there anything on it?"

"Yes, there was. A depiction of the Eye of Horus. The drawing covered most of the paper, done in the ancient Egyptian style, you know, only showing the right eye, which represents the sun. Of course, I found this most peculiar. Mystified, I tried to reason why anyone might have done this. We're speaking of a time more than forty years ago. I was busy, but not too much to delve into some old texts relating to Michelangelo's intentions when he created the Moses for Pope Julius's tomb. Nothing very revealing came from this—some ambiguities—but the puzzle's remained with me ever since." He smiled. "Until, that is, I read your translation of the scrolls and understood at last—that Eye of Horus had been a revelation connecting Moses to Akhenaten."

Camberini abruptly looked over their shoulders and said, "Good afternoon, Capitano."

The others turned around to see an officer of the Blackshirt militia with another man, tip his head to the cardinal.

29

Later that day

iorelli pursed his lips in thought, adjusting the cincture that held his simple black cassock at the waist. He looked at the baroque tall clock in the corner. It was that time of the late afternoon when a particular—and possibly most telling— opportunity just might present itself. Why not give it a try? He paused in the next room of his apartment to grab a black topcoat and passed through one of its doors into the corridors of the palace, which he hoped someday to occupy as suzerain.

Emerging into the Vatican gardens, he lingered for a moment at the top of broad steps leading down into the extensive landscape. Crinkling the muscles around his eyes, he surveyed the scene. A late rain had left everything smelling of damp soil and soggy autumn leaves. The tall, contorted pines with their umbrella tops appeared somber in the darkening sky.

No sight of his quarry. Still, why not take the chance? Fiorelli grabbed the skirts of his robe, headed down the steps, and struck out into the maze of paths. After half an hour of touring its nearer precincts, he gave up and quit the garden by one of the farthest gates. On a hunch, he made his way to the private chapel used by many of the Vatican workers.

Bells for the Compline had begun to toll their gentle call to evening prayer. Figures in black suits and robes trickled into the chapel from several directions. Fiorelli waited outside in discreet shadows. His vigil was rewarded. The Jew's new puppy dog arrived—alone.

Fiorelli waited several moments before entering the chapel. Antique chants hummed like an undertone to their devotions. He sat just behind his quarry who had knelt and was already absorbed in murmuring a prayer. He studied the tonsure cut into the novice's red hair. There were freckles on the back of his pale neck.

The novice lifted himself and settled back in his pew. His eyes rose up to the chapel's windows and vaulting, lost in his thoughts.

In a low voice, but loud enough to be heard, Fiorelli spoke in a matter-of-fact tone. "Fritzi."

The man's head and body jerked about only to be confronted by the long, narrow face of Cardinal Fiorelli who sported his triangular smile. Triumph shot like sparks from his eyes.

Fritzi rose from his pew and strode for the doors to the right of the altar. He was followed at the same pace by the cardinal. When Fritzi stepped outside, night was setting in. He started to run toward the Vatican gardens. The chase quickly became complicated by the many twists to the paths, which gave the athletic Fritzi an advantage.

He finally leaped off a graveled path toward an area where a grotto crouched in the hillside. Hoping not to have been noticed, he entered the grotto guarded by leering grotesques at the entrance. The side walls of the cavity in the hillside extended in two sweeping curves to the rear wall. In its black shadows, he could hear the water falling from a high shelf of rock into a large pool at its base. Other footsteps soon echoed in the small cavern. He dodged behind the first outcrop of rock, now completely immured in darkness. No sound. Just the cascade splashing to his left.

The ambient light coming from outside threw a faint moving shadow onto the wall opposite his hiding place and to the right of the small cascade. He coiled himself and tried not to be heard breathing. A faint movement of air, a hand brushing on the damp volcanic stone, something alerted him that the other presence lurked close by his hiding place.

Tense and alert, his opportunity came when the breathing from the throat of his pursuer exhaled almost next to him. The two bodies touched and began to grapple. The novice had once been used to carrying heavy stones. He was younger and far more fit than the cardinal. It did not take long before he had him in a stranglehold. With an effort not to kill the man, Fritzi squeezed his throat just long enough to make the thrashing arms fall limp and his pursuer lose consciousness.

He used the long, braided rope that belted the cardinal's robe, to bind the man's wrists to his ankles. He turned him on his side and ran the rope behind so he could not move when he awakened. With that, he rose and straightened his robe, trembling with anger and disappointment.

30

Earlier that day

"So, Your Grace, Brother Andreas, that completes the story of how Michael and I have come to sit here this afternoon. Standing before Moses together, I did have a curious thought." Rupert exhaled the smoke of his Turkish cigarette. "It may well be neither of you has been to the Museum of Antiquities at Cairo. A large depiction in stone of Akhenaten flanks one side of a doorway. That statue bears absolutely no resemblance to the image created by Michelangelo. They could not be more different. But, with that said, both project an immense aura of mystery. As if they were party to secrets, we will never have fully revealed. All-knowing in some divine symmetry between the two sculptors' visions."

The hours had passed, and the November daylight was beginning to darken. Camberini looked at his watch. "Gentlemen, I think we should address the question of what to do with the treasure. As we've seen from your account of events, there are forces prepared to go to any lengths to have it.

Brother Andreas and I have even considered burying it under the stones that pave the floor in front of the very statue where we met. But the casket itself, the original ark, if you will, would be difficult to place there.

"No bank vault in this country is secure with Mussolini in charge. The Papal Treasury under Pius is hardly any better. And we cannot keep it where it is much longer, especially if something should happen to either of us."

Rupert said, "Until this storm of fascism and persecution has blown over, we shouldn't give others ammunition to demean Judaism or treat the Covenant with irreverence. I think that rules out its public display anywhere for now."

Andreas said, "Perhaps we can continue this later? I must go now to my Compline devotions." He stood and shook hands with the two visitors.

The three remaining men continued to tease the subject as day disappeared into twilight and then deep darkness relieved occasionally by clouds scudding away from the moon.

Camberini put up his hands and said, "It's time for a drink." He rang, and a steward soon arrived. They settled around one end of a table filled with books and a pair of antique globes. The subject had changed to Europe's fate under the aggressive regimes metastasizing at its center.

Loud sounds of people arguing outside the great salon's doors soon interrupted them.

With a rush, the doors sprang open—and Brother Andreas broke into the room. Camberini shooed away the uniformed young man who had scuffled with the novice. The doors were closed again.

Camberini had risen. "What can be the matter? You're white as an unholy ghost."

Trying for more breath, he spat out, "It was him. Fiorelli."

"What do you mean?"

"I was kneeling at prayer this evening, and I heard a voice behind me say my real name. Dear God! Like a fool, I turned around. It was him. How could he know who I was?"

"Then what happened?"

"I left right away and ran like the wind through the gardens. He followed, and it got darker. I hid in the grotto. He came into it, and I caught him from behind around the throat. I don't think I killed him. He was unconscious, and I tied him with his own cincture. He could be there till someone finds him. But how could he have guessed?"

Camberini nodded. "Fiorelli's got his hand in every fascist pot you can imagine. Clearly someone's told him about you. I can't think who. I'm so terribly sorry to lose you, and so soon, Fritzi. We'll send you to a safe monastery, and I'll come to visit. You'll be enrolled as Brother Valerian. You'll be down the road from the convent where Solange went when you arrived last week."

The cardinal walked over to a curved corner of the room and made an invisible door in the carved paneling open. "Until I get you out of here without being noticed, I want you to take these stairs up to the next floor and go to the last door on the left and lock it from the inside. I'll tell my overly protective young guard you've gone away by a back entrance."

Fritzi seemed now ready to weep. "I don't want to leave, Your Grace."

"You know you must, my lad. You will be brave."

Fritzi pulled himself together and nodded, jaw clenched. He shook hands with Rupert and Michael. "You've got now what was rightfully yours. Save it—at all costs."

With his head bowed, he passed through the secret door, which the cardinal closed after embracing him.

Camberini turned to Rupert and Michael. "Well, everything's changed. Prepare for the worst. You can't imagine how profoundly cynical and ambitious Fiorelli is. You had dinner with him. His ruthlessness knows no boundaries. And he's a creature of Mussolini. An alliance of tyrants."

"The Nazis have already murdered brutally for this prize," Rupert said. "Would Fiorelli, a man of the church, be capable of going that far?"

"Without a shred of doubt. And his ambition brooks no limits as to who his victims could be—even the pope himself."

"Then you are, I hate to say it, also in serious danger, Your Grace."

Camberini nodded.

31

Later that evening

iorelli opened an eye, then the other, slowly dawning to his situation. A rat had been crawling over him in the dark. His neck was sore, and his throat felt as if it had been stabbed. But he breathed. And a passion for revenge brought a rush of strength, enough to send out a piercing call. His hoarse cries reverberated in the grotto, which amplified his voice like a loudspeaker. Still, it seemed far too many hours of desperate calling had passed before rescue arrived. At which he managed a smile. At least this wasn't going to be his tomb.

"You say he gave his name as Charles Wakely?" Cardinal Fiorelli fixed on his informer as if he were about to pin him like an insect specimen to the door behind him.

"Yes, Your Grace. The porter said a gentleman of that name, with a friend, visited Camberini for lunch today. No idea if they're still there." He studied his watch. "Very late now, long past dinnertime." The obsequious man in his black robe smiled. It had the charm of an adder yawning. "I was told

Wakely's evidently English, and his friend has a Greek accent. They were in the room when Camberini's puppy dog crashed past the guard. He told me everything."

Fiorelli studied his fingernails, which were ragged stubs from clawing at rope and stone during his confinement in the grotto. "So, no one has seen any of the four people leave Camberini's place since the puppy dog made his entrance?"

"It does not seem so, Your Grace."

"All right, you may go now."

"Thank you, Your Grace."

When the doors closed behind the sycophant, he picked up the receiver from his desk phone, rubbed one of his sore shoulders, and spoke for enough time to set in motion a plan already formed for just this contingency.

✞

At about eight in the evening, Rupert, Michael, and Fritzi were taken to one of the rear entrances to Camberini's quarters. They were led unnoticed in the darkness through several courtyards and gardens to a barely visible and nondescript door through the wall dividing Vatican City from the city of Rome. Using the cardinal's key, they slipped from the pastoral peace of a tree-filled park onto a street charged with urban life. They hailed a cab. At the second stop, Fritzi paid the driver and went around to open the boot. There sat the casket and treasure, which he carried into the little pensione.

In the meantime, Camberini contacted a Roman police captain whom he had both baptized and some years later performed his marriage. The man sent four of his most able people to the secretary of state's apartments, ostensibly to discuss a visit being planned for a foreign delegation to Rome and the Vatican. When they arrived, the uniformed policemen sat in the cardinal's grand salon where he gave them details of their mission for the night. They deployed afterward to station just inside each of the four entrances to his quarters.

Around one o'clock in the morning, two Vatican guards came to the main entrance of Camberini's apartments. Six more deployed in couples outside each of the other three entrances. When the rope of the main doorbell had been pulled, the policeman just inside opened it a crack. The guards pushed the door hard against him, upsetting his balance. The pair of Vatican guards stood over the Roman policeman who got to his feet and said, "By what right does any jackass force his way into the private quarters of the cardinal secretary of state?"

The guards sneered at him. One responded, "Inside these walls, His Holiness's guards have jurisdiction, not Rome's police. So, you will stand aside." They tried to move past the policeman, but he put up both arms to block the way. "We said to move aside. We're here on Vatican business. We've reason to believe a violent criminal is hiding in these quarters. We must protect His Eminence. He could be in danger."

"Enough," bellowed Camberini, striding into the room, majestic in his satin dressing gown with large silk-corded lapels and panels running down the front. "There's no excuse for this invasion. You must leave immediately."

"We can't, Your Grace. His Holiness's magistrate has given us a warrant to search your apartments for a spy and enemy of the church—and for contraband that properly belongs to the church. So, we ask you, please, to cooperate for the good of all concerned." The Vatican guards bowed toward him as this was said.

Camberini barked, "Stand down. You need go no further. I can assure you there's nobody here but me, and there's certainly no 'contraband' as you call it. My word as a cardinal, a member of the curia, and as your secretary of state."

The guards shook their heads. "We've got orders from the magistrate. No one is above the law, as you know, Your Grace. Please let us do our job."

By this point, the Roman policemen and the guards from outside the three other entrances had collected in the salon to witness with some satisfaction this confrontation.

Camberini sat down in a throne-like armchair beside the massive fireplace. With sarcasm oozing from every syllable, he smiled. "Then if you must keep us all awake, and worry your families, uncertain of your return to their bosom, at so late an hour, and, most important of all, cause a rift between the Holy See and the administration of Rome, by all means obey the magistrate. But do so with speed and care—and do no damage to these magnificent quarters." He stared for several seconds at a small Faberge clock, which he had lifted from a table. Setting it back with a deliberate clatter, he squinted up at the Vatican guards, "So, what are you waiting for, gentlemen?" He spread out both his arms. "Search away to your heart's content. You will find nothing and no one."

They tested the paneling for hidden doors and found the secret access to separate servants' quarters, both stories of which were inspected to no avail except to awaken several members of the cardinal's staff. The bookshelves were taken apart and restored to their original order. The long chest made of predella panels was opened, and the tapestries were removed and replaced.

The Roman policemen had joined the cardinal before the fireplace and been served coffee and refreshments. They were chatting about the coming elections and making bets as to their outcome.

The Vatican guards, all eight of them, assembled in the salon after their search. One of them said, "So, why, then, Your Grace, have you deployed Rome's constabulary at your doorways if you had nothing to protect or fear?"

Camberini smiled. "I think you might just divine that for yourselves. Just analyze what you have done this past hour. The smell of intrigue was high tonight like rotting garbage. I called the garbage collectors just in case matters were to get out of hand. Now please go and know I shall never forget any of your names ... and I might add, it shall not be for any sentimental reasons."

32

The next day

*R*upert went shopping the next morning and returned having purchased a small steamer trunk, which was delivered to his suite at the Hassler after having its entire interior fittings removed. He had called an old Roman friend and was able to take loan of one of his motorcars, a spacious and elegant Lamborghini.

The hotel restaurant prepared a picnic for four, which was placed in baskets with assorted elegant glassware and plates and cutlery and patterned linens. By noon, the car was packed. With Rupert at the wheel and Michael beside him, they set off. The day was exceptionally warm for mid-November, and the sky was a crystalline blue with occasional creamy white clouds piled up like a Tiepolo painting.

They navigated through the city to a small pensione that Rupert had known as a youth. He went inside. Nothing had changed, and for a moment, he was deluged with memories of a girl he had met in Rome and brought there when he was a stripling student at Cambridge checking out the charms of Italy. It had been the first time for both of them. He snapped back to the present, approached by a man of sturdy build wearing sunglasses, a striped shirt, and a belted brown jacket of heavy cotton corduroy. His head had been completely shaved, and he wore a large, floppy-brimmed fedora. It was Fritzi transformed. They both smiled at his new incarnation.

Michael turned and welcomed him also with a laugh as Fritzi helped Rupert remove the steamer trunk from the back seat and carried it into the pensione. Ten minutes later, the two of them carried it back and replaced it in the Lamborghini. Fritzi squeezed into the back seat beside the trunk and pulled his door closed as they drew away from the curb.

They headed northeast in the direction of Umbria. Twenty yards behind them, a little black Fiat truck had also pulled away from the curb. It had followed them from the Hassler and now continued for the next hour or so until the Lamborghini slowed before the gates of a convent on the left side of the road. The Fiat passed them by and turned into a small dirt road on the right and parked in a copse of trees. A man emerged, tall with dark brown hair cut like a medieval page. His sunglasses had perfectly round lenses, and his body was padded slightly to make him appear heavier. He carried a *Fodor's Guide to Italy*. He walked over to the convent's entrance and strolled through into the courtyard where the Lamborghini had parked. Bent slightly over the *Fodor*, he looked up occasionally to study the heavy block walls of what had once been a fortified castle. Approaching the freestanding chapel, he positioned himself where he had a clear view of the comings and goings at the wide entrance, while managing to appear more interested in the architecture of the chapel than anything else.

Some fifteen minutes later, the three men returned to the courtyard with a woman whose cheekbones were sculpted and eyes of deep blue-green were placed far apart like a basilisk. Her hair was completely hidden under a white starched hat with little wings. They opened the rear compartment of the Lamborghini and withdrew the steamer trunk, which they carried, led by the woman, down a passageway that opened into another courtyard. The tourist-plus-Fodor casually crossed the entrance yard and hurried down the passageway in time to see them turn left and carry their load into what looked like a dormitory.

He strolled around the corner of the building and saw them through a window placing the trunk in a corner of the ground-floor cell. Strolling slowly past a couple of other windows, he glimpsed more cells with their occupants' luggage as well. He came to the next staircase entrance. Stepping inside, he saw the building was bisected by a central corridor at the other end, and he caught the backs of the little group as they left the dormitory. He strode quickly back and watched the Lamborghini pull out of the entrance courtyard and turn left.

He ambled through a small group of tourists and beyond the convent gates to the little lane hiding his Fiat truck. On the passenger seat lay a green cap, which he pulled over his pageboy locks. It bore the same logo as the freight delivery service displayed on the vehicle's side panel. He checked the effect in the rear-view mirror; satisfied, he started the ignition and drove slowly back into the convent courtyard and he parked neatly and out of the way. No one seemed to pay much attention when he wheeled his upright metal carrier with an air of confident purpose through the passageway and into the cell. When he had worked the trunk onto it and wheeled his load back to the truck, he had to struggle a bit to get it up into the rear compartment.

A nun approached at the sight of his efforts. "Signore, may I know what you are doing?"

He turned, startled. An elderly face, wrinkled and wise, looked at him, skeptical under the white wings of her immaculate headgear.

He calculated with speed and responded in Italian. "Mother, Sister Solange wishes to have this trunk taken to her family in Germany. Our company's been in business for many years. I'm responsible for collecting the trunk and taking it to Berlin."

The abbess appeared alarmed by this. "How do you come to the name of this Sister Solange? No one here uses that name. You're from England I would assume, given your accent. What brings an Englishman to drive for a Roman transport service?" Her hands were tightly squeezed together, and tension had drawn her face into a frown.

He walked around to the front doors of the vehicle and extracted a delivery document that he had just now filled out before reentering the courtyard. It showed the full family name of Solange and an invented address in Berlin. Returning to the open pair of rear doors, he handed the paper to the abbess.

She was not impressed. "Sir, I must insist you wait till the owner returns before taking her property. Please remove this trunk immediately and return it to her cell."

He looked at the small group that had collected to watch. Bluster seemed to be the best offense. "I can't wait till then, Mother. I've got strict instructions to make this delivery without delay. It must be important to her German family."

She shook her head. "Not acceptable, young man. You must wait. That's all there is to it. So, please remove the trunk right now."

He glanced about the courtyard, which still had little throngs of tourists. No one appeared likely to throw up much resistance to his sudden plan. He turned and smiled at the abbess while he slammed the rear doors shut with a shuddering bang. Bolting to the left, he leaped into the driver's seat and switched on the engine. People scattered as he ground the shift stick into first gear and headed toward the gate. The abbess had gotten there ahead of him and stood in the center of his path with her arms outspread.

He swerved to his left, trying to use the space available without running full tilt into her. The right side of the van struck the determined woman and propelled her against the right-hand stone pillar and the side of the open wooden gate attached to it. She landed upon the gate with her arms still spread, appearing to hang for a moment as if from a crucifix, before she slumped to the ground.

The van careened onto the road and sped toward the north. A rumbling sound came from the van's rear compartment as the young Englishman trembled, knuckles white on the steering wheel.

♀

Long angles of afternoon November sunlight came in shafts through the creamy white clouds onto the sparkling surface of Lago de Bolsena. The remains of the Hassler's picnic delicacies lay scattered on the cloth spread over the wild grass. Three men and a woman lolled alongside on a little slope overlooking the water. A sleepy idleness pervaded them in the day's unusual warmth.

Rupert found himself dreamily focusing on the beautiful young face of Solange without her stiff novice's winged head covering. Her eyes had closed, and her breath moved the petals of a little cluster of wildflowers that he had plucked and were now clutched in her two hands. She still bore the bruises from von Vranken's angry hand. He imagined her back in Alexandria, dressed for her performance in the most ephemeral of garments. When he had placed his hand on her bare back to dance, its silk-velvet smoothness had startled him. Now, the desire to touch it once again whelmed over him like a drowning wave.

Coolness finally set in with the further descent of the sun and the beginning of evening winds that carried a chill. They rose one by one and began to collect the picnic things. On the drive back to the convent, the day's more serious matters resurfaced. Solange had laughed at Fritzi's transformation upon first seeing his completely shaven head. He had rapidly put the fedora back to cover it. The whole effect was of a raffish thug, rather than the buttoned-up, serious Nazi insider. Now, he outlined their predicament. "We've got the ark, and the cardinal is safe from Fiorelli, at least for the moment. On the other hand, I'm in permanent danger now that Fiorelli's uncovered my true identity. He's known as 'Il Duce's pope.' Was made a cardinal under pressure from Mussolini with the obvious intention of making him this pope's successor. The Nazi intelligence system clearly has gone into full search mode after events in Alexandria. Just like you, milord, they reached poor Father Stanislaus. As you described, they found my father's grave as well. In the early days, nobody did much investigating when someone joined the party. We were all hotheads, young, idealistic, and when I realized how deep was their hatred of my people, I resolved to be on the inside of my enemy's bastion. The Trojan horse, if you will, hiding someday to open the gates.

"But I was also seduced by the power we all felt. We received respect and inspired fear. Many flocked to our cries for a new Germany with honor and glory. The country was sick of being held hostage to the demeaning dictates of Versailles. So, I lived two lives at once. Strange it was. From the beginning, I became one of the Fuhrer's favorites because I always told funny stories, and I was physically strong. He admires physical strength, you see.

"So, the years passed. Yes, sometimes I wear a uniform, but my real function has long been what might be called special operations. Which brings us to today. When word got out in Berlin of Ludwig Borchardt's translation, I was sent to Alexandria. My instructions were to do everything possible to find the treasure and bring it back to Berlin. From the outset, I was never going to let Berlin come near it. I secretly make contact with Camberini and arranged to bring it to him. I could think of no one better placed to take control of its destiny and keep it out of Nazi hands, Which is just what happened as we all know. At least until last night.

"Vranken went crazy when I arrived in Alexandria with my orders. He started by feeling upstaged and burbled stuff about being a hero, maybe a field marshal, all sorts of delusions. I finally calmed him down, and we plotted the theft together. Anyway, his obsession to have the ark, believe me, means he won't relent for a moment from trying to find its trail.

"The ark should be OK now with Solange. Just another personal belonging of the convent girls who stay for a spell and then leave. But it's not the long-term solution. We've got to decide where it will be safe."

Rupert, at the Lamborghini's wheel, nodded. "Yes, it's been top of mind since we three left the Vatican last night. It might conceivably be safe in England or America. But don't forget, danger will follow it everywhere."

♀

When the Lamborghini turned into the convent's courtyard, they were stunned. Several police cars and an ambulance sat among a crowd of tourists and nuns and postulants. Their revolving lights flashed beams like tiny lighthouses on the frightened faces. A stretcher was just being loaded into the ambulance. The face of its occupant had been covered.

"Oh my God, it can't be." Solange covered her face with her hands and wept.

Fritzi put his arm around her to keep her from trembling. "What do you mean?"

"I'm sure this is all because of me … because of the treasure. I always knew that trouble would follow it here."

Rupert had an intense frown. He emerged from the car and asked a man standing close by, "Do you know what's happened?"

The man was eager to deliver tragic news. "The abbess has been run down by a fellow in a truck. He was stealing something, I think, and she tried to stop him."

"It's gone," Solange almost screamed. "I'm sure it's not in my room."

Rupert and Michael ran down the passage and dashed through the entryway to her room. Solange's pessimism was warranted. They studied to see what clues might have been left. All they found were faint tracks of sand and grit from two wheels and, efficiently, a receipt for the trunk. It lay on the bed like a taunt.

"Goddamn it!" Rupert hit a wall with his fist.

Michael was shaking his head and tensing his jaw muscles at this twist.

They hurried back to the main yard.

Fritzi stood at the rear doors of the ambulance with his arms still around Solange. She stared ahead, frozen in silence, eyes ringed with dark circles of anxiety.

Fritzi said, "They found a piece of paper with a pencil stub in the abbess's robe. She wrote down the license number and the name of the transport company that owned the truck.

Descriptions of the driver from several observers suggest someone maybe wearing a disguise."

The Lamborghini had attracted the attention of two policemen. They asked one of the nuns whose car it was, and she pointed at Rupert's group and said they had delivered the same trunk earlier in the afternoon.

The carabinieri, spiffy in well-cut uniforms and polished boots, strode over to Rupert. "*L'inglese*, signore?"

Rupert nodded. "Yes. I'm English."

"You bring trunk to this convent? Now stolen, yes?"

"You are right. We did bring a trunk here today."

The two policemen exchanged glances, and one of them asked, "So, what made someone come to steal trunk and kill old lady?"

Rupert was cautious. "Frankly, I don't believe the ancient documents contained in the trunk were the reason why the abbess was killed. It sounds to me like an accident caused perhaps by the thief's panic in trying to get away. The trunk contains some old scrolls mainly of interest to archaeologists. The thief must have imagined there was something else of greater value—or else he would not have taken such a risk."

"So, why you leave trunk in private cell of young novice?"

Rupert gave the man his most engaging smile. "Actually, signore, we just took the young lady," he gestured toward Solange in her starched white wimple, "on a picnic and planned to collect the trunk when we returned. We needed to make room in the car for her."

The carabinieri nodded. "I see. Well, we now send all stations alert to find vehicle and man who did such terrible thing. Abbess was tough old lady, but very good person. She help poor and was friend to everyone in this *cantone*. We will catch this man and make him pay for his crime."

Rupert nodded. "I'd like to help, signore. Please let me have your description of the thief and his vehicle. Give me your telephone number. I can let you know if we find any trace of the wanted man."

The carabiniere responded, "Yes, we give you this information. Now you please to show me your passport."

Rupert handed the officer his papers.

The man studied them for several minutes. He looked up, nodded, and smiled. "I see, milord, you are important person. We will send notice if we find your trunk."

Fritzi summoned the other three to follow him through the passage into the little park behind Solange's cell. They sat on two small benches facing each other. Fritzi leaned forward and said, "We must have been followed from Rome. No one else could have had the slightest idea what we were doing except going on a picnic. Somebody in Rome must have seen you, Rupert, and Michael, who perhaps recognized you at the Hassler. But who could that be who also knew you might be transporting the ark?"

"Anyone who'd seen us go to Camberini's quarters and happened to be in touch with Fiorelli." Rupert contemplated his cigarette as if for inspiration. "But that requires a degree of information unlikely in an accidental observer. Too much improbable coincidence. It boils down to this. The person who took the ark this afternoon had to have recognized our faces, knowing exactly who we were, and of our connection to the ark, and that it had been taken with us from Camberini's quarters last night."

Michael shrugged. "Sounds far-fetched such a person could even exist."

"A person who had to be familiar with the entire episodic history of the ark," Rupert said. "That narrows it down to someone connected to the von Vranken camp and the original plot to steal it. We can also deduce he'd got to have received the most recent key bit of information from Fiorelli alone sin e no one else knew this fact, either last night or this morning—that is, the ark had presumably been taken from Camberini's Vatican apartments by persons unknown except for one probably being English and called Wakely and another one Fritzi and called Brother Andreas." He stomped out his cigarette on the gravel path with his heel. "And he had to be able to deduce Wakely was me, which is something Fiorelli now could easily have assumed."

33

Several days earlier

$\mathcal{L}$othar von Vranken had reason to be worried. He'd not heard from Fiorelli in several days. His first frustrated letter to Fiorelli had simply blown off steam to an old friend after Fritzi's betrayal, which led to the loss of the treasure. He'd then gone on to describe triumphantly how he'd alerted the gestapo agent in Athens to Delacorte's imminent arrival with the brilliant result of the latter's eavesdropping on Delacorte's phone conversation at the Athens airport. And he had told the story of Fritzi's unveiling in consequence.

Now, more than anything, Lothar had but one overarching mission—to get his hands on the ark and deliver it himself to Berlin. But what about Fiorelli? After all, Lothar had by now filled him in on everything to do with the contents of the casket and its current thief. But not a word back in return. The thought had suddenly intruded like an uninvited guest crashing a party. Was his old friend Fiorelli playing his own game now? Paranoid theories began to pile up pitilessly in

Lothar's mind, fevered by his ambition. He marched to his desk. Only one thing would do now. He picked up the receiver of his telephone.

Some two hours later, Fritzi's young English cohort in stealing the casket from Caridis had appeared at Lothar's Alexandrian headquarters. Ushered into the man's impressive office by a uniformed Nazi underling, the anxious German aristo summoned him to be seated for his instructions.

"I need you now to finish the job we gave you." Von Vranken continued pacing from the windows to the fireplace and back again. "We were both betrayed by Vogel. Now we both can have our revenge. Here's your plan. You'll be flown by an official Luftwaffe pilot to the Rome airport." He stopped and put his hand on his forehead as if a moment of dizziness had gripped him. Recovering quickly, he continued, "If our deductions are correct, and these are based on very thin evidence so far, you may find the treacherous Fritzi Vogel somehow linked to the apostate Jew cardinal, Giovanni Camberini. He's the pope's secretary of state and very powerful."

He paused again to catch his breath. He had kept up his nervous pacing. "But first you must approach my old and very close friend, the famous cardinal Fiorelli. He's known, in whispers, as Mussolini's pope-in-waiting. Still, even with him, you must be careful. You see, I've kept him informed by letters and a telegram of everything to do with Fritzi and the ark. The latest being what we gleaned from overhearing Delacorte's call to his private investigator—Fritzi's possible connection to Camberini. You know, typical Jew conspiring with Jew. Yet I'm concerned. Since I explained this latest theory to Antonio, I've not had a word from him."

The young Englishman leaned forward in his chair. "If you're correct, and Fritzi's somewhere at the Vatican, then I should be able to recognize him. If this Cardinal Fiorelli has already found and unmasked him and got his own hands on the casket, I should be able to find that out."

"Exactly right. I've always trusted Antonio. I confess I'm not so sure anymore. You, I can trust. After all, you came on your own from England—like a genie with the magic words to open Aladdin's cave. You'd found clues to the combinations to his vault sent by Caridis to your father. That proves you're one of us. A true Nazi."

Orlando Delacorte, the Viscount Cressy, squirmed in his seat. "Do you think my father knows about me?"

Lothar von Vranken frowned. "No reason for him to know. As we arranged, no one here, including Fritzi, ever has had any notion of your real identity. Only the gestapo who sent you. We've reason to believe your father may be heading to Rome. We lost his trail. But if he's thinking the way Nazi headquarters in Berlin are thinking, then he would follow his own clues connecting Fritzi to Camberini."

Orlando Delacorte stared at von Vranken without seeing him. His mind had begun to race along the same lines as this driven man pacing about the room like a restless inmate of an asylum, completely preoccupied with his private fantasies. Orlando was finally catching this strange disease. The thirst for glory in the eyes of the party had gripped him as well.

It was for lesser dreams that he had come to Alexandria in the first place—after steaming open and reading the letter sent to Rupert by Michael Caridis. How could he resist impressing his Nazi control person with his report that Caridis's vault in Alexandria contained what was referred to as one of the greatest archaeological finds in history?

Attracted by the rise of the fascist movement in Britain, Orlando had fallen into the clutches of London-based recruiters for the German Nazi party. They'd had no difficulty persuading him to act as a spy on his father who figured prominently in the House of Lords. They were concerned that Ravenstone was allied with Churchill's faction in raising alarms over Germany's massive arms buildup and relentless incursions into its neighboring countries.

When he'd read aloud the Caridis letter containing clues to opening his vault in Alexandria to his primary Nazi contact and told him of his father's hasty departure, the fellow had reacted with excitement. An uncanny coincidence. He explained he'd just received word from a colleague in Berlin telling of some important archaeological events just then unfolding in Alexandria. Orlando's control agent said they could reasonably involve Caridis and Lord Ravenstone. He got back to Orlando within twenty-four hours and explained how the party put the highest value on his immediate cooperation. He must leave now for Egypt to meet with the Nazi chief in Alexandria.

Orlando's thoughts snapped back to the present moment, realizing his lapse of attention may have been noticed. He focused on von Vranken's questioning expression. "Colonel, of course I accept your charge. Indeed, with pleasure. Alexandria's airport, then, this afternoon, ready to fly at 2:00 p.m."

The German stopped his pacing and smiled. "Good. I knew you could be counted on. My recommendation of Viscount Cressy's performance to headquarters in Berlin will surely deserve to be of the highest order. If you find the treasure, contact me immediately—and I shall fly to you on the spot and bring it to the Fuhrer myself."

Orlando stood from his seat, a hint of a smile in his eyes, and extended his arm in the Nazi salute. "Heil Hitler!"

Von Vranken did the same.

34

November 1938

The carabiniere in charge of the criminal investigation came through the passage. He possessed a serious demeanor and was spotlessly uniformed. At his approach to the group seated together behind the novices' dormitory, Solange had cringed. He looked at Rupert and said, "Signore il Marchese, just now we inform International Criminal Police Commission of what happened. They send out alert to police in all countries near us. We hear description of murderer, and it sound like he wear disguise, no? Maybe we have no good idea of way he really look. Other witnesses say he is tall with thin face, young, and speak Italian with very English accent."

Fritzi looked at the policeman and then at Rupert. "Of course, that's the answer." He knocked his knuckles against his shaven head. "Damn! Why didn't this come to me sooner?"

Rupert felt the same flash of inspiration. "Was he your partner that night of the theft from Michael's vault?"

"Yes. Had to be. No other explanation. Had all the

knowledge you suggested was required—except we don't know how he might have recognized you or Michael—including last night's details."

A fearful suspicion grabbed Rupert's gut. "I think—yes, I'm afraid I may know how. What did he call himself?" Rupert eyed the German. "I should've asked before. Please, tell me what name did he give you, Fritzi?"

"Lothar von Vranken introduced him to us as William Sebastian, a British partisan of our Nazi philosophy." He shrugged. "Who knows if that was a real name?"

"Oh Christ!" Rupert collapsed back onto the bench. "Oh my God. I must have blocked this without realizing it. I'd figured it was Stephanos who'd got the combination codes." His hands started to tremble as he extracted a cigarette from his case.

With an affected calm, Michael said, "Fritzi, how did this English fellow come into the picture?"

"He was sent by our people in London, in fact, because he had the codes. Stephanos said he'd overheard Caridis give a fair number of clues to the codes, but this Britisher had the key clues to get everything right. At least that's the way I figure it. You see, he and Stephanos hit it off right away. An instant attraction. I ignored the obvious. Only interested in getting the ark from your vault and saving it from the Nazis."

Rupert shook his head. He felt a despair clutch at him like nothing he had known before. "You see, my brother's first two given names were in fact the same as the ones he used." He looked at Caridis. "And you posted the codes to me as a precaution in case something happened to you. My boy must have seen the envelope and opened it. He knew I'd dropped everything to come here when you asked me. When he read your letter, he probably connected my sudden departure for Egypt with something terribly important."

Fritzi said, "Makes sense. According to von Vranken, he was sent by our Nazi infiltrator in London. Your son must have discussed your departure and that letter with him. The rest is pretty obvious. As for me, I was sent to Alexandria because Berlin had just read Ludwig Borchardt's astonishing document—the one kept for years at the Society of the Seraphim. News traveled fast to our outliers that something major was happening in Alexandria. They needed someone from Special Forces."

Rupert looked at Michael Caridis and said, "I'm so, so sorry, old friend. About all this. It didn't have to be."

"Don't be. I should have been more careful about Stephanos. There were clues. He's been more guarded lately. Frankly, I've accepted all along that he's an opportunist through and through. Probably a promise of some sort of reward—even possibly an attraction to your boy—could have made him betray me."

The carabiniere had witnessed this exchange in silence and said, "Lord Delacorte, I think we maybe now have a real name and description of the criminal, no?"

With a resigned shrug, Rupert nodded. "I can give you details." His son had betrayed him and everything his family stood for, and now he must give information that might lead to his capture. All the love he had tried to give, in his own perhaps understated way, over the years, and the bitter rewards of ingratitude and insolence, passed through his mind. Something else struck him. The earlier, and first, Covenant of the Hebrews with their God was right now somewhere with his boy. Nothing good was going to come of this sacrilege. He smashed his cigarette under his shoe and pounded one fist into the other. "Signore, all I ask is you find my son and let me know before any German authorities can get their hands on either my boy or his cargo. Please promise me this small consolation."

"Of course, milord, we try our best."

Rupert sat with his elbows on his knees and looked up at him with the saddest eyes since they had witnessed his parents lying at the base of Aphrodite. "If you find him, please explain to anyone concerned that he must have my lawyer present. Try to keep him in Italy, I beg of you."

☥

Fritzi and Solange sat in the rear seat of the Lamborghini on its way to Rome.

Gripping the wheel, Rupert deliberately sat up straighter that usual as if to pull himself together. He glanced over his shoulder toward the two behind him. "You both should be thinking of next steps. Will you try to leave soon, maybe London, Paris, Brussels?"

Fritzi looked at Solange. "Yes, we've got to move quickly. We're marked people. We know von Vranken much too well. He'll be obsessed with revenge." He took a deep breath. "But we'll manage. We'll find a better place." His hand slipped into hers. "If you're in touch with Camberini, please tell him how much we thank him for everything. He's a saint in a vipers' nest." Fritzi stared out at the passing moonlit countryside. He turned back and said, "Rupert, your son might save himself by teaming up with von Vranken and staying in Germany. That way, he could probably avoid the international police."

"Not bloody likely to happen, teaming up. My boy's a loner. A cold fish. I'm sure he plans to do his own thing with the ark. No way he's going to let Lothar von Vranken play in his sandbox. The question is, what's next?"

"He may try to go through with the original plan on his own. Take the casket to Berlin and hope this buys him respect and protection." Fritzi leaned forward and touched Rupert on the shoulder. "Your boy's a strange one, as I think you may already know."

Rupert looked back at him in the rear-view mirror. "Has been since an infant. It seems heredity can be pretty ruthless in the tricks it plays. There's some bad blood in our family line."

"I really am sorry. It took me a little aback when he asked for details of our detention camps. Wanted to know what techniques were used to punish the enemies of the state. Seemed to be excited by the infliction of pain, especially the details." Fritzi sighed. "That was ironic, no? You see, these things were absolutely the most hateful part of my job."

Rupert squinted at the oncoming headlights. His thoughts veered back into the past. "My older brother, his uncle, tried to torture me when we were kids. The butler or a nanny would hear my screams and come to my rescue. They'd untie me and take away whatever he was hitting me with. So, when I recall finding my son breaking the limbs of frogs or strangling rabbits as a child, it was pretty obvious the sadistic strain hadn't yet run out."

Rupert took a deep breath as if to bring himself back to the present. "So, you think he'll bring the ark to the Seraphim in Berlin?"

Fritzi said, "Most likely, but I don't think you fully understand. The ark's a living thing. It's been awakened from a long sleep. It knows the difference between those with good and others with evil intentions, and it reacts. There's a mysterious force inside that box. If and when he might get it to Berlin, it's hard to imagine what could happen there."

Rupert's eyes stayed fixed on the road. He nodded. "Are you referring to what happened in Michael's vault when you first touched the ark and then Orlando did? Stephanos said the whole thing became quite agitated when my son got near it. If so, he's going to have his hands full."

35

The next day

The reckless killing of the Mother Superior made Italy's morning papers the following day. A reporter had drilled down to get details, which included a description of the steamer trunk and the novice from whose room it was taken. Cardinal Antonio Fiorelli let his paper dangle in one hand while he took a sip from a delicate porcelain demitasse of espresso and allowed his thoughts to play about this story. He noticed the motes traveling through the sunbeams that had penetrated the heavy curtains and slanted in a swathe of gold that ended at his feet. The germ of an idea had gradually shaped itself into a coherent form. He let the newspaper crumple to the floor and stood up from his throne-like armchair. His step was determined as he headed for the door.

Cardinal Giovanni Camberini looked up from the desk at the steward entering his study. "Eminence, the Cardinal Fiorelli waits in your salon and asks if you would be so kind to speak with him."

"In his case, Steward, I am rarely inclined to be kind. However, I shall see him to satisfy my curiosity." The man, faintly smiling, nodded and withdrew.

Fiorelli, examining a painting, turned around. "Ah, Giovanni, I always marvel at your good fortune to have this divine Raphael at your beck and call."

"Yes, Antonio, and I shall resist any and all efforts to reverse that good fortune. Now tell me why you're here."

"No need to be so arch with me, Giovanni, especially this early in the day." His unctuous manner and air of injured innocence added to Camberini's irritation. "Have you read the papers this morning?"

"Yes. Why?"

"Well, Giovanni, I suspect you might have a very good idea of my answer, no?"

"Not the slightest, so let's have it."

Fiorelli's eyebrows gathered in a frown. "Indeed, you shall. Having been severely beaten by your protégé, the puppy dog who followed you about for the past week, I feel entitled to make this visit. It seems he's a traitor to his country, which is a strong ally of ours, and you gave him shelter."

"I will remind you, Antonio, that 'our country' as you call it is not Italy; it's the Vatican State. So, carry on with your little diatribe to which I have a ready response when you've quite finished."

"I will. Through an impeccable source of information, it's been made quite clear you not only protected this questionable character *and* received from him stolen goods of considerable if not inestimable value. At no time did you report to His Holiness that you had in your possession a treasure of the greatest consequence to Mother Church. He would most certainly have negotiated with the proper owner to acquire this treasure and preserve it as one of the most revered objects of our faith—and of that faith that you so famously abandoned."

Camberini repressed his disgust. "Assuming such a treasure had been in my possession, the puppy dog, as you call him, would have been happy to have the treasure under the protection of Mother Church. But no such moral consistency drives you. Under your theories of rightful ownership, sending your fascist allies on the Vatican force to take it from me in the middle of the night was just fine. And not, I'm certain, with any intention of allowing to His Holiness the glory that you must have relished the thought of having come to you. In any event, this is all theoretical, isn't it? Because no such treasure exists within these Vatican precincts."

"Of course it doesn't. For the very simple reason you returned it to your puppy dog and to his concubine. He compounded his felony in abducting her from a distinguished member of our closest ally's aristocracy, one Lothar von Vranken. And I shall carry my deductions several steps further. One must conjecture that the novice described in this morning's story was the very same concubine. Do I detect your fine hand in placing her in that convent? It's come to my attention, Giovanni, she's a member of the Jewish faith and not even a convert, which makes this all the more puzzling.

"I won't even dignify this conjecture with a response. What else do you have to say? Why are you really here?"

Fiorelli smiled. "Because I want us both to find the person who stole the treasure, which I am sure was in the steamer trunk reported this morning. My sources have provided me with descriptions of two visitors to your quarters who were with you the day of my beating by your puppy dog. Their descriptions conform exactly to two gentlemen who happened to dine in my apartments only recently. England's wealthiest lord and an aesthete from Alexandria, a Greek known for his collection of antiquities and the person responsible for finding the treasure. My German friend tells me he believes the thief who killed the Mother Superior was none other than the son of our English marquess. Now, you look more than a little surprised, Giovanni."

"I see. So, you think I'll help you find this treasure because your Englishman may have the key to finding his son—and I'm the key to the Englishman."

"Exactly. You've always been clever and quick, Giovanni."

"Well, Antonio, let me react to your novel proposal. You and the pontiff are not exactly on the side of the angels. It's well-known you're his practically anointed successor, if Italy's totalitarian buffoon has any say in the matter. It doesn't take much deep reasoning to conclude the original Covenant would be a fascist tool against the Jews. Why? And how? I will tell you. From the altar of Saint Peter's would come the pronouncement: 'See now the truth about the Jews. Not only did they kill Christ—they murdered the man they call Moses because he really wasn't a Jew at all. He was a brown-skinned Egyptian called Akhenaten.' Now guess what? To cover up their crime, they installed a humble Jewish scribe, who was in service to the great pharaoh, as the Father of Israel and their great lawgiver. All this, therefore, is yet another example of why the Jews are anathema."

Fiorelli smiled. "My, my, Giovanni. How paranoid you sound. So, that's why you were so reluctant to share the Covenant with Mother Church. You've lost faith in her goodness. Like a hybrid plant that sometimes reverts to the flowers and leaves of its original rootstock, you've gone back to being a Jew. Well, your fears are groundless. Come to grips with reality. We're living in a new age where demagogues are seducing the masses. Vatican City sits right in the path of this totalitarian comet sweeping through Europe. If we're seen to be an obstacle, we could be swept away in a cosmic flash."

Camberini shook his head. "No, no, Antonio. You really miss the whole point. Ambition has clouded if not disabled your moral compass. Remember, our Christ died because he was a willing sacrifice to redeem mankind from its sins. You're saying we must go along with the great evil that is being released by Hitler and Mussolini and Franco. On the contrary, I'm insisting the church stand up to evil even at the risk of its temporary destruction. Goodness is profound, and evil is shallow. In the end, we will triumph."

Fiorelli played with his rosary beads. His face had become flushed, his voice somewhat hoarse. "It seems I can't reason with you. Don't you see if we don't find the man who's got the ark, he'll be captured by the enemies whom you decry, and the ark will end up in Berlin. Just think for a moment, wouldn't you rather have it in Rome?"

"What difference does it make, Antonio? In either case, it will be used against the Jews who are already being rounded up and expropriated and killed or put in detention camps. I would rather hide the ark until this comet as you call it has burned itself out. And I assure you it will, in time."

Fiorelli stood up abruptly, anger showing in every movement. "You Jews are all the same. High and mighty with words and ready to exploit every angle. I don't know what you've got to gain by not being my partner in finding the ark, but something must be brewing in that conniving mind. I'll be keeping my eye on you, Giovanni. Don't make a false step. Anyway, the future belongs to me and my kind. Yours? Well look at history. Your kind have always provoked persecution. With good reason, I must add."

Camberini laughed. "Ah. So, easy to bring out your true colors, Antonio. I'm surprised how quickly your sophistry collapses. Let me give you a warning. I'm not making a deal with this devil I know or any other. But your fate, whatever it may be, will be one of utter and complete loneliness. You've no faith, Antonio. God and Christ aren't your friends and your spiritual companions. Only power moves you, and the hunger for it will consume your soul and leave you frightened and empty, staring into the chasm."

After his enemy had stormed out in a black cloud, Camberini addressed a letter to Ravenstone Park. He poured some wax on the flap and pressed his signet ring into it. Next, he asked the operator to connect him to his friend in the Roman police force. "Captain, I've got a big request to make of you. Have you read the papers this morning?"

"Yes, Your Eminence. Why do you ask? Of course, I'll be pleased to help you any way I can."

The cardinal leaned back in his chair and looked up at the clouds and cherubs painted on the ceiling. "Lorenzino, it seems a Mother Superior was wantonly run over yesterday."

"Indeed, a tragedy."

"Certainly that. She was a good servant of the Lord and the church. I've reason to believe the person who did this is a young Englishman. The steamer trunk mentioned in the article is of some concern to me. I think the article made clear the crime happened because he was stealing this object. I am asking you to do everything you can to find this person and to retrieve the contents of that steamer trunk and let me know immediately that happens."

"I see, Eminence. Interesting, I must say. You're now the third party to make a similar request. The first was an all-department alert sent to every force in the country, to find this person and bring that steamer trunk to headquarters in Rome. The second came earlier this morning from the Vatican. I'm sure you're more than able to guess who was behind that call."

Camberini frowned. "All right, then. Please consider mine the most important of the three. To some extent, Lorenzino, our very civilization depends on that object not getting into the wrong hands. I hope you'll keep that point to yourself. It is critical."

"Of course, Eminence. As you can imagine, this is going to be a little complicated, but I'll do everything in my power to find the Englishman and bring the steamer trunk to you."

"Once again, you have my blessings, Lorenzino. I and the good Lord thank you.

36

November 1938

*L*othar von Vranken's mind wandered as he looked from the window of the Luftwaffe plane at the island of Sicily below. Smoke curled up from the volcanic craters of Aetna off to the right. It was early afternoon when they landed in Palermo for refueling. He disembarked and strolled over to the terminal. When he entered the office of the airport superintendent, the man stood up and saluted the Nazi colonel dressed in full uniform. The man's desk was covered with papers in such chaos it made von Vranken wrinkle his nose at this typical evidence of the legendary wantonness of Italians everywhere.

"Superintendent, please assure my plane will be refueled and able to leave as soon as possible for Rome. Must make it before sundown."

"Of course, Colonel. May I have some coffee brought for you?"

"Yes. Give me the latest news. First, weather conditions in Rome?"

"Cool, but clear skies for landing."

"Headlines?"

The Italian rummaged for his afternoon paper. "Ah, here it is. Let's see. Il Duce and the Fuhrer are planning to meet again soon. No date given. They speak of common goals and friendship, and now that Austria's part of the German empire, the border with Italy in the northeast is 'unchangeable,' according to Berlin." He looked at the Nazi colonel. "I hope that's true for the future. What do you think?"

Von Vranken smiled and waved his hand as if to dismiss any doubt. "Of course, of course. Our two nations share a common destiny. We're partners in a great enterprise. I'm sure the Fuhrer has been making this very clear to Il Duce. Now, anything else of importance? I don't read Italian, so give me a quick rundown."

When the Italian got to the news item about the hit-and-run event at the convent, von Vranken's attention became riveted. "You say the driver was stealing a steamer trunk? Do they say why? Anything about its contents and a description of the driver?"

The superintendent translated aloud the entire article. Its bottom line was speculation the fugitive was probably a young Englishman. "He was wearing what appeared to be a disguise. No one believes they have a good description of the real person except his youth, that he was rather tall, and spoke Italian with an unmistakable British accent. A major manhunt has been ordered through the International Criminal Police Commission, the ICPC. The Italian authorities have expressed confidence they'll capture the fugitive before he's got a chance to cross any borders."

"I see." Von Vranken showed a sudden change of mood. He seemed to forget the other man existed until he finally said,

"Where's the telephone? I need privacy for an important call to Berlin."

Twenty minutes later, the little Arado Ar 96 was back in the air, and by late afternoon, they were flying low toward the city. The plane's shadow moved like a large dragonfly across the Colosseum and ancient Forum below before alighting at Ciampino Airport.

Von Vranken strode rapidly to the waiting Mercedes sent from the embassy and urged the driver to make the Vatican with all speed. He recalled the useful word and kept on repeating "Pronto" to the Italian chauffeur struggling with Rome's evening traffic.

Upon being ushered into Cardinal Fiorelli's apartments, the sight of Fiorelli standing in the middle of the grand salon sent a shock of dismay through the German. The cardinal was shaking his head, and his hands had spread out in an attitude of exaggerated helplessness.

Lothar von Vranken figured him in a flash. The longstanding friend of his skiing youth had always been unable to dissimulate with him. Yes, Tonio possessed the arrogance, self-assurance, smooth Jesuitical logic to deflect most suspicions that others, less perceptive, might have about his intentions. What Lothar knew with certainty was that Cardinal Antonio Fiorelli was not going to be his trusted partner in a race to retrieve the treasure.

Lothar had the advantage. He'd always been a gambler. His call to Berlin from Palermo was his bet, a toss of the dice, which, if correct, would give him at least some chance of success. So, he would now dangle some red herrings before Fiorelli.

"Ah, Tonio, we've deduced the driver who killed the Mother Superior was in fact the fellow I sent to you, Orlando Delacorte, to find the Jew Fritzi. It seems he too has gone rogue. So, what will he do with it? Sell for a fortune? No, he's too rich already. Will he want to use it for personal power? If so, how would that work?"

Fiorelli allowed his imagination to play with the question. When he gave voice to some theories, Lothar encouraged him into wild-goose chases.

Meanwhile, in the back of Lothar's mind, revenge continued to fester. Those two. Treacherous Jews. He should have known. Every time he thought of Fritzi Vogel stealing both his mistress and his treasure from under his very nose, the upsurge of fury could hardly be contained. He would find them, and he would capture them, the way he was going to find and deliver the Seraphim treasure. And how exquisite would be his pleasure when he delivered the particular punishment he had in mind.

37

1914 and 1938

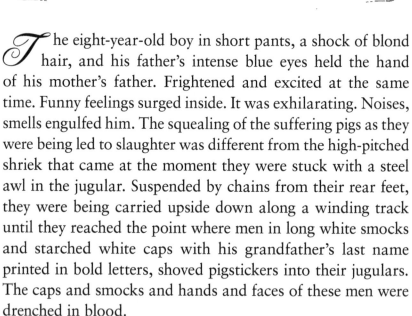

he eight-year-old boy in short pants, a shock of blond hair, and his father's intense blue eyes held the hand of his mother's father. Frightened and excited at the same time. Funny feelings surged inside. It was exhilarating. Noises, smells engulfed him. The squealing of the suffering pigs as they were being led to slaughter was different from the high-pitched shriek that came at the moment they were stuck with a steel awl in the jugular. Suspended by chains from their rear feet, they were being carried upside down along a winding track until they reached the point where men in long white smocks and starched white caps with his grandfather's last name printed in bold letters, shoved pigstickers into their jugulars. The caps and smocks and hands and faces of these men were drenched in blood.

After the kill and the terminal screams, the pigs continued to squirm for a while, spurting blood in all directions on their way to being skinned and dismantled into numerous parts and pieces.

The little boy looked up at his grandfather before he leaned over and vomited his breakfast onto the blood-puddled floor.

The big man, with his silver hair swept back on the sides of a strong, handsome face, looked down and broke into a loud laugh. "Now that you've been baptized, my boy, shall we go?"

The boy wiped his mouth with the sleeve of his little smock and smiled back. "No, Grandpa, I feel better now. I want to see some more."

He'd never forgotten that smell of raw life and death that emanated from the Chicago Stockyards. Feces and blood and guts mingled with the smells of burning fur and tanning tanks. It was diabolical, powerful, disgusting, horrible, and incredibly compelling. All this was at the basis of the fortune his father had married into when he left England at the age of twenty-three.

His father had loved his job as a popular and underpaid schoolteacher at Eton. However, the lure of adventure grabbed him, and he left England to start afresh in the New World. Within a year of his arrival in America, he had the good fortune to fall deeply in love with the daughter of one of Chicago's great meatpacking barons. Within two years, they produced a girl and this boy.

Later that same summer, which had seen the eight-year-old boy's baptism into the sanguine mysteries of his American family's abattoir, also witnessed the boy's first visit to his English great-grandmother who lived in the charming dowager's cottage on the family's fabled Wiltshire estate. She welcomed him with an immense hug, and for the next days, she told him stories about his father who had come to stay with her at the same age, albeit for much sadder reasons.

The boy spent hours exploring this new terrain, spreading miles around an ornamental lake, and he loved to delve deep into woods that covered the sides of long, sloping hills. It happened on a late August afternoon when he'd been chasing a rabbit and some colorful birds fluttering in and out among the trees. Damp smells of dark brown soil and rich mulch paving the ground beneath the endless trees, enchanted him— as did the caressing coolness beneath the towering oaks after the shimmering warmth of open meadows. When he heard footsteps scrunching on the mulch some distance away, he slowed down his antic running and hid behind a tree. Someone came into view and disappeared and then reappeared as if he were on a search.

Orlando saw the rifle in his left hand. Was the man going to shoot at any of the animals he had been chasing? Was he in danger of being mistaken for one himself? The boy wondered whether to call out or simply hide. For the moment, he felt safer doing the latter. As he drew closer, Orlando thought how like his own father he looked. Similar eyes and hair and build, but no naval-cut beard, which his father had just adopted.

The man stopped, looked around, and tilted his head up at the high canopy of branches and leaves. He leaned the rifle against a tree and walked over to a notch between a tree trunk and a branch. He extended his hand at eye level into the notch as if to check it out. Apparently satisfied, he walked deliberately over to collect his rifle. He anchored its butt in the notch so that it rested there securely. He put himself, with feet spread slightly apart, at the open end of the rifle barrel and aimed it into his mouth. His left hand reached out to feel the trigger. He rested his left thumb in the trigger guard so that its padded tip gently touched the trigger. For a moment, his eyes rose up again to the intricate vaulting of branches and leaves through which some rays of sunlight were penetrating in long shafts, one of which suddenly touched the top of his head and made it glow as if a golden light had been turned on inside. His left thumb tensed.

It seemed that all the birds in creation scattered to the winds at the explosion. The boy tiptoed slowly over to the tree where the rifle had tumbled from the notch and was lying between the spread legs of the body, which had been blown backward and lay splayed upon the forest floor. The eyes were intact and stared upward as if amazed. Blood began to trickle from its mouth.

Little Orlando stood above the body for a long time. He had never seen a dead man before. He lingered in its rather cool, almost detached contemplation and noticed where the pool of blood, spreading in the dead leaves under the ruined head, had touched the edge of his shoe. Finally, he released himself and ran through fields and over small bridges to the dower cottage and appeared before his great-grandmother with the news. His description of the man left her in no doubt that she had lost her only son a quarter century before—and now one of his sons, both by their own hands.

The deep sockets into which her ancient eyes had sunk began to fill with tears. She gestured for the little boy to kneel beside her so she could wrap her arms around him. Her silent grief was almost unnerving. With one hand, she pressed the back of his head so that his face lay in the crook of her shoulder. He would never forget the musty smell.

Driving through the Italian countryside along small, deserted roads, he couldn't shake the feeling he had today killed that loving and needy old lady of his early youth. The trembling in his arms and hands gradually subsided, helped in part by the simple activity of operating the truck.

Darkness wrapped itself around him. With a nervous motion, he snapped back to the present, realizing he could barely make out the road. He flicked on the headlights. Which way to go without finding himself winding in circles and ending up in the middle of a town? There was much to do, and he had to be calm to think straight. First, get rid of this truck without leaving a trace and take whatever new means of transport he might turn up. The best place to abandon it would be deep in a forest or submerged in a lake.

Then there was that damned noise, the rattling of the trunk on the metal floor in the back of the truck. At times, he thought he could make out voices. Whispering and suffering sounds would sometimes flow from the steamer trunk as if it housed supernatural creatures. That was not going to be helpful. How was he going to get all the way to Berlin with this temperamental baggage capable of betraying him at any moment? The journey would take a number of days to complete. And he had two borders to navigate—Italy to Austria and Austria to Germany—where anything could happen.

That night, he drove where his instincts and the occasional road sign took him. At about two o'clock in the morning, he passed through a sleeping village and stopped near some woods about half a mile beyond. Burying the truck in a copse some distance off the road, he let his exhaustion take over. After locking the doors, he curled up on the front seat and fell into a nightmare-ridden sleep.

By six in the morning, he was awake. Changing out of his disguise, he became the slim, fair-haired young man he was, dressed like a traveling student with a backpack and a stick. He needed a map and to find a certain train station. And a crate for the ark, not the steamer trunk. Something with screened openings, which he could say were for air for small, noisy creatures that he was transporting to a Berlin experimental laboratory.

By nine in the morning, he had walked into the nearby village with his backpack. There he acquired a makeshift crate, which a cooperative carpenter modified for him with some opaque screening framed at one end. Having purchased a map, he looked about for an old and dilapidated vehicle to buy. After several minutes of walking about and wondering if he needed to come up with another solution, he spied a fellow parking an old run-down car outside a feedstore. When he proposed a sum well beyond its value to the elderly farmer, the latter was delighted to take full advantage.

He drove back to the copse where the truck was hidden. With some difficulty, he transferred the ark from the steamer trunk into the crate and screwed down the cover. Grabbing the crate's rope handles, he hauled it over to the car's rear compartment. With a length of rope, he tied the trunk lid tight down as far as he could on top of the crate and to the bumper. Ungainly and typical of a poor farmer transporting something in a jalopy.

He left the car hidden in the trees and drove the little van deeper into the woods, skirting dead branches and rugged boulders. When he came to a ravine, his heart pounded as he recognized the opportunity at hand. He got out and searched for the best spot. At a curve in the ravine, it seemed to be deeper than the rest. He threaded the truck through several trees until he reached an unobstructed edge near the curve.

After aiming the wheels and setting the gear stick in neutral, he got out, closed the door, and reached through the rolled-down driver's side window to steer as he pushed until a last mighty heave tipped it over the edge and started its pell-mell course through small rocks and brush down to rest on its side in a small crater. He looked about and found enough dead branches, which he dragged and pushed over on top of the truck. To notice it now would require someone to come to the edge of the ravine and fix their attention on that spot beneath the array of broken tree limbs. As he trudged back to his car, he prayed no one would stray that far into the woods before he was well away.

38

Back in Rome

upert parked the Lamborghini before the pensione where Fritzi had emerged that morning. While Michael was wishing them well, Rupert studied Solange. Desire and regret flooded over him. He felt a premonition of loss, all not going to go well for her.

Fritzi held out his hand. "Milord, you're an extraordinary man. Keep on warning your colleagues in Britain about the menace here. Time's not on your side. The Fuhrer meant nothing when he signed that pledge with the pathetic Chamberlain. Nothing. If your boy reaches Berlin with the ark, they might well celebrate him as a hero." He shook his head. "But they could throw him to the wolves because von Vranken is upset at being upstaged by him in bringing the treasure on his own. Or they might want just to punish you. So, save your son and the ark from their clutches. But don't let them trap you by making fantastical charges of interfering in their dealing with Orlando. You're their enemy, their outspoken critic in your

Parliament. They might be happy to find a reason to detain you as well—or worse."

Showing the steely side of his British nature, Rupert nodded and smiled with a shrug. "Thanks for that. Now, your business is to save Solange, both of you. If the Italians get hold of you, they're certain to turn you over to the Nazis. Anything to curry their senior partner's favor."

Solange nodded. "That would be unspeakable."

Rupert said, "I know." Their eyes connected for a telling moment. He said, "Godspeed you both to safety, and if you somehow make it to England, please find me and let me know." He took Solange in his arms. "Such a good and beautiful soul." He kissed her with tenderness on the cheek. Then he hugged Fritzi and patted his back.

He and Michael drove in thoughtful silence on to the Hassler where the concierge handed them a message. "Mr. Wakely's friend would like to have another interview. Please contact at the earliest." No signature.

☥

Sitting in Giovanni Camberini's private study, the two men noticed their host's hesitation to form his words. His fingertips touched, and his heavy brows were pulled together. Finally, he said, "I cannot tell you, Lord Delacorte, how serious is the crime done by your son."

"So, you've learned this already, Your Grace. Yes, a terrible, awful thing. Did you know the good lady?"

"Indeed, I delivered the German woman to her because I knew she'd protect her from my enemies here. But how were we to divine the intervention of your son, of all creatures? What could be a motive for taking the ark from his own father?"

Rupert felt for the first time in his life the burden of sin.

Partly for the sins of his boy—and also the quirky reverse. For the bad blood that had found its way into his son's veins. "I must take some blame, Your Grace, for being the vessel that passed this on to him. I am so sorry." He paused and cleared his throat. "It seems my son's fallen into the clutches of British fascists sympathetic to the Nazi party. A chain of circumstances hard to imagine ever happening, in fact did happen. I'm convinced he's set on taking the ark to the devil himself."

"You mean to Berlin?"

"I do."

"So, how can we stop this? Can you, Lord Rupert, knowing your son, imagine his next steps?

Rupert asked, "May I light a cigarette, Your Grace? And if so, would you join me?"

Camberini smiled. "Yes to both."

Through a swirl of bluish smoke, Rupert touched on the psychological peculiarities of the man he had spawned. "Given all that background, Cardinal, you will see how Orlando is clever and resourceful—and self-indulgent with the means to plot whatever mischief might beguile him at the moment. Of course, he'll continue to be hunted down, and this may finally stop him in his tracks. One thing is certain: he'll do anything to fulfill his malign obsessions."

"If you're right, he'll probably try for the Austrian border."

"He might well." Rupert touched a hand to his forehead. "We both want the ark to come back to the right hands. I must also confess, I want even more badly to prevent my boy from arriving in Berlin and becoming ensnared, if you will, by that diabolical machine. He committed a terrible act by killing the Mother Superior. He panicked. And he should pay for that. But what I see for him in Berlin is worse. By far. They could capture and consume his soul. He'd become someone else. My son will have died."

Camberini reached over and held his forearm. "Milord, I hesitate to say, but it could already be too late. Your son may have reached that point—even without Berlin. He may have abandoned long ago, or perhaps never possessed, what we call a soul. This sounds terrible. But there are such people in this world, and these days, as I've heard you English say, they're coming out of the woodwork like termites. A new age is dawning for the soulless."

Rupert stared into space, his eyes flat and bleak, and he remained silent for some time until he flinched. The cigarette had burned itself into his finger.

39

November 1938

O
ut in the distance, Venice's bell towers and domes glinted in the sunlight across the azure lagoon. Orlando parked in the crowded lot next to the railroad station. He walked to the rear of the jalopy and untied the rope holding down the lid of the trunk compartment in which the crate was resting. He dragged it out and placed it on the ground. Closing the lid of the trunk compartment, he turned the pitted chrome handle to secure it. Looking about, he found some dead weeds, which he draped from the handle to obscure the license plate.

It took some minutes to drag the crate over to the entrance of the station where he nodded to a bicycle taxi. Soon he stood on the landing where a water taxi was just arriving. Speeding across the broad reaches of the lagoon, the breeze felt cool on his face and ruffled his hair. Stress began to drain away like the widening wake of the motorboat. Fear suddenly loosened its grip and gradually was replaced by anticipation of what was to come. For the first time, he was relaxed enough to take stock of those recent surprises, and a new feeling surged within. He was suffused with a new sense of power. It was like a revelation out there on the sunlight-sparkling waves. Yes, he was becoming a master of his own fate, not its pawn. The adrenaline rush made his throat tingle along with the back of his neck. He laughed out loud against the winds.

They arrived at a palazzo on the Grand Canal, not far from the Rialto. The driver helped him place the crate on the little quay recessed deep into the base of the palazzo. A gondola rocked gently next to the stone dock. It was carved and gilded on its elaborate bow and stern. Several feet away, a broad staircase led up to the interior of the palazzo. Next to it was a booth where the boatman might wait until called upon to navigate either the gondola or the motorboat docked beside it.

Orlando pushed the crate into the booth and closed the door. He ran up the steps to a magnificent space crowned by Tintoretto-painted vaults and filled with statuary on many-colored marble pedestals. His footsteps resonated, and he could almost hear himself breathing. "Delphine," he called out as he looked into several smaller rooms.

At the front, with five tall windows overlooking the Grand Canal, there was a salon that was even more rococo than the entrance hall. Heavy satin brocade draperies cascaded the twenty feet from their massive mahogany rods in a riot of golden tassels and fringes. The furniture was massive, carved to excess with animals' heads, bodies, and feet, gilded and contorted.

A pale arm reached up from the back of a sofa facing one of the two opposing fireplaces surmounted by towering mirrors. The graceful forefinger of the hand beckoned him forward. He hurried to the other side of the sofa and found her lying back among its immense cushions, dressed only in a black leather G-string and holding a glass in her other hand.

She had a boyish body, taut, muscular, firm, uplifted breasts, small but perfectly formed. She shook her silky black pageboy hair so that it rippled deep blue highlights from the chandelier overhead. "My naughty, naughty boy. Come to Mama."

He knelt beside her and placed his head between her legs. She reached around and patted his bottom with little slaps. "I'm superior to the mother you ran over, aren't I?"

"Yes, Mama." His voice was muffled.

40

November 1938

Rupert slapped the arm of his chair and stood abruptly. "Now I really must go, Your Eminence. Something quite obvious struck me. Just could be a chance to intercept Orlando before he might leave Italy."

Camberini straightened up, alert. "I see. Perhaps I can help?"

Rupert shook his head and gave a sad smile. "You see, my son's, shall we say, rather different. He's got bizarre tastes—and the means to slake them. One day last August, my private secretary came with an accounting of Orlando's expenses. I normally never look over these things, but my chap thought I should. You see, rather substantial gifts, including money, were being transferred to a woman in Venice. A young woman, shall we say quite known for her exotic sexual proclivities. Known also, it must be said, because she comes from one of Italy's oldest noble families."

Camberini interrupted him with a sly smile. "Which indeed never rules out bizarre proclivities as we both know."

"Of course it doesn't," Rupert pulled out his cigarette case and snapped it open before the cardinal.

Camberini shook his head and gestured. "But please, come here and sit down again. Let's see what we can do."

Rupert continued to stand, facing him, intense and serious. "It's possible Orlando's got other bolt-holes to hide in Italy, and he might even choose not to go to Berlin at all—but not bloody likely. I know this boy. He's a creature fixated when his mind grabs onto something. For example, his mad obsession with the political movement in England whose folks strut about in their fencing shirts, singing fascist anthems and scaring little children. Or in this instance, recovering the ark and taking it to today's high altar of fascism."

"So, you suspect this woman in Venice could be just the place for him to hide for a few days instead of racing across borders to Berlin?"

"Yes, I mean just that. He's an arrogant, spoiled young monster. That's just his sort of arrogant indulgence, flaunting danger. So, I pray we find some understanding police types and have a look. This is where your contacts could be helpful, Eminence."

Camberini had already picked up a telephone. After he gave the number, he waited with eyes veiled until suddenly snapping alert. "Capitano? My dear Lorenzino, I've got a specific request tonight. It relates to our earlier conversation today. Ah, I'm so pleased you're anxious to hear it. Well, it's somewhat speculative. We think there could be a place in Venice where our quarry may have tried to drop out of circulation for a while. Just a suspicion. It actually comes from someone who knows him quite well. What can you do to help us here?"

After several minutes without speaking, except for a few reassuring sounds, Camberini said, "I see. All right, then, Lorenzino, we'll proceed. My friend will come to see you tomorrow morning at eight, and you can execute the plan together. Thank you, and again, God bless you. Good night."

Camberini turned to Rupert. "I'll give you where to meet Lorenzino. He's ready to move early tomorrow. By late afternoon or early evening, the two of you should be in Venice. Lorenzino's most grateful to you for suggesting the Venetian connection. If he's successful, it will be a big feather in his bonnet—or whatever you British say. In the meantime, he's alerting the police there to follow any clues they've got. An old car was bought from a farmer in a village to the northeast of Rome the day after the incident. The buyer sounds like Orlando."

Rupert frowned. "If we find the boy, will your captain keep him rather than giving him to the Blackshirts?"

"Milord, I really can't say what the fascist thugs will do. I can tell you Lorenzino will jealously guard his prey if he's successful in finding your Orlando."

They embraced as he departed the cardinal's quarters.

The churchman said, "Be brave, my friend. May God give you strength."

Back at the Hassler, he was handed a message from Elizabeth. He'd asked the housekeeper to have her call him. He dreaded having to give her his news.

41

November 1938

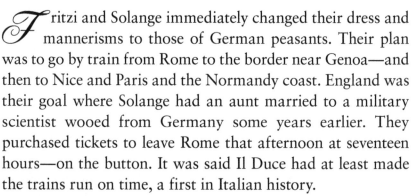

*F*ritzi and Solange immediately changed their dress and mannerisms to those of German peasants. Their plan was to go by train from Rome to the border near Genoa—and then to Nice and Paris and the Normandy coast. England was their goal where Solange had an aunt married to a military scientist wooed from Germany some years earlier. They purchased tickets to leave Rome that afternoon at seventeen hours—on the button. It was said Il Duce had at least made the trains run on time, a first in Italian history.

Lothar von Vranken left his old friend in his Vatican apartment with a slap on the back and a litany of red herrings to worry over. Berlin was pointedly not included in any of his hinted destinations for the young Britisher. He strode through the Vatican City gates and out into the Roman traffic. Face flushed, he was already seething again with rancor over his pivotal deception by the redheaded Jew traitor whom he was ready to throttle with his own hands. And now to have the junior Delacorte make mincemeat of his plans was really too much.

He arrived a quarter hour later by taxi at the gestapo headquarters in Rome. One of the helpful gestures the toadying Mussolini had made to the Fuhrer was to provide a rather elegant palazzo to the Nazi government for their embassy and several other of their more secret government organizations stationed in Italy.

Vranken marched up the stairs without a word to the receptionist and barged into the ambassador's outer office. "Is he here, Fraulein?"

The assistant stood up and pushed back the hair from the side of her face. "May I know who is calling?" She was visibly unsettled by his aggressiveness.

"Just say it's Graf von Vranken."

"Of course, your honor."

He paced about until she opened the door and ushered him into her boss's office. With a little curtsy, she closed it behind him.

"Yes, Lothar, what can I do for you. Here, have a seat. A cigar perhaps?" The diplomat had come from the old regime. He was one of Vranken's class and rather less fanatical about the current ruling faction. With a small giggle, he continued, "Oh, sorry, I sometimes forget." He flopped his arm out over the desk. "Heil Hitler."

Vranken jerked his hand up and repeated the formula in a mumble. "Now, Georg, I've got something to ask you."

"Yes, so what is it? You look hesitant."

"Don't worry. That I am not. Anything but hesitant. It's only that I'm asking you to take several shots in the dark. You see, I've been betrayed by someone who's a threat to our party and to our nation. He has abducted my mistress as well. I want him brought to justice, in Berlin. He's stolen a priceless asset, one of the greatest prizes imaginable, which I had destined for the Fuhrer. I think the traitor's still here in Rome, or if not, I'd guess heading for the French border. Probably by train, bus, or car. I want you to post the secret service—in as large a force as you can muster—to check all trains and motor vehicles that stop at Ventimiglia before they cross over into France. Do this starting immediately and keep it up for at least two or three days if we don't get results sooner."

"Interesting, Lothar. I assume this is not just a private vendetta but can be justified by a genuine raison d'etat?"

"Come on, Georg. Of course, it can be justified. These are traitors. They should be executed."

The ambassador lifted his cigar up in the air and said, "All right, then. How tall, what kind of build, general impression, and all that sort of thing to help us identify what we're meant to be looking for?"

"Ah, yes, I do have a photo of the woman." He withdrew from his pocket a folded picture that had appeared in a brochure for the nightclub where Solange had danced. "Here, see this? Maybe you can have some kind of sketches made for others to use. I will write down their names, and I can give you a description of the man as well. He's assumed a disguise, quite ridiculous because it almost makes him more identifiable. We got his newly created description from the Italian police who've just investigated an incident where he had been present."

The ambassador unfolded the picture and smiled. "Ah, Lothar, now I know why this is a matter of national import. We can hardly let a creature of this beauty escape, can we? Both a traitor and a national treasure, I assume."

"Cut the sarcasm, Georg. Get to the point. Will you do this for me?"

"Of course, Lothar, my old friend and fencing mate. Fear

not. We've infiltrated Italy with more of our people than even you realize. This can be handled rather efficiently, I believe. At least by our side. We won't rely much on the Italians, I'm afraid. But no matter."

"Thank you, Georg. Be quick, please. Time's of the essence here. They could already be on their way to the border."

The ambassador sat up straight, put down his cigar, and turned on the speaker to his assistant. "Fraulein, send the gestapo chief up or his next in command. I need both of them, in fact." He looked over his glasses. "The plan will now be launched, and by this evening, Ventimiglia will be a dragnet. These people will find it almost impossible to get through if that's actually where they'll be trying to escape."

☥

Solange could not hide her agitation. She paced the station floor back and forth before the large board suspended above giving arrival and departure times and track numbers for the trains. Theirs was leaving for Ventimiglia in only forty-five minutes.

Some miles away, in a run-down neighborhood marked by dirty, narrow streets and tenements, Fritzi stood tapping his nails impatiently. They made a little clatter on the glass showcase that served as a counter for the sale of pistols and rifles and shotguns. He stared about the walls. Several firearms hung along with four stuffed animal heads that were far from their original condition in life or the taxidermist's art. He called through the partly closed door. "Giuseppe, what's the matter? I've got a train to catch. Come on, you've got all the information and the photographs. Hurry up!

"Hold your horses, I'm printing your new name right now. Don't forget who you are as of this afternoon, Herr Joachim

Sartorius. Your lady companion's is already done. Now let me concentrate."

Fritzi turned and walked toward the front door with the thought of breathing in some of the crisp autumn air. As he opened it, two men in Blackshirt uniforms appeared it seemed out of the blue sky. They looked at him with an impatient smirk and practically pushed him aside in order to enter the little shop.

Fritzi tried to appear relaxed as he sauntered back to one side of the counter. "I say, Giuseppe, you've got some customers. Is my little pistol ready yet?"

Slightly muffled, he said, "Yes, yes, Joachim, your things are all wrapped." Within a couple of minutes, a hunched-over man in his sixties emerged like a troll from the rear. He walked to the end of the counter where Fritzi stood and laid a package wrapped in newspapers on the counter.

One of the Blackshirts with a bull neck, small hands, and tiny ears said, "You have a permit for this pistol?"

Giuseppe said, "Of course. The permit was shown to me, and everything is the way it should be. Now, gentlemen, may I be of service to you?"

The pair of thugs took a last look at Fritzi and turned their attention to Giuseppe.

Fritzi had twenty minutes to make the train. He clutched the precious package, and his adrenaline pumped as he bolted after a taxi that appeared to be unoccupied. Diving into it, he glanced over his shoulder at the two thugs standing outside the shop and looking his way.

What he did not see was their return to confront the elfin proprietor. One of them grabbed him by the shirtfront and shoved his big head into the man's face. "Give us the name of that fellow right now. And we want his real name."

The little man tried to smile and retorted, "Joachim

Sartorius. A German chap. Wants to do target practice with his pistol."

The thug stretched his lips against his teeth. "If you're lying, we'll be back." He signaled to his companion. "Come on. Let's go make our report." They slammed the door, and one of the stuffed stag heads dropped to the floor.

Solange stood tense at the gated entrance to the platform where their train was about to leave. Her eyes were so worried that passersby were tempted to ask what was wrong. Conductors had begun calling out their last warnings to board.

Just then, Fritzi appeared out of the crowd, running at full tilt. Out of breath, he practically lifted her up into the train and swung up and in himself as the starting whistle sounded twice. The sleek engine's steam blew up into the elaborate steel vaults covering the platform, scraping metal sent sparks that smelled of ancient fire, and a chorus of clanging joints was raised as the railcars, one by one, were jerked into motion.

42

November 1938

"We're alone, my dear. All alone for three days and nights. No servants, no callers. Our world is sealed and safe. You must relax and concentrate. This is a special moment for me."

Orlando studied Delphine, curious, as he rose from his knees next to the sofa. "How special?" He stretched his arms and back and walked over to a table with a tray of bottles. He took the stopper out of a decanter and was about to pour when she interrupted him.

"Be careful, my darling. Absinthe. Of course, one way to celebrate your graduation could be from that bottle, but I've got something better. Look in that little Faberge box—with the oval of pearls around a large cabochon sapphire."

He opened the exquisite box and found it filled with a white powder.

She smiled and arched an eyebrow. "Am I right?"

He put a small pinch on his wrist and sniffed. "Certainly not snuff."

"Give me some. Come over here and sit with me." She curled into a large cushion at the end of the sofa.

He brought the box over and snuggled up beside her in the voluptuous array of brocaded and fringed silk cushions.

She took it and sniffed it directly from her own wrist. "A little wasteful and inefficient, but a nice beginning this way, no?" Her eyes had begun to shine like glass.

"I don't have three days, Delphine. I must leave tomorrow. It's complicated."

She put her arms around him and buried her head in his shoulder. "What's so complicated, darling? You've now raised yourself above the herd. You've entered a new realm."

He looked her in the eyes. "You mean because I killed that old woman?"

"It doesn't matter who it was the first time, my brave boy. You did it. That's what counts. Now you've tasted a new kind of power. This is the power of our new age. And you're now one of its initiates."

At last, he smiled. "Coming across the lagoon in a vaporetto, you know, I did have that feeling of power. As if I was in control of things. Of people, of circumstances."

"Perfect. Then you understand what I'm talking about. Power like this will banish what they call, out there, the conscience. Only cowards worry about such things as conscience. You and I are destined to be above all that. We can attain the ultimate." She reached into his crotch and held him firmly.

"How is that?" He shuddered with excitement. "I'm not sure I understand?" He took another pinch from the jeweled repository.

"You will find out, my young Viscount. The sublime awaits

you tonight. But for now, I want to know what it was you've abducted that was so important the old lady wasn't allowed to stand in your way?"

He twisted from her erotic grip, turned to rest his head on her lap and looked up at the carved putti cavorting on the edges of the ceiling. "You see, Papa was called by an old friend in Egypt. Archaeologist, collector of antiquities, like Papa. He'd found something so important he needed Papa to translate it. Ancient scrolls only the best in the field should do."

"What can be so important to make the famous Marquess of Ravenstone travel all the way to Egypt?"

"Well, you'll be surprised. These scrolls come from around 1350 BC, written by a scribe who was part of the intimate entourage of the pharaoh known as Akhenaten, husband of Nefertiti and father of Tutankhamun."

"Their message?"

"It's a story. Simply that Akhenaten, not Moses, was the person who led the Israelites out of Egypt across the Red Sea and part of the way to their promised land. Akhenaten, not Moses, was the man who ascended Mount Sinai and had the dialogue with God that produced the great Commandments. Akhenaten came down from his first such exchange with God and was so annoyed at Aaron for allowing their people to worship the golden calf, Baal, that he threw down the first tablets upon which had been written the Laws of the Lord, and these broke into pieces. So, Akhenaten went up again to receive anew the Laws of the Lord, which are the ones people follow today. This time, when he came down, Aaron was really upset. Not long after, he used his great rod as a weapon that did in both Akhenaten and Nefertiti. That's when the great rod finally broke.

"In the meantime, his scribe, Ishmael, whom Akhenaten always called 'my other Moses,' for personal reasons, had collected the broken pieces of the Covenant, the first Covenant, to be clear, not the one in the Bible, and placed them in a chest. He sent it back to Akhenaten's mother with the scrolls. It's now downstairs in the boatman's booth on the inner docking platform."

She looked at him in wonder. "You mean the very first Ark of the Covenant is in this house!" She began to laugh. "What an irony. Of all places for this sacred object to be—in a place where nothing is sacred." Her laughing, which was rather musical, continued until she had to force herself to stop.

He said, "I can tell you one thing, it's not happy around me. Makes all sorts of noises and bounces around sometimes like there's an angry creature inside."

"And where're you taking it. I assume you must leave by tomorrow because it's going somewhere important?"

Orlando's eyes shone. "I'm bringing it to the Fuhrer."

43

November 1938

*R*upert appeared at the police captain's station at eight o'clock the next morning. The slightly rotund, mustachioed gentleman exuded Italian charm. Nonetheless professional, he confabulated intensely with Rupert over strong coffee served in mugs by an attractive young woman in a police uniform. They prepared to drive through the day to Venice and begin investigations as soon as arriving. As for any clues, there had been only one fairly reliable sighting of someone who might have been Orlando out of many that had been called in from various quarters of the Italian peninsula. That was reported near a little hill town called Montefiore Conca on the Adriatic coast. This lent some credibility to their plans for heading to Venice.

As they dined the night before, Michael had realized Rupert was roiling silently at the specter of Orlando's terrible fall from grace and needed to follow this particular leg of their investigation on his own. So, he tactfully remained in Rome to await events. The next morning, when Rupert had already set off, the Hassler reception desk handed him a written invitation to lunch with Cardinal Fiorelli. It was puzzling to have been singled out—just as if his host knew Rupert would be away.

At the prelate's quarters the next afternoon, it was nothing less than a performance. The cardinal waxed effusively polite, a bit of grand guignol that made his thin, beaked face seem even more sinister. He expertly guided their conversation into ancient arts and cultures, and Caridis wondered when he would learn whatever it was the slippery fellow wanted.

Smoothing his way through these topics as they ate, Fiorelli came at last to the point. "Michele, if I may call you by your Christian name in my language, would it be indiscreet of you to give me some sort of report? It must break your heart that this great discovery of yours is once again stolen. It was so perfect here with Mother Church and so sad it had to be taken away."

Caridis put down his knife and fork with a small clatter. "Eminence, and what would you have done with it had your policemen succeeded in wresting it from Cardinal Camberini? Placed it on the altar of Saint Peter along with scrolls that rewrite the accepted history of a terribly persecuted people?"

"Ah, my dear sir, you really misunderstand. We feared the good cardinal was under duress by the thieving Jew. We came to rescue both Giovanni and the ark from that man's clutches. Our impression was he'd some sort of hold over our secretary of state."

Caridis smiled. "I see. Well, as you may have surmised, I happily helped remove the ark from the Vatican. You certainly can't fault its return to the discoverer?"

Fiorelli looked upward disingenuously as if seeking divine corroboration. "Well, I think one can argue the original Ark of the Covenant is the property of all humanity, and it doesn't belong even to its finder—with all the more respect and admiration for your remarkable achievement."

Michael laughed with appreciation for this Jesuitical sophistry. "All right then, Cardinal, does this make the Church of Rome a priori the custodian of what belongs to all humanity? A bit presumptuous, don't you think? Your pope isn't exactly a friend of all humanity, is he? Only of one part and that part's in sympathy with a tidal wave of inhumanity that's about to crash upon the shores of civilization. Heaven knows what will get washed away and destroyed."

"Come, come, Michele. That's a distorted view of things. Our church is navigating a difficult path located as it is in the heart of that new order. Fascism's very demanding, as you know." Fiorelli waved away a butler who wanted to bring in the next course. "In any event, someone else now appears to have taken the treasure. What will he do with it?"

"Frankly, Cardinal, if I'd the slightest idea, why should I share it?"

"For the simple reason I've got the power to help you get it back. This is Italy. If this thief's still here, there are strings to be pulled by me." Fiorelli stared at him without blinking.

Caridis shook his head. "You really amaze me, Cardinal. In any case, I'm pleased to say strings are being pulled already, so your kind offer's really unneeded. Anyway, I thank you. Another topic, perhaps?"

"Ah, yes. I see. Let's speak then about your missing friend?"

44

November 1938

ritzi tensed and pulled back his arm from holding Solange, huddled in a corner of a third-class coach. The conductor had pulled open the door of the compartment with a slamming sound, and the others in the compartment jerked their heads around to see what was happening. Fritzi smiled and showed him their tickets. The conductor seemed to size them both up and down and then returned the tickets after they were punched with his little machine.

When he had left the compartment, Solange reached over and put her arm across Fritzi's chest as if to hang onto him for security.

He patted her hand and kissed her forehead.

When the train pulled into Genoa's station, they took their modest bags, joined the crowd surging into the main hall, and found the listing for their train to Nice. The wait was about an hour, which they decided to spend at a café that was fenced off in a corner of the main hall. After they were seated, Fritzi left to buy a newspaper. She looked up as he returned, shaking his head, which was focused on the front page.

"What is it?"

"Terrible," he whispered. "Hurry and tie a scarf around your head like a peasant would. Let it hide some of your face on each side. At least my head's shaved, and this stupid, phony mustache makes me look very different, certainly older."

In a low voice, she said, "You mean our pictures are in there." She pointed at the *Corriere Della Sera*.

"Front page, no less. Vranken must be behind this." He pulled a pair of horn-rimmed glasses from a pocket and put them on. The lenses were ordinary glass. "Let's go somewhere less well lighted than here. I think we're probably all right at this point. No gestapo types." He knew what to be looking for as he checked the crowds.

Forty minutes later, they came forth from the shadows of a poorly lit passageway lined with shop windows they'd been pretending to check out. Their train had already docked at its platform and was loading passengers. Walking to a third-class car, they kept their heads down. Inside the compartment, they pulled the shades and sat across from each other with their heads angled away from the entrance door.

A kind of momentary relief flooded over them when the train pulled out of the station without incident. They sat with heads buried in magazines for most of the two-hour journey, and when handing their tickets to the conductor, they made as little eye contact as possible. The whistle blew occasionally in the darkness as they rattled over vehicle crossings with gates down and red lights blinking. The regularity of the sound of the wheels rolling over the steel rails lulled them into a low-keyed level of fearful excitement as they neared the French border and freedom.

The train finally slowed down for its approach to

Ventimiglia. The platforms and their surroundings had tall poles with bright lights that were sweeping back and forth in long, slow arcs, illuminating the several platforms and tracks almost to a daylight level.

Fritzi was facing forward, and upon seeing the lights, he galvanized to action. He signaled across to Solange to grab her bag from the rack and follow him. He did the same and led her into the corridor where people had begun to collect. He pushed his way past and into the next cars, toward the rear of the train. The two of them persisted, bumping and squeezing through passengers and luggage. They were tense and expectant as they came almost to the end by the time it drew to a stop along the platform.

At the rear of the last car, there was nobody waiting to detrain.

Fritzi unlocked and opened the door on the side away from the platform. He jumped down onto the roadbed and took Solange's valise before he reached up to grab her waist and carry her down to the ground. He looked at the sweeping lights and at the parking lot next to the tracks. "Stay low and follow me over to those cars." Several had their headlights on waiting to pick up passengers.

They stumbled across the rocks and gravel until they came to a wire fence that separated the parking area from the tracks.

Fritzi searched frantically left and right, an impenetrable barrier without a single opening. They moved further along the fence away from the station. Several drivers started to honk their horns, and more turned on their headlights. The two figures raised their arms trying to duck away from their beams.

Fritzi threw a desperate glance across the four sets of tracks to the other side. There was no fence, but what appeared to be a small knoll dropped down and out of view.

They ventured onto the tracks and realized that one of the rotating lights from the towers had cast a broad beam smack in their path. There was no option but to dive quickly across and somehow disappear down the knoll. They tripped in their haste and caught themselves from falling on the lines of steel and wood and gravel.

When they reached the other side, the knoll turned out to be a steep slope, plunging down through trees to a street below. They slipped and stumbled, sometimes catching onto the trees to prevent themselves from falling and rolling the rest of the way down.

Sirens had begun to blare. One of the klieg lights had stopped moving and was fixed upon them. By the time they reached the street below, gasping for breath, police cars had lined up—and a truck of soldiers disgorged a dozen armed men in military uniform arrayed out with rifles aimed at the two of them.

Fritzi and Solange froze, chests heaving and eyes staring. He took her hand and faced the phalanx of threatening men.

One of them stepped forward, impeccable in full gestapo regalia, and said, "Your passport, Herr Vogelberg? I assume you are currently calling yourself Joachim Sartorius?"

45

November 1938

A snappy, straight-backed lieutenant was admitted to the inner office, crossed the floor to the desk, and saluted Josef Goebbels. "Heil Hitler!" The messenger handed him a dispatch in an envelope, which Goebbels tore open and began to read. He waved the other fellow out of the room.

After several minutes of frowning, he took his phone with long, bony fingers and asked for the grand master of the Society of the Seraphim. When he answered, Goebbels said, "I think it's time we call the council together. Things are moving now. They've captured the traitor-Jew Fritzi Vogel at last. Thanks to von Vranken who got himself to Rome and organized a dragnet at the French border."

After several more exchanges with the Seraphim's grand master, he replaced the receiver and looked out the window for a long time without moving.

A small gilded statue of the golden calf stood in the center of the polished onyx table. Seated around it were the twelve elders. An empty ebony chair loomed at the head of the table. On the inside back of the chair was carved the rod of Aaron in bas-relief. The walls, floor, and ceiling of the room were of scarlet lacquer.

Goebbels sat enthroned at the other end. He looked at the men on either side. Familiar faces—two great industrialists, a famous scientist, three of the highest-ranking members of the German nobility—were included among them. Their faces spoke of comfort with power, used to being served and obeyed, and several were addicted to unspeakable practices in their pursuit of ever-more exotic sensation. Even two elders descended from families that had converted sufficient generations before from the Hebrew faith to nominal Christians, were by now, like the rest around the table, at the edge of a spiritual abyss—mostly unaware. They had no beliefs, no faith, but served as stewards of the Seraphim's immense power backed by limitless riches accumulated over the thirty-three centuries since Akhenaten and Aaron had confronted each other.

Goebbels nodded to the grand master seated to the right of the empty throne. "Brother, you should explain why we've called this meeting of the council."

If Goebbels instilled terror with his hawklike skeletal features, the worldwide leader of the Society of the Seraphim inspired an entirely different response. With a family heritage that had been an ornament of German history dating back to the earliest days of what had been termed the Holy Roman Empire, he radiated benevolence and charm. Tall and erect in posture, fair-haired, middle-aged, attractive, one would never intuit that he led an organization committed to exploiting every institution through the ages that could be used to manipulate as many people as possible to serve its ends.

The grand master addressed the council. "As you all know, the Ludwig Borchardt translation of an ancient scroll found when he discovered the head of Nefertiti has led us to a much greater discovery. In fact, what has been unearthed may well be the most important physical object in existence today." He paused. "It is nothing less than the original Ark of the Covenant. It contains the remains of the first set of tablets brought down from Mount Sinai by Moses. He threw them in anger and broke them on the ground when he discovered Aaron had led the worship of our beloved Baal. It contains, as well, three scrolls inscribed by the hand of a man, Ishmael, who was affectionately called Moses by the very man who later came to be revered as Moses by the Jews. Only now we know for sure the true Moses who led the Jews from Egypt was none other than Pharaoh. Moses was Akhenaten himself."

A gasp of astonishment came from those seated at the table. Heads turned as if to question each other at this.

"A translation of these three scrolls was made by Rupert Delacorte, Marquess of Ravenstone, the Fuhrer's great detractor in Britain's House of Lords. His eloquence, along with that of Churchill, has been a nuisance to say the least. These messengers have put Britain on notice of our intentions. By that, I mean the war machine Germany's been building is going now, sooner than later, to be matched by Britain, probably with the aid of America in due course. Therefore, we must act with some dispatch to marshal all our assets to see that the horse we're backing at this stage in the long history of our Society will be the winning horse."

From the other end of the table came a snort and laugh. Heads turned that way.

"Of course we're backing the right horse as you put it." Josef Goebbels hit the table with his fist. "National Socialism's the horse, and Fuhrer is its jockey. You couldn't have made a better bet!" He leaned back with a smug smile.

One of the industrialists said, "Grand master, where's the ark as we speak now?"

"I was coming to that. A bit bizarre on the surface. We've reason to believe it's now in the possession of Ravenstone's son and heir, of all people. Orlando, Viscount Cressy, to be precise. He took it from under the nose of one of our own members, the now-infamous Friedrich Vogel. Not dreaming of his real character, Vogel was sent by Brother Goebbels to Alexandria. His mission was to obtain it from the discoverer by whatever means possible.

"By sheer luck, Cressy told his German control in London he'd found a letter to his father with the combination to open the vault where the discovery was kept. So, Berlin had Cressy and Vogel meet in Alexandria. Together, they succeeded in removing it from the vault. But Vogel upset the plan to bring it here and took it instead to the Vatican with the help of Cardinal Camberini, their secretary of state. Not long after, events set in motion by Brother von Vranken unfortunately caused the ark to leave the Vatican, and that's when Cressy came back into the picture."

Another councilor asked, "Have we got any idea where Cressy is now? His intentions? And why's he acting against his own father?"

The grand master smiled. "Cressy's our biggest catch in Britain. He's been carefully molded and shaped by our very capable head of recruitment there. Cressy's greatest ambition, it seems, is to meet and please the Fuhrer. With that possibility dangled before him, he became one of Berlin's tools. At this point, however, only slim clues exist to his whereabouts."

Germany's most important banker asked, "But you think he may, ultimately, bring it here to Berlin?"

"Yes. What else would he do with it?" The grand master shrugged. "Cressy won't be able to sell it, and hiding it just for himself gets him only a very private and personal satisfaction. No, I am persuaded by von Vranken his purpose is to bathe himself in glory by laying it before the Fuhrer himself." The grand master's voice fell, and he almost appeared to find that conclusion distasteful.

Goebbels said, "A police captain from the Roman force has been reported to be on his way to Venice. This is interesting because he's said to be accompanied by Ravenstone himself."

The banker shook his head. "Like my brother here, I just don't get why the son's taken such a radical turn away from his father."

The grand master gave the man a patronizing smile. "Come, come, now. Why've you yourself become such a rabid Nazi? None of us, we of the Seraphim, ever needs to believe in the ideologies of our beneficiaries. Our interest is more simply pragmatic. But like you and Brother Goebbels, Cressy's become a believer."

"Perhaps, Master, but Cressy's not German. His situation has to be very different."

"The Fuhrer's quite infectious. His appeal has spread well beyond our country's borders. But let's move on. Our goal's now to find Cressy and bring him, *avec bagages*, to Berlin."

"And then what, if we're successful?" Germany's foremost steelmaker leaned forward, his hooded eyes eager.

The master sat up quite straight on his throne. "We will make the most of such an occasion, I assure you. As you know, this treasure has got one true home now that it's been resurrected from its ancient hiding place. Here, in the sanctuary of the Seraphim."

Goebbels looked at the master, the muscles of his jaw throbbing in and out.

46

November 1938

*R*upert sat with Lorenzino, the Roman police captain, in the small Fiat 500, which the latter expertly threaded through the narrow, winding roads of the Emilia-Romagna region, heading northeast. They drove among undulations of softly rounded hills covered in velvet carpets of green and brown, punctuated occasionally by stands of pine and oak trees.

The loquacious Roman had been holding forth on many subjects, delighted to share with this famous Inglese. He exuded the easy charm of his race. With an enthused gesture, he pointed up at a little cluster of buildings gathered precariously about a seventeenth-century church perched near the top of one the highest hills. "My village. Growing up in places like that makes your legs and lungs strong. Nothing's flat. I'd love to show it to you." He turned to look at the tense man beside him. "I know, signore, you don't need to worry. We haven't time to indulge this little opportunity for my fat and funny

Tia Elena to pour for you the best limoncello in all Italia. She makes it herself from the lemon trees on her *terrazza*. Another time maybe when so many important things have not got us in their grip, as you say, no?"

Rupert laughed lightly. "My new friend, you certainly know about human nature, don't you? So, tell me about this country of yours. It seems filled with so much laughter, *vino fino*, delightful pasta, and the most feminine women in the world. What's happening in Italy that makes you want to join the brutal partners you've adopted from the north? It just seems a rather odd match, don't you think?"

The Roman smiled and maneuvered the car around a slow farmer's wagon just in time to avoid an oncoming truck. "You *Ingleses*, you see everything in black and white. Good or bad. Here, it's something else. We're a Catholic country. Here we can sin during the week and be given a clean slate on Sunday after a debauched Saturday night, just by confessing to some frustrated priest who wants to tickle the breasts of the young things making their First Communion—or maybe only heaven should know what else they might desire. So, we've got a government that calls itself fascist. That's supposed to mean they control our lives just like the church. But we're a messy, conniving people. We need a little order in our lives. So, this kind of control is not all so bad. As long as you keep your nose clean, like they say in your country, the government isn't going to pinch it. Now our streets are clean when they used to be filled with garbage. Yes, Il Duce is a bit ridiculous. A strutting, self-important guy who makes you want to laugh at him— privately, of course. I will tell you this. If he ever gets too big for his boots, you say? Then, we'll take off his boots and string him up by his feet."

Pulling a cigarette from his case, Rupert said, "Want one?"

The other fellow nodded and received it helpfully lit.

"All right, then. But you still haven't explained why this partnership with the devil from up north. It seems to me they want to do much more than bring order to an unruly people."

The Roman scratched his chin. "Ah, yes. That is an interesting question. History, my friend. Inferiority complex, maybe. Those barbarians have always stood for order. None of this Latin forgiveness for our sins. We from the sunny south have always been looked down on by them. Ever since they sacked my city fifteen hundred years ago, the same savage, unforgiving martinets as today. Il Duce says to us, 'See, now that we're fascists, we've got the respect of the Huns, at long last, and we're now the Fuhrer's equal partners.'" He shook his head. "Of course, not true. Mussolini fools himself. We're still treated with condescension by these Huns who've infiltrated Italy like microbes. Someday, the infection will become intolerable, and then—and then, God knows, it might be too late. We'll have become a slave state like the rest of Europe. Hitler wants to make us all his vassals."

They stopped in the little independent principality of San Marino to refuel and eat. The Roman parked at the police station and emerged several minutes later, full of newfound information. "It seems, signore, you know your son quite well. I've just been on the *telefono* with the police in Mestre on the edge of Venice. They've actually found the car bought from a farmer yesterday morning by a young man answering to your son's description. It's parked in the lot next to the Venice railroad station."

Rupert looked blankly out the windscreen. "So, what did you tell them? The name of his friend and her palazzo?"

"No, don't worry, signore. I want us to be there when we follow up on your suspicion. We'll take them to the palazzo, together, tonight. We should be in Venezia for dinner."

☥

She pressed her hand hard between his legs. Still lying on the sofa, the two of them high on cocaine, she smiled as she felt his reaction through his trousers. "I want to prepare you, my young lord. Ah, what is to come!" Her eyes lit up. "Tonight, we'll know the sublime that can happen only once between two people. When I learned you'd killed the abbess, I prayed you would come next to me. And see? My prayer was answered." Skill guided her to the next stage. She gave his ear a light bite and pressed her other hand into his solar plexus.

"That's why I'm here, Delphine." He caught his breath at her next move. His voice broke slightly. "Tell me how the abbess changed things."

"Because it baptized you. What I want with you I've wanted for some time. But only someone who shares my path to ecstasy would do. Not any ordinary brute who can simply kill."

"The someone to do what?"

"To fuck me till I die."

He laughed. "What do you mean? That's sort of what we do always, no? The longest, most tantalizing tease known to man or beast before the universe explodes?" He gasped as she found another spot to touch. "I mean, it always feels like we've died and been reborn. How much more can you imagine, my bewitcher?"

She stroked the side of his face and focused her gleaming light brown eyes into his, as if she were about to hypnotize. "This time will be the last. I have been ready for this. Waiting for this moment. My life has been dedicated to sensation. So, too, will my death. And you, my perfect disciple, will be the instrument."

He spoke to the ceiling, head back on the masses of sofa cushions. "Come, come. Why, my mysterious Delphine, only twenty-three? You're still gorgeous—gifted like no other in the arts you practice. So much more to share and feel. Why now?"

"Are you just being selfish, my *Visconto*, so you can have a convenient trip over the moon every now and again? Or are you ready to become the super being and stand above other men, sure of your destiny, your power, your unique place in the universe?" She put her hands around his throat and thrust her tongue between his lips and deep into his mouth. Her hands squeezed enough to make him feel light-headed. Her knee pressed into his groin. He groaned and grabbed her ass with both hands.

She pulled away. "See, that's a hint of what you're going to do for me tonight. My hands will be tied, my legs will be free, and you will press until … until … ah, Orlando, you will just follow … until you will lead. And then we will both be beyond thought, beyond reason, in a whirlpool of stars. Worlds will collide. The gods will smile. Everything will happen just as I say, and you will be reborn, a new man, a superman, and I will know such sublime pleasure as only Olympus could imagine. My life will be complete—and yours will just begin."

☥

Somewhere between San Marino and Venice, it happened. The Roman was gesturing to him as he drove around a bend in the hilly road. Smack in front of them loomed a wide and tall wagonload of winter animal feed piled high in bales. Pulled by a tractor, it was impossible to pass on the left because one could see nothing of the road ahead.

The Roman captain automatically jerked the wheel to the right and flew off the road, landing for the moment upright speeding down a gentle slope arcing toward the right between several stands of trees until the car careened onto its side. They skidded toward a cluster of pines and were stopped abruptly as the nose of the car was caught between a pair of closely spaced trees.

Rupert found himself lying on top of the captain, pressed against the driver's door. The man was unconscious. Rupert could feel warm blood against his cheek. He raised his head off the other's shoulder and saw that it was oozing from his companion's nose and mouth and running down his front. Rupert sniffed and could smell gasoline, but no hint of a fire. He pushed his right arm up at an awkward angle in the confined space to hook his fingers around the door handle. He pushed hard to swing the door up and back until it fell with a bang against the right side of the car above them. Twisting himself, he grabbed the sides of the opening and pulled up, trying not to press too hard against the Roman's body beneath him. The man was still breathing and occasionally moaned.

When he had succeeded in pulling himself completely from the little Fiat, Rupert stood outside and peered down at the broken body of the captain who had stopped moaning. He heard cries and looked up the hill. Men, slipping occasionally, were rushing to their rescue from the roadway above.

One was a doctor. He arrived first and nodded as Rupert pointed inside the car. He looked and directed the other men to try to push the car away from the trees that had saved it from gaining momentum and descending farther toward its possible complete destruction. The seven men managed to maneuver it out and tip it back upright with a shudder of the car's frame as it landed on four wheels.

The doctor directed one rescuer to kneel on the front seat and hold the captain from falling while he carefully opened the driver's door and examined the unconscious man's limbs and back. He directed the fellow inside to guide the Roman's legs as the doctor and another man slowly withdrew him by his shoulders until both of them could support his back while the man inside lifted up his legs and carried them across toward the driver's door.

The captain was laid on packing blankets from a parked truck above. The doctor began his closer examination of the victim. But he first called on his fellow rescuers to find a way to call for an ambulance. Rupert realized he'd hit his head against something when it began to throb. He ignored the small amount of blood oozing from a growing bump and marveled at fate's caprice, which had left him substantially intact. In Italian, he asked the doctor how serious the captain's injuries might be.

Answering in heavily accented English, the doctor said, "He maybe have concussion. Problems also with leg and arm. We see later."

The Roman remained unconscious and breathing heavily.

The doctor covered him with another blanket from the truck driver's collection.

Within twenty minutes, they heard the singsong of the ambulance's siren.

At the hospital, the captain was whisked away for close examination.

Rupert felt tense as he saw how many hours late he was going to be in Venice, assuming he could leave the hospital in good conscience.

The hospital doctor finally emerged to give an update. "Your friend will be all right. He has bad twist to his right leg and a small fracture in left arm as well as concussion, which may be serious, but we hope he gains consciousness before morning."

Rupert asked, "If I leave now, can I call the hospital for reports on his progress. I must be somewhere tonight. It can mean life and death to someone else."

The doctor smiled. "Of course. When he becomes conscious, I will explain to the captain why you have gone. You must think he will understand."

"Oh, yes. He will. Thank you, signor. Are there any taxis in this small town? I need one to get me to Venezia."

"We have several people the reception desk can call. They will let you know as soon as they find one."

Rupert smiled. "We were very fortunate to be near your hospital. I think my friend is in good hands here."

"Thank you, Inglese. We try do our best." He walked through the swinging doors to the reception and returned in five minutes. "Your taxi will be ten, fifteen minutes. I hope you have success in Venezia, maybe a couple hours away."

Rupert shook his hand and faced the abyss that lay ahead.

☥

It was late. He had called earlier to explain the cause. Rupert sat with the Venetian chief of police.

"We expected you this afternoon. I am sorry about the Roman captain's accident. You say the hospital thinks he will recover?"

"Well, they were fairly optimistic, but one will know better when Lorenzo regains consciousness." He glanced at his wristwatch. "I see it's now past two in the morning. We're dealing here simply with an intuition on my part. My question for you is are you prepared tonight to move without waiting until daylight?"

The chief smiled. "I can answer that better if you give me more information such as who's the person who might be sheltering your son?"

Rupert explained he'd learned only recently of his boy's relationship with a Venetian aristo, one *principessa* Delphine

Palestrina, including its erotic aspects and his son's bizarre proclivities. He did so with a heavy heart and sadness in his voice.

"Ah! I'd not even speculated it would be her. I see. So, you think the suspect's with this woman? She's something, I must say. All Venice knows what she is. She walks through the streets and over the bridges, and all the men—and many women—turn to look at her. Her ass moves like an angel's, and her long black hair lies like a mysterious curtain partly over her face. The lips pout as she adjusts her dress over her breasts and hips. And for her, any man, even on the run from the law, might well be tempted to stop, and the devil damn the consequences, eh!"

Rupert nodded, his face taut, and said, "Sounds like Circe to me."

The chief agreed. "Indeed! So, there's probably no risk he'll be leaving tonight—assuming we're correct."

The chief's female colleague laughed. "My friend, but for the marchese here, how could anyone even suspect the fellow would be in Venice with *La Delphinetta*? After discovering that dilapidated car at the railway station, who'd make this kind of connection? No, we'll be advised to go now, tonight, while they're likely to be, shall we say, distracted by other things."

The chief poured another round of grappa into their small glasses and said, "Not a bad idea. Catch the fly at the honey jar. No?"

☥

The moon's reflection broke into dazzled fragments on the Grand Canal. Santa Maria della Salute's statues looked down from the dome they surrounded like a diadem, silent witnesses to centuries of that particular decadence for which Venice has been a byword. The calm, lapping waters licked the ancient, barnacled walls of the buildings slowly sinking into them over the ages. From deep inside the arched docking area of one of the grandest palazzi, a practically silent electric motor sparked to life, and within moments, a polished mahogany boat with brass trimmings glowing in the moonlight emerged from the bowels of the mansion.

For anyone who happened to be awake and listening from a balcony or open windows, the soft sound of wailing angels' voices wafted over the waters. The Covenant of the Lord lay within the boat, as if in a state of shock, not agitated, but like a tomb—even its ethereal chorus could have been taken for whispers of the wind.

The boat wound its way past sleeping gondolas and colorful striped docking posts. Occasional late-nighters could be seen in their long capes and dresses weaving through the shadows.

Orlando steered the craft out into the open waters of the lagoon. He aimed it to the east and sat back in the dark leather seat with his hand steadying the wheel. He could not see the vaporous emanations joining with the wailing voices as they drifted out behind him over the great expanse of water.

His thoughts were a blur. A great excitement filled his breast. He felt he could fly. A sense of invulnerability to ordinary menace flooded through him. Power. A mad desire to sing. The past six hours cloaked in mystery. A sensation of something extraordinary having happened. As if he'd just received a gift, unexpected and sublimely uplifting.

Dawn at last began to tinge the open sea with shafts of roseate gold, soon broadening into bright reflections, at moments almost blinding him. Shipping traffic became more congested as he drew further out into the Adriatic. He was hungry. He would conjure a good English breakfast once he got to land. By late morning, he could see the building-studded skyline of his destination, the port of Trieste.

The beautifully cared-for craft flirted with buoys, crossed the bows of tankers, playfully and dodged in and out of the early-morning sailboats capturing the wind on their exhilarating reaches. Fishermen shook their fists as the wake of his swooping boat swished over their gunwales.

He had taken from the vessel all signs of its name and ownership, along with its papers, which he had found in a waterproof metal box. He tossed the box and the boat's bronze name plaque over the side along the way. By now, the only clues to the boat's identity were nestled among the ancient debris at the bottom of the Adriatic.

Heading around the promontory, he found a yachting harbor away from Trieste's major docks and the cranes silhouetted against the cloudless sky. He maneuvered into an empty spot with his stern to the land.

A young crew member from one of the docked vessels happened to have stopped to admire the sleek craft. He came over and poised himself to receive the stern line that Orlando threw up to him.

As he tied it to a cleat, Orlando asked, "I've got a special reward for you if you also tie up the bowline, find me a dolly, and help me with my crate. It's rather heavy. Could use your muscle."

The fellow smiled and nodded. Having tied up the other line, he came back soon with a small handcart. They got the crate onto it, and Orlando straightened up. "A nice surprise for you. Here are the keys to my boat. I don't need it anymore. No papers. You can have it. Take it someplace where no one'll find it for a while—and it's all yours."

The fellow said, "What am I to do with it? We're sailing later today."

Orlando shrugged. "Look, here's enough money to put it in dry dock for a year. You can come back for it, use it, or sell it. By that time, no one'll ask any questions. It's worth a fortune, no? Be smart and get it out of the way for the time being."

The man inspected him more closely. "You Inglese?"

Orlando shook his head. "No, German, Tedesco. I suggest you get a move on if you want to be rich."

The fellow stared at the key in his hand. "Electric, no?"

"Of course. But it's got an auxiliary petrol motor for the open sea. Very special. I don't need it anymore, and I'm leaving for a place where I can't even use it."

The fellow, whom he took to be about twenty-five, gave the elegant vessel another look, taking in the enclosed cabin with leather seats, beveled windowpanes, and polished brass fittings throughout. This persuaded him to grab his good fortune while the gift horse was still waiting. "Yes, yes. I go do it now. *Grazie, signore. Grazie.*"

Orlando waved at him from the main pathway to the marina's parking lot. He smiled to himself as the fellow waved back, now steering out to sea. There were several taxis standing by the main vehicle entrance of the marina. He took the first one and directed the driver to find a place that sold fancy motorcars.

Before long, Orlando parked his brand-new car—with the crate locked in its boot—in front of a small café where he ordered a large breakfast and mapped out his next moves. The waitress, who had seen him pull up in his drophead Mercedes, placed his order on the table, wiped her hands on her apron, and openly admired the thirty-year-old customer with his shock of blond hair and the lines on his handsome face that emphasized his high cheekbones and gave him an air of someone who had lived beyond the reaches of ordinary men.

He was too preoccupied to notice. He studied the car's

papers, using the false German name his London Nazi contact had assigned him in the new German passport issued when he'd left for Alexandria. It was to be his escape hatch from any pursuer who might inconveniently be looking for Viscount Cressy, but it represented more. He was now evolving and growing. He was now going to be someone else. A new man. This brought on another surge of puissance, the feeling that. had been washing over him all morning. She had been right. The night before had been his time of transformation. He had been annealed like a Damascene blade. He saw himself, that blade in hand, invincible, basking in the blinding light of his destiny.

47

November 1938

$\mathcal{T}$he police boat turned from the moonlit canal and entered the shadows of the inner docks of la Principessa Delphine Palestrina's palazzo. The three men had to adjust to the sudden darkness.

Rupert looked around, making out the elegant porter's cabin with its gilded carvings and red leather interior. The flashlight shining on the owner's gondola revealed what could have been a flashy member of one of Canaletto's colorful festival regattas of grandly outfitted vessels.

The chief said, "My colleague here says this belonged to a famous ancestor of the princess, one of the greater doges of Venice."

Rupert frowned. "Are we sure no one answered when the station telephoned the palazzo?"

"Yes, signore. We tried several times." The short, bearded Venetian police chief shook his head. "Also, now we ringed the bell from next to the porter's cabin. No servants, no signs of anyone here in the palazzo. Very unusual for such an establishment. And all very dark."

Rupert walked over to the wide staircase. "Shall we be breaking too many laws if we go up without an invitation?"

"Not to worry, signore. We go now." The little man bounded ahead, leading the way up to the main reception hall. Each armed with a flashlight, they explored the piano nobile, finding only the remains of a meal for two, several opened bottles of wine, and the small jeweled casket with its hinged lid laid back and some of its white powder scattered on the silk, brocaded sofa.

The Venetian captain looked at Rupert. "The *visconto* uses this sort of stuff?"

He nodded. "I'm sure that and other things." Pointing at the low table, he said, "At least we've got signs of two people having been here, and I should think very recently. The remains of this meal haven't yet congealed, can't have been here for very long, probably several hours ago at the earliest."

A carved and gilded staircase swept upward in a dramatic curve. Calling out, the three men moved slowly up the broad steps. Their voices rebounded from soaring walls inlaid in patterns of colored marble. No response.

At the landing, they looked both ways. At one end of the wide hall, which was filled with paintings, mirrors, consoles, and chairs, there was a slightly open pair of tall doors. They looked at each other and moved as if by tacit consent in that direction.

When they reached the doors, Rupert pushed one inward. The room was dark. In the beams from the flashlights, they could make out the heavy pillars of a majestic canopied bed with draperies flowing from a gilded crown suspended from the ceiling.

The Venetian captain waved his assistant to find the light

switches. A moment later, the space awoke in a blaze of colors. Lights glowed through red silk lampshades on table lamps, standing lamps, and sconces on the elaborately upholstered velvet walls. But their attention was riveted on the bed.

A magnificent female form lay gracefully torqued partly on its back with arms spread out and tied to the thick, carved spiral bed pillars by tasseled golden cords. Her hips were turned so that one leg was drawn up over the other more extended leg. Her flesh was the color of alabaster and seemed to be just as smooth. The nipples were pink, like enamel caps adorning breasts rising upward and shaped to erotic perfection. As the men approached the bed, they could see that her head was turned to their left and a sweep of silken black hair covered her face and neck.

Rupert moved to the left side of the bed and reached over to push back her hair. As he did so, with gentle care, the three of them recoiled. It revealed a horror that would be hard to forget. The eyes bulged from their sockets like bright ivory orbs with onyx inlays. The tongue was swollen and distended from her lips. And the woman's neck was covered with blue bruises. Rupert replaced the sweep of hair so that it covered her face once again. Tears had begun to well up in his eyes. He turned and put his hands over his face and sobbed.

The Roman captain approached and put his arm about his heaving shoulders and led him from the room.

The assistant to the Venetian captain emerged from the bedroom sometime later and found the other two seated in a small library off the same hall. "I've got some news for you. In the bathroom on the washbasin was this ring with a crest engraved into it. Here also is a partly smoked cigarette with an English marque printed on it." He handed them to his boss.

The Venetian turned to Rupert and said, "Signore, does this crest mean anything to you?"

"It does, I'm sorry to say." He had regained his composure. "It has belonged to the eldest son of every Marquess of Ravenstone since the sixteenth century."

"Ah, signore, I'm so very sorry indeed. We'll have to hold onto it as evidence. It will, of course, come back to you. Now just for further insight, do you think the visconto uses this brand of cigarette?"

Rupert nodded. "I'm afraid so, Captain. But may I ask a favor? Can you do your utmost to find my son before he leaves Italy? This terrible incident seems to have just happened, so he mustn't yet have gotten very far. For lots of reasons, we've got to find him now."

"Yes, yes. He could be in Venice. His car's under constant watch, so we'll know if he goes back to it. Let me assure you, the manhunt has started."

"Grazie, Captain." Rupert walked over to several windows. He opened one and stepped onto the balcony. Lighting a cigarette, he looked through its pale cloud at the Salute across the water. Camberini's words kept repeating. The boy, simply, may have been born without a soul. Perhaps a living metaphor for a world without moral bearings? He shuddered. Berlin. A possible cocktail of his only son, those mad Aryan narcissists, and their control of the Ark of the First Covenant was more than he could bear to imagine. Anything could—and probably would—happen, and well beyond the orbit of outrage.

When they'd finished, the police and Rupert descended to the official boat docked below. They piled in and drew out of the dark enclave into the sunshine. Swinging to the right, they headed in the direction of the Rialto Bridge. A vaporetto loomed toward them, slicing the water like a knife. Five members of the gestapo stood motionless, facing forward, their dark figures eclipsing the sun. In their midst, Lothar von

Vranken glowered. Both men twisted their heads to stare as their vessels crossed each other's wake.

♀

Orlando shifted into fifth gear and eased out the clutch, relaxing into the prospect of the long stretch ahead to Ljubljana. He had presented his new papers without incident at the border of Slovenia. The passport and customs officers had been much more interested in his nice, snappy convertible. The admiring looks he got driving through villages tickled his vanity. Much better than that jalopy he'd ditched in the ravine. The truth was, it's always better to project power. The power of the new man. The wind felt good as it whipped the longish hair back from his arresting face. He felt higher than any cocaine he'd ever tried.

The ark was acting up again. Sometimes he could feel the thumping vibrations throughout the vehicle as it rocked about in the trunk of his two-seater. The rush of wind past his ears drowned out any other of those strange sounds that might be coming from the crate.

Racing along through the lush countryside, he noticed fields had been plowed up after the harvest and lay in rich dark patches on the undulating landscape. Copses of trees mixed the naked limbs of ancient oaks with luxuriant stands of towering pines. The far-off Alpine crest of Europe gradually took form, in dim and teasing glimpses, mere mountainous hints in the distant haze.

He entered the outskirts of the Slovenian capital by late afternoon. It was already darkening with each November day advancing another step toward winter. The River Ljubljanica coiled through the unspoiled city's handsome buildings and boulevards. Several baroque churches and neoclassical monuments studded the cityscape like jewels. Orlando stopped and asked a policeman for the best hotel in town. With an approving nod at his car, he was directed to an esplanade overlooking the river and its adjacent canal where the five-star staff helped unload the crate and bring it to a large suite. He had reason to be grateful. The agitation of the ark within the crate had been unusually subdued.

Although a painting of the Yugoslav king, Peter II, hung above the concierge's desk, it was clear the culture of this charming city was far more Austrian than Slavic. He noticed there was time before the shops closed. Recent events had forced him to travel light. By dinnertime, several handsome leather valises had been delivered with all the necessaries to make his triumphant appearance three days later in Berlin.

He smiled to himself. How secure he now felt with his new name, a German identity freshly minted and unlinked to anyone the international police would be seeking. While he'd been out shopping, the concierge had arranged the ticket for his train journey to Berlin. A special railcar for his drophead Mercedes, stopovers, transfers, everything was organized with a large private compartment for his comfort all the way. The route was set through the Austrian Alps and across to Prague and then Dresden. What a relief. He was finally about to enter friendly territory.

He reflected as he was taken to his room. Just this last March, Austria had willingly allowed herself to be grabbed by Hitler for his growing new Germanic Empire. Only seven weeks ago, western Czechia, called the Sudetenland with its largely German population, important banks, and industrial base had succumbed to Hitler's advances just ten duplicitous days after the gullible Chamberlain had obtained the Fuhrer's signature on a scrap of paper pledging peace in our time at Munich. Orlando felt pride over Germany's ability to have its way.

He watched the hotel dining room's uniformed butler refill his cut crystal goblet with a fine chilled hock and mused with great satisfaction on the obvious. He was riding the crest of history's wave. It was much more than a wave, a virtual tsunami steadily building in depth and power and preparing to engulf Western civilization.

In the hotel's dark-paneled bar after his meal, the attendant brought a single malt of great age and smiled at the young aristocrat's satisfied first sip.

A voice, cultured and difficult to place, spoke to him in German. "I overheard your order. Rare to have a connoisseur of single malts in this outpost on the Slavic fringes." The man was tidy and compact. Dark, slicked-back hair, immaculately tailored, small black mustache, eyebrows slanted upward like his eyes, longish nose, pale graceful hands. He had leaned over from his chair where he sat alone with a brandy snifter and a demitasse on a tiny black marble coffee table.

Orlando, not quite alarmed, remained somewhat guarded. He wasn't yet entirely out of the woods and into what he soon expected to be super-friendly territory. He nodded, gave a deliberate smile, and lifted his glass.

The other fellow raised his and said, "Must have spent some time in England. Shows in your accent. School? Nanny? Parent?"

"All three." Orlando was now tensed in every muscle but kept his outward cool. "And you?"

"Ah, a bit polyglot. Turk by birth and raised mostly in Rumania. Mother part of its royal family. I deal in antiquities, mostly Persian and Greek. You a collector, perhaps?"

Orlando gauged his interlocutor. Seemed a good sort and probably not a real threat, but why even take the risk? He decided to keep things on a superficial level and soon extract himself. "Not really a collector. Amateur admirer, always curious, but not very acquisitive."

The other man said, "Well, I can't help myself. Things keep on speaking to me, insisting that I must have them. Take this walking stick, for example." He reached over to where it was leaning against a small corner in the wall. The top of the stick was made of blue enamel threaded with an intricate pattern of inlaid golden stems and leaves. "Here, go ahead and unscrew it." He handed the cane to Orlando.

The shaft was polished ebony, and it was surprisingly heavy. He gave the enameled cap several smooth turns on finely cut metal threads until it came off in his hand. Nestled neatly inside the shaft was a tube of polished gold topped with a small, fitted ruby-studded crown.

"Go ahead. See what's inside." The man smiled encouragingly.

Orlando did as bidden. He withdrew the golden tube, which was rather long, and it glided out with a slight suction effect from the shaft. Its ruby crown turned easily and was laid next to the enameled outer fitting.

The Turk's eyebrows went up in a questioning gesture.

Orlando looked into the narrow opening of the tube and saw it was filled with a white powder.

The other man smiled. "Perhaps you'd like to try it?"

With a small flutter of excitement, Orlando tapped a small amount on the back of his hand and sniffed it like snuff. A miasma of well-being enveloped him with such speed he was caught by surprise.

The Turk coughed lightly and nodded as if seeking his approval.

"What is this?" Orlando asked, as if in a dream state.

"Ah, something special. Do you approve?"

Orlando's pupils had dilated. He took another sniff.

The Turk studied him silently for several moments and then put one graceful white hand on Orlando's arm. "Shall we take a walk about the town? Good for the digestion, and who knows what we may find?"

A stroll of some fifteen minutes along the embankment brought them to the porticoed entrance of an eighteenth-century mansion house. Its polished dark green door happened to open just as they approached, and two persons emerged throwing kisses over their shoulders at a bearded giant just inside. One of the two squeezed the arm of the other and caressed a well-rouged cheek. This produced a giggle and a shake of curls attached to a dark blonde wig.

The Turk smiled at Orlando and raised his eyebrows. With a tip of his head, he directed him through the open door.

Orlando stepped inside. A head-spinning mixture of cigar smoke, piano music, laughter, and scented candles filled the bordello's public rooms. Champagne bottles lay empty on the floor, and handsome young waiters wearing only loincloths carried trays of drinks and small sandwiches and pastries among the revelers. Occasional squeals could be heard as one or another of their bottoms was pinched.

The Turk was directed to a throne-like chair where he patiently peeled off his gloves and handed them with his hat to an attendant. Using his walking stick, he pointed to the seat next to him, and Orlando sat down. When they had both been installed with a glass of champagne, and their cigarettes lighted, the Turk crossed one leg over the other and leaned toward Orlando. "Well, milord, what might be your taste tonight?"

Suppressing his shock, Orlando pretended not to notice the term of address.

The Turk touched his arm and repeated the question.

This time, there was no way but to look confused. "Are you speaking to me?"

"Of course, the selection here will be as good as any you might find in London, Paris or ... Venice, perhaps?"

Orlando felt a chill as if a wind was blowing at him from a bottomless chasm at his feet. "I ... I'm not sure ... I do think you may have me confused with someone else."

The Turk's triangular smile was lit from a candle flickering below on the table holding their drinks. Orlando shuddered at the sight of those cold, dark eyes with their flashing reflections and found himself rising from his chair.

The Turk pressed him back down and cleared his throat. "Surely you don't want to leave now. A connoisseur of sensation perhaps teasing himself by pretending to hold back, to deny himself the delectations before him. Ah, yes, I see it in you. How clever! The ecstasy of renunciation ... but only for so long, of course." The Turk unscrewed the enameled cap of his cane and handed the golden tube to Orlando. "This enables many things to become clearer, to sweep away the mists of self-doubt. We're throwing off our shackles, aren't we? Hearing voices awaken our destiny after a long sleep. You are joining the ranks of the great, milord. It is obvious you will stay the course."

With that, Orlando inhaled the powder from the back of his hand, wiped his nose with a handkerchief, and realized someone was waiting for him. He looked up into the light blue eyes of a well-proportioned young man, almost naked, hand held out to take him upstairs.

48

November 1938

*B*ritain's secret service had contacted Rupert with the news. MI6 intelligence officers had done their search quickly. He'd asked for any information on Orlando's contacts with German spies in London. He reread their response sent in the high-security, sealed pouch to the British embassy in Rome.

After the shattering trip to Venice, clues had suddenly petered out for the Italian police, one of whom was driving him back to Rome. They stopped at the hospital where the ever-positive Roman police captain was now conscious and grinning when he saw Rupert at the doorway. The doctors reassured him his injuries would heal and he'd probably completely overcome the effects of his concussion within six months.

Rupert's driver, the assistant to the Venetian captain, had continued to ask questions along the way. Doubtful about capturing Orlando in Italy, he dropped him off at the Hassler and wished him luck with a little shrug, which suggested much was needed. The trail was now chilling to the point Orlando was almost certainly going to reach Nazi territory before they could find him.

☥

Back in the bar of the Hassler, Michael grinned and stood to welcome him with an understanding hug. Over a Bellini, Rupert's favorite mix of champagne and peach juice, Michael led the conversation deliberately by describing in brief the details of his meeting with Fiorelli.

Rupert shook his head at Fiorelli's desperate argument for cooperation to capture the ark. "The fellow's clutching at straws, old man. This thing's got way beyond his reach."

Michael said, "Don't you think von Vranken must be mostly in control at this point? Our fascist cardinal looked quite dejected when I mentioned his name."

Rupert produced an ironic smile. "This fascist cardinal's got no idea of the dangers lying in wait for Italy—and the papacy—once the Nazi juggernaut has assembled the European empire spelled out by its leader for any and all to read in his book." He gestured to the waiter to refill their glasses. "Yes, Lothar von Vranken's our immediate devil. The fellow'll spare nothing to get what Orlando's stolen." Michael's stratagem had worked as Rupert volunteered his account of events in Venice. "My poor boy's in way over his head."

Michael gave him a sympathetic nod. "I feel what you're going through. Damned unfair your kid should end up this way."

"It those goddamn genes. Lizzie calls it the Ravenstone curse." He crushed one cigarette into an ashtray and pulled out another, which he lit with a slight tremor in his hand. "I just learned from MI6 that Orlando's holding a German passport with a new name that's got shadings of French connections.

Gives him an alibi for a reasonable but still not native German accent. MI6 also reported that the International Criminal Police Commission has been officially charged with finding and arresting the boy. Miko, do you believe, the ICPC seemed to feel compelled to note he's 'the son of the most eloquent voice in the House of Lords raised against the coming crisis with Nazi Germany'? Just imagine all the goodwill that's going to get with his potential captors."

Michael signaled for refills as he downed the remains of his Bellini. "You know it's going to be tough. Orlando must now officially be charged with double murder. From what you've just described in Venice, I'd say the boy's only footing's on a legal tightrope—at risk wherever he goes—including Berlin. But I've got to believe, like you, I'm sure these things happened in a way different from what they seemed. I can't imagine the fellow's at heart a cold-blooded killer."

"Miko, you're damn right. There's no alternative now. I've got to send my own people on a private mission to find and, I hate to say it, *capture* Orlando. We've put one of our finest generals—a hero of the Great War—in charge. We're going to run our own manhunt. He's been given carte blanche to lead the search. Already casting a dragnet of spies to capture any helpful information."

Michael was impressed at this grand scheme, but he was still alert to the uneven odds. Laughing lightly, he said, "Only you'd have the balls to pull this off against not only the police forces of Italy and Germany, but all the resources of the Seraphim! With Berlin at their helm, they too are now the enemy, alas."

49

November 1938

*O*rlando awoke the next morning, his memory clouded, uncertain where he was or where he had been the night before. Swinging his feet to touch the floor, the mists began to clear. A surge of excitement passed through him. He was puissant, yes, one of the new men, far above the herd. It was indeed his right to do just as he pleased. Without really grasping the fullness of what was happening to him, he stood up and stretched with a smile. He had willfully taken the first steps out onto the highest emotional tightrope of his life so far. And it made him feel high with power, almost indestructible. His nose itched as well. What pleasures had come by way of it last night.

His train was set to leave that afternoon. It was only ten-fifteen. He walked into the sitting room of his suite to check the crate. It hadn't moved from the far corner where he'd placed it as distant as possible from his own regular movements. When he approached, almost on tiptoe, there was little reaction. Just a small bounce up and down at one end and a soft sigh.

His morning proceeded with a shower and a shave by the hotel barber who came to his suite to perform this ritual. How satisfying to have that sense of smoothness that only came with a fine razor wielded by an expert. His hands ran over his face and throat after the barber had pulled off a hot towel and massaged the tight skin stretched over his high cheekbones. Once he had completed dressing in the well-cut clothes acquired the day before, he turned with delight before the dashing image captured in his full-length mirror.

On his way down to the lobby, a nagging unease—he'd kept it at bay—squirreled under the surface of a perfect day. How had the Turk known to call him *milord*? Well, no matter. That episode was done. Now he would think only of the glorious conclusion to the journey ahead.

The crate was locked into the trunk of his two-seater, and his leather valises were strapped to the shiny rack on the outside of the trunk lid. At the railway station, the car was taken to be loaded onto a special flatcar for the trip to Berlin—where he would appear in style as befitted his mission. Porters carried the crate and his valises to the double suite. He was met by the butler assigned to service the two suites that filled up the coach.

"Good afternoon, *Mein Herr.*" The butler wore a green and silver striped waistcoat and a small green bow tie. "The private parlor car's just next door. You'll find newspapers and refreshments while I install your things." Picking up the two suitcases, he looked at the crate and at Orlando with questioning eyes.

"Just leave that in the corner over there. No need to open it. Experimental creatures going to a laboratory in Berlin."

The butler's eyebrows went up a bit. "Do I have to feed them?"

Orlando laughed. "No, no. That's already taken care of. Usually pretty well behaved. Only sometimes act up." With that, he nodded and turned to leave for the next carriage. A table was covered with newspapers from Italy, Slovenia, Austria, and Germany. He ordered a coffee from the waiter. As he scanned through each of the newspapers to see if any items dealt with him, he could not suppress a tiny stab of fear. He finished. Nothing. At least not yet. No photos nor even mention made of any search for him. One more day to feel safe. And why not? After all, his disguise had been outrageous and misleading at the convent, and nobody could have had the slightest idea who might have been in the Venetian palazzo with the famously promiscuous Delphine. He should relax. Once he was in Germany, everything would change. He would be protected. They'd certainly understand. Everything that happened was done because of his mission. He'd saved the ark from Fritzi, after all. He felt himself straightening up. He was a man of destiny.

On schedule, the train's whistle blew, and steam clouds billowed back into the station as the engine's wheels were engaged. With a series of jerks and clangs, each of the cars began to roll.

Orlando sat in a comfortable armchair with his cup and saucer on a ledge beside him surrounded by a small brass rail to keep things from sliding off. He had selected the *Frankfurter Zeitung* from the others to read more completely. The headlines had intrigued him. They announced that tens of thousands of Jewish men were being transported to three internment camps: Buchenwald, Sachsenhausen, and Dachau. The article referred to the Kristallnacht earlier that month when throughout German-speaking Europe, the "people" had risen spontaneously and sacked and burned about two hundred synagogues. The Nazi High Command was quoted. Offended citizens had cleaned out thousands of Jewish shops to avenge those who had been "cheated" by their proprietors.

The nation was now on its way at last to purification. All Jewish children were to be expelled from German schools, and all retail establishments owned by Jews were to be turned over to Aryans.

Orlando leaned back with satisfaction. These people were so far ahead of his own country. Germany was the place for him. Progress and purity. And soon to possess the original Ark of the Covenant. He tingled at the thought and took a deep breath.

The regular movement of the train, rocking from side to side, had lulled him into a dream state. Images folded in and faded out, inspired by these news items as well as by his father's translation of the scrolls in the ark, which he'd read aloud to Delphine that incredible night.

She had insisted he do this—as a final sacrilege, she'd said. After he had finished reading, she'd asked, "Why on earth did the ancient Egyptian government even want to stop Akhenaten's Exodus? After all, the Jews were conveniently cleansing Egypt themselves by leaving in those huge numbers. It's going to be so much more complicated for Hitler, isn't it?"

Orlando was drifting now through a swirling miasma, fixed on something that had stuck in his mind from the translation. He wanted, in fact he needed, to know the untold story implied in the scrolls: the fate of Tutankhamun, the son, heir, crown prince. Things began to come into focus.

He could now clearly see the boy mounted on his horse and hear him saying goodbye to his father for the last time. To his sudden surprise, Orlando shared the emotional tug of the boy as it became vividly clear he was now to be forevermore on his own. The ten-year-old prince set his jaw like a man and gave the whip to his horse as he turned his chariot southward toward Thebes. Orlando felt he was riding with the boy-god as he headed for the first time in his young life to the ancient capital. Perhaps to be its ruler. With his return, Thebes would at last be restored to its traditional function as the center of the world's most powerful empire. Tutankhamun's unease was compounded by a vivid awareness. He would be used by the infamous General Horemheb as hostage, the key to exercising the powers through him of Pharaoh himself.

Orlando was now completely under the spell of his daydream. He was there, witness to events. Sounds, smells, tension, and fears of each moment were all awakened to his senses.

The veiled woman, charged with pretending to be Nefertiti and Horemheb's great prize, had hidden in her carriage beside the boy-king's chariot all the way to Thebes. What would Horemheb do when he learned she was not in fact the object of his obsessive desire? That scenario now took shape in rich detail.

The nearer they came to Thebes, the larger loomed the certainty that Horemheb's anger would probably be taken out on the boy as well. At the thought, bravely driving his chariot toward this destiny, he trembled more than ever before in his young life. On their arrival, the two of them were escorted without ceremony by a phalanx of spear-carriers straight into the presence of Horemheb.

When Horemheb walked with glowing eyes and a smile over to her, she backed away. He grabbed her arm and pulled aside her veil. She had known all along the journey from Akhetaten to Thebes that her fate had been determined. She fainted at his touch. It turned out to be a gift—she was blessedly unaware when Horemheb grabbed his dagger from its sheath and slit her throat with a sweep of his arm as she fell.

Seeing his chance, Tutankhamun ran at speed into the arms of the priests waiting just outside to welcome him as the rightful pharaoh. When Horemheb, bloody dagger in hand, ran after him, the priests formed a human barrier around the boy and declared that he was protected by the ancient gods. And now, at last, so were they. He was their salvation. His name and birthright would cancel the sins of his father's aberrations into monotheism. The old gods were now restored in the person of this young king, and no ambitious general was going to upset that applecart.

Horemheb saw instantly where his primary advantage now lay. Before the defiant priests, he announced he would marry the eldest of Akhenaten's five daughters by Nefertiti and thus become regent for his new brother-in-law. With arms folded across his bull-like chest, he stared them down.

The priests consulted each other briefly and gave agreement—at the same time spurring him on at speed to chase Akhenaten. This stratagem was a way to be rid, at least for the time, of the troublemaker and perhaps to be rid of him forever if Akhenaten's troops should gain the advantage.

But Horemheb had indeed come back from his expedition. Yes, admittedly with only a small number of survivors from his army's mass drownings in the sea whose waters had parted. But, like many leaders of history's failures, he announced the whole thing had been a remarkable success. Egypt would never see the heretic king again. The loss of his men had been the necessary price of peace and restoration of the old ways. He laid claim to the highest honors the nation could bestow. He was to be made a prince as well as the boy-pharaoh's regent.

The priests gathered in council for two days. They returned to the Temple of Karnak's main plaza to make their announcement. They arranged themselves in a large semicircle within the enormous pillars of the temple. Their white robes were embroidered with multicolored stripes and symbolic figures. The high priest declared henceforth that Tutankhamun would be under the priests' physical protection night and day as the living symbol of the ancient religion. Horemheb would be made a prince—and Pharaoh's regent—only until he reached the age of nineteen.

The newly minted prince-regent was still not happy.

Something interrupted this vivid reliving of events and made Orlando surface, semi-awake. He felt uneasy in the pit of his stomach. Why? He could not shake the image of Tutankhamun, the lurking threat, the smell of danger, and his fear of Horemheb. He was now conscious, and then he knew why he'd identified with the boy-king.

His eyes snapped all the way open and stared into the triangular smile of the Turk.

50

November 1938

upert picked up the telephone in his suite at the Hassler. The operator announced his wife was calling from Ravenstone Park.

"Lizzie, darling. Are you all right?"

The voice crackled over the long-distance wires. "Yes, I'm fine. But I can't bear what's happening. Your letters keep coming, and it gets worse and worse. What've we ever done to bring this about, Rupert?"

They continued for some time on the terrible turn Orlando's life had taken.

She said, "Two things … why I called. Happened to look into the little locked glass cabinet where you keep the small pistols."

Pausing to catch his breath, he said, "My parents' pistols?"

"That's right, darling. Well, one's missing. It can't be any of the staff—and only you and I know where the key is."

Rupert's jaw muscles flexed. "Damn it. Orlando gets into

everything. Christ! This whole mess started when he read a confidential letter from Michael with the codes he wanted me to have for his vault in Alexandria. I'm sure it's him. Who else would even want such a tragic object as that pistol? Certainly not our daughter!"

Lizzie said, "You're right. The other thing is Coutts bank called for you, and I spoke with them. It seems Orlando's been drawing large sums from his account, and they wondered whether we knew about this, and if it really was Orlando who was receiving these funds. The last big drafts were from Trieste and Slovenia. Ljubljana to be exact. I thought you should know this. I gather you've still got no idea where he is?"

Rupert's voice was excited. "My God, Lizzie, that's the first useful lead we've had. Of course, he must have taken that sick-minded woman's boat to Trieste—and then got himself up into Slovenia. We speculated about something like this, but we had no real leads to hang onto until now. Must go and call the fellow who's leading our search. Wish us luck, darling. I'll let you know as we go along, my love." He hung up and let his hand rest for a few moments on the phone.

His distinguished general, who'd been a remarkable tactician in the Great War, knew what to do. He set in motion all the forces he'd assembled at Rupert's request, and within five hours, he had gleaned the clear lines of a plausible story. It seems someone corresponding to Orlando's description was using a new German passport name. He'd engaged half of a special railcar and a special flatcar for moving an extremely expensive motorcar corresponding to one purchased from the payee named by Coutts Bank. The train had left the afternoon before from Ljubljana, and the special railcars were engaged all the way to Berlin. There were no records anywhere showing any other wealthy German with the name used for these transactions. The general's intelligence team had concluded the sums transferred by Coutts bank corresponded to the levels of spending required for the lavish style of the German with Orlando's new passport name. He recommended the search now be focused entirely on intercepting this person. Presumably, he was still on that train. They would have a contingent of special forces present at the train's next scheduled stop.

☥

Orlando had flinched at the sight of the Turk. He turned his head away as if returning to sleep. His eyes sneaked back to see if he was still there—and looked away again.

"Ah, milord, now don't you seem comfortable here in our private lounge car. Quite a coincidence we should be sharing this epitome of luxurious travel, no? Well, I'm ticketed all the way to Berlin. And you? Getting off sooner, perhaps in Salzburg? I hear the skiing's quite good now. Season's started a bit early, you know."

Orlando's hand went to the bridge of his nose and massaged between his eyes as if to clear them. He pondered whether his dream had been reality and if the Turk was now just a dream.

"Ah yes, now I see it's you on the train. That explains something. Of course. It has to be you who owns that absolutely divine motorcar they loaded onto the train. Am I right? I was really quite curious, you know. Not everyone can afford that sort of thing. Have you had it for long?" The Turk sat down in the leather lounge chair next to him, arranged himself, and pulled a long cigarette holder from an inner breast pocket. He laid it carefully on the same small shelf where Orlando's half-finished coffee sloshed about in its cup. He pulled out a cigarette case, snapped it open, and leaned over to offer one.

Orlando waved his hand. "No thanks, not now. Must be

going back to my room." His voice was barely audible. He placed both hands on the sides of his chair as if to rise.

The Turk smiled and held down his forearm. "We've got to enjoy the leisure of our surroundings, my dear fellow. You ought not to be rushing off. One really must adopt a bit of the Italians' approach. *Far niente* and all that. I recommend complete relaxation with a fine glass of your favorite drink. What was it you enjoyed so much last night? Ah, yes, the absinthe. Well, now I suppose you'll have to settle for something else. Shall I order a bottle of the '29 Krug rosé? Awfully nice stuff, you know." He pushed the call bell in the mahogany paneling. "Had some bottles delivered to our steward—who, I see, is coming to take our order."

The Turk twisted a cigarette into the open end of his golden holder.

The steward, without missing a beat, struck a match and held it ready. "Will you be having your champagne now, sir? It's chilled and ready to be served."

The Turk turned to Orlando who had collapsed back into his chair. "Do you like coupes or those nasty flutey things some slaves of the latest fads are making all the rage?"

Orlando shook his head. His eyes were now a little bloodshot.

The steward spoke, "Afraid we've only got the coupes. Will that do, sir?"

"By all means, my good fellow."

Outside, the day had turned dark earlier than usual. The train chugged along through the crepuscular light that was beginning to be flecked with bits of snow striking the windows of the train, tiny explosions of white crystals lit by the sconces of the parlor car. As the train gathered speed on the straight stretches, the snow flew by in streaks.

"How do you know?" The words came out almost as a whisper.

The Turk leaned toward Orlando. "What? What is it I'm supposed to know?"

"I don't think you need to be told what I mean. Not really. You already know." Orlando was on the verge of weeping.

The Turk gave him his ghastly smile. "Be strong, my good fellow. Strength is what justifies everything. You've given your soul for it. Might as well practice its use. Now please tell me what I'm supposed to know that mystifies you."

Orlando bowed his head and spoke as if to himself. "Who I am … that's what." His lips twitched as did the muscles in his cheeks.

The Turk laughed. It was high-pitched, thin, almost a cackle. He swept his long cigarette holder through the air in an arc. "I know everything, milord. That is to say, men have secrets, but they reveal them because they have them. A secret changes a man. I can read those changes. Very simple, after all." His eyebrows pitched down and met in a little frown, emphasizing their upward tilt in a V even more. "But I can also keep secrets. You need never be afraid of what I know."

"But … I … am … afraid." The words hung, suspended, waiting for a response.

The Turk's lower lip curled out. "Now I really am disappointed, I must confess. After last night, you were in the full bloom of your powers—radiant, fulfilled, sure of yourself—why has it come to this?"

As if on cue, the steward materialized and topped up the Turk's glass. He turned to Orlando. "Haven't touched your champagne, sir. A wonderful vintage. You'll certainly appreciate it once you try it." He smiled and replaced the bottle in a bucket recessed in the mahogany counter.

Orlando reached over and took the glass. Some of its contents had splashed onto the polished surface. Their train had a way of rocking around the bends as it cut through the mountains. Peaks were visible in moonlit flashes piercing the veil of snowfall.

"Now that's better, isn't it?" The Turk spoke in a soothing, caressing tone, as if to a child. "We all need reinforcement every now and again." He reached into his waistcoat pocket and extracted a small, jeweled pillbox. With almost exaggerated delicacy, he placed his thumbnail under the catch and lifted the golden lid.

Orlando studied his movements, curious. He backed away slightly as the Turk's hand dipped in and pulled out a small dark-green tablet, which he reached across and dropped into Orlando's glass. "This will bring things back to an equilibrium, my dear fellow. You will see."

Orlando watched it disintegrate, a little dark cloud dispersing in the champagne. It was accompanied by an enhanced release of tiny bubbles. He took a sip, and then another, and then he drained the shallow glass.

The steward suddenly appeared, smiling, and refilled the glass. "Now there you are, sir. Let no pleasure go to waste, I always say."

Orlando looked at him, his voice slurring a little. "You're British, aren't you?"

"Why, how did you know? Is my German so telling? Would I be right in guessing you might be the same, sir?"

Orlando caught himself. "No, no. German. French mother. First language. Perhaps that's what you hear."

The steward bowed, "Of course, sir." He turned away, stopped, and asked, "Dinner will be ready anytime you wish. Will you be sitting at separate tables?"

The Turk tapped off the ash from his cigarette. "Thank you. We'll share a table."

51

November 1938

*A*t the suggestion of his general, Rupert had flown that morning from Rome to Salzburg. The weather changed as they crossed the Alps. Whipped by winds and snow, the small aircraft was blown about and prone to sudden up and down drafts that tested even the pilot's courage.

When they landed at the modest airport, the snow was sheeting across the runway. Rupert had wondered if the plane would be flipped over by the wind even while it was taxiing to the terminal building. He huddled against it as he emerged down the little steps that had been dropped to the tarmac.

Two men in business suits and overcoats waited beside the plane and tipped the fedoras they were clutching. Despite their discreet dress, they were part of the special forces his man had convened here at Salzburg, the next major stop of the train that was probably carrying his son.

The Austrian police were polite at passport control. In

response to the usual questions, he explained he was just a tourist to see Mozart's birthplace and attend some concerts.

The leading policeman asked if he was planning to attend *Don Giovanni* that very evening.

Rupert gave a delighted look to his two attendants, and they nodded. "Why, that does seem quite a good idea. Must arrange for a ticket."

The two men brought him to the Hotel Goldener Hirsch. The streets were becoming slippery with the constant snowfall. Passing through the heavy wooden doors carried on huge wrought iron hinges, the warmth of the small reception room was welcome.

The clerks in snappy green and black uniforms handed Rupert a heavy wax-sealed envelope.

"Thank you. By chance could you find me a good seat for *Giovanni* tonight?"

"Certainly, milord. I'm sure we can find a ticket. Just one?"

Rupert turned to the two men who both shook their heads. "Yes, just one seat, thanks."

The two men guided him to the small bar where they sat over coffee and schnapps. They explained the train with a passenger presumed to be Orlando was scheduled to arrive the next morning. He could spend the evening as he wished. They would fetch him at the hotel at eight in the morning. The envelope contained a list of the special forces and the tactical maneuvers that had been planned to remove Orlando from the train and take him back to the airport where he would fly with Rupert to England.

"I see, gentlemen. Well, let's hope the Austrians haven't yet linked this passenger with someone known to be important to Berlin."

One of the men said, "That's likely to be a certainty, I'm afraid. The Germans have clearly been out looking for your son, if our current information's correct. Of course, they're aware of his false passport identity. On the other hand, they won't know you have that information. Therefore, they won't necessarily be aware we're waiting in Salzburg. But we've got to act quickly and precisely. We know the special railcar he's in, and there are only two suites in that car. The special flatbed with his fancy motorcar, we'll worry about later. It can always be retrieved. We'll have just twenty minutes before the train resumes its journey."

Having freshened up in his room, Rupert descended the stairs to the lobby and left the hotel from the back door in the dining room. He was bundled into a heavy overcoat and gloves, with the brim of his fedora pulled down tightly to shield his eyes from the driving snow. It was slow going on the sidewalks. He managed to stay standing and reach the Great Festival Hall within a few minutes. He felt disgusted when he saw a great row of identical flags with huge swastikas ruffling in the wind along the facade. A large contingent of gestapo were gathered by their motorcycles, flanking a Mercedes limousine.

In the lobby, people's voices rose in a confused babble, and commotion reigned.

Rupert asked one of the doorkeepers, "What's the matter?"

The man, standing rather stiffly as if he were being reviewed by an army officer, responded, "Herr Reichsminister Goebbels has arrived unexpectedly. Maestro Toscanini has just refused to perform, and Maestro Furtwängler agreed to take the podium tonight."

"I see." He nodded and produced his ticket. Directed by the same attendant, he headed up a staircase where an usher showed him to a seat on the aisle. Checking out the crowd, he concluded that mostly prosperous Austrians were present, ladies in long dresses and fur wraps and men in dinner jackets and black ties. After the audience had been seated, the orchestra filed in followed by Wilhelm Furtwängler, who was booed by several of Toscanini's more intrepid stalwarts.

The conductor took his position and raised both arms to launch the orchestra into a rendition of *"Deutschland Uber Alles"* with a full-throated vocal accompaniment from the seats. As it concluded, there was a roll of drums and a trumpet fanfare. Three men emerged from a side door and were escorted to their seats in the center of the first row. The man at the rear was Joseph Goebbels.

Rupert felt a visceral tug of revulsion at the sight of the insect-like, pallid face of the man who had sent Fritzi to Alexandria and was no doubt this moment hot on his trail—if he had not already found the poor brute and the gorgeous Solange. Furtwängler turned around to face the audience and reached down to shake Goebbels's hand. There was some applause, and a few shouts of "Heil Hitler" sent shivers through Rupert.

Three hours later, the well-deserved final retribution for the arrogant and unfeeling rogue, Don Giovanni, was underway. The *commendatore* whom he had killed at the outset of the opera was now back from the dead, brought by the Don's own taunting invitation to dine together. The commendatore's voice rang sepulchral and resonant as if issuing from the depths of the earth.

He called three times for his murderer to repent, but the Don refused and stood his ground. The commendatore grabbed his arm and gave a chilling cry of condemnation. With the orchestra building to a thundering climax, Don Giovanni fought the demons as they inexorably pulled their victim to eternal damnation through a wall of flames. At this moment, a side door opened into the audience, and one of the two men who had met Rupert at the airport rushed in, shaking off an usher's restraining grip on his arm. Rupert turned to look and left his seat as soon as he recognized him. They moved quickly back and over to the side door while Don Giovanni plunged forever into perdition.

The man murmured, "I'll tell you in a minute. Let's first get past the gestapo gang out there. Walk casually and speak to me as if we're having a pleasant conversation." These instructions were delivered with the usher fuming, keeping pace alongside them. The special service man turned and stared the usher into silence with his threatening stance. "Enough, now go away!"

They turned the corner at the bottom of the staircase and sauntered along to the lobby doors, adjusting their hats and gloves. Heads down, ignoring the now almost frozen contingent of gestapo guards outside, they turned left and then right toward the rear of the hotel and out of the guards' view.

"All right, now, we've got an emergency. Very little actual information, but here's the story. The train's way behind schedule. Last heard, the train hasn't passed an automatic signal point that should have registered their passage some hours ago. That fact combined with reports of unusually heavy snowfall and possible avalanches in the mountains has us very worried."

"So, what do you propose we do, if anything?" Rupert's natural habit of reacting coolly had taken hold. "I can't think there is much we can do."

The special forces man spoke quickly and to the point. "The general has sent instructions to various points along the way to where we think the train might have stopped. Right now, snow-removal vehicles mobilized by us are clearing the mountain roads. It won't be easy, and we may be thwarted by avalanches obstructing the roads, but we'll give it our best effort. Do you want to join us?"

"Of course, I'll go with you. I assume you've got vehicles that can navigate in these conditions?"

"We do." The special services man signaled to the driver of a four-wheel-drive Mercedes Overland vehicle parked near the hotel's rear doorway. It drew forward, and both men climbed in. They began their journey passing under the brooding castle commanding the heights over the city and continued through the little villages that lay along their route toward the mountains.

"A number of our forces are well ahead, sir."

Rupert marveled at what had been engineered by his general, increasingly convinced he deserved his reputation for tactical and strategic ingenuity.

They drove along roads that had been cleared just for his people, moving gradually higher into the mountains. They passed their first snow-removal vehicle in a little cleared spot next to the road, waiting for whatever more needed to be done.

"Brilliant," Rupert said to the man who had fetched him from the opera house.

The other fellow smiled and remained silent. They were all focused on the road ahead. The snowfall was now a bit lighter, and glimpses of jagged peaks came and went against a moon-backlit sky and clouds.

They passed another snow-removal truck. Hands waved from each side with thumbs up. The road wound deeper and higher into the mountains. They passed through mounds of snow piled tall in some places where the trucks had coped with minor avalanches. So far, there were no major rockfalls, and the going was slow and deliberate.

Rupert could not help speculating about the meeting he might be about to have with Orlando. His anxiety to find him had blocked any subtler considerations of what it would be like if and when they did meet. Now, there was the fullness of time playing out to an ending that he found difficult exactly to predict. Would he even know the man? His and Elizabeth's only son, a moral ruin caught in a vast drama of his own making. And there could be no happy conclusion.

What the three men did not see, even though they were in the rear guard of the general's operation to find the train, was the tidal wave building in their wake.

52

November 1938

*T*he Turk raised his glass of Haut Brion '28. "Here's to the good life, my friend." The train was now moving more slowly through the snow-blown darkness.

Orlando had been restored to confidence. He was back again perched on his emotional tightrope. The little pill had done its work. He once again saw himself in glory, a shining knight bringing the grail to King Arthur. He tapped his glass against the Turk's. "Papa always says this vineyard's '28 was better even than the '29."

Flourishing his triangular smile, the Turk leaned forward. "In most cases, I take it you don't always agree with your father?"

Jerked up a bit like a fish just caught on a hook, Orlando stammered, "Not in politics."

"Is that all?"

Orlando stared through his companion, taken by a sudden onrush of feelings. He was gripped by a reprise of his daydream—that imagined moment charged with menace when Tutankhamen had met Horemheb. And he was pierced to the gut now by the boy's longing for the protection of his father whom he knew he would never see again. But this surge of feeling passed, banished by the pill, and he said, "Well, Papa's never really appreciated me. Tessie's got most of his attention. She walks on water. I may be his heir, but he'll never understand me. Anyway, we believe in different gods. He's a family person, devoted to his profession and to his rather grand position in our British world. He wants to do good, but he doesn't aspire to greatness."

"How is that?" The Turk's eyelids had fallen to cover half of his eyes.

Orlando took the initiative this time. "Why don't you tell me what you see as greatness in a man?"

The Turk looked up at the ceiling. "Ah, from you, an interesting question. Indeed, you've parried my thrust. Still, I'll go along with your little game. Let's see. We can either make this what they call a moment of truth—or we can take the easy way. Which do you prefer?"

"I'll take it straight. Let's have the truth."

"All right then. We'll start with human desire. What's the greatest driving force of mankind, the very reason for life existing at all? Desire, of course. Desire to survive, desire to copulate, desire to dominate. These are the cardinal desires. There are lesser ones like protecting a child, helping the poor, being a good citizen. But with these, desire is muddied by virtue. It loses sight of the transforming beauty of the cardinal desires carried to their ultimate state."

Orlando said, "So, the cardinal desires are those that come mainly from appetites and basic instincts?"

The Turk's smile for the briefest moment looked like a death's head. The triangle of his smile had become part of the cavity left by the missing flesh of the nose and lips that stopped covering the two levels of teeth. It was just a moment, a flash of revelation, enough to make Orlando want another of those little pills from the Turk's bejeweled repository.

"You've focused exactly on my point. Good for you." The Turk placed a cigarette in his glittering holder and held it to a votive candle on the dining table. Drawing the cigarette into flickering life, he said, "Have you ever scratched some part of you that itched terribly until you felt relief? Yet the aftereffect left things inflamed even worse than before you'd scratched. Greatness occurs when you know how to distract yourself from the soreness by satisfying another of the senses. And so forth. Greatness comes from directing, focusing, and moderating your cardinal desires to a higher purpose. It comes from being willing to dare to indulge to their limits without losing the powers of rational choice."

Orlando attempted to rephrase the Turk's prescription. "So, you're saying greatness comes from satisfying our cardinal desires only up to a point? That point is where indulgence becomes immoderate. Scratching the itch, but not until it gets sore?"

The Turk shook his head. "No ... I'm afraid you're missing the real message. Greatness comes from indulging the cardinal desires to excess—to their very limits—but knowing how to avoid the consequences of scratching an itch to soreness. It's all right to drive yourself to ecstatic pain as long as you've got the antidote. The antidote is an intoxicating awareness you've transcended ordinary men."

Orlando had never been inclined to self-examination. He'd a life spent mainly fulfilling the caprices of desire. This chaotic theme had repeated itself for years like a scratched record incapable of passing a certain point. But now, something else was touching him for the first time, a new, quite different insight.

Far removed from that bloodline driving his grandparents to suicide and their older son the same. Those facts had always hovered like a black crow on his own singular branch of the family tree. But in this very moment, a ray of comprehension had come to him—and it came now, unbidden, directly from the wisdom of Rupert, his father, mercifully untouched by the Ravenstone curse.

He looked the Turk calmly in the eyes. "You're arguing greatness only comes to those who can kill their conscience. Because conscience can bring the worst pain of all."

His companion stared at him without speaking for some moments. He spoke at last. "I see. Perhaps I misjudged you. You've really grasped the nettle. You've had that moment of truth. Yes, conscience is the bane of greatness. It is the begetter of cowardice. It can lead only to mediocrity."

Orlando's eyes were haunted. They had become gray hollows in his handsome face. He had understood finally, confronting at last his many years of self-deception, dulled by indulgence and by drugs. "It seems I can murder men, but not my conscience." The muscles of his jaw were drawn tight to the point of twitching. He stood up.

The steward rushed over to help with his chair. The obsequious man looked at the Turk as Orlando pushed him aside.

Everyone's attention shifted at the sudden, jolting arrest of the train, brakes grinding, screaming aloud with the pain of steel meeting itself in friction to awaken and torment the dead.

Orlando was almost toppled to the floor as he grabbed a fixed armchair for support.

Outside the windows, the world was suddenly lit as if stage lights had banished the darkness. They were perched on a bridge high above a chasm between two mountains. The light got brighter and then pushed past them, and the view was canceled by the engine and freight cars of another train heading in the opposite direction. It too was braking with the same terrifying sound of steel in desperate pain. At last, it slowed and shuddered to a stop. The two trains now rested in an uncanny silence beside each other on this trestle bridge.

The Turk had a look of mild amusement. He leaned back in his chair and drew smoke once again from his cigarette holder.

Orlando rushed past him to the platform at the end of the car. He stood at the window away from the other train and looked down into the river rushing through the bridge supports far below. The moon had emerged from shifting clouds. Everywhere on the mountainsides was snow captured in a spectral light. He turned and walked back through the car without speaking to the men who were studying his movements. He entered the corridor outside the two suites and opened the door to his. Inside, all was in order. His bed had been turned down, and clothes had been hung in the mirrored closet. Shaving things were laid out on the lavabo top along with his hairbrush. He looked up at his reflection and recoiled.

Voices, muffled sounds, he thought, were coming from the ark. He approached. This time, the ancient chest in its crate did not react. It remained perfectly calm, docile—even when he touched it. The commotion got louder and closer. It was clear now, coming from somewhere outside. He let down his window and stared up and down the blank sides of freight cars strung along the tracks parallel to his on the bridge. People's excited shouts, babies crying, female and male calls out to others, so close but not to be seen. Why would people be in those windowless freight cars? Babies? It all struck him as surreal. The strange hoarseness of scraping doors suspended on rusting tracks cut through the silent night like screams.

Turning his head toward the engine of the other train, he could see a white moonlit wall gleaming in the distance. The engine seemed to have plowed into the wall, but he thought this could not be—until it occurred to him. The massive amount of fresh snow must have accumulated so quickly it could not stay put. An avalanche. He snapped his head the other way to look at his own train's engine. A shiver suddenly jittered down his spine. Two avalanches. Such symmetry surely was not going to happen. But it had. His mind discovered how both trains were able to be stymied by avalanches caused by the other train passing onto the bridge at the same time. When each train had entered simultaneously upon the structure that was now bearing both trains, avalanches had been triggered by a freakish coincidence at each end, stopping the other from leaving the bridge and passing onto the mountainsides.

Behind him, a thumping, agitated sound began to come from the crate. The ark was beginning to act up. He turned to look. It had actually moved closer to him. His attention was caught by the sound of someone outside his door. It was sibilant, like something hissing. The ark's voices were now moaning as if in sorrow—or pain.

A movement outside the window. He turned to see a large, bearded face looking up at him lit by the light from his room. Fierce and questioning. Almost biblical, it struck him. Someone was trying to open the door of his suite. With every shaking of the nob, the ark reacted. Orlando rushed over and pulled up the lock's latch.

As Orlando swung the door open, the Turk leaned back and brought his cigarette holder up to his lips. With a little smile and a coy tip of his head to one side, the Turk said, "I think, milord, you are about to have a visitor. I would pay no attention to him if I were in your shoes. He will want something you have. And he will want it very badly. You will see. Be strong and sure of your mission. People like this are the enemy. They want to thwart your destiny."

In the background, the ark in its crate had skittered as far from the doorway as possible. The Turk watched it and stepped past Orlando into the room. At this, a howling sound arose from the ark, and it bounced up and down as if possessed.

A large man in a dark suit and overcoat suddenly filled the doorway. His beard was full and long, and he wore thick glasses in a silver wire frame. An aura of purpose radiated from him. His eyes fixed on the crate, which had now stopped all sound and motion. The visitor strode over to where it lay and dropped to both knees. He bowed his head and rested both hands on the crate. From his lips came words that Orlando could not understand.

But Orlando had an inkling of what he was witnessing. New voices could be heard from the corridor outside his suite. He saw the steward rush past his doorway. A commanding voice ordered the newcomers out of the railcar. They resisted and argued.

Orlando heard a gunshot and ran to look into the corridor.

A small contingent of bedraggled men were looking down at one of their own writhing on the floor from a wound in his leg.

"Now get out of here, you Yiddish rabble. Get out!" the steward screamed.

The group helped the wounded man to his feet and backed out of the car. Orlando returned to the scene inside. The rabbi had stood and was facing the Turk.

"This is not to be yours. Your people lost all rights to it the moment they abandoned the man who ascended Sinai to receive the so-called Word of his God. And a good thing that was, it seems to me. Now I suggest you leave without any commotion."

A loud laugh emerged from pink lips nested in the dark beard. "Sir, you cannot be serious. It was the hand of God that stopped our trains. He meant for us to find this. You cannot change fate."

All heads turned. A shudder ran through the railcar. The sound of something snapping, loud and sharp, was followed by another tremor.

The Turk waved his hand with the cigarette holder. "Now, sir, that is fate. Yours is coming sooner than you thought. I suggest you move aside and let us take this thing to a safer place."

Alarm and determination mobilized the large man. He reached down and grabbed both sides of the crate. He stood up with it securely in his hands and pushed past the Turk and Orlando. "We will save this. My people on that train, that's taking us to perdition, will be saved as well. I will lead them from our death train with this to protect them."

The Turk backed away from the rabbi and his burden, putting one arm up before his face as if to protect himself from them. The rabbi continued through the doorway and entered the corridor where the steward pressed himself hard against the windows, his head turned away as the large man approached him.

Without a word, Orlando, ignoring the Turk and the steward, followed the rabbi. He reached him at the steps leading onto the space between the two trains. The exit door had been opened by the contingent of men waiting outside with their wounded companion. Orlando said, "Let me help you."

The large man stood at the top of the steps where he had put down the crate. He looked back to Orlando and nodded. Another shudder of the bridge made them both clutch at the walls until it had passed with a series of new snapping sounds. The two trains now appeared to be leaning slightly away from each other. Voices cried in alarm inside the freight train.

Several of the men left them to retrieve their families for an exodus from the bridge.

Orlando moved around the crate and jumped down the steps. He stood at the bottom to accept one end and helped the rabbi bring it down to the level of the tracks. The two men stopped to assess the situation. The crate had been placed across two ties running perpendicular to the rails. They looked down at the wide spaces between the rail ties and could see through the complex understructure of the bridge, down to the moonlit waters of the river rushing around its pylons far below.

Orlando said, "Let's head toward the engine of my train. It's closer to us and away from wherever you were being taken—probably the better bet."

The rabbi nodded, and they reached down to pick up the crate and began gingerly to navigate the ties to safety.

53

November 1938

The special agent cursed when he got back into the rear of Rupert's Mercedes Overland vehicle. Pointing at the snow-removal truck next to them, he said, "Just got the radio report. Damn little certainty just where the train's stopped, you know. We've got it narrowed down to about a two-mile stretch. But that's not ideal, given snow conditions and mountainous terrain. They've got search parties out on snowshoes, and with dogs, but it's real tough going out there. We can go a little bit further in this truck, but the rest will be on our feet—over the snow and whatever else is underneath it."

Rupert agreed. "We'll do just that. Now the night sky's clear—there's a large moon. Do you think the train crew might have been able to clear the tracks and continue through whatever might have stopped it?"

"Not likely, sir. It's likely to have been an avalanche of snow and rocks, something like that. They won't have anybody coming on the railway line itself with emergency equipment until daylight. We're the first responders right now, and nobody can predict what, if anything, we'll find."

Another truck was standing where they made their final stop. The driver and his assistant were perched high above them behind the truck's windscreen, boiling tea over a burner placed on the dashboard. The flame cast a bluish tint on their faces, turning them into flickering masks with eerie expressions. They opened a window and explained where the search parties had gone and suggested they hold on until more information had been radioed in.

Rupert, however, was not about to wait. "Let's put on our snowshoes and take our ski poles to search for the railway line, which we can follow until we find the train."

The two agents nodded. They all changed shoes and put on jackets with fur-lined hoods that covered all but their eyes and noses.

When the snowshoes had been strapped on, one of the men from the truck appeared similarly protected against the elements. "OK. You'll follow me. Here, strap these lights to your foreheads. Sorry, should have given them before you fixed your hoods."

They set out, a little band of moving lights like deep-sea divers in search of treasure. They ascended over rising and jagged terrain, across small plateaus and through occasional stands of pine trees. A good hour passed before their first sighting of the railway tracks. The terrain was precarious enough to make one wonder how laying the tracks had been managed in the first place.

"Which way should we go?" Rupert stood at the barely visible tracks with mounds of snow swept into soft undulating forms highlighted by the moon.

"We're going to the right. That leads to a gorge spanned by

a trestle bridge, maybe a mile from here." The leader adjusted the flashlight on his forehead. "We probably can see enough by the moon's light. Just follow the tracks. The forward party should already be at the bridge. Maybe they've even crossed it to the other side."

"How many of our special forces do you think are out there?" Rupert picked up one snowshoe and then the other to set them in the chosen direction.

"We've mobilized a total of sixty top professionals. Fully trained by the British government to handle the most sensitive jobs. These guys can do anything and leave the most minimal traces." The leader lifted his hand to signal they were to proceed. He started with the zest of an athlete and made his ski poles swing in a regular rhythm.

Rupert kept up with him, feeling strong but with the altitude adding a touch of light-headedness. They entered a stand of pines, tall loads of snow piled on most of their spreading upper branches. A sudden wind caused one of these to tremble, sending a cloud of snow down upon their heads.

Unseen hands held a pair of special binoculars that could make out clear images in the moonlit snowscape. Lothar von Vranken handed them to his companion. "These night eyes are amazing. Our German engineers are the world's best, no? I see the sitting ducks are moving toward the south, winter's early, no!"

"Yes, Mein Oberst Graf, these new binoculars give us a nice advantage. The British have nothing like them."

"We must thank those nice people for clearing the roads for us too." Von Vranken sucked in his cheeks and meditated on their strategy. "Best of all, our pigeon's been using a new name provided by our London team when he agreed to get involved in this operation. No one but our people should know our

Lord Cressy's new identity. He's traveling in first-class style as befits a titled member of the Hanseatic nobility. An invented title that sounds real and matches the young poppycock's self-delusions." He rubbed his hands with their thick gloves over his face to stimulate circulation against the cold that made his face feel frozen into immobility.

The young noncom looked at his superior with a puzzled expression and hesitated about how he was going to express his next thought. Gathering courage, he said, "Still, Oberst Graf, the ducks have somehow figured out where to look for the pigeon in spite of his new identity. How did this come to pass, do you think?"

Von Vranken's pale blue eyes clouded over at this dissection of his selective alternate reality. "Oh, I'm sure that'll be fairly easy to explain. And, as we've found tonight, it's really been quite helpful to have the ducks search for our pigeon. Once we knew their movements, we were able to use them in this freak storm. Tonight, we've got power over the ducks, and they've no idea. We know where they are, and—most wonderful of all—it's on German soil."

The Austrian noncom straightened his stance. "Right you are, Oberst Graf. As of these past few weeks, Austria's become a proud part of the Reich. Heil Hitler!"

"Indeed. Heil Hitler! And without spilling a drop of blood. It's our destiny, young man, and you are privileged to be part of it." His eyes blazed with conviction—and scheming ambition.

Other members of the Seraphim's forces converged upon von Vranken from among the many trees overlooking the railway line.

A captain asked, "Do we follow now, Oberst Graf, or wait for news from the front line?"

Von Vranken raised an eyebrow and said, "No need to

advance yet. We've got the advantage. They don't know we're here, and that's all that matters—for the time being. We're in perfect position to cover their only route back to the roads, which they've so very kindly cleared for us."

54

November 1938

Orlando picked where he was stepping. One slip between the ties could mean a broken leg—or much worse. Another girder snapped off the structure shedding itself astride the chasm. He glimpsed it tumbling in cartwheels down to the river far below. By far the noisiest crack so far, it was followed by the first indications of swaying. Orlando concentrated all his faculties even more, obsessed with making it to safety. Now driven by a complete reversal of his earlier motivations, his single-minded thought was to save the ark and deliver it into benign hands. He felt its warmth passing from his hand on the robe handle of the crate, traveling up through his arm to his neck and his face. In the freezing night, his face was hot, his body was not cold, and his heart was beating at double its normal rate. He turned to look back at his companion. The rabbi was weeping. Loud sobs lurched out from his throat. He was intoning in an ancient tongue Orlando had never heard.

They passed along the blank sides of the freight cars between the two trains, while the growing stream of passengers slowed down the two men with the ark. The multitude somehow knew what was passing among them and began to chant. The rabbi swallowed back the tears and joined their voices. The chorus of jubilation seemed to gather force from the swaying bridge, drowning out the terror they felt as more girders snapped and the swaying increased. The ark was their inspiration and their protection as long as it remained with them on the bridge.

Nearing the end of the bridge, Orlando looked up and saw a swarm of men shoveling away the avalanched snows that had stopped his train. Although the firm footing of the mountain was gradually being exposed, there was barely enough room for two or three people at a time to leave the bridge.

As people ahead of Orlando and the rabbi reached the end, they were helped onto the rock and handed up to others staged at different levels on the pile of snowy debris. When Orlando placed his foot onto rock, he felt a huge depletion of energy.

A man holding a shovel looked at him as if he were one of the condemned Jews and said in English, "You're safe now. We're friends." Orlando allowed his end of the crate to be taken by someone who appeared to understand what it was while the rabbi insisted on stumbling with it up over the mound to safety.

Orlando turned around to help the stream of Jews making their way with frightening slowness. He was suddenly aware that something so malignant as to be incomprehensible was taking place before his eyes. The Turk and the steward were moving swiftly toward his end of the bridge, wielding walking sticks like weapons to beat aside the men, women, and children struggling to cross from rail tie to rail tie. People screamed in pain as they fell partway or completely through the ties. Others tried to fight back and grab the flailing sticks, but to no avail.

Orlando helped the lucky ones reaching the rock. He took

children from the arms of parents so they could find their footing on the slippery surface. The prisoners' faces were haunted. They seemed to have no good choices even if they survived the immediate danger. No escape from this forlorn place seemed possible. Only the British voices of their rescuers gave some a tiny sense of hope.

Two more girders shot off the upright framework of the bridge. The Turk and the steward had almost reached safety when the roadbed at the other end of the bridge began to tilt to the side. The engine of the freight train teetered on its left wheels for a precarious moment and then tumbled over the side, dragging the freight cars one by one, ripped from the tracks and still containing the souls of those unable or unwilling to traverse the bridge to safety.

This sent a violent shudder as the bridge twisted like a huge snake trying to turn itself over. Orlando's train followed quickly the other. Its contortions dragged the prisoners still hanging onto the bridge as it tipped over and slid down the collapsing rails like an out-of-control roller coaster to the river below.

Just at the brink of safety, the Turk had reached out his hand to Orlando for support while he tried to get his right foot up onto land from the bridge falling away beneath him. Behind him, the steward had already been sent screaming into space with this last undulation of the span.

Orlando, about to extend his hand, hesitated for a moment—just long enough to be too late. The Turk flashed his triangular smile as he slipped away. Orlando stood at the jagged edge and stared at him cartwheeling into the chasm. He remained in place, not moving. Alone, no one left to rescue.

A voice spoke up beside him. One he recognized. "My son, my poor boy. At last." Rupert had climbed through the now well-worn groove in the avalanched snow. He looked down to the tangled mess below and took Orlando's arm. "Come away from the edge. You've been too close to it for far too long, dear boy."

The younger man turned and looked at the older one, standing now face-to-face. His expression ran the gamut, as if it was a silent film of rapidly changing and exaggerated emotions. "Papa? How did you get here?" His voice sounded confused. His thoughts were indeed muddled. The daydream that had haunted him on the train was playing out again. The prince Tutankhamun is saying goodbye to his father. Is it forever? The danger posed by Horemheb, the ambitious general? But that perhaps disappeared with the Turk? Where was this story going? Was there only one ending?

"Where are your thoughts, my boy?" Rupert reached up and smoothed his son's hair. "Come back to me from wherever you are."

Orlando reached into a pocket and withdrew a small pearl-handled pistol. He stepped back and said, "No, Papa, I can't ever come back. It's over." His voice caught. "I've gone too far." He started to weep. Huge quantities of tears poured out, and his body convulsed with pain.

Rupert reached out his hand. "Give that to me, son. It's not meant for you. It's done enough damage already."

Orlando shook his head and took another step back. "I've been so wrong, Papa. There's no way I can fix what I've done. I'm terribly sorry, Papa. I've shamed you. I've brought dishonor to a great man." His shoulders heaved in a shrug, and then his arms spread apart in a hopeless gesture. "I just wanted to make my own rules. Live my own way." An ironic laugh. "Pretty stupid, no?" He dried his eyes with the back of the other hand.

Rupert said, "There's redemption, my boy. Orlando, come to me. Let me hold you … like I did when you were just a boy." Rupert extended both arms, and Orlando let him move forward until he found his father's arms wrapped around him. Both men remained thus while the wind picked up and blew gusts of snow that powdered their heads and shoulders.

"My, my. What a pretty picture, no? Really now, Rupert. Consorting with criminals? What will the prime minister think the next time you give one of your virtuous diatribes against Germany in the House of Lords?" Lothar von Vranken stood above them with hands on hips at the apex of the defile cut through the avalanched snow. He started to laugh. "And as for you, our confused young Anglo-Nazi turned Jew-sympathizer—the rabbi was full of praise for the way you helped him carry the ark. He called it *his* ark, actually. Well, I'm pleased to advise it's no longer his. As they say, you can't take it with you—and even rabbis know that before they die. Which he did, but only after asking me to convey his thanks to you, my young Lord Cressy."

Orlando backed away from his father. The pistol was still in his hand. His eyes narrowed, and his jaw muscles flexed. "Take a good look at the sordid world you're trying to build— you sick, fucking bastard!" He raised the pistol and pulled the trigger.

Two shots resounded in a stream of echoes from the surrounding mountains. Rupert, stunned, watched Lothar von Vranken tumble forward down the hard-packed pile of snow. At the same time, instinct made him whip around to catch sight of Orlando clutching his side and struggling to catch his balance.

"No-no-no!" Rupert lunged forward to grab his son's arm, but it was too late. A sharpshooter posted on top of the avalanched snow smiled to see his target stagger backward to the jagged edge of the rock, totter for a moment, and finally lose his balance. Rupert saved himself when he tripped and fell while trying to catch Orlando. He now lay gasping out the boy's name, time after endless time, with one arm dangling over the chasm.

Within minutes, two men clambered over the avalanched snow, helped Rupert to his feet, and continued to hold onto his arms. He paid no attention to his captors and kept jerking his head back toward the chasm, sobbing his son's name, as they moved him firmly up to safer ground.

The limp body of von Vranken was bundled on a stretcher and carried toward the medical vehicle for Rupert's forces. He finally focused on the current situation and realized the tables had turned. The enemy had followed his people's tracks and taken over. He looked about the moon-cast shadows of the pine glade where Seraphim troops were rounding up his forces at gunpoint and shepherding them into their own trucks.

The British colonel leading Rupert's field operation was escorted to the same medical vehicle as Rupert. A guard said, "You two are going with Oberst Graf von Vranken. He's still alive, thanks *Gott*."

At the steps of the ambulance, Rupert was startled by a blast of bullet explosions that cut through the night. Then another. Shouts and cries and pleading could be heard. And yet further fusillades. He realized not one of the poor occupants of the freight train who had made it off the bridge would leave alive.

Their captors strapped Rupert and his colonel for safety onto a side bench opposite the stretcher. They gazed down on an unconscious Lothar von Vranken. One of Rupert's special forces medics attended him. He turned to Rupert, shrugged, and said, "The god of healing before all others."

Rupert nodded and leaned back against the inside of the ambulance. He was numb with exhaustion. It was over. They'd lost. The poignancy of those last moments wrenched his gut. He realized he'd just now been more demonstrative with Orlando than for most of the boy's lifetime before. Had he been more involved, could he have stopped the boy's seemingly inevitable descent to self-destruction? Perhaps it was grasping at a straw, but Rupert felt the lad had at last come on his own to the point of contrition, of repentance. He seemed to have died trying to destroy the face of evil to which he had once been attracted. Yes, he had acted as ever, up to the end, according to his own voices, but these seemed at last to have called him to the side of the better angels. And that was where, Rupert prayed, he'd finally gone in spite of all he'd done to deserve otherwise.

Rupert composed himself and offered a cigarette to his companion. Their smoke drifted into the driver's compartment where the Austrian guard from the Seraphim's brigade, sitting next to the British driver, turned around and indicated he'd like one as well.

The way down through the mountains passed more quickly than their ascent and had remained cleared. The domes and steeples of Salzburg came into view just after they passed through the outlying village of Anif, and the driver was directed by his passenger to take the left fork in the road. They snaked in switchbacks up through dark stands of trees until they came to the gates of the massive castle brooding high over the city on the Monchsberg, the singular mountain some ancient convulsion had caused to erupt from the flat plain beside the winding River Salz. Rupert gazed at the baroque town below touched by streaks of pink dawning light through the morning clouds.

At the tall iron gates, two guards in Nazi uniforms stopped them and inspected the rear compartment. When they saw von Vranken's inert body and pallid, waxlike face, they closed the rear doors and nodded them through to the inner courtyard.

Rupert and his field colonel were directed to come down the rear steps of the medical vehicle by two armed men in

Nazi uniforms who gestured them across the courtyard to the main entrance. In the meantime, several other soldiers carried the stretcher through snowy slush to another entrance where a group of Austrian medics took over.

Once inside, their footsteps echoed from the vaulted spaces as they were led by an armed contingent through many rooms and corridors of the immense castle. Rupert felt the oppressiveness of its fortresslike stone walls, relieved by occasional tapestries and lighted torches stuck into wrought iron sockets. Their march continued through halls and galleries overlooked by balconies and occasional stands of medieval armor and arms. He was becoming more and more curious about their destination when it suddenly became clear.

Two massive doors of oaken planks were pulled open by the soldiers. Rupert alone was nodded to go inside a grandly furnished space with an immense fireplace at the other end in which six-foot logs were burning robustly.

A thin, rodent-like man sat in one of the armchairs by the hearth. Every aspect of the man repelled Rupert as it had the evening before in the opera house. Sporting a rictus smile, he called out in a reedy voice, "Come here, your lordship. We've been expecting you." At the same time, with a wave, he gestured the armed guard to take the colonel away.

"Well, now, it seems our strategy was successful. Especially in a contest with one of your nation's most brilliant and charismatic noblemen. Come, sit across from me." His skeletal hand pointed at the high-backed armchair flanking the other side of the fireplace. It was Josef Goebbels.

55

November 1938

*T*he Vatican operator connected Camberini to the Hassler. A message for Caridis was left with the concierge, giving only a telephone number. Later that afternoon, after calling the cardinal's private line, they agreed to meet that same evening in his apartments.

Michael was surprised to see how worried the large man appeared. The cardinal greeted him perfunctorily and launched straight into what was on his mind. "I've got bad news for you."

Michael studied the Italian's demeanor. He seemed far less collected than usual. "You've had reports of Ravenstone's whereabouts?"

"Much more—and nothing's good. Terrible, in fact." He stopped and looked up at the sound of the steward entering with a tray.

Placing two glasses on a table with a carafe of brandy, the steward poured some into the snifters, which he handed with a little bow to the two men. Withdrawing, he pulled the pair of doors behind him and then, looking around the outside hallway, pressed his ear against the tiny opening.

Camberini sipped a small amount and put down his glass. "I'm told a bloody confrontation happened high in the mountains near Salzburg where one of nature's freak snowstorms caused an avalanche that stopped a train carrying Lord Cressy and the First Covenant. I'm not sure you already knew your friend had mobilized an impressive force to take his son from this Berlin-bound train when it got to Salzburg. After a tremendous operation to clear their way through snow and ice, Ravenstone's people succeeded in saving the ark from the bridge's collapse, but the boy was shot and killed. To everyone's surprise, the enemy had discovered Ravenstone's plans and pounced at the last minute. They captured him on the spot, and they've now got the ark. At least so my spies report. Sad to say, our greatest foe here isn't just the Nazis. We're up against the most powerful secret organization that exists. The Society of the Seraphim. And worst of all, they work hand in glove with the Nazi leadership and now together control the ark."

Michael shook his head. "I see. I think you should know both Rupert and I belong. Also that the Seraphim were the source of the conundrum with clues to the whereabouts of the treasure. Alas, the Nazi party exists only because of the Seraphim's initial support. And with Rupert and the ark in their clutches, don't you think we might just need divine intervention to rescue them?"

Camberini gave a wry smile. "You must be reading my mind, Michele. Time's come to take this to the Holy Father. Between you and me, not very holy, alas, but he's still got a certain moral force on the world stage. He's never been told about the ark, I'm certain. Fiorelli won't have mentioned it to him. So, when I break the news, it will give me a leg up. The pope actually fears Fiorelli most of all men. That alone should drive him to do what we need."

Caridis reflected for a moment. "How do you explain holding onto the ark yourself even for a brief moment without telling His Holiness?"

"You've no idea how byzantine the business is of getting it physically to him. In the meantime, Fiorelli would have found a way to get his hands on it and then Berlin's. You saw what he did with the Vatican thugs who ransacked my quarters. He's obsessed with reaching the throne of Peter. He knows his future depends on Nazi support. Now, of course, that's moot. Berlin's got control of the ark. So, the only resource we've got is for the pope to appear on the world stage and demand that such an object be placed in the Vatican for safekeeping. I think Mussolini will get behind the pope's request. He'll back anything that brings the world's positive attention to Rome."

Michael pondered where this was leading. "Am I hearing this tonight because I found the treasure—or perhaps just because I'm Rupert's friend? There's more, no?"

With a nod that made his jowls spread, Giovanni Camberini smiled and came to the point. "Of course. First, you *did* discover it. Without you, all this would be moot. Also, you're a most respected member of the Seraphim." He pointed at him. "I've got a surprise that I hope you'll accept."

Michael raised his eyebrows and wondered what was coming next.

"I'm appointing you the Vatican's emissary to Berlin, with the rank of ambassador, to lay what will now be the pope's proposition before the powers that have control of the ark."

Michael was somewhat taken aback. "The Nazis and I are, to say the least, at odds, Your Grace. Don't forget they're the ones who stole the Covenant and scrolls from my house.

The Berlin Seraphim directed that operation. The Nazi commandant of Alexandria is a leading member of the Berlin headquarters of the Society. He's now my bitter enemy. How then can I be of use to you?"

"I know all this, Michael. Anyway, as an ambassador of the papal state, you've got unimpeachable standing to make an objective case. You're absolutely not claiming for its return to you, but, in fact, only to the pope as custodian."

"Are you really sure the Holy Father will cooperate? It's pretty well-known he kowtows to Berlin."

Camberini chuckled. "Oh, I'm certain, Michael. When he learns what's at stake, he'll rise to the occasion. He'll simply insist this extraordinary pillar of both Judaism and Christianity be placed in the custody of the church. Even if the request is denied, the church will have done its duty."

Satisfied, Michael rose and said, "Well, Your Grace, it's a very long shot, but it's worth trying. At the same time, I hope to God I can get Rupert released from their clutches. What about you? Aren't you moving out on a limb when you tell the pope that Fiorelli tried to take the ark by force from you? This means open war with Fiorelli. Dangerous, no?"

With a long sigh, Camberini nodded.

Outside, the butler saw someone coming along the hallway. He pretended to be closing Camberini's doors and turned to walk away.

56

November 1938

*R*upert sat down before the blazing fire, alert and curious to learn what was coming next. He responded to the self-congratulatory greeting he'd just received from the Reichsminister opposite him. "Yes, you do have the advantage at this point, Minister. Thanks be, you can no longer have my son."

The Nazi bigwig raised his eyebrows. "He performed remarkably well for the Reich, you know. One of our finest recruits. A shame something turned him at the end. Do you think it was seeing you, perhaps?"

A spasm of nausea gripped Rupert. He recovered and said, "No, I think it happened sometime on his journey, just before we saw each other. He seems to have met a rabbi whom he helped carry the ark to safety. This was not the act of your recruit. He was evidently lost to you by then."

"Well, thanks to him, we've got the treasure, don't we? Really nothing else much matters, does it? Oh, sorry. Of course, you've got a somewhat different perspective. Anyhow, I must commend you. Your translation of the scrolls, which was handed me shortly before your arrival, sheds a fascinating light on the real Moses and the original Commandments. An extraordinary story. Not that the party puts much stock in such things, but the Reich will grow to encompass many who do, one way or the other. Anyway, the story will upset the Hebrew faction in particular, and that is all to the good."

Rupert allowed himself to unload with bitter pointedness. "Come now. What's the Hebrew faction ever done to hurt Germany? They've given you some of your greatest achievements in art and science. They've bankrolled Bismarck in the very creation of the nation you now govern. They bring acumen and civility and do not even proselytize others to their faith. Surely they're an asset that it would be mad to destroy. Yet that's what your leadership says is necessary to the future of Germany. Frankly, I just don't get it." His voice quavered with feeling.

The other man remained silent for a long time. He finally said, "Lord Ravenstone, you're a politician, in fact rather too able one for our taste. As such, you understand these things better than most. In a nutshell, people unite when confronted by a common enemy, especially one that is uncommonly talented and powerful and which has aroused through history feelings of envy and fear. Partly for their power and partly for their differences with the common faith of our European civilization. Now we're trying to build a clean, clear, pure culture of Germanness. All pollutants will be scratched out, eradicated, and cleansed from the race—no matter how much such creatures may be deemed to have contributed. The Aryan must be liberated from his bonds of servitude to alien philosophy and habits. The new German will throw off the shackles of the Jew who sits next to him in classrooms.

Pisses next to him at the toilets. Runs the banks where he keeps his money. Invites his children to their religious feasts. Cheats him in the marketplace. Tries to marry their sons to his daughters. Who are eternally out only for themselves and wish to subjugate the Aryan's culture to their greed. And, Lord Ravenstone, when all is said and done, the great majority robustly support the government in this. The Fuhrer knows this feeling runs deep."

Rupert stared at Goebbels and thought, *What a little shit you are. A nonentity raised to prominence by a charismatic madman who tapped into the unhappy, war-defeated, inflation-impoverished German psyche.* Rupert spoke, "I suspect when you call on the worst in human nature to underpin your power base, someday the whole edifice is bound to collapse. Building a consensus rooted in hate and fear will turn on you eventually. It's happened again and again throughout history. The only way then to delay the inevitable is to maintain total control of people's minds." Rupert laughed lightly. "And that's like trying to stop nature in its tracks." He pulled out his cigarette case, snapped it open, and raised an eyebrow. "Like one?"

The German must have sensed the dismissiveness of this gesture. He moved in his chair as if he found his position uncomfortable. A faint flush infused the pallor of his skintight death's head. "It might be well to keep in mind that you're now my prisoner."

Rupert exhaled and stared at the smoke rising to the ancient carved beams high above. "Indeed, that's a fact. So, what do you have in mind to do with a key member of the House of Lords who has just tried to rescue his son from a bridge that became a pile of matchsticks at the bottom of a chasm? Was this an act of war against the so-called Third Reich?" He flicked some ash on the stone floor.

"An interesting question, Marquess. You massed a

force under the direction of one of your more distinguished generals—yes, we have ways of knowing these things—and engaged that force against the keepers of order in Austria, which is now a part of the Reich. Surely that would seem to qualify as an act of aggression, no?"

Rupert sat erect and calm, keeping the German in his gaze. "Our force, as you call it, was there on a peaceful mission to deal with the rescue of a private British subject and to leave the country. In the course of that effort, our people were attacked. We did nothing out of order under any of the international conventions. Each person had a passport they had presented at Austria's border, including the colonel whom you have in your charge along with me."

The German said, "These people were in our mountains with arms. Does a rescue party require such things? Clearly you anticipated interference, and quite rightly so. Because the person you so nobly set out to rescue was a guest of the Reich and was here under his own volition. Your so-called rescue plan is a pile of nonsense. It was a planned kidnapping."

Rupert studied the man before him to the point where discomfort made the other get up from his chair and stand before the fire with his back to the room, pretending to warm his hands. "I think the kidnapping argument's quite a leaky one, Minister. My boy felt threatened by his so-called host, von Vranken, and he shot him. I think you must come up with another rationale for attacking our rescue party. We lost a number of men, and, to boot, your people murdered the man who helped my son bring the ark to safety. And who knows how many others died along with the poor bastard."

Goebbels turned to face Rupert. "Simple fact: you wanted your boy, and you wanted the ark. Let's not beat about the bush. The ark is ours and will stay with us, whatever you might wish otherwise. You're now under our control, and you're coming with us to Berlin. We've got a rather remarkable surprise arranged that you, in particular, will appreciate."

"What if I tell you this is most inconvenient? You know very well our prime minister's just signed a nonaggression agreement with your leader. I must be back in time to ratify it in the House of Lords. I assume you'd like our side to honor what's said in the agreement?"

The German's eyes narrowed even more than usual; placed close together, they became two slits touching the bridge of his nose. "Your presence in Parliament won't make any difference. The British are feeling quite relieved. Their government has so wisely averted conflict. It will be approved without you—I'm certain of that. It would be most unfriendly for you to refuse a personal invitation to meet our head of state and be part of an immense historical event I'm sure you should hate to miss once you're there."

Rupert shrugged. "I see. I've got no choice. Then what?"

The German put his hands on his hips and looked down at Rupert. "Ah, yes. I suppose we shall just have to wait and see, won't we?"

The doors opened and a uniformed officer strode in. He said, "Herr Reichminister, we've got a problem."

57

November 1938

The grand master of the Seraphim, Joachim von Wittgenstein, was for a moment jubilant. He spoke into the telephone and continued, "You mean the ark is now ours? What incredibly good news. And the English chap, Ravenstone's son? Oh, how sad. And von Vranken was his target? What could have changed him like that? The young man was so helpful to us. Now what about the ark?" He paused and listened for several minutes while a frown deepened the furrow between his eyes. "Yes, I see, we'll have to do something to deal with the problem. It seems more and more, we've unleashed the whirlwind. I must think. These people are grotesque. We'll just have to deal with it at this end. What a revolting idea of killing two birds with the proverbial same stone. No, we'll wait and see. More when you get to Berlin. Goodbye. And don't, for God's sake, say Heil Hitler!" He replaced the receiver on its cradle. Sitting there for a few minutes motionless, he stared at the small golden calf on his desk. At last, he spun around in his chair and looked at a photo of the Fuhrer behind him. He picked it up, slammed it facedown on top of the credenza, and rang the intercom. "Bring me the keeper of the rod. We've got some serious matters to deal with." He rose from his desk and strode over to a window.

He turned around when the door to his office opened and his associate entered. "You called me, master?"

"Yes, yes. The partly good news is that we've got the ark. Which is to say the Nazis, most particularly, have got it. That doesn't necessarily translate to being able to take it into our custody. Already they're beginning to play games."

"How so, master? It was well understood from the beginning this treasure belongs, without the slightest question, to the Seraphim."

The grand master smirked. "What do you think? Hitler apparently said to Goebbels that the Nazi Party is equated with the Seraphim, inseparable. We know that's rubbish. We made Hitler. We funded his rise. He's our creation. Now he's conflating his power with ours."

"It's not the first time, master? Napoleon did the same thing. Once they achieve supreme power, they're rather more difficult to manage. It's the risk we always run."

The grand master shook his head. "This is different. No one would have even known to look for a treasure that turned out to be the ark but for the legend carried through the ages by the Aaronites. Ludwig Borchardt was an Aaronite. When he found that little scroll near the bust of Nefertiti, he would not have been able to make sense of it without knowing of our legendary enigma. And, foremost of all, is our amazing Aaronite, Caridis. He searched and found the ark only because our predecessors had passed down the story of a mysterious treasure."

"I agree, master. Of course, there should be no question about ownership of the ark."

The grand master sat down heavily in his desk chair and pressed his hands together. "And now to complicate things even further, I've just been told Michael Caridis has arrived in Berlin. You'll never imagine why."

"I suppose to claim the ark as his own property. Finders keepers, that sort of thing, no? But, tell me, how could he even know the Nazis have it?"

"That's easy. Who's got the best spy system in Europe? The Vatican, of course. Now here's the real surprise. He's presenting his credentials tomorrow to the foreign minister as the Vatican's special cultural ambassador to Germany."

"How bizarre. Why? Where on earth is this leading to?"

The grand master raised his eyes to the ceiling. "Let's say there can be only one conclusion. He was sent by the cardinal secretary of state, Camberini. Clearly Michael Caridis is going to claim the ark for the Vatican."

The keeper of the rod shook his head. "It seems everyone's racing to the trough. Still, we've got to have a talk with Caridis. His first loyalty in every instance must be to the Seraphim. He made this commitment years ago, and he agreed to be bound by it for life."

The grand master nodded. "And that's not all. I need help with a much more complicated question, and I don't quite know yet how to deal with it." He shuddered.

The keeper of the rod gave a questioning look.

"It's those fucking sadists that we've enabled!"

58

November 1938

*T*he Reichminister ignored Rupert and walked to the
door to speak with the uniformed officer who had just
entered. Rupert watched the flames dancing in the massive
fireplace. He could just hear their voices, too indistinct to
understand. His options were few, and the most logical was
to follow the ark as long as it was in Nazi hands. How to
wrest it away appeared insurmountable without help. There
was always his co-captive, the field commander of their failed
operation. But the castle was immense. Where was the fellow
now? And the ark?

The Reichminister returned to stand before him. "Your
colleague attempted an escape. Most ill-advised under the
circumstances. Our people had no choice but to put an end to
him." A faint smile flickered on his emaciated lips.

Startled, Rupert looked back at the door where the officer
had remained as if waiting for him.

"It seems he wanted first to find the ark. But never got

close. He wrestled with a guard and managed to make his way out of the courtyard. Our soldiers finally caught him in the forest. But we do have another small problem, Britisher. This officer's waiting to take us to the ark. You'll join us." He pointed toward the door.

The three men's footfalls resounded in the vaulted corridors. They passed the castle's private chapel and arrived at a doorway where several guards were gathered. They parted to let them through and saluted the minister. Inside the simple stone room, there was very little else than an oak table on which had been placed the ark.

Rupert studied its condition. A few scratches in the durable ebony during its recent rescue from the collapsing bridge and the snow and ice into which it had fallen with the rabbi who'd carried it to safety.

When one of the Nazi soldiers approached, a moaning sound could be heard. When the man got closer, it began to shake, rattling on the table. And when he touched it, his hand drew away quickly from the glowing casket, its bronze bands as hot as a burning coal.

"Now, your lordship, let's see you touch the ark. I'm sure you'll be quite pleased to do so."

The soldier backed off and watched Rupert step slowly to the table. There was no disturbance of any kind. He laid his hands with gentleness and reverence on the wood and the bronze bindings of the casket. It was cool and silent.

"Now open the casket, your lordship. Let's see what's inside." The minister leered at the box as if were an object of perverted sexual desire.

Rupert removed the bronze rod that ran through the three small bronze hoops of the clasps. He lifted them off their hoops and raised the cover. Everyone remained silent. The creaking of the stiff hinges made the only sound.

"Now remove what's inside." The minister appeared to be holding his breath.

Rupert lifted away the linen cloth and reached in to take out the first scroll. He held it in his two hands and turned around. "Now what?"

The minister advanced a step and hesitated. He pointed at the soldier who had first approached the casket. "Bring that scroll to me, Corporal."

The soldier looked frightened.

"Go ahead, Corporal. Bring it to me."

The young man straightened his back, clenched his jaw, and moved toward Rupert's outstretched hands. When he placed the papyrus scroll, light as a thought and heavy as time, into the boy's reluctant hands, the lad's eyes opened wide as if he had received an electric shock.

"All right, bring it here."

The soldier did not move. His body appeared to have been taken over. Rupert alone could see his face. It was that of an innocent child, confused and amazed. His fingers very, very slowly bent outward from the scroll until they tipped down and dropped it back into Rupert's waiting hands. And then, as if he were a statue struck by lightning, his eyes rolled upward, and his body stiffened until it fell backward, straight as a board, cracking his skull on the stone floor at the minister's feet.

"Put it back in the box," the minister screamed.

Bowing his head with a small private smile, Rupert replaced the scrolls and closed the casket. When he faced the Nazi once again, Rupert adjusted his expression to a neutral indifference. He looked down at the corporal who remained ignored by the others. "Poor lad, that." Rupert tilted his head to show sympathy.

The minister folded his arms. "For better or worse, your

lordship's found a new calling. You will be the only one to touch the ark. And when it's moved, you will always be next to it. That should give you some satisfaction?"

"Whatever you say." He withdrew his cigarette case and offered one again to his adversary.

Goebbels waved him off, spun about, and stomped out of the room.

59

November 1938

*W*earing a morning coat with swallowtails and a gray silk cravat, Michael Caridis stood the image of a suave diplomat and man of the world. He removed his gray felt top hat and handed it to an attendant when he entered the official reception room of Germany's foreign ministry. Waiting on the dais at the other end of the large room, von Ribbentrop looked diminutive in front of the enormous swastika on the wall behind him.

A uniformed functionary announced, "His Excellency, Michael Caridis, emissary of the Vatican."

Striding to the dais, he mounted the steps and stood facing the foreign minister.

Von Ribbentrop extended his hand.

Clasping it, Caridis said, "I am here, Excellency, to present my credentials, which His Holiness will be honored to have you accept."

The German bowed and said, "The Fuhrer and the Third

Reich are pleased to receive this papal emissary and would like to be informed, in due course, of the purpose of his cultural mission."

"Indeed, sir, and the Vatican welcomes the earliest opportunity for such a meeting." With these formalities accomplished, the appointment was fixed.

Michael returned to his quarters at the Vatican's embassy. That evening, the grand master of the Seraphim invited him to dine at the Society's world headquarters.

The three men sat alone in the master's palatial private dining room. The keeper of the rod had been a Jesuit priest until he'd lost his faith. He said, "Brother Michael, first, we must say how honored we are to receive you. You solved our ancient riddle—and what an incredible discovery it turned out to be. It may have taken you thirty-five years, but your reputation will now be timeless."

"Thank you, Keeper. There's more at stake here than my reputation. The treasure's fallen into unfortunate hands. Yes, our Society backed the rise of the present regime, but now our power seems to have fallen under the sway of this regime. It's not only sad; it's humiliating."

The grand master nodded. "For centuries, we've been the greatest economic force on the planet. What you say, Brother Michael, concerns us every day. But I've got another question. We're a cult that grew strong as a haven for people searching for something to believe in. And here you come in the bizarre role of representing the very church that many of our members—such as the keeper—have abandoned or even reviled. What can be on your mind, Brother?"

Michael smiled. "I agree. All dogma, religious or otherwise, is anathema. My mission's simple. Find a safe place for the treasure. It's now in the worst hands. In all candor, it's evident the Society will find it difficult to keep the Nazis from using it for mischief. Our Society's got some real risks here."

The grand master looked at the keeper. They both nodded in agreement. "Yes, Brother Michael. And for your ears only, you'll be pleased to know the bulk of our considerable assets rest far out of reach of the German regime. In fact, we're funding both Washington and London toward creating a counterforce to the Nazi madman's Wehrmacht. Ironic, no?"

The keeper said, "Still, there are obviously high stakes here. The Society still has major interests in Germany's industrial complex and vast tracts of land and buildings. These are indeed hostage to the will of the so-called Fuhrer and his stooges."

The grand master shook his head. "Your mission, Brother Michael, I'm sorry to say, is doomed from the start. Goebbels is already planning the opening of the ark in a dramatic ceremony. Alas we're being forced by the Nazis to play the central role in that unveiling. Goebbels wants to stage this in our Berlin Sanctuary. He's even inviting important Aaronites from around the world to the spectacle. Hitler plans to keep the ark always near him. The evidence Moses wasn't even a Jew sends him high as a kite. He brags he'll make routine public gestures to defile the ark. His sickness has got no limits."

Michael shrugged. "We'll see. It might be a bit uncomfortable for the braggart to be so near to the ark. In any case, I've got a makeweight argument on my side. The pope is, shall we say, cooperative, if not helpful, to the tyrants here in Berlin. If he became custodian of the ark, it would be placed in the crypt of Saint Peter's. In return, the pope could call on the vast membership of his church, shall we say, to look tolerably on the Nazi regime."

"I see your point. The propaganda value of the Vatican's offer could greatly outweigh keeping it in Berlin. But, candidly, Brother Michael, the pope's recruiting all his flock to back up the Antichrist seems a little farfetched. Can he be that frightened of the Nazis?" The grand master looked puzzled.

Michael gave a wan smile. "I've heard it's just possible he agrees with them in some things."

"What a horror." The keeper grimaced.

"Well, I suspect not every Catholic's going to go along with that—even if it comes from the papal throne." Michael looked up at the ceiling. "And popes have successors who certainly can change the official dogma."

The grand master said, "What if that fascist Fiorelli gets the vote when the time comes?"

Michael responded, "My bet would be on Camberini. Unless, of course, Mussolini surrounds the Sistine Chapel with cannons when they vote."

60

November 1938

"The Reichminister's left for Berlin. You're to come with me." The speaker was a uniformed Nazi officer who entered the room where Rupert was seated alone beside the ark.

Behind the officer, two guards carrying rifles were at the ready. They stared past him at the ark. One of them said, "Captain, how're we going to get that thing into the plane? Nobody wants to get near it."

The officer gestured toward Rupert. "You must be there while two of the castle's nonmilitary employees deal with it. We'll see if that's enough to keep it quiet for loading onto my plane."

"I take it, Captain, we're about to fly somewhere?" Rupert's manner was relaxed, almost incurious.

"That's right. Berlin. My Siebel Fh 104's being prepped. Be ready to leave in forty-five minutes. Your things are being collected from the Goldener Hirsch Hotel and will be brought to the airfield."

Two castle workmen appeared and carried the ark to a small truck, which one of them drove. Rupert was directed to sit in the front seat between the driver and an armed guard, and the other man remained in the rear, holding onto the ark to keep it from sliding about.

They drove through the black slush of both courtyards of the castle and zigged down the backside of the Monchsberg and into the winding streets of Salzburg. Shopkeepers were closing up for their lunchtime meal, and traffic was light all the way to the little airport on the outskirts of town.

The small twin-engine aircraft sat ready on the runway. Its light gray metal fuselage still had the polished sheen of a recently made plane. The metal-clad plywood wings were designed for their strength and lightness.

The pilot's door stood open, and a mechanic sat at the controls and watched as the engines revved. He waved at the truck when it pulled up beside the plane. Climbing out onto the wing, he helped a workman haul the ark up into the cockpit area. They placed it just behind the copilot's seat. The guard stood clutching his rifle at the ready, between the truck and the plane. He flinched as the ark was carried past him. The fate of his young colleague was still fresh in his memory. He moved over and helped the workman jump off the rear edge of the wing and onto the tarmac, wondering at the man's apparent immunity to the powers of the ark.

The pilot gestured to Rupert to sit beside him and in front of the seat to which the ark had been strapped. Rupert turned to look behind him at the casket, which was showing mild signs of agitation. He reached back his hand to touch it. This brought a state of perfect calm.

The pilot said, "You'll do that whenever necessary, Englishman."

The plane was cleared for takeoff, taxied to one end of the single runway, and turned to face the north. The engines were gunned, and the plane gained acceleration until it appeared to pop off the tarmac and surge into the cloud-specked sky.

They circled the foothills of the Austrian Alps, which were covered with the fresh November snow of the day before. Rupert tried to find the place where the bridge had been and the chasm into which Orlando had fallen. Would they ever find him and return him to them? Rupert almost preferred to spare Lizzie the trauma of receiving the battered body of their tormented child.

His eyes glazed as he thought about what might be waiting in Berlin. Automatically, his hand reached into a breast pocket for the cigarette case. He offered one to the pilot who grabbed it without speaking. When he flicked on his lighter, the pilot leaned over to be the first to light up.

Rupert leaned his right elbow on the tiny window ledge and stroked his tidy, short beard with his thumb. A calculus raced through his mind. What was waiting for him in Berlin? Freedom, of course. He was, after all, an invited guest to some sort of event involving the ark. Enforced attendance was probably all that was expected of him. The fate for the ark would be obvious. The odious Nazi command would appropriate it along with other purloined treasures from confiscated collections of wealthy German Jews and others. But the ark was simply too special to be left to their perverted purposes. It was possibly the most powerful material artifact in existence. It seriously revised the history of the Hebrew faith, and it possessed their original Covenant with their Lord. How much did it really matter that their intercessor with the Lord was an Egyptian rather than a Jew and that Aaron killed the man now called Moses? To some, it would be intolerable, of course. But the original Covenant itself? How could it be allowed to suffer the desecrations the godless Nazi sadists no doubt had in store for it?

In his favor, one fact, vital to the moment, had been unreckoned with by his captors. He, Rupert, was a licensed pilot with many hours of solo flying under his belt. How best to use this? Wherever he might force a landing in Germany would result in his immediate capture—so nothing to be gained. One option was to aim for Switzerland, which was still near enough, but crossing back into the Alps had huge risks. He had no idea where the nearest airports might lie among its jagged peaks. In truth, the ideal option was to land in a field in northeastern France or Holland, which was flat and further to the west, well off their present route.

Above all, he would have to depend on the ark to make this work. In truth, that should prove to be simple—and fraught with danger, of course. Enormous danger. They were in a small plane, which would become the stage for a confrontation of forces that could bring the plane down at any point. But there were just the two of them. Once he grabbed the controls, everything would depend on the pilot's instincts to self-preservation.

They passed through a cloud that obscured the sun and the earth below. Beads of moisture gathered on the windscreen like drops of rain and then were whipped away by the forward motion of the plane. As they emerged back into the blue afternoon sky, Rupert grabbed the copilot's column and pulled it back slightly to make the plane climb.

The pilot looked at him, alarm etched suddenly on his face. "What the hell are you doing?" he screamed above the roar of the two engines. He reached out and slapped Rupert's hands.

With this, the ark began to vibrate and strain against the

belts that held it fastened to the seat behind Rupert. The more the pilot wrestled with Rupert, the more agitated the ark became. This made the plane pitch from side to side, amplified by the shifting of the ark, which was gradually coming loose from the belts holding it to the seat.

Rupert shouted, "Do we all go up in smoke? You, me, and the ark. The ark has control of the plane, Captain. As long as you resist, our lives are about to end. Your choice."

The pilot's eyes were popping as he braced himself against the plane's erratic movements. "God damn you, Englishman." He let go of his steering column.

Rupert was finally able to stabilize the plane and set it on a westward course. He grinned at the German who was glowering in his seat, impotent—at least for the moment. "I suggest that you help plot our course to Strasbourg, Captain. The cuisine is incomparable, wine sublime, and your people haven't yet tried to take it back from the French."

"You will pay for this, fucking Englishman."

61

Late November 1938

oreign Minister von Ribbentrop rose from his desk. "May I introduce Herr Reichminister Goebbels? Ambassador Caridis, cultural emissary from the Vatican."

The gaunt figure remained seated and signaled for Michael to sit in the other chair in front of Ribbentrop's desk.

Von Ribbentrop turned to his colleague. "Herr Goebbels just arrived today from Salzburg where he met your friend, Ravenstone."

"Correct. Now I wish to speak privately with the papal emissary. There are matters that cannot be shared."

Von Ribbentrop stood up, smiled, and let himself out by a side door—but not before discreetly flicking on the switch of his intercom.

When the door had closed, Goebbels rose and paced the room. "We're both members of the Seraphim. As we know, your friend, Ravenstone, is one of our numbers. I left him this morning in the Salzburg castle. He's coming by a separate plane with one of our most trusted pilots. They are bringing the ark of the Jews to Berlin."

Michael leaned toward the ambulating German and noticed his stubby, ragged fingernails. "That's why I'm here, Minister."

Goebbels leered at him. "Because your friend is coming? Or because the ark is under our control?"

"Officially, the latter. Personally, both." Michael sensed the other man's stress. He wondered what was behind it. "May I ask about your plans for the ark, Minister?"

"Ah, yes. We indeed have plans. You will, of course, receive an invitation."

"An event?"

"Yes. It will take place at the Sanctuary of the Seraphim this Sunday evening."

Michael cocked his head. "So, the Seraphim will remain the custodians of the ark with full powers to protect it?"

"Why are you so concerned about who are the custodians? The Reich and the Seraphim operate together these days in Berlin. As we're a secret society, it will be better for the ark to remain visibly in the hands of the Reich. The world has to know what you've discovered. It's too important to keep under wraps by the Aaronites."

Michael marshalled his thoughts. "Minister, even though we're both Aaronites, committed to no system of religious belief, you know as well as I do the ark is more than the word of someone's god. It's a force of nature. It's got a life of its own."

That was the moment Goebbels showed his true colors. "Indeed, I know this. I've seen evidence with my own eyes. One of our corporals received the scrolls from Ravenstone and literally suffered rigor mortis on the spot. That's why we've made special arrangements for its transport to Berlin and for our ceremony and for keeping it afterward."

Michael shook his head. "You're playing with fire, Minister. You clearly know that by now."

Goebbels stood next to his chair, folded his arms, and looked down on Michael. "Fire can be contained."

Michael studied the man's face. His expression belied these words of self-assurance. There was a trace of fear of the unexpected. And that gave him his opening. "My mission, sir, is to relieve you of this responsibility. The Holy Father proposes the ark be placed in the crypt of Saint Peter where it will be secure and available for all the world to see."

"Ah, Brother Caridis, you don't know us well at all. Try to think as an Aaronite. We've both read the translation of the scrolls. They show Aaron as an outcast and the killer of the man who is both Moses and Akhenaten. Aaron gave his people the golden calf. The Fuhrer is giving the world himself and the creed of Nazism. Imagine giving up the symbolism that discredits the identity of the Jews' greatest prophet and lawgiver and shows the broken words of their god?"

Michael asked, "Why does your Fuhrer need to possess the ark? Let it rest in Saint Peter's crypt, and you can still adopt whatever symbolism your leader chooses."

"Not the same. He'll want to humiliate the Jews by selective acts of its desecration."

Michael was already revolted by the rodent-like creature before him, but this last bit had tested his self-control. "Can you be serious, Minister? We've just spoken of its being a force unto itself. This is not some passive artifact you can desecrate at your pleasure, without consequences."

Goebbels straightened up and pursed his lips. "Aren't you forgetting my function in the Reich, sir? After all, I am the chief of propaganda. Interesting, no? That very word comes ironically from the Catholic Inquisition. In order to enlarge the circle of obedient adherents, they created the Office for the Propagation of the Faith. Hence the word 'propaganda.' And, as you well know, the office was most rigorous in assuring fidelity to the church and its beliefs. Its punishment for any deviations was severe. Burning at the stake was, shall we say, a kindness compared with some other methods used."

"I see. And your brand of inquisition is not to test the faith of the Jews, but rather to destroy it—lock, stock, and barrel?" Michael's voice trembled slightly. He was suddenly chilled by this cold-blooded creature sitting before him, a demon in a blue suit that seemed to hang loose like an afterthought to make its wearer's skeletal frame less alarming.

"Exactly, sir." Goebbels flashed his horrible smile. "What could be more useful for this project than the original Ark of the Covenant? And just imagine, we've got you to thank for this treasure."

Caridis remained impassive. "How about Ravenstone? What are you planning for him? As a diplomat for the church, I would ask you to show compassion for a man who just lost his son and whose fate is of great concern to his government and the royal family."

"Well. You may have a certain claim to immunity because of that, but your partner doesn't have the same privileges. You might recall one evening, quite recent, when the two of you assisted the traitor Vogel, or should I say Fritzi Vogelhardt, in escaping from the Vatican along with our treasure." His voice suddenly went shrill and rose by almost an octave. "Yes, you helped the traitor escape, the thieving Jew, stealing our treasure! And that deception will cost Vogelhardt the most exquisite punishment imaginable!"

Caridis bit his lip and said, "Do you mean he's been

captured? What are you going to do with him? Was she with him?"

"Yes, yes, yes! To all three questions. My answer's simple. They, those two conniving Jews, are part of our plan for the event this Sunday. I need say no more. Just be thankful your British friend, who's no friend of Germany, will be spared their fate."

Michael stared at him for a time and said, "You really are playing with fire—and you really are very likely to be burned, sir."

62

Late November 1938

*R*upert noticed the captain's impeccable grooming. His fingernails were perfectly shaped and lacquered with clear polish. His haircut was recent and military in its simplicity. An aura of crispness surrounded him like virtue. And Rupert knew it would not be long before the airman's sense of duty would overcome all fears, including death.

They had flown about forty minutes due west. Munich had been visible to the north. The German was doing nothing to help set their course. He had turned to stare at Rupert in silence since surrendering control of the plane. Rupert would occasionally turn and smile, suggesting the captain focus on navigating. Silence remained the only response.

Flying low enough to follow the countryside with his eyes, he calculated the Alsatian border would be another hour and a quarter or so, which meant that he might have to swing into northern Switzerland instead. He could see the Alps in the distance off to his left. He set a more southerly course in order to approach Swiss territory where he might be able to recognize some landmarks. Then it struck him. Of course, the most obvious would be Lake Constance, the source of the Rhine. It straddled both sides of the German-Swiss border. He pulled the plane higher to have a more extended view and looked for a large sheet of water. There was nothing yet.

Finally, the expected.

"Englishman, I've had enough. You will now return control of the plane to me." The German placed his hands on his steering column.

The ark began to quake, sending vibrations through the small aircraft.

"You'd better simmer down, Captain. What you're doing is foolish in the extreme." Rupert gripped his controls with determination and tried to counter the contrary movements of his companion.

The German snarled. "You won't get away with this. If we die, we will die on German soil. Someone will find the ark and do whatever must be done with it."

"If we crash, the ark will be destroyed. You know that. Don't let heroics push you to madness. No one will blame you. They will know it was the ark's fault that you lost control of the plane to me." Rupert's cheek muscles were flexing and both arms stiffly tried to maintain their westward course.

The German struck the side of Rupert's head with his fist, and Rupert retaliated with a sweeping swing of his left arm against the German's throat. The man coughed and lurched forward for several seconds, letting go his steering column. The ark went into full agitation mode, and the plane rocked from side to side.

The German recovered and screamed, "*Verdammt!*" He tried to get his right arm hooked around Rupert's neck and succeeded in pulling him off his controls.

Rupert clutched at the German. At the same time, he saw in the distance a large body of water that had to be Lake Constance. A sudden, inspired awareness reared up before him. Of course, how could he not have divined it already? The ark did not want to be destroyed. It would not cause the plane to crash. That would only happen if one of the two men did so in reaction to the ark's provocations.

The German's right arm was strangling him. Stars danced before his eyes. With a huge effort, he pulled the German's forearm off his windpipe and swung his left elbow in an arc that landed on the German's temple.

The man collapsed unconscious onto his steering column and caused the plane to pitch into a sudden nosedive. It took several precious seconds for Rupert to dislodge the inert body that had become entangled in the controls. The earth was rushing up with horrifying speed.

Rupert steadily pulled back on the control and managed to level off the plane just yards above a grassy meadow. The momentum of its downward plunge prevented him from elevating any further, so with quick reflexes, he tried to drop the landing gear—but it was too late. The plane's belly skimmed the wavy grasses and then struck the hard earth with a violent impact. They skidded across the meadow toward a grove of trees. The left wing was ripped off by the first trees, and the fuselage was sent spinning in a quarter circle until the other wing was sliced off as well. Both engines burst into flame at a small distance from the fuselage, one side of which, deeply dented, was wedged against some trees.

Rupert's head had struck the windscreen, and he needed several moments to recover his senses. He reached across the inert body of the German and opened the pilot's door. He unstrapped him and pushed the German through the door so that he slid several feet down to the ground. They were almost surrounded by trees that were now aflame. Rupert unbuckled and pulled the ark across the seat behind the pilot's. He then dropped down to the ground and shifted the pilot out of his way. With a mighty effort, he was able to maneuver the ark from the rear seat down to the oil-covered grass.

Flames were spreading across the underbrush at speed. Rupert was finding it difficult to breathe, and smoke and heat filled his lungs. Out of a corner of his eye, he saw a figure moving through a gap in the burning trees.

A man dressed in farm clothes shouted at him in German to help him carry the pilot to safety. They each took hold of the unconscious man and carried him out to the open meadow.

Rupert gestured toward the fuselage and pulled the farmer by the arm back into the circle of flames. He grabbed one end of the ark, and the man took up the other. As they turned toward the opening to safety, a thin pine tilted toward them, a torch of burning sap and needles. They just managed to exit the furnace before the tree plunged across the fuselage of the dismembered plane.

Sirens sounded on the road beside the meadow, and the pilot was beginning to stir.

The farmer spoke in German. Knowing the insignias of his rank, he addressed the man as Captain and asked if he could move his limbs.

Lying on a bed of grasses, the pilot rolled his head in both directions until he saw Rupert. His eyes were charged with loathing. Looking back at the farmer, and doing as he had suggested, he responded that every limb was intact, but he had problems with his rib cage and pain in his right knee.

Two fire trucks and an ambulance crossed the field. The trucks sped toward the remains of the plane, and the ambulance stopped beside the three men. Two medics emerged in spotless white cotton coats. One came to Rupert, and the other walked quickly over to the pilot. He looked up at the medic and read out loud the wording on his lab coat. "Reichenau Infirmary." He lifted his head slightly but could see nothing but the field and the burning plane. "Is this the Reichenau with the ancient monastery? On the island in Lake Constance?"

"Yes," the medic responded.

"So, are we in Switzerland or in Germany?"

The medic smiled. "Captain, this little island belongs to Germany, the next one to Switzerland, so you're at home. Don't be at all concerned. We'll take good care of our great army's officer."

The pilot tried to sit up, groaned, and fell back with the medic catching him before he was again prone. He spoke in a low voice. "You must get the police here as soon as possible. Don't let the Englishman escape with a casket. You must have seen it somewhere around here, maybe on the other side of your ambulance. He's a prisoner of the Reich and will try to steal it. It's the property of the Reich and must not leave your sight until the police have it and have agreed to get both the casket and the Englishman to Berlin."

"Understood, Captain." The medic looked over and could barely overhear his confrere and Rupert. He wondered what they might be saying.

The other medic was speaking sotto voce to Rupert. "Yes, your lordship. But we'll have to report your presence here to the police. As you know, it's rather irregular to fall from the sky, so the police must have a record of your arrival, especially as it's so unorthodox."

Rupert frowned and looked down at the pilot. He sensed he'd been the topic of discussion between the pilot and his medic because the latter had repeatedly turned his head toward Rupert during their exchange. "It's terribly important I get to Switzerland. You said it was just a short trip by boat to the Swiss shore of the lake. If I can leave right away, there should be no need to report my accidental arrival here. In any event, I originally entered Germany quite properly through immigration. You can see, if you like, the German stamp in my British passport."

Rupert's medic was adamant. "My lord Englishman, do you want the Nazis to arrest me, maybe send me away? You don't know how strict they are now since five years."

"Well, then, why don't you simply ignore me and take care of the pilot. He looks to be in pretty bad shape." Rupert noticed the other medic had left his patient and returned to the driver's seat of the ambulance where he was using some sort of speaker device. Standing up, legs still a little shaky, he walked casually over to the farmer who was standing with his hands clutched together, as if waiting for someone to give him instructions.

"I want to thank you, sir," Rupert began in German. "You saved the life of the pilot and helped me to save that box over there."

The farmer shrugged and said, "Nothing else to do, sir. I could see you were in a bad way."

"Well, I'm really most grateful, my good man." He pulled out his wallet and counted a large sum into the man's surprised hands. "Let this be my way to say thank you. I would ask you another favor though. It's getting dark. I don't know how long these medics and the pilots will be before they all get into the ambulance. I suspect the pilot may be trying to take my chest on the other side of the ambulance where you helped me remove it—and at great risk to yourself, as it turned out."

The farmer nodded, visibly perplexed by where all this was leading.

"I would like you to do me a huge favor. Discreetly hide the casket and, if asked, say it was burned in the plane. Hide it when no one can see you drag it into the woods. The firemen are too busy putting out the mess caused by the burning petrol. They won't notice anything. Give me your address and if you've got a phone, the number. I will contact you to pick it up and bring it to me when I've gone through formalities with the police."

At that word, the other man looked uncomfortable.

"Not to worry, just to explain we arrived here by accident and had no bad intentions. Is that all right, then? This plan?"

The farmer scratched his thick hatch of light brown hair. "Will do my best, sir."

Rupert strolled back to the pilot and asked, "So, how are you doing, Captain? Seems we're still in Germany. Sorry to miss that meal in Strasbourg though."

The pilot was shaking with anger. "You've ruined my plane and my reputation. God damn you."

Rupert laughed lightly. "I did save your life, after all. Perhaps, by now, only a small blessing given the fall from grace you expect from your beloved Nazi overlords."

The medic returned from the ambulance and said to the pilot. "All's in order, sir. Not to worry. I think it's time we got you to the clinic. And, Englishman, you'll have to come with us to the clinic as well. We must do a thorough examination to see if everything is all right."

Rupert played a delaying game while he saw the farmer disappear on the other side of the ambulance. "Surely I'm OK. Just a little shaken up, truth be told. Used to that in the last war. Managed to get through intact. So, now I'm told we'll have to report to the police, given our unusual means of arrival on this island." As if to demonstrate his unconcern with these formalities, he asked, "Are there any interesting tourist attractions to soothe the hunger for self-improvement?"

The pilot spat out. "You won't have time for such things,

Englishman. You're going straight to Berlin—and who knows what fate there. They won't be too pleased when they hear what's happened."

"Well, I think they'll understand quite well the ark took control of the plane. That's just what happened, of course."

"A lie—and you know it. You made the ark behave like that."

Rupert wagged his finger. "You should try to recall how it only got upset when you tried to rough me up." He noticed the farmer had reappeared and stood once again with his hands folded in front as if waiting to be told what to do. "Anyway, the ark finally took its own life, if you will."

"What do you mean?" snapped the pilot.

"Captain, it was a question of triage. One of us had to go: you, me, or the ark. Happily for you, I didn't choose the ark. It's gone up in the conflagration that the firemen are still trying to put out."

By then, the sun had fallen, and the forest was lit by fires that continued to spread through the underbrush. The wooden wings of the plane had become a blackened heap of their metal cladding. The fuselage was not even a vestige of what had been. It had disintegrated in the inferno fed by the plane's fuel and the wood and other combustibles used in its interior.

The pilot stared at this devastation "Oh my God in heaven!"

"Not your fault, Captain. Don't worry yourself. If they ask, I'll explain it was all the fault of the ark. Bad idea, don't you know, to have taken it on an airplane. Too many unpredictable possibilities. Anyway, Berlin will understand. Your minister of propaganda saw with his own eyes that poor chap who for all purposes turned to stone when I handed him the scrolls. I doubt they'll be needing me now in Berlin. It's time I headed home."

☥

Reichminister Goebbels had finished with his interview of the pope's special emissary. The late November evening had settled in at its usual early hour. Michael Caridis stood up with an aura of deep disappointment. "It seems, then, Minister, you are determined to use the ark as an object of desecration and not as a treasure of our grand human heritage."

Goebbels let go one of his shrill, almost feminine laughs. "I think by now, Mr. Ambassador, you've understood whatever's sacred to the Jews is anathema to the Nazi dream."

Michael thought, *What an irony. Calling this horror a dream? This thing that had come like a black whirlwind upon the earth. Calling it a nightmare would even be too kind.* He turned abruptly at the sound of the side door.

Foreign Minister von Ribbentrop ran into the room. "Josef, oh my god, you won't believe what's happened."

Goebbels shouted. "The ark?"

"Yes. It's been destroyed. The plane crashed on Reichenau Island in Lake Constance. Burned beyond any recognition of its contents."

Michael feared the worst. "Any survivors?"

Von Ribbentrop nodded. "Both men survived. The pilot's in the hospital, but he will be all right. Ravenstone walked away from the plane and has told the police in Reichenau that he wants to go back to England."

"No! Ravenstone comes to Berlin." Goebbels's fists were clenched. "Let me speak to the pilot if he's conscious."

Fifteen minutes later, the phone rang on Ribbentrop's desk. He picked it up, listened for a moment, and handed it to Goebbels.

"Yes? Captain, can you speak?" His eyes and bared teeth showed his rage. "All right, then, what happened?" He listened, leaning forward with his elbow on the desk, and his forefinger beat a little tattoo on its mahogany surface. "I see.

So, Ravenstone made the whole thing happen. Damn him. But I'm not surprised. We should have sent him by train even if it was going to take an extra day.

"Are you sure the ark was destroyed? Was there nothing left—not even the bronze bindings? Surely they would have been recognizable no matter what?" He waited for a response. "Did you hear what I asked you?" Another pause. "Ah, I see. So, in fact, you say there was someone helping Ravenstone to get you out of the plane while you were unconscious. Could that fellow have helped him take out the ark as well and then hide it?" Goebbels looked with malice at Michael as if to blame him for what had happened. "That's right. It's possible there was time to rescue you and the ark, no? Of course. You weren't conscious. I'll call them there right now. Thank you." He turned to Ribbentrop. "Get me the gestapo office in Reichenau."

Less than an hour later, the farmer had visitors at his house. He answered the door, expecting it would be Rupert. When he saw the gestapo uniforms, he looked beyond the two men and recognized the truck used to transport prisoners. They grabbed him and pushed their faces into his. He'd had to give his address to the medics as a witness. Now he was a collaborator in something far more dangerous than he had ever imagined. It took no time for him to agree to cooperate.

The three men drove to the woods, which loomed in jagged and charred silhouettes against the night sky. The farmer led them to a place where the trees were intact. He had hidden the ark under some debris of underbrush. When the two officers approached it, the ark began to glow in the dark. They had been warned. They ordered the strong young farmer to pick up the ark, bring it to the truck, and sit in the rear compartment alone with it.

At gestapo headquarters in the small town's police station,

Rupert sat disconsolate in a barren room. His conscience felt heavy. On Goebbels's order, he was under a double guard. They'd told him the farmer had been identified and would be asked about the ark. Rupert made it clear the man hadn't the slightest idea of subverting the police. He had only followed Rupert's request to put the ark in a place where he could find it later.

When the farmer entered struggling with the heavy casket, Rupert looked at him with sad eyes and shook his head. The farmer was ordered to deposit the ark next to him. He was grabbed by the two men escorting him and hauled down the hall to an interior courtyard. Rupert could hear his screams of terror before two shots resounded through the building, and then silence.

The guards on duty over Rupert ordered him to stand. A janitor helped him carry the ark to the waiting prisoner transport vehicle. Once it had been chained and padlocked in place, they ordered Rupert to sit on one of the benches running along each side of the prisoner compartment. They clipped his seat straps, which were attached to the wall, across his chest and lap.

"Where are we going, gentlemen?"

"With us, Britisher." The speaker sneered.

"Berlin?"

"Could be. You'll find out soon enough." He climbed out and slammed the rear doors. Rupert heard the lock turn and could see there was no way to open them from his side. He pulled out a cigarette and snapped open his lighter. A spark leaped from the flint onto the fragrant Turkish tobacco. He inhaled and let his mind drift back just twenty-four hours to the ambulance that had taken him with his colonel and the wounded von Vranken to Salzburg. What a fraught time. He felt a tug in his throat once again as the image, seared into his memory, of Orlando, apparently repentant, toppled over the edge and into the chasm. This was the worst, but it wasn't all. His colonel had been shot, and the poor bloke who'd hidden the ark was no more.

Too much pain was following in the wake of this object. When would it all come to a head? He sensed that might not be far off.

He took in his little prisoner's cell, mobile and austere. A six-bottle metal rack with a handle, containing six empty milk bottles with screw caps evidently served as an improvised toilet facility. The small windows in the two rear doors were covered with steel grills. He mulled over his likely reception at their destination. Frigid, at best. Goebbels would not be at all pleased by the recent turn of events.

His captors peered through the glazed and steel-grilled opening that separated the front seat from his quarters. He would give them little cause for alarm. The night passed in considerable discomfort. Sitting on a hard bench—and feeling every bump in the road magnified by the lack of shock absorbers—made sleep impossible. He did catch an occasional glimpse of the places they passed through. Usually out of the small rear windows, and sometimes through the window to the front of the van when it wasn't blocked by one of the guards. Stuttgart was the first city he was able to identify in this fleeting way, which meant they were heading north—and Berlin was probably their destination.

In the morning, the two guards parked the van at a roadside restaurant. One of them opened the window from the front seat and asked if he wanted coffee and some bread.

He nodded. When they had gone inside, he undid his harness and stretched his limbs. He lay down on his back and moved his arms and legs to restore his circulation. Then he crouched at the rear of the van to look out at the parking lot.

There was evidence they were probably near Nuremberg by this point, further confirmation of their trajectory.

As he scanned the scene, a face appeared suddenly at the window, just inches away, startling him. It was not an ordinary face at all. Dark, slicked-down hair, parted in the middle, a long, triangular shape to the head, thin, pointed nose, laughing eyes, and a perfectly triangular mouth in a disturbing smile. Two narrow lines of mustache pitched above his mouth, and a Vandyke goatee accentuated the image of inverted triangularity.

There was hint of the familiar about the face. Where had he seen it before? *Once seen, not easily forgotten,* he thought. Then it dawned. It dawned with the brightening morning light that accentuated the chalky pallor of this face. Of course. That moment when he had crawled across onto the icy ledge from over the drift of avalanched snow and seen Orlando at last. The boy was standing frozen before this haunting visage. Hesitating at first, Orlando had almost reluctantly held out his hand to help the creature onto the ledge. But it was too late. Reaching from the bridge as it was convulsing into its total collapse, the other's hand had barely grazed the tips of Orlando's fingers before crashing down with the disintegrated span into the riverbed far below. And he'd kept the same smile all the while.

Rupert shivered and turned to look at the ark. It was beginning to act up. Bouncing on the metal floor of the van, the noise made the two guards—who had just emerged from the restaurant—start to run toward the van. Rupert could see them through the interior window and windshield. When he turned to the rear door and checked the scene, the face had disappeared, and the casket was calm once more.

63

Late November 1938

Goebbels and von Vranken had never lost a moment of love for each other. The German aristocrat actually found the man repulsive. But the Fuhrer regarded the rodent-like creature as his brilliant, and admirably ruthless, deputy and thus conferred upon him enormous power. In point of fact, the Reichminister of propaganda had advanced his master's image and message with great effect. And Goebbels was not unaware of the condescension that often dripped from von Vranken's offhanded asides.

Sitting in a wheelchair, partially paralyzed from the shot fired by his despised enemy's son, Lothar von Vranken listened to Goebbels, enrapt, as the words he heard slowly crystallized a plan in his mind.

Goebbels was pacing about his office, touching this object and that, occasionally stopping before a large photo of his crony on the wall to stare into Hitler's eyes as if for enlightenment. "Caridis naturally wanted to have some say in his discovery's whereabouts, which is why he answered Camberini's call. We know this whole idea of turning it over to the pope is the brainchild of the Jew who wears a cardinal's cap. And we also know the pope had never even heard of the ark until Camberini made his move."

Von Vranken nodded. "Which is why the pope's conceived a sudden and intense respect for Camberini. Yes, I do see your point, Josef. He persuaded the pope he'd wanted to protect the ark from our Cardinal Fiorelli. Camberini claimed Fiorelli was trying to take it to advance his own ambition to keep the throne of Peter from anyone other than himself. This enraged the pontiff who knew full well his potential successor's ambition but not the degree of cynicism and opportunism propelling it. Feeling threatened by this revelation, the pontiff's anger rose to the point where he refused to receive Antonio in private audience—not even to let him present his own defense."

"Precisely, my dear Lothar. Which is why I've asked you here today. We need someone to rid us of this damn priest. Any thoughts? I recall you and Fiorelli were competitive skiers in your youth."

"Indeed, Josef. We've remained close ever since." Von Vranken smiled wickedly. "But I would like to be clear. Which damn priest? Camberini or the not-very-holy Father?"

☥

Berlin's Tempelhof airport was busy these days. Leading members of the Seraphim were arriving from the corners of the earth. This perhaps had caused Goebbels his worst indigestion ever.

Even imagining the ark had been destroyed in the crash had made him double over in pain. Humiliation was the least of its consequences. The Fuhrer would never have forgiven his own embarrassment on the world stage. This could well have meant the end of Goebbels's glorious career. Maybe also his life.

There would be no real peace until the van got to Berlin—and he actually had physical possession of the ark. In the meantime, preparations were underway to impress the incoming visitors. The Fuhrer had originally insisted on using the occasion to hold a monster rally to include more than elite Aaronites mainly sympathetic to the Nazi cause. Goebbels, however, had persuaded him their planned program would be too controversial to share on such a large stage. It should not take place in the stadium that had been designed by Albert Speer for Hitler's Imperial Roman-inspired spectacles.

Churchill declined his invitation and asked the whereabouts of Rupert Ravenstone. Berlin reacted with silence, which worried him. At least Lizzie had kept him updated on events since going off to Alexandria. The embassy in Berlin had also reported details of Orlando's violent death to him. This had stoked his already apocalyptic fears of the dangers for everyone posed by the Nazis despite the scrap of paper Chamberlain had got Hitler to sign several weeks before in Munich.

The abdicated British king, now Duke of Windsor, had already arrived, as had the crown prince of Japan, Benito Mussolini, and King Farouk of Egypt. They and an international host of other Aaronites and their wives had been invited to a banquet on Saturday evening before the midnight ceremony.

Goebbels was terrified by the Fuhrer's hourly calls to know whether the van had arrived. The Seraphim's grand master had also insisted on being told when the ark would be delivered at the Sanctuary. At last, an hour after sunset, the van pulled up before the Ordenspalais, the eighteenth-century palace in which Goebbels's ministry had its headquarters across the street from the Fuhrer's chancellery.

Goebbels ran to the entrance where it had parked. The

gestapo officers saluted him and opened the rear doors of the van.

Rupert sat in the far corner, leaning back with his legs crossed and holding a cigarette. "Minister, I think fourteen hours of travel in this luxurious transport would confirm the awesome possibilities for comfort only the Germans could devise."

Goebbels looked with relief at the ark and snarled. "Enough of your cheek, Englishman. I know the whole story. You're goddamned lucky to be who you are because the firing squad would have been far too good for you. Now come out of there and get in the car that's waiting. You'll stay put under guard until the Seraphim event on Saturday night. If you misbehave, the German government will bring charges of high crimes, and believe me, you'll be found guilty. Now begone with you. This time, we're taking permanent charge of the ark."

64

Late November 1938

*C*ardinal Giovanni Camberini received the full report from his spy network, which was probably the best in the world, and Caridis had recounted his full conversation with Goebbels from a secure telephone provided by the papal embassy in Berlin.

His voice trembled, and he shook his head. "You mean that craven Austrian corporal plans to urinate on the ark?"

"Among other unmentionable forms of desecration. Your Grace, his superman delusions won't be tempted by favors from this pope or anyone else. Wouldn't give a farthing to see the ark placed with reverence in the crypt of Saint Peter. We're dealing with Lucifer, but this one never fell from grace. He was conceived fallen."

Camberini clutched the telephone and said, "You do understand better than most, Michael, the powerful force that's alive in that chest. I know from my ancestral faith what potential it's got."

"I'm sure you're right, Your Grace. But these people are literally obsessed with hate. They feed on it. They believe anything connected to Jews or their faith must submit to the scourge the Nazis have in mind."

Camberini said, "Of course they're wrong! But even more, the ark doesn't just carry the traditional Word of the Hebrew God. It's much more than that. Received from the Lord by an Egyptian pharaoh, transcribed by a Jew, it's the bedrock of Christianity as much as Judaism. These are the commandments of the Lord of billions of humans today. Trifle with the Word at one's peril."

"Even I, Your Grace, an agnostic who still searches for faith in something I haven't yet found, I regard those commandments as our code for a civilized society. In the balance, I think preserving this treasure is even more important both for your church and for all mankind than finding Christ's Chalice itself would be."

"Absolutely, Michael! No question at all. But I suppose any efforts to stop whatever they plan for Saturday's ceremony are futile?"

"Alas, that's the simple fact. Sometimes I almost wish I'd never found it, you know." Michael took a long breath and soldiered on. "Your Grace, something else. We discussed this before my mission."

"Yes, my friend?"

"Please be very careful. The Nazi command now look on you as a threat. They're ruthless. They speak openly about Fiorelli succeeding the Holy Father—and that you must not stand in his way, especially after this futile mission of mine."

The cardinal laughed. "Not to worry, thank you. I can take care of myself. And as they say in my country, *Que será, será.*"

Giovanni Camberini slowly replaced the receiver on its cradle, rose from his chair, and decided his stiff joints needed some exercise. He rang for the steward and asked for his plain overcoat and an ordinary fedora. He was handed his willow-wood walking stick, adjusted his scarf, and pulled on his leather gloves.

He feet took him toward the river. Few, if any, people along the way had the slightest idea about the identity of the rather tall and portly man who was strolling and inspecting all about him with his eternal fascination and curiosity.

As often as he could, he took rather obscure little streets instead of the boulevards. With some inevitability, as if all roads led to it, he found himself in the park of Hadrian's fortress tomb, the Castel Sant'Angelo. Standing before the looming facade, he shrugged and decided to walk up to one of the roof platforms and enjoy the marvelous views.

With some effort, he pushed himself up the narrow staircase that was reserved for church officials. Stopping occasionally to catch his breath, he thought about his age. He was only sixty-two, but time lately seemed to have brought new burdens. Well, perhaps it wasn't time but the times. The thought of that sadistic little Austrian corporal defiling the Ark of the First Covenant kept coming to mind. How he wished he'd been able to hide it where no one would discover its treasure until the terrible storm now gathering in Europe had passed.

He looked up and wondered how many more steps before reaching the highest platform. The sound of feet treading on the stairs below interrupted his musing. He'd seen no one else so far in his ascent. Well, at the best of times, except for festivals or the occasional fireworks display, there wasn't a lot of traffic this way to the several levels of the brooding building. The footfalls became louder as they grew closer. It now was clear several people were coming up behind him. Something made him want to reach the roof as soon as possible. He pushed himself, moving as quickly as his weight and strength would allow.

Rounding another turn in the tower staircase, he was relieved to see daylight from the opening onto the roof twenty steps ahead. His heart was beating rapidly when at last he stepped outside into the bright sunlight, his eyes dazzled a little after the gloom of the poorly lighted stairs. He caught his breath and looked up at the statue of Michael the archangel, triumphant and huge on its massive substructure, wiping the blood from his sword on his tunic.

It was lunchtime, and Rome, enjoying the sensory pleasures of the table as much as anything else, was taking full advantage of the hour. A few tourists were inspecting the view, but there were no guards in sight. Those people who had been behind him now emerged. Instinctively, Camberini walked over to a parapet as if to check the view himself.

Two of the recent arrivals walked up to the tourists and said something that made them nod and take leave by the public staircase.

Within moments, Giovanni Camberini was alone on the highest roof of what once had been the tallest building in Rome—except for five men in dark overcoats and fedoras like his.

65

Late November 1938

upert looked out from his bedroom window in the state guesthouse at the artfully wooded Berlin park surrounding it. Clouds moving across the early afternoon sky were reflected from the lagoon just beyond the end of a manicured lawn and hedge. To his great satisfaction, he was being allowed to meet with Michael Caridis in ten minutes.

The guard stationed outside his bedroom escorted him down to a small salon.

Michael was removing his gloves and overcoat and hat. "Ah, thank God you're all right, my dear Rupert. I don't know what I expected, but I'm so pleased to see how fine you look. What you've been through! Just surviving a plane crash, for one example."

Rupert winked. "You might recall I'm a licensed pilot. The other chap's rather worse for the experience." He laid his forefinger on his lips and cupped the other hand to his ear. He then continued in rapid Arabic. "If I'd landed the plane on a patch of meadow several hundred yards over, on the next island, the ark would have been in Switzerland, and things quite different this weekend." He gave a mischievous smile.

Michael responded in Arabic, "I must tell you our hosts, if we can call them that, are so furious with you that they've seriously considered a kangaroo trial regardless of the international commotion that would cause."

"I know." Rupert laughed. "They were quick to point out my rank in the British government was the only thing that saved me from the firing squad. Well, I guess getting their clutches into the ark at last might have made their appetite for vengeance a bit less compelling."

"Evidently. I don't know how much they've told you, but they're preparing a celebratory presentation of the ark tomorrow night at the headquarters of the Seraphim. You'll be astonished who of the world's elite came for the unveiling."

Rupert smirked. "Yes, and to think I was ready to leave Germany on my own and miss all this. But, frankly, my recent treatment's given me a certain schadenfreude. The ark's got a pretty stroppy mind of its own. It's not bloody likely to stay calm under our so-called hosts' control." He paused to light up. "So, where're you staying?"

"With the Vatican ambassador." Michael described his bizarre mission and his temporary diplomatic appointment.

Rupert's eyes twinkled. "You, of all people, representing the pope? A man committed to questioning all ecclesiastical authority. Nice. On further thought, not so implausible, since most leaders of great religions realize how much hocus-pocus lies behind it all." He dragged on his cigarette. "I take it you weren't successful."

"Never had a chance. Just a long shot, no illusions. I must say, the cast of characters is outrageous. As you know, of course. After your friend, the minister of propaganda, spent some time with you in that quaint Austrian town, which I won't name, he met with me when he got back to Berlin. His message was simple. The big fellow at the top here wants to use my discovery to torment the race they're cleansing from the planet."

Rupert turned as his guard entered the salon. "Your time's up, Englishman."

Rupert whispered, "Sounds like the call to the gallows. Suppose I'll see you all dolled up tomorrow evening."

They both laughed and stood.

Rupert helped Michael on with his overcoat.

Turning to look over his shoulder at Rupert, Michael whispered, "I shudder a little wondering what these barbarians actually have up their sleeves."

66

Late November 1938

The headquarters of the Society of the Seraphim sat well back from the boulevard, with a broad curved driveway and surrounded by formal gardens. Its facade was flanked by a tall colonnade that ran in two arcs from the central core. Centered above the core's two levels of soaring two-story windows rose a shallow dome reminiscent of the Roman Pantheon.

Hundreds of spectators crowded outside the gates. Word had flown that world figures were in town for a fete given by the Fuhrer. Technically, the hosts were the Seraphim, but that was in name only.

Michael, driven in a Vatican car, stopped at the guesthouse where Rupert was lodged. His ever-present guard dropped into the front passenger seat with a surly nod to the driver. Behind them, the two were immaculate in their white ties and tailcoats, Michael wearing a high award of the Egyptian monarchy while Rupert, outfitted by a superb tailor sent by the

Seraphim, could not have cared less to be without his Order of the Garter, his monarch's highest honor.

Rupert sensed immediately something was amiss.

Michael sat rigid and tense. After several minutes, he leaned over and whispered, "Must speak at the Seraphim. Something terrible's happened. Found out just now leaving the embassy."

The Vatican car, flag fluttering at its prow, entered the curved driveway and was gestured to stop near the main steps. The guard waved aside the costumed attendant and opened Rupert's door.

Rupert said, "All right now? You've got me here safe and sound. Why don't you have a relaxing drink and enjoy the scenery?" Without waiting for a response, he took Michael by the arm and walked quickly with him to one side of the entrance steps. "What is it?"

Michael was suddenly emotional. "These people stop at nothing. Camberini's dead. The official Vatican story is he jumped from the highest parapet of Castel Sant'Angelo because he was depressed by the plight of Jews all over Europe. Absurd as we both know. Now there's no obstacle to Fiorelli. Hitler will have his own puppet there when the present pope has passed away." He paused and gave an ironic smile. "And even that could be hurried along." He shook his head. "Giovanni shouldn't have sent me on this mission. I'm certain he'd still be alive."

The muscles contracted in Rupert's cheeks. His expression changed briefly, like a passing shadow. "These are animals. Camberini deserved so much better. But by the end of this evening, don't worry, I'm sure we're going to have some measure of revenge. I can feel it." He squeezed Michael's arm. "Come now, put on your party face. Let the games begin."

Inside the entrance hall, the guests glittered. Waiters wove in and out among them serving drinks and hors d'oeuvres. The occasional German prince stood out in colorful nineteenth-century uniform replete with gold braid, shining jeweled buttons and buckles, and sashes and medals. Rupert glanced about, smelling the perfumes and sipping a superb rosé champagne, as he took stock of the guests.

A small orchestra consisting only of violins was playing a Lehar waltz at one end of the room, adding to the high level of decibels and the atmosphere of excited expectation.

Michael was deep into discussing the origins of his staggering discovery with King Farouk when he noticed a wheelchair being pushed by one of the liveried men. Looking extremely fragile, Lothar von Vranken had spied Rupert and directed his assistant to propel him there.

A couple walked up to Rupert and became quickly engaged in conversation. It was the Duke of Windsor and his duchess. Rupert bowed to his cousin and kissed the hand of his new wife. He knew of the former king's sympathies, and he deliberately asked the duchess what she thought of the Nazi regime.

"Perfect," she responded. "So clever and efficient. They've figured how to run a country. It's refreshing to be somewhere that has its political priorities straight. And that charming Fuhrer, he addressed me as 'Your Royal Highness.'"

Her husband smiled with happy indulgence at this solipsism.

Lothar von Vranken's wheelchair stopped beside them, and all three separated to see who it was. Lothar extended his hand and said, "Your Highness, or may I even say, Your Majesty, I'm so pleased you've come to honor us with your presence."

The duke hadn't a clue who this was but nodded politely. He was also still secretly pleased at the Fuhrer's misuse of "Royal" for his wife who had been the subject of a heated debate among the cabinet and parliament and Edward VIII's successor all of whom rejected resoundingly a Royal Highness title for Wallis Simpson. And, of course, since his abdication the year before, Windsor was no longer a "Majesty." Lothar continued, "Like our friend here," tilting his hand toward Rupert, "we've got family in common. My great-grandmother was your great-grandfather, Prince Albert's, sister. Your return to his native land must give you some feelings of sentimental pleasure?"

Rupert wanted to throw up at this but said nothing.

Windsor perked up and said in his high thin voice, "Oh, yes, as you must know, Germany's the place most of my ancestors came from since George I."

"Well, then," von Vranken said, "you must do everything in your power to make Britain understand an alliance between our two great nations would be the lighthouse for the world. Our mutual beacon would shine into all corners and bring our values to dominate everywhere."

Rupert was disgusted and watched Windsor take the bait. The duke vowed to explain this to the British government. The very government, Rupert reflected, that had insisted he abdicate and that wanted him as far away from Germany and particularly England as possible. Rupert had already discussed with his ally, Churchill, ways of finding a post for him, perhaps in the Bahamas, as the governor of a crown colony. At least this would put some physical distance where it was sorely needed.

Rupert felt a touch on his arm and turned. It was Michael. Rupert turned to Windsor and said, "Sir, do let me introduce someone extremely important. Michael Caridis, the discoverer of the surprise to be revealed later this evening."

Windsor inclined his head in respect. "Congratulations, sir. Many people of consequence have come great distances to witness what you've brought to light. We're all dying of curiosity. Can't you possibly give us a sneak preview of what's coming?"

Michael smiled and said, "I must explain, sir, this isn't my show at all. In fact, I'm not sure what the hosts have got in mind. But one can say in advance the discovery itself was inspired by our Seraphim's most ancient legend." He smiled. "I'm afraid you'll have to figure out the rest on your own."

The duchess showed her own rather predatory smile. "Ah, nothing like a good mystery. And then finding out the solution tonight. I can't wait for the whole surprise."

Michael and Rupert exchanged knowing looks. Just then, a gong echoed through the entrance hall, and a loud voice announced dinner was about to begin.

The glittering gathering promenaded into the grand banqueting hall. Passing through its doorway, they were given directions to their places. The broad table was 120 feet long with sixty seats on each side and a throne-like chair at the far end. A liveried servant stood behind each chair. They were dressed in colorful uniforms with high-banded collars and elaborate gold-braid and brass trimmings.

The table was laden with the legendary Hohenzollern silver-gilt *plateaux*, salt cellars, and candelabras that had been given in appreciation to the Seraphim by Frederick the Great. Mirrors in towering, gilded frames on both sides reflected the opulence into infinity.

Rupert was directed to his seat near one end of the table. He remained standing and waited for other guests to come beside him. He noticed Michael seated near the table's center.

Michael nodded to him, turning away to greet the lady arriving on his left. She was the very young queen of Egypt, wife of Farouk, clearly relieved to be next to someone she recognized. He'd always been avuncular and charming with her. The chair on his other side was at the central point of the table's length. He glanced down to see the grand master's place card.

An orchestra on the balcony above the room's entrance began to play *"Deutschland Uber Alles"* in full-throated and majestic cadences. A voice commanded all to rise. At the other end, double doors opened onto its high balustraded platform. The grand master stepped out followed by two handsome women who appeared to be sisters and then two men. They descended eight broad steps, and, spreading apart, they flanked the steps and turned to look up at the Fuhrer who appeared in the doorway to applause and cries of "Heil Hitler!" He came down and was ensconced at the head of the table with one of the two women placed to his right. Guests remained standing while the grand master took his seat beside Michael. The other fashion icon and the two men headed to Rupert's end. She smiled brightly and kissed him on the cheek before sitting beside him, while her husband took his place across the table and tried not to look directly at Rupert. His skin crawled slightly as Josef Goebbels, rat-like as ever, passed by to take the foot of the table. Rupert suspected he was placed so near to Goebbels in case he tried to disappear before the unveiling.

Goebbels took Diana Mosley's hand and kissed it, glancing at Rupert with a malicious hint of a smile, and turned to the woman on his left. Rupert enjoyed this small attempt at retribution and winked as Diana gave him a look of complicity. She radiated offhanded sophistication, wore well her slight debutante slouch, and managed to be witty, charming, caustic, and utterly desirable all at once. He recalled Evelyn Waugh's saying that her beauty "ran through the room like a peal of bells."

"Darling," she trilled, "how's your divine Lizzie? Oh, my dear, of course, you're both grieving—for that poor boy. Oswald was devastated when he learned. Orlando was his finest recruit, destined someday to succeed him as head of the British Union of Fascists."

Rupert gave a sad smile and replied, "Thanks, my dear Diana, let's speak rather about your son who was born, what, only ten days ago? I must say, you're doing awfully well for all that."

"How'd you know? Word has it, Rupert, you've been rather naughty of late, at least according to our friend here." She gestured toward Goebbels.

"Naughty may not be perfectly apt. I've indeed been occupied with trying to find Orlando and to rescue the very object you've been invited to see tonight. In the event, alas, I've lost both."

She gave him a flirtatious flutter of eyelids. "I suppose you won't tell me any more about that thing than Joseph here's done? He's been terribly coy, you know. Maybe a little peek before the ceremony?"

"Not my place, especially as I don't approve of anything your friend Joseph is about."

"Except, darling, sitting us together like this."

Rupert nodded. "Yes. Odd it seems, puzzling, because he spares no energy in loathing me possibly because those feelings are mutual. Anyway, I'm certainly grateful for this one small redeeming act. Now tell me, how is it you've followed your rather infamous sister down there at the other end sitting with the man whose name I find it difficult to speak?"

"Oh, Rupert, darling, they're madly in love, didn't you know? Unity thinks he's absolutely marvelous. Guess what? The stars foretold all this. Truly. Unity was conceived in a town in Ontario, Canada. The place was called Swastika! Really. Clearly a foretelling. Then another omen. She was christened Unity Valkyrie Mitford. Grandpa knew and loved Wagner, it seems."

Rupert asked, "Do you think marriage is in the air? She's rather taller than he is, for starters. At least she looks like a particularly ethereal Brunhilda, which he might let overcome any other inhibitions."

Diana shook her head. "I doubt bells will swing for their nupts. He's not going to let a foreign girl be the Fuhrer's missus. He stands for pure German blood and all that. But, on another matter, I'm telling you in *confiance totale*, Oswald and I were married right in Josef's office." She pointed at Goebbels. "And now our newly arrived little gent is legit. Ain't that terrific?"

Rupert hated to show enthusiasm for anything to do with either Mosley or Goebbels, but he gamely smiled, marveling, yet again, at these eccentric sisters he'd known most of his life.

Meanwhile, dinner was drawing to dessert. The grand master leaned toward Michael and said, "I've got a copy here of Lord Ravenstone's translation of the scrolls. I want them read aloud—to give everyone background for what's about to take place. What do you think? Should I do this or leave it up to you or Ravenstone?"

Michael, without missing a beat, said, "Rupert, of course. He's a marvelous speaker, and it's his translation. No question, in my mind."

"Very well." The grand master walked down to Rupert's seat, and Goebbels looked up at him with satisfaction. They nodded to each other as the master tapped Rupert's shoulder.

Diana said, "Rupert, darling, the grand master himself. What an honor."

The master leaned over Rupert's shoulder and explained in a quiet voice what he wished.

Rupert nodded slowly, beginning to see the reason for his placement. "I think it better if I give a synopsis, a brief commentary. Would that do?"

"Whatever you think best, Brother Ravenstone." The grand master straightened up and handed Rupert a copy of his translation of the scrolls. "Here, just as an aide-memoire, perhaps." He smiled and gestured for Rupert to join him at the center of the table.

The grand master led Rupert to a beautiful baroque lectern with a microphone mounted on top. He tapped on it and called for everyone's attention. "Fuhrer, majesties, princes, dukes, all other nobilities, ambassadors, state ministers, and honored guests, we're gathered tonight for an extraordinary occasion. In the annals of this Society to which we all belong, a legend has persisted for more than three thousand years. A treasure was said to be buried that would reveal great and surprising secrets. It was accompanied by a single clue: a fragment of stone upon which the following enigma is inscribed: 'Be the King a Prophet, or the Prophet a King, what was broken remains true since truth cannot be broken ... Until I am found, you must seek something in which to believe ... I alone shall lie with the truth ... somewhere between twelve twice and God.'

"It took one of our members who happily is with us tonight, Brother Michael Caridis of Alexandria, to solve the mystery. He devoted thirty-five years and finally succeeded. He divined the location of a tomb in the sands surrounding the capital city constructed by the pharaoh Akhenaten. What was found I will leave up to another distinguished member of our cult to explain. I give you the greatest scholar of Egyptian hieroglyphs and Middle Eastern languages in the world today. His lordship, the very distinguished Marquess of Ravenstone."

Goebbels glowered but managed to join in the applause that greeted Rupert as he took his place behind the lectern. He placed his translation on the lectern's deck, looked up, and smiled. "Brothers and sisters, I don't know what's been planned for us inside the Sanctum tonight. My message deals only with the extraordinary nature of what was discovered by Brother Caridis in that tomb. When he penetrated its stone door, it was clear he'd come upon the very simple, rapidly constructed tomb of Pharaoh Akhenaten and his wife, Nefertiti. Their coffins, alas, had been stolen, probably shortly after burial thirty-three centuries ago. The greatest revelation, however, lay behind a wall within the small tomb. It was that very treasure of our Aaronite. A casket made of ebony and bound in bronze. Within were three scrolls revealing one of the most intriguing tales of all time."

The audience sat mesmerized.

"I marveled at the unfolding message of these texts as I translated them. They'd been written by a man who was the scribe for the pharaoh as well as his most trusted servant and friend. Not too surprising—as Pharaoh had saved his life. The scribe's given name was in fact Ishmael, but Akhenaten called him by a diminutive of his own mother's pet name for himself, for reasons that you will learn later when you read my entire translation. That pet name," Rupert paused for effect, "was 'my little Moses.'

"The scribe addressed the scrolls to Pharaoh's mother whom he called 'blessed' and 'divine.' He used these words for a very good reason. It seems her son was conceived when she was very young and had never known a man. So, apparently born of a virgin, her son grew up to be the first monarch in all known history to insist one God alone was fit to worship. As you'd expect, the priests and many adherents of the old religion of many gods fiercely, dramatically, opposed this heresy.

"These established groups were alarmed by the many who found Akhenaten's faith compelling. These included the Hebrew people, Egypt's captives for the previous four hundred years. Dissension between Pharaoh and the old guard was also fanned by a fiercely ambitious general seeking to rid Egypt of its heretic king. Without much hesitation, traditionalists supported the general and authorized him to negotiate with Akhenaten.

"The outcome was a deal. Akhenaten would take the Hebrews, now to be liberated, and seek another place to set up a monotheistic society. He would let his young son, Tutankhamen, succeed to the throne. The general also insisted, obsessed by the beauty of Queen Nefertiti, that she be given to him as a wife. He would then assume the role of regent for the boy-pharaoh and govern with Nefertiti at his side.

"This plan was put into motion. However, Akhenaten could not bear to let her be taken to the general. Instead, he substituted a veiled lady of considerable beauty to travel with Tutankhamen as if she were the queen herself. Their journey south took some days to reach the old capital of Egypt now restored as the center of Egyptian power.

"Akhenaten looked with a pang at his departing son as he prepared to lead the Hebrews and hosts of Egyptian believers in the One God northwards in search of a land where they could settle and be free of spiritual and physical subjugation.

"The exodus of Akhenaten and his flock had been in progress for several weeks when a furious general, deprived of his promised bride, caught up with them at the edge of the Red Sea. All appeared to be lost until a great comet flashed through the sky over the heads of the general and the Egyptian army poised on a cliff above the Israelites and Akhenaten. The gravitational force of the comet blasted apart the waters of the sea, and the masses of fleeing people stumbled their way through the open gully until they reached high land on the other side. By the time the general and his army were able to descend from the cliff and enter the opening carved by the comet, its gravitational pull had been spent—and the water collapsed upon the army in a cataclysmic rush, killing most of them. The general, by the way, had been at the rear not the head of his army and thus was saved either by a premonition or a natural fear of those walls of water suspended in trembling towers on either side of his lemmings."

Rupert looked to his left and saw, to his mild amusement, Hitler shaking his head. He continued the narrative. "So, the fleeing masses had put a major barrier between them and the Egyptian army, the meager remains of which gave up and returned to Luxor. The great exodus of pilgrims proceeded for some months, moving slowly and feeding off the land. When they reached what we call today Mount Sinai, Akhenaten had a revelation. The voice of his One God spoke and commanded him to ascend and receive the Law by which his people would govern their lives.

"Akhenaten took his scribe Ishmael, who carried water and clay and trays and a fine-pointed tool to inscribe whatever words his master might receive. They spent many days without any communication from his One God. In the meantime, the traditional spiritual leader of the Israelites, the very Aaron of our cult, was importuned by his people for something to worship. They were spiritually hungry and impatient for Akhenaten to come back with his message. They had clearly begun to doubt that outcome. So, Aaron said they could create an idol to receive their prayers. They made the crude image of a calf draped with a golden shawl and called it Baal.

"And the people were pacified for the time being. At the end of forty days, Akhenaten descended from the mountain with three tablets of laws revealed to him under a barren tree that had miraculously erupted in a fullness of new leaves as the Word was received. When he saw the idol, he threw down the tablets in terrible anger, disappointed at the weakness of his flock and especially of Aaron whom he excoriated before the people, now fallen upon their knees. The tablets had shattered into pieces, and everyone was shocked at themselves for causing this confrontation. With great foresight, the scribe, Ishmael, managed to collect these pieces and keep them safe.

"From that point on, there was bad blood between Akhenaten and Aaron. Akhenaten went back up the mountain. The Word was given again, and the tree remained robust, but it was covered now with fewer leaves. He carried the new Commandments down the mountain and gave them to the people who pledged on their lives to obey the Law forevermore.

"The first Law stated there would be only One God and none could come before Him. Akhenaten pointed at that law and told Aaron he lacked real faith. That, ladies and gentlemen gathered here in this home of the Aaronites, is the reason for the existence of our cult. We're searchers who've seen false truths take the form of answers to the longings of people for something in which to believe. Many of us have yet to find that 'something.' But others believe they have found it. Some of these answers have stood the test of time. But others have not and will not. Our cult is based on skepticism and a desire for a truth that we often find eludes us. Akhenaten was fixed to his perceived truth. The laws he brought back down that mountain have become the foundation of three great religions, those of the Hebrews, Christians, and Muslims. This, I believe, deserves at the very least, our respect, if not our awe.

"Now for the miracle. Contained within that casket are also the broken pieces of the original Commandments given by their Lord to the Hebrews. These pieces, picked up and preserved by the scribe, Ishmael, were placed with his scrolls inside the casket. It thus became the true Ark of the Covenant. It is here in this building and contains, among its admonitions, a wonderful law that is not mentioned in the later, sterner commandments. Hear it now: *Whoever does not love does not know God because God is love.* Can we not admire the beautiful idea behind this?"

An affirmative murmur came back from the guests.

Rupert looked at the left-hand end of the table, where, seated on his throne-like chair, Hitler folded his arms, wore a disgusted expression, and shook his head once again. "Much more lies within these scrolls that we haven't the time to mention. I hope you'll learn their full text at some point. I'm pleased to have left you now at least with their essence. I salute the real Moses, an African monarch and mystic. He was a man for all of us to admire. Thank you."

Amid the applause, there were a few shouts of "*Nein, nein!*"

Goebbels stood up and passed by Rupert with a look of cold contempt. At the podium, Goebbels bent into the microphone. "You've heard one interpretation of the treasure of the Seraphim. Yes, it can be said to be the Ark of the Covenant. But whose Covenant? It reveals the man whom the Hebrews worship as the prophet they call Moses wasn't even a Jew. He was an African, dark-skinned, and the king of a nation that held Jews as slaves for four hundred years.

"It also shows the deep doubts Aaron felt about the Hebrew god when he permitted his people to worship the forbidden golden calf. Aaron's a symbol. He's our apostle of pragmatism. We Aaronites have supported many doctrines and regimes through the ages, including all the major world religions and history's most notable leaders. It's because we have chosen until now to exercise our power through those different doctrines and regimes that we've been able to survive and prosper for so long."

Rupert wondered where it all was leading. The man was skating out onto pretty thin ice. But it was worse than that.

Goebbels said, "The miracle is that now, at long last, we've found the final solution to our Aaronite's endless search for something in which to believe. He's sitting at the head of our table tonight. He alone commands the future, and it will be permanent and pure. No more will the world be polluted by races and religions and regimes that deviate from the vision of perfection granted to our leader. *Deutschland Uber Alles!* Heil Hitler!"

Cries of "Heil Hitler!" rose from about half the places at the long table. Other guests exchanged uncertain looks.

The grand master winced at the thought of what was to come and wanted to absent himself entirely from the proceedings. But to disappear now could mean both that his life and the welfare of the Seraphim would be in jeopardy. He stood and nodded to Goebbels who sensed his comments had been rather ham-handed at best and appeared defensive and even more arrogant. He waved a flippant hand at the master and returned to his place.

At the microphone, the master announced, "Please proceed now to our robing."

The liveried steward, who had served each place at the table, escorted his charge to the robing rooms. On the way, guests chattered in a state of high excitement and anticipation. The ladies had their room, and the gents had theirs. A robe on a hanger hung on each of the many hooks that circled the room. There was a name in large print above each occupied hook.

The stewards helped their wards with the deep maroon velvet robes and woven gold masks that covered just the eyes of each Aaronite.

Rupert, fully outfitted, walked over to the other side of the room as Michael was having his mask tied behind his head with a maroon velvet ribbon. "What did you think of that display of tone deafness?"

Caridis's eyes rolled visibly behind his mask. "These people are simply unhinged. I'm not at all sanguine about what we're about to witness." He tilted his head toward the grand master who had just entered. "I can tell you that man is suffering. He loathes the fellow walking up to him." It was Hitler, robed and ready.

"God help us," Rupert said.

The grand master called out, "Please form a line of twos for our procession." He left with the Fuhrer, entered the ladies' robing room, and gave the same command. Both rooms spilled out into a wide corridor. The men's and women's lines merged together with two abreast and the master with the Fuhrer at the head followed by Goebbels, the Duke and Duchess of Windsor, the king and queen of Egypt, and the crown prince and princess of Japan.

The column filed through large arched double doors and into a rectangular room covered entirely in red lacquer, including the floor and ceiling. Mirrors punctuated the walls, set in tall panels of red molding. The only lighting came from candles in vermeil chandeliers hanging in front of each mirror. At the other end of the room stood another pair of lacquered red doors. The first pair of doors was closed when everyone had gathered in the anteroom.

With a certain solemnity, two of the stewards slowly opened the far doors. Admiring sounds came from the procession as they beheld the Sanctuary, which was also lit only by candles. A large octagonal space rose up to the broad shallow dome, underpinned by a balcony running across each of the eight sides. The entire space, including the dome, was covered in jet-black Belgian marble, polished to a mirror finish. Centered under the dome rose an imposing octagonal structure of black marble. Seven steps ran the length of each of its eight sides. These led to an octagonal platform about six feet high from which rose a black-marble octagonal altar holding an octagonal pedestal. Poised atop, the golden calf gazed out in mute splendor. The statue was beautifully modeled in highly polished solid gold that glowed strikingly from the many black marble surfaces. Jittering flames from a thousand candles reflected from marble walls and dome—and from the golden calf with its sly expression, as if it had a little secret it was dying to share.

The Aaronites entered and were led once around the full perimeter of the great altar. They were divided into two groups, flanking an aisle leading to the great altar, and they admired the statue. At last, slow soft drumbeats broke the silence. From the shadows behind them came the sound of chanting.

Rupert turned and saw a procession led by a man wearing a scarlet robe from neckband to floor. Upon his head, perched high, was a helmet of red gold upon which leered the hairy head of a wolf with crimson eyes, jaws apart, razor-like teeth, and pointed ears. The high priest carried the rod of Aaron. This was encircled by a sleeping cobra; its hooded head jutted above the carved leaves, arch and menacing.

Rupert wondered how long the drug's effect would take to wear off before the sinuous creature awakened, but his most pressing concern was the face of the man himself. That face had stared into his through the rear door windows of the prisoner's van when they'd stopped before reaching Berlin. It was an unforgettable face, triangular head, triangular smile, mocking eyes, and black goatee. That smile seemed impudent as the man nodded left and right on his way to the altar. Rupert felt an icy draft and shivered. He could not blot out the image of Orlando hesitating and then extending his hand, too late to save this same man from plunging into the chasm.

Next in the procession appeared sixteen men in black hoods and robes to the floor. They carried torches and chanted. Following them appeared two muscular young men dressed in ancient Egyptian-style short kilts and sandals with laces crisscrossed around their ankles. The torch flames reflected from their well-oiled upper bodies. On a small platform between two poles held at either end by these men, the Ark of the Covenant brooded in silence on its way to the altar of the golden calf.

The audience murmured as the litter was put down. The two men carried the ark up the seven steps to the altar and placed it below the idol with its clasps facing the celebrants. The bearers stood with arms folded before the ark.

The black-hooded figures arranged themselves in two lines of eight on either side of the altar. Each man inserted the foot of his torch into a small hole in the marble floor and remained standing behind it. The torches were gilded and shaped like the symbolic Roman bundles of wheat stalks tied with bands of golden rope, which were called fasces in Latin. Borrowed now from the ancients, they had become the symbol of the eponymous fascists.

The chanting grew urgent and louder, as did the drumbeats, and Rupert turned back to see what might follow.

Two barefoot figures in loose white gowns of fine cotton emerged from the shadows. Each one was flanked by two young men in Egyptian kilts like the carriers of the ark.

Rupert turned to Michael and whispered, "Good God. It's Solange and Fritzi! Damn! I meant to tell you, they never made it to England."

"Those poor bastards." Michael choked up. "Nothing good can possibly come of this for them."

The two barefoot figures were brought down the aisle to stand before the altar. Their heads were held high, and their eyes gleamed as if they had been drugged. But they had not been drugged. Their ecstasy came from within as they faced the ark. The four men lined up behind and crossed their arms.

Standing on the base platform with his back to the audience and holding the rod of Aaron, the high priest began an incantation in a language no person present had ever heard.

Rupert said, "Strange. The ark isn't reacting. Yet, it's literally surrounded by anathemas. It's practically underneath the golden calf itself? Is it being lulled by the diabolical sounds of the fellow who seems to be playing Aaron up there?"

Michael nodded. "I think this might be a strategy. We're dealing with an intelligent force. The Covenant operates in its own mysterious ways. In any event, the Nazis haven't got a clue."

The high priest turned to face the two white-gowned figures. Wearing his perpetual triangular smile, he raised the rod and lowered it three times to strike the marble base, sending out an echo with each stroke. He said, "Herr Graf Lothar von Vranken will introduce two participants in tonight's ceremony." He pointed with the long fingernails of his other hand at the carved mahogany wheelchair next to Goebbels, from which Vranken was being assisted to stand up. The Nazi aristocrat was held up by two of the kilted men as they walked haltingly to stand beside the leader.

Von Vranken focused into Fritzi's eyes and spoke in a voice filled with venom. "This is Friedrich Vogel, one-time confidante of the Nazi high command. Now exposed as a traitor and betrayer and Jew. Posing as a Gentile since joining the party at its very beginnings, he has further betrayed the trust of his colleagues and his country by trying to steal the Ark of the First Covenant and bring it to a now-defunct cardinal who was also a Jew. For all this, Friedrich Vogel has been condemned to die."

Turning to Solange, he scowled and said, "Solange Falkensberg, lewd dancer, Jewess, and spy. She, too, has betrayed her country. Probably a witch as well. In like manner, Solange Falkensberg has also been condemned to die. For reasons that will become evident later, these two have been chosen to reveal the contents of the ark to our fellow Aaronites." He bowed and was lifted back to his wheelchair.

An audible intake of breath was heard from the assembled Aaronites.

Rupert found this intolerable. Her magnificent features and proud bearing had not been a jot diminished. The candlelight had made the green of her eyes seem crystalline, and his desire for her mounted before the imperturbability of her movements, as if she had complete control of her life.

Fritzi's hair had begun to grow back. His well-formed head was capped now in sandy-red curls. He, too, had not a trace of visible concern for his fate. Only an excitement that made the two radiate a sense of exaltation.

The high priest descended the seven steps and walked past the two barefoot celebrants to stand behind them and their four attendants. He faced the altar, raised the rod, and intoned, "Let the ark be opened."

Fritzi and Solange mounted the steps and faced the casket with reverence. They looked at each other as if to ask what to do next.

The two kilted men flanking them moved in front of the ark and withdrew the bronze rod from its three clasps. They nodded and gestured for them to take over.

Fritzi lifted each clasp. Holding the sides of the cover, he raised it to rest against the pedestal beneath the golden calf. There was no reaction at all from the casket.

Solange reached inside and withdrew the sacred cloth. She placed it on the altar beside the casket and lifted out the first scroll.

Fritzi received it and unrolled it slowly.

They both held up the opened scroll to show its hieroglyphic inscription to the audience. The papyrus started glowing as if a golden lamp were lighted within.

The high priest, not pleased, gestured them to put it down on the altar, continuing to radiate its golden light. His words seemed to come from the vicious open jaws of the wolf's head on the high priest's headdress. "This is the first part of the letter addressed to the queen who was Akhenaten's mother." The high priest's voice sounded reedy and mocking. "It reeks of its scribe's sadness, the trusted servant who was called Little Moses by his master Akhenaten. Sorrow because the scroll accompanies two embalmed bodies. Her son's and his wife's. Yes, Akhenaten and Nefertiti." He stopped and nodded for them to continue.

Fritzi lifted out the second scroll. They unrolled it, and as its hieroglyphics were exposed, the beige papyrus assumed an intense watery blue inner light that changed like sunlight seen from beneath the moving sea.

Gesturing impatiently for them to lay it upon the altar, the high priest said, "This scroll recounts the story of the escape through the riven waters of the Red Sea and the slow progress of these people up to Sinai." He appeared uneasy as the final scroll was being lifted from the ebony casket.

Slowly unrolled, the papyrus shone a bloodred light, radiating enough to bathe their two faces in its glow. Solange and Fritzi looked at each other, sharing a sense of the sublime, and held it like the others. This ancient text was in Hebrew and included a copy of the complete inscription on the original tablets. Those with good vision in the audience immediately recognized the significant difference in appearance to the other two texts.

The high priest pointed with his forefinger's talon-like nail at the altar, an imperious gesture that brooked no delay to lay the final scroll upon it. "This is the most important scroll. It describes Akhenaten's ascent of the mountain to receive the first commandments of his god. Then Akhenaten's breaking of those tablets upon the golden calf in anger at, for him, the insufferable affront of Baal. And finally, the death of

Akhenaten and Nefertiti. Aaron is the cause. At a feast where the two monarchs are being honored and thanked by the thousands of refugees they'd brought to this point, the terrible event occurs. In a fit of humiliation and resentment, Aaron swings his mighty rod across both their heads. He could not abide the anger of the man he considered an Egyptian interloper in the religious affairs of his, Aaron's, Hebrews. Thus, Aaron the searcher and improviser became the inspiration for our own cult."

There was a sound behind the high priest, and he whipped around.

Solange and Fritzi still faced the altar. Before them, the three scrolls had furled and lifted themselves to stand on their ends, emanating light upward in red, blue, and golden tones. Barely audible voices of a female choir seemed to shimmer with the shafts of colored lights that rose like a rainbow over the ark.

The audience exchanged questioning looks.

The high priest stormed back up the steps to the altar and raised the rod to knock down the scrolls. In mid-swing, he froze as if a hand had suddenly gripped the other end. Recovering poise, he lowered the rod and turned to the pair of kilted attendants flanking the altar. "Raise that box high!"

The men closed the lid, lifted the ark from its ends, and held it firmly above their heads.

The high priest addressed the four kilted men standing at the foot of the altar steps. "I'm told one of you can release the false bottom inside the box. Do so now."

A man mounted the steps and told the two to raise the box higher so he could see its bottom. Finding the cartouche, he pressed it hard with both hands. Upon hearing the click inside, he straightened and nodded to the high priest.

They lowered the ark to the altar beneath the shimmering

rainbow of lights pouring from the scrolls. The invisible choir grew more audible and insistent.

Rupert glanced over at Goebbels's profile; his triumphant smugness had begun to fray.

Solange and Fritzi paused before the ark and bowed their heads in reverence for several moments.

The high priest barked, "Get on with it."

Solange smiled joyously at her companion. He nodded and lifted the lid, again resting it on the pedestal holding the golden calf. Reaching inside, he withdrew the false bottom, a heavy slab of ebony, laid it beside the ark, and gestured to Solange.

She brought up from the secret compartment two small packages of different sizes covered in burlap and tied with leather laces. Placing these with great care on the ebony slab, she continued to retrieve the rest until none were left within the ark. The array of packages covered the slab.

Fritzi untied a package. Its leather laces were brittle and fell apart in pieces. Peeling aside the folds of the supple burlap, he withdrew a jagged piece of stonelike clay inscribed in hieroglyphs and Hebrew. These inscriptions broke off at the shard's edges. He studied the readable bits of Hebrew, smiled at Solange, lifted the piece to his lips, and kissed it.

The high priest pushed aside the kilted men in front of him and began to mount the steps, waving the rod and calling out, "Just do your task." Resonant bass sounds of sighing came back in response. It could have been the moaned warning of a giant imprisoned beneath the Sanctuary floor.

Fritzi held up his hand. Its exposed shard now began to show sporadic pulsations of inner incandescence.

Angered, the high priest struggled to advance up the other steps, but he fell backward. The kilted men caught him just in time.

Rupert leaned toward Michael and whispered, "The dark angel seems about to have had a second fall."

"Rather gratifying so far, I must say." Michael could not contain a wry little smile.

The two, oblivious to all else, went on unwrapping the shards. Fritzi examined each piece with excitement as he handed it back to Solange to replace on the ebony slab.

Rupert wished he could be next to them trying to put them together like a puzzle to reveal the text as it was first inscribed. He spoke softly again to Michael. "Glad we'd the foresight not to unwrap the Commandments ourselves." He gestured toward the altar and grinned.

Goebbels turned and flashed a malignant look over his shoulder, suspecting their low voices were gloating.

The deep sighing had continued like the moans of a monster in a cave, underpinning celestial voices swelling and receding as if waves against the shore. As the shards were emerging from their ancient cocoons, each piece pulsed with inner light. They could very well have been alive on the ebony slab.

The high priest remained impassive behind the four kilted men. His triangular smile never flagged. By his posture, he seemed to be biding time before the next phase of a plan, which he had determined would not be frustrated by any forces—not even by the invisible wall that had blocked his attempt to reach the altar.

Solange and Fritzi, condemned prisoners, had become unanticipated acolytes of their Lord and apparently protected by their very reverence for his Word. Nobody had ever imagined in the planning for this event, the two Jews could possibly have invoked such powers. So be it. This was a challenge the high priest knew how to meet. It was not the first time—and it would not be the last—that he had confronted a formidable adversary. He spoke quietly to two of the men in front of him.

They nodded and ascended the steps. No invisible obstacle prevented them from bringing the slab down from the altar.

They carried it among the assembled Aaronites. As they passed Hitler and Goebbels, it radiated such an intense burning light their eyes had to be covered.

Goebbels reached out apparently to knock the slab to the floor, but he couldn't see at all for the moment. His lashing hand simply sliced the air.

The kilted men carried it on to be viewed by all the other celebrants. Several picked up one or two shards and inspected them. The pieces still pulsed faintly with light, but they could be touched without incident by those without malice.

Rupert and Michael inspected pieces longer and more intensely before replacing them on the slab.

After presenting the broken pieces for the last rows of guests to inspect, the kilted men placed the Covenant on the side of the altar away from the celebrants. They circled the altar, picked up the ark, and brought it to rest beside the shards of the original Commandments. The three scrolls no longer sent out their shimmering rainbow. Pleased with himself, the high priest could now mount the altar steps without impediment. He directed the four kilted men to lead Fritzi and Solange to stand below him with their backs to the audience.

Tension gripped the room.

The moaning giant's sighs became louder as if it wanted to stop what was coming next.

"Every brother and sister present tonight recalls why our cult bears the name of Aaron. So, we will now avenge the humiliation Aaron suffered from his leader for allowing the people something in which to believe when they needed it most." The high priest turned and pointed at the golden calf. "What many of us have forgotten is the fullness of the man called Moses's anger. Not only did he throw his God's

Covenant on the ground to be shattered as you've just seen and touched. Not only did he thereby destroy the very Word of his God in a fit of pique. But he then went on to order three thousand of his followers killed for having the temerity to worship an idol whom they celebrated with joyous abandon and sensuality. These people weren't traitors. They were merely satisfying human hungers for which they could easily have been forgiven."

Rupert whispered, "What crap. These Nazis give hypocrisy a good name."

The high priest came to the point at last. "Now we shall atone for the sins of Akhenaten against Aaron. These two condemned traitors," he dipped his hand toward Solange and Fritzi, "will have their execution carried out here tonight as a sacrifice of atonement." The man looked around at the Aaronites while maintaining his horrible smile.

The crowd gasped in disbelief, and sobs could be heard while a very few tried to silence those who showed these reactions.

Goebbels and Hitler nodded approvingly.

The high priest commanded, "Bring the woman to the altar."

As the two men flanking Solange took each arm to lead her up the steps, the giant's sighing and moaning now became multiple voices pulsing in urgent waves of complaining sound from every direction.

The men hesitated.

"Bring her to me!" The voice of the high priest had changed. It seemed disembodied.

The two men holding her did nothing. It wasn't clear whether they had the power to move at all.

The high priest held up a small vial before the sleeping cobra. Within seconds, its hooded head begun to move as its body stretched along the rod. He set the staff on the altar and grasped the creature just beneath its malevolent head. Turning, he raised it aloft by neck and tail and descended with slow, menacing movements. Standing before Solange, he let go of the cobra's tail and ripped away her flimsy white gown. It dropped in a puddle about her feet. She held herself erect, chin firmly up—naked and beautiful and proud. The tail of the cobra undulated across the gap between them and touched her breasts. The high priest brought the creature's head closer to Solange, its twitching fangs a millimeter from her cheek.

Rupert let out a great cry, as if he were suffering unspeakable pain, which seemed to awaken many of the Aaronites from their trance.

Shouts of "No!" rang out.

Rupert bolted toward Solange.

The high priest jerked about to see what was happening as he prepared to lay the cobra around her neck. Already startled by Rupert, he looked up at the dome. Rumblings as of an earthquake seemed to possess the Sanctuary. A great fissure zagged across the dome, and guttural rolls of thunder gained in force, racing toward them all like a monsoon.

Terrified, many of the Aaronites held each other tightly against the whirlwind that surrounded them. It whipped about the space in a huge vortex that blew out every candle and torch. From the darkness, a thousand voices surged in and out of the howling of the wind. The celebrants watched as the scrolls were sucked up from the altar into the maelstrom, three cylinders of light spiraling like little spaceships caught in a collision of stars. From this chaos, a glow began to brighten on the other side of the altar, silhouetting the golden calf. It grew into a shimmering aurora borealis that filled the dome with layers of fluctuating colors that changed constantly.

Within the aurora, a form began to take shape in fits and

starts. It emerged and then faded, like the shaky images of the earliest moving pictures, and the full lips, shaved head, and hooded eyelids of Akhenaten gradually became recognizable. Clad only in an Egyptian kilt, he towered above the altar beneath the damaged dome. He was encircled by the winds and shimmering lights. A faintly mocking smile accompanied his movements. With a commanding gesture, he pointed to the side of the altar not visible to the celebrants. Another roll of thunder shook the Sanctuary, and the fissure in the dome widened so that the darkness of a moonless sky was visible.

He spread out his arms. Piece by piece, the shards of the Commandments streamed up from the altar like the trail of a comet. Light as a thought, each piece found its place as if celestial creatures were assembling a jigsaw puzzle. Suddenly, three tablets had taken form. Akhenaten folded his arms over the tablets and hugged them to his chest.

Rupert held Solange tightly. Reaching down, he grabbed up her white shift from the black marble floor. He felt no fear. Only caution as he viewed the spectral scene taking place beneath the crippled dome.

The high priest appeared frozen. The cobra had wrapped itself around his neck, and its hooded head was arched back as if to inspect his face. They stared fixedly into each other's eyes.

Rupert looked over his shoulder at the Nazi bigwigs in the front row. Goebbels had taken Hitler by one arm and Unity Mitford by the other and was about to lead them toward the exit. They cowered under the shower of starlight that poured from the tablets clutched by Akhenaten above them. With alarm, their heads jerked up to witness another towering form emerging from the chaos of light, sound, and wind. It was Nefertiti.

She gave her husband a smile so enchanting that Rupert's breath was taken for a moment. Nefertiti laid her hands flat on the tablets. A whistling sound came like the wind and grew louder. The drums of thunder were pounded once again in a series of hammer blows. The rift in the dome grew larger, and the golden calf teetered back and forth as if about to topple over. From out the swirl of cloud and light and celestial voices, finally came Aaron. Dressed in a prophet's robes, bearded and turbaned, he nodded to the couple. Extending a hand, a stream of light shot down from his fingers to the rod on the altar. It rose from the black marble and sailed up the light stream until he had it in his grasp.

Nefertiti shimmered between the two men. Myriad voices began to chant, and the winds subsided. Flickering colors and vaporous clouds continued to fill the atmosphere surrounding the trio. With her regal bearing and ethereal charm, she turned to Aaron.

He inclined in a slight bow and said in Hebrew as he handed the rod to her, "I no longer have need of this."

She turned then to Akhenaten.

He also made a small bow and said in Egyptian, "These now belong truly to Aaron." He placed the tablets in Aaron's arms, and Nefertiti passed the rod to Akhenaten.

He thrust it aloft. Something so ominous was conveyed by this gesture, and the Aaronites moved en masse and at speed from near the altar to the outer extremities of the octagonal Sanctuary. The only ones remaining by the altar were the high priest and Lothar von Vranken whose chair's wheels had refused to work.

Rupert hugged Solange and tried to find Michael in the crowd. Just then, he appeared by their side.

Goebbels and Hitler pushed and screamed at people blocking the entrance doors. The jam-up came from those torn between fear and a desire to witness what would be coming next.

In desperation, von Vranken cried out to the high priest for help, ignoring the rigid state that had come over the man upon the appearance of Akhenaten's specter. He called again and had to watch the frozen form begin to fade. Within seconds, the high priest became a transparent form and then disappeared entirely, leaving behind only his robe, the cobra, and the sinister vulpine headgear. Von Vranken pushed himself out of the useless wheelchair and tried to crawl toward safety. He looked up at the figures in the dome. Terrified, he strained to turn around and find a different rescuer. He noticed the cobra slithering down the altar steps.

Fritzi had edged away from those who hovered by the walls. He stopped halfway and cocked his head with an amused twinkle.

Von Vranken silently implored him, but Fritzi simply shook his head, folded his arms, and smiled. Von Vranken spat out, "You pig of a Jew. Damn you to hell."

Solange pointed up and buried her head in Rupert's shoulder. Tongues of flame leaped from each of the twenty-four carved leaves of the rod. With both hands, Akhenaten had launched it straight up into the center of the cracking dome. The three shimmering figures seemed to vaporize and were replaced by a pillar of fire with the rod at its core.

The column of flame surged up through the dome and into the sky and shot down until it engulfed the golden calf. The idol's insouciant smile shone unperturbed through the flames until its lips began to melt along with bright eyes and pointed ears and the rest of its solid finely molded body.

The heat grew more intense, and von Vranken writhed by small degrees, trying to get away from the inferno—and the cobra.

The gold of the idol, becoming ever more molten, began to cascade from the pedestal down onto the altar and steps where it formed a thick, voluptuous stream that crept across the floor toward the crawling man. He gave a terrified look over his shoulder at the advancing flood and saw the cobra, which had begun to make its slow, sinuous way toward him. He tried to move faster, but the serpent reached him first. It hooked up over his left heel and started to undulate along his leg and back.

Lothar also felt waves of heat from the advancing gold. It was alive, fed by a constant fire within that kept it able to flow faster toward its victim. His screams could hardly be heard in the massive roar of the flaming pillar. The gold began to spread around his legs and hands. He could no longer move, and the gold rose higher and higher onto his inert body. His last sight was the cobra, which had arched over the back of his head and started to enter an eye with its quivering tongue.

Guests struggled through the entrance doors, pushing and trampling on each other.

Fritzi led Rupert, Michael, and Solange to the place from which he and Solange had approached the altar. The four stood for a moment and watched the river of gold engulfing Lothar von Vranken. They witnessed the serpent sliding off to safety while the puddle of liquid gold finally reached the man's face. Its erased features melted with the heat, consumed by what had once been the golden calf.

With this, the building shook as if struck by an earthquake. The walls of the Sanctuary shuddered and loosened their support for the dome. The four of them watched pieces of the dome fall in large chunks. They left as the Sanctuary became a pile of rubble under a huge hole in the sky.

The four found their way through the building, which was echoing with the noise of its falling pieces and the screams of the fleeing guests. They emerged by a side exit into the park surrounding the grand palace of the Seraphim, which was now entirely aflame. Fire engines kept arriving in numbers, and the invited guests were being treated by medics or taken away in their cars, which had been waiting before the melee and confusion had begun.

No one bothered them as they walked away from the conflagration and through the trees and pathways and ponds. As they approached a side gate, they looked at each other fearful it might be locked. Fritzi grasped its knob and turned. The metal gave a grinding sound that was prolonged until the latch finally disengaged. Filled with relief, they emerged into the street. Traffic was normal, and before long, a taxi stopped for them. The driver showed a blasé indifference to the rather odd foursome. Two of them were in bare feet and wearing white cotton robes, which Rupert told the taxi driver, offhandedly with a laugh, was the result of a costume party. As the temperature was quite cold, the driver just shrugged and looked doubtful.

"Take us to Tempelhof, please. The private aviation side." Rupert turned to the others and whispered, "We'll have to improvise a bit. Didn't actually expect we'd be four. I'll explain later."

☥

At the airport, Rupert left the others in the taxi and entered the private aviation section of the terminal. He looked around the enormous interior—with its clean rectilinear columns and soaring windows—and recognized one of his senior staff executives reading a newspaper alone in the vast deserted hall.

The man looked up, leaped to his feet, and rushed over. "Milord, how good to see you, at last."

"Thanks, George. You too. We've got some special issues to deal with. Is the embassy's first secretary here?"

"Yes. Waiting, just as you asked. Brought your new diplomatic passports with, shall we say, different identities for you and Mr. Caridis. He'll do what's necessary to manage any difficulties should that be needed. But I'd guess these are just a backup that you probably won't need to use. Only if the rest of the plan runs afoul. I don't see any complications—unless, of course, your 'special issues' give us some."

Rupert shot him a wry look. "Well, they do happen to have two particular complications, I'm afraid. Look, in a nutshell, we've got a couple of political refugees to get out of Germany tonight. If they stay, they'll be given the coup de grâce by dawn. So, they've got to be spirited onto that plane either as embassy staff going home or sub rosa. Any ideas?"

His colleague smiled. "Just up my alley, sir. Leave it to me. They're going to be dressed as airline personnel. I snooped a bit while waiting for you and chanced to see a changing room where upper-echelon flight service personnel have spare uniforms. Nearby, the baggage handlers have a dressing room for their coveralls and the like, including fancy little caps with serial numbers on them. We've got to get your refugees to a place where they can change."

The airport was undergoing a major renovation supervised by a well-regarded Nazi architect. It already boasted being one of the largest buildings in the world with its two curved hangars reaching out from both sides of the main building like the wings of a hawk. The whole thing was more than a mile long, and very early on a Sunday morning, there were no personnel on duty in the immigration control or customs office. One or two police guards and the odd loiterer were the most visible signs of life. Aircraft mechanics were servicing some planes parked under those great curving shelters.

Fifteen minutes later, two people emerged from the toilets. Each had managed to make it to the bathrooms without being challenged for their weird gowns and bare feet. Rupert smiled and said, "Solange, with your hair tucked into a steward's cap, your shoes stuffed with newspaper, and that male steward's uniform clinging to your slim figure, you could be a new Charlie Chaplin. A career is foretold." He paused. "Assuming we make it from here, of course."

There were nervous smiles.

Fritzi's strong physique produced the opposite effect. It bulged through the tight outfit chosen by Rupert's colleague who had found just a few lockers unlocked from which to source their costumes. Both their military-style steward caps and jackets normally bore insignia of Deutsche Luft Hansa, the national airline. They had removed these from their otherwise simple dark blue uniforms. Solange had ripped part of her white cotton gown and tied it around her neck with a bow flaring to one side of her face. This little change separated her from the commercial airline employees. Fritzi, to give a consistent uniformity, had taken a strip of white gown and made a neat ascot in lieu of the dark necktie normally worn by the airline's stewards.

"Now for the moment of truth." Rupert stiffened his back and gestured for them to move through the somewhat Byzantine temporary pathways lined with plywood construction. At the double doors to the airplane parking hangar, they encountered a bald man with a suave gray mustache. He was dressed in a striped Savile Row suit and wore a calm, almost benign, expression.

Rupert's man announced His Majesty's Berlin embassy's first secretary, and they shook hands all around.

The diplomat winked and said, "So far, so good. I don't think we're going to have a passport issue. No police in evidence yet. I suggest you walk together in a tight group to the plane and keep your heads down until the plane's doors are closed and it's set to take off down the runway."

Rupert addressed the group. "We've submitted a flight plan for 0800 hours, later this morning, but of course that's changed. Our official destination's Stockholm, but in fact, it's London. Our chartered plane's got instruments for taking off and landing and flying at night. We're using a straight unlighted runway here, and that should be easy. It will be dawning enough to land with good visibility, weather permitting, at the other end. Time's of the essence. Who knows what obstacles the Nazis may put in our way, but if we can get off the ground, we should be all right." The diplomat raised two hands with crossed fingers and gave them an encouraging smile.

They filed slowly out into the overhanging shelter where a twin-engine de Havilland Dragonfly was waiting, one of many planes of different sizes, wingtip to wingtip down the sweeping curve of the east hangar. The pilots were in their seats, and the steps up to the wing were in their place.

A man in coveralls smiled conspiratorially and helped them up the steps. When everyone had entered, he withdrew the steps, ran to a small vehicle connected to the underside of the plane, and began to pull it out of the hangar. Several technicians working on planes down the line looked up, incuriously, and returned to their jobs.

About one hundred feet away from the hangar, the man in coveralls disconnected the plane from his tug vehicle and waved at them with a large smile and thumbs up. The pilots started the engines, which attracted everyone's attention in the hangar, and several people came out to see what was happening. The tug vehicle made haste back into the hangar.

Propellers revved up to speed, and the plane began its way to the first of the two runways.

Rupert had his eyes fixed out the window on one side of

the plane, and Fritzi scanned the airfield from his seat on the other side. Several men in police uniforms were running after the plane with rifles in hand. Following behind them came a vehicle with a spinning light on top, emitting a piercing sound from its siren. Someone leaned out of the passenger window and aimed a rifle at the plane.

The pilots called back for seat belts to be secure, and everyone prepared for a rapid takeoff. Several times, Rupert though he heard bullets ping against the fuselage, but it was difficult to know over the roar of the engines and the shriek of the siren. The police on foot had stopped and aimed their rifles, but they lowered them without firing as the plane drew too far away.

A fiery shell passed along the portside of the plane as it was lifting off.

"Anti-tank missile, probably," muttered Fritzi. "We're too obscure now to be a good target unless they get lucky. In twenty seconds, we should be safe."

67

Late November 1938

"So, where are they? Buried in the rubble along with our gilded margrave?"

"I don't think so, Fuhrer. Von Vranken tried to crawl to safety, we're told by eyewitnesses, because his wheelchair probably jammed. He never made it. I'm sure the others must have escaped." Goebbels rubbed his hands together nervously.

"You never know, Josef. Masonry from the dome might have struck the two Jews—and maybe that goddamn interfering Englishman as well. It would be a good riddance. *Scheisse!* Couldn't get away with putting him in the camps. I know. Especially not right after we made that silly Chamberlain believe he'd produced everlasting 'peace for our time.'" Hitler unleashed a mirthless laugh. "When it really was peace to give us time."

"Indeed, Fuhrer. Ravenstone would just be a distraction from our next big move. Adding the next piece of our great empire. Poland! Poland, so vital to your vision of the unconquerable Germania!

An officer entered the room in the chancellery where the two men were sitting in their tailcoats still marked with the dust fallen in clouds from the disintegrating dome. "Heil Hitler!"

"Yes, Captain. What is it?"

"Tempelhof called, Herr Fuhrer. A chartered plane has made an unauthorized takeoff from the airport. It contained two pilots and four passengers, we think. Two passengers wore uniforms. They looked a little like our national airline uniforms. No one is sure. Two were dressed like you are."

Goebbels snapped out. "Was there a flight plan, Captain?"

"Yes, sir. Stockholm at eight this morning. The gestapo office at the airport reacted quickly and pursued the departing aircraft in a ground vehicle with a machine gun. We don't believe any damage was done to the plane."

Hitler said, "Tell Goering to have a fighter search the skies. No matter that it's nighttime. Get a pilot with good night vision. We must be much faster and more agile than their plane. Contact every airport between Berlin and Stockholm. For good measure, also between here and London. And shoot down that plane no matter where or when it's found."

⚥

Twenty minutes later, a young pilot climbed behind the controls of his almost new Messerschmitt Bf 110. He'd calculated several probabilities after hearing a quick capsule version of the facts. The leader of this escape plan clearly had to be the Englishman. His cohort included two renegades from German justice and an Alexandrian Greek. Why would he go to Stockholm? What he would do first is head as quickly as possible out of German airspace. That meant he would indeed head north toward the Baltic. There he would either continue northeast to Stockholm or cut west over southern Sweden and Denmark, intending to land somewhere on the British coast. Along the way, both planes would need to refuel at least once—and perhaps twice.

His fighter plane was much faster than the Dragonfly, and he'd been blessed with the night vision of an owl. The skies were pretty clear, and his plan made as much sense as any. He set his course on a straight line to Stockholm. He would go halfway there and search the skies all the way. If he saw nothing, he would make a hard turn to port and set his compass straight on to London. In the meantime, radio contact with Tempelhof would tell him of any sightings or news that could be helpful.

Few places along the route to Stockholm existed where any sightings might be made and reported. When he had reached Oland Island and had been told by Tempelhof no useful information as yet had been received, he made his hard turn toward Malmo, Sweden, and Copenhagen, sure that he'd be told if the de Havilland landed in either place. He had another advantage besides his extra speed. He could also cut across the northwest corner of Germany, which he knew Rupert would avoid. This meant Rupert's route would be longer by staying out to sea. Better than being shot down over German soil.

Refueling in Copenhagen, he learned his prey had not stopped. When he prepared to take off again, Berlin let him know the Dragonfly had refueled at Malmo's Bulltofta airport within the past thirty minutes. A triumphant smile creased his face; he was now confident his strategy had been correct.

The fighter pilot maintained his high altitude, which provided a sweeping view below. Clouds were now practically nonexistent, and long-range visibility was excellent under the stars. He was certain they'd have kept the de Havilland Dragonfly's wing lights turned off, as indeed were his.

As he was nearing Amsterdam, a voice crackled, disembodied, from his earphones. His eyes widened, and a smile flashed from his face. A message had been intercepted by the radio tower at Schiphol. A de Havilland Dragonfly had announced five minutes ago they were setting course for Croydon Airport and would expect to arrive within one hour and ten minutes. He sucked in his cheeks. That gave him a good hour to hunt and kill his prey.

The Messerschmitt headed out to the North Sea and followed the compass setting between Amsterdam and London. A glow of light was beginning to tint the horizon far behind him. Small clouds were popping up beneath as well. These as yet had presented no big problem, but he had to act fast since daylight could bring a change of temperature and the forming of a typical November cloud cover over the sea. He put the aircraft on autopilot and scanned the airspace below with his binoculars. He spied only a heavy transport plane heading toward the Continent. He continued to check the skies like an eagle ready to pounce.

Twenty-five minutes later, the Tempelhof voice asked what he was seeing.

Impatient at being bothered, he responded, "Nothing. Nothing. Nothing."

His temper suddenly improved. He'd seen something, a flash of silver disappearing beneath a cloud. Yes, indeed, it was the de Havilland Dragonfly emerging from the other side. Jubilation erupted from his voice on the open line to Berlin. He grabbed the steering stick, turned off the autopilot, checked his gun alignment controls, and prepared to press the firing button. He slowed his speed and dropped to the altitude of the de Havilland Dragonfly, which was now only two hundred yards ahead of him. He checked out the skies and seas beneath them. It was going to be a nice clean hit. The plane might sink and never be found. He accelerated slightly to close the gap. His prey appeared to be unaware of the predator on its tail.

☥

Rupert leaned over toward the pilot. "We're getting pretty close now, aren't we? No planes sighted so far?"

"Right you are, milord. A couple of transports about a half hour ago. Probably didn't even notice us overhead."

Rupert thought with excitement about finally holding Lizzie. How he missed her—and how he needed to comfort her. Several things had changed for him. His daughter, Tessie, would see more of him. He was going to listen better and express his deeper feelings, opening up much more to her. They were, after all, the most important people in his life. A nagging fear gnawed away at him. Had he been different with Orlando, could he have warded off the curse that consumed him? He was lifted a little by the thought they'd been able to save Solange and Fritzi. Would that had included Orlando as well. He stared out the window into banks of clouds forming over the sea as the dawn began to cast its fiery light upon them to splendid effect.

☥

The pilot's thumb pressed on the firing button. The response sent a thrill through him. He shuddered with pleasure as he let go a second fusillade. The de Havilland Dragonfly's fuel tank caught fire this time, and one of its engines stopped. He lifted the fighter sharply and set it in a tight arc to encircle the spot where the de Havilland Dragonfly was plunging several thousand feet into the English Channel. Berlin could hear his whoop of triumph and crackled back a volley of bravos. This was pure joy. He watched the spinning plane enter the icy waters below like a whirligig.

☥

As instructed, the radio operator telephoned Goebbels at his residence. It was six o'clock in the morning.

With a groggy voice after only a couple of hours of sleep, he asked who the hell was waking him up. When he heard the word Tempelhof, the mists cleared, and he pressed the receiver tightly in his grip. "Yes. What news?" He listened to the full report. "This is excellent. But you must tell the pilot to evade detection. Get back into German airspace without being discovered. We don't want anyone to make the connection with our plane. No publicity should leak out. You mustn't discuss this with anyone, and I want you to destroy the logs. The pilot must be given the same instructions. He will be honored by the Fuhrer himself in a private ceremony. But quiet is the word."

The radio operator was silent.

"Are you there?" Goebbels wondered if he'd been speaking to a dead line.

"Yes, Herr Reichminister, but there could be a small problem. You see, we kept an open line between Berlin and the plane so that all information could be exchanged without interference. There's always the chance our conversations were intercepted. Further, we were in contact with many points along the way, trying to track the course of the de Havilland Dragonfly."

Goebbels frowned and struck the bedside table with his fist. "I suppose we'll just have to make a blanket denial of our involvement. Your conversations aren't helpful, but they were necessary to the task. Anyway, we'll say our interest was because the plane carried two condemned persons fleeing from German justice, which is why we were tracking its movements to know from whom to seek extradition of our escaped prisoners. But we will deny shooting it down."

"Understood, Herr Reichminister. Heil Hitler!"

☥

Rupert caught his first sight of England's shores through a small cloud of smoke from his cigarette. He called out to the others. "Looks like we're going to make it." Dawn was breaking upon Saint Paul's dome as they made a wide bend over the city and the Houses of Parliament. His heart leaped at the sight of Big Ben, and he thought about the grilling he would get for the entire story from his colleagues in the House of Lords. And Winston would be full of comments as he was told its details, especially where they involved several of their prominent fellow countrymen and women.

Their plane received clearance and approached Croydon. The ribbon of its runway lay before them like a welcoming carpet spread upon the land. Their wheels touched down, and the four passengers broke into cheers. When the plane had come to a full stop and steps were being brought to the wing, the four embraced as tears poured from Solange and Fritzi.

The door of the plane was opened, and Rupert looked out at a rotund figure waiting beside the steps. The man was sporting a huge smile and an even larger cigar. Rupert laughed with delight. "Good God, Winston, rather early for you to be up and about. What can possibly be the matter?"

"I'll tell you what's the matter. We had the worst fright. Another de Havilland Dragonfly was up there at the same time as you. Flying from Schipol to London. Shot down. Managed to see their attacker and radio word to Croydon. Obviously meant for you, old man. Messerschmitt. Clever to have tracked you, and goddamn lucky for you the other plane played decoy to the Nazi brute."

"Well, maybe it was this that protected us." Rupert pulled a fragment of an ancient clay tablet from his pocket.

His traveling companions wore expressions of complete astonishment.

Michael smiled. "Of course, when they passed around the broken pieces for everyone to see and touch, you kept one, no?"

"You are, as usual, quite right, dear friend." Rupert held it out in his palm.

Winston took it and turned it over. "Looks like Egyptian hieroglyphics and Hebrew. What on earth is this all about?"

Rupert said, "You're holding the only surviving piece of the original Commandments brought down from Sinai—in reality by an Egyptian pharaoh." He pointed at the inscriptions. "To add further to your apparent astonishment, it represents one word in both languages."

Churchill threw him a quizzical look. "If you must confound me with contradictions, go ahead and tell."

"It's a word never used as a noun in the second rendering of the Commandments, but in the first go, it's part of a wonderful sentiment. 'Whoever does not love does not know God because God is love.'"

Churchill shrugged. "I see. It's used in that inspiring admonition as both verb and noun."

"Indeed," responded Rupert.

Churchill pulled the cigar from his lips "Well, I can tell you all that we're not going to see much love lost in the coming cataclysm." He handed the fragment back to Rupert. "I devoutly wish this charm, which may well have saved your lives, might do the same for all those millions now at unthinkable risk."

Finis

EPILOGUE AND
ACKNOWLEDGEMENTS

Some have asked what does the word seraphim actually mean? It refers to the very highest order of angels in the Christian hierarchy of the heavenly hosts—the seraphim comprise just six such angels, and these are the very closest angels to God. This goes some way to explain the vision of their own power and importance held by some members of the Society of the Seraphim in my story.

I would also nominate several candidates for seraphim-hood amongst my friends and loved ones who gave time and perceptive thought to my journey down this narrative path. First, I owe much to the patience and encouragement provided by my beloved wife Boulie whose criticism is always unsparingly objective while also pointing in helpful directions. Her older son, Timothy Nugent-Head, read the earliest manuscript and gave some valuable insights on its form. My older nephew, Robert Garrett Jr., helped to fine-tune some character development which improved the flow of the story. A kind friend, Tim Burrill, a noted British film producer, was perhaps my best cheerleader and gave my spirits a bounce when they needed it most. A friend of some forty years, Ilaria Ratazzi, generously studied the first part of the story and fired a critical broadside which alerted me to some necessary changes which I made with gratitude. Finally, another dear friend and author, Patrizia Chen, suggested I meet Maria Campbell, a much respected beacon of literary perceptiveness who had the kindness to shine her light on an earlier version which led me to appreciate that sometimes less is more.

ABOUT THE AUTHOR

James Constantine Marlas grew up in the American Midwest and attended Harvard and Oxford before becoming an entrepreneur, a world traveler, and a lover of historical fiction. He has been writing stories since the sixth grade, when he composed a fictional adventure about ancient Mayan culture. James and his French-born wife of thirty-three years live on the American East Coast and in southern France.